Adara

Louise Furley

Adara

ISBN- 978-1-7357712-4-3 (Paperback)
ISBN- 978-1-7357712-3-6 (eBook)

Cover design by Pixel Mischief Design

The characters and events portrayed in this book are fictitious. Any similarity to real persons, living or dead, is coincidental and not intended by the author.

ADARA

Chapter One

The gaggle of girls wearing plaid skirts and white blouses, skipped down the walk in black patent leather shoes past clusters of men hanging around the street corners.

Every few blocks, a different gathering of mostly males loitered in front of bodegas or bars or restaurants, huddled in furtive conversation while sucking down beers and toking cigars.

Giggling with the abandon of girlish giddiness, every time after they passed a group of men, the chattering girls' heads came together. Out of the men's earshot, they whispered about the fearsome chills and dangerous mysteries they sensed as they had hurried by.

Fluffing her sophisticated blonde curls, "Oh, Adara," twelve-years-old going on sixteen, Selena gushed, "Paulie is so hot, I'm gonna marry him, ya know."

Tripping along in her little heels that she was the only one of the group allowed to wear, Selena's head swiveled back to see if the boy she liked was looking at her.

Her grin stayed but stiffened when she saw Paulie never raised his head from the huddle he was in.

Paulie was in his late teens, he had no interest in what he and the rest of the guys would consider babies.

Throwing her haughty chin up at the perceived affront, Selena clutched to her chest the Hermès bag that matched the designer heels, both she was way too young to wear.

The girls continued on their way.

Braids bounced around Dominique's shoulders as she shook her head at her flighty friend. Rubbing it in with rolling eyes, sounding like a young professor, she tutored, "Selena, please, Paulie is practically an adult, almost a grown man, and you are a little girl, he wouldn't look twice at you."

Her vocabulary impeccable, Dominique was the oldest of the group with pretty cinnamon colored skin, and almond shaped dark brown eyes encased behind neon pink glasses.

"Huh," tossing her long blonde hair, young fashionista Selena shot her a grimace, then smiled.

Glints of hazel darted slyly at Dominique, Selena said, "Maybe not, but," she glanced at Adara, "Vaclav Braşov's spooky eyes might be mostly hidden by those lids so low they're barely visible, but he never took them off you, Adara." She wiped her slightly too long, too pointed nose with the back of her hand.

Crystal giggled nervously, plucking at a long, light-brown curl she pulled in front of her chest. "That's nothing new, Selena, he never does. He never has. He's seldom in this country, but when he is, those icy-blues follow Adara's every movement. So creepy," she gave a little shiver.

"He's like maybe ten years older than you," Crystal went on. "Makes me think of a hawk sitting hidden on a branch, only his eyes visible, waiting for the sparrow to fly too close."

Keeping her expression bland, Adara suppressed a shudder. The youngest of the group, even at ten-years-old she was well aware that Vaclav Braşov's inscrutable piercing eyes bore into her every time the girls scurried past the corner he hung at when in town, or when they ran into each other at community events.

At some occasions like weddings, the Italians and Russians, and other gangs, warily mingled, keeping safe distances and a ready hand on a hidden weapon.

Pudgy, redheaded Margaret struggled to keep up with her thinner, quicker friends.

Huffing, she said, "Obviously he digs really huge, seriously dark eyes, Adara. Yours are like molten chocolate. And those velvety curls, like wavy dark syrup," her voice held a twinge of envy.

"Geez, Margaret," skinny, bookish Crystal reproached the chubby girl. "You are always thinking of food, and now you're making me hungry. Anyway," Crystal glanced at Adara.

"My dad always says you have doe eyes. He says they're richly dark, pure and intriguing. My mom says that's so…klee…uh, cliché, then she hits him and he calls her jealous of a child and then they start fighting again."

Rolling her eyes at Crystal, Selena said to Adara, "Wouldn't Vincenzo be mad if Vaclav laid a hand on you? I mean, your brother is moving up the ranks of your father and uncle's organization, the Italian Brotherhood, the Lambogliá." The other girls nodded.

Selena continued, "The Lambogliá has always had a restless truce with the Russians, but if he thought you were in danger, wouldn't Vincenzo drop Vaclav like a rock in a pond?"

Dominique shook her head solemnly, answering for Adara, "I don't think so. My cousin Jamil says the Russians are the most violent, dangerous gangsters there are. You know they call Vaclav Braşov *Vâjâi* or like *Vâj,* for short. Jamil says it means 'raging storm' in Russian." She blinked through the pink glasses trying to remember what Jamil had told her.

"I mean, maybe he said Vaclav is Romanian, not Russian. Whatever they call him, Jamil said that even though he is quite young, he is a majorly dangerous man, a brutal enforcer for Viggo Garatteo and they all steer clear of him when he's around."

Adara grumbled bitterly, "My big brother is too busy keeping mama and dad from killing each other, and is too involved with the gang to pay any attention to me."

Crystal patted her arm with sympathy. "I'm sorry, Adara. Your parents have always been horrible."

"Crystal!" Dominique snapped, appalled at her.

Shrugging, Crystal replied, "I'm only saying the truth. Everyone knows. They act like we kids don't know anything, but we do. At the top of a New York bloodthirsty syndicate, her father is not a nice man, and my mom says her mom cheats on him like a robin plucking at every worm in the ground, while her thieving brother-"

"Crystal, *please*," Adara shot her a 'please shut your pie hole' look.

"Huh," Selena grunted with a dirty look at Crystal, scolding her for talking about their friend's parents that way. "Anyway, you guys ever really looked at the guy? Vaclav Braşov?"

Everyone but Adara snuck surreptitious peeks over their shoulders at the young Romanian male.

Standing many inches over six feet, his unusual hair was dark on the closer cut sides and lighter blond on the longer top. A dark blond lock shaded one malignant eye shadowing his gaze even more.

Selena sighed. "He may have a hard, mean-looking face with that scar by his temple, but my older cousin Althea says he's hot. One scary bad-ass dude, but so buff, girl, that guy has muscles on top of muscles."

"And tats on top of tats," Margaret cooed with young salient interest. "Even his thick accent, it's weird and scary too."

Crystal looked at her young friends as if they were freaks. "Geesh, you guys, you talk like you're twenty-years-old for heaven's sake. We're not even teenagers yet!"

She didn't mean to, but Adara couldn't help peering over her shoulder at the Russian. Romanian. Whatever he was.

"Huh," Dominique expelled a shivered breath. Straightening the pink glasses she said, "You pegged it, Selena, scary as shit. He's one of the meanest, toughest looking guys I've ever seen. Gives me the willies," a chilling shudder wriggled over her athletic shoulders.

She added, "Like Jamil says, I sure wouldn't want to be alone in a dark alley with him!"

"Potty mouth," Margaret scolded her then grinned when Dominique stuck her tongue out at the chubby admonisher. Pushing

4

red springy curls out of her face, she returned Dominique's impudent gesture.

As if he knew they were talking about him, Vaclav Brașov slowly turned his head in their direction and pierced Selena with a narrow prickly gaze before shifting it to Adara.

His strong jaw covered with an afternoon's worth of scruff, he had diamond hard cheekbones, a low, masculine ridged brow, and his mouth, full yet the sharply slashed lips never smiled.

Adara promptly jerked her head forward and walked more quickly.

Suddenly uncomfortable, the other girls rushed after her.

Selena hurried to walk beside Adara, her little heels clacking on the worn and cracked cement sidewalk.

Catching her breath, she said with a slight pant, "Crystal's right, that guy is creepy. He shows up every so often to meet with his gang, mob, whatever they call themselves, they say he lives in Russia." Her steps quickened to keep up with Adara who was striding faster.

Scooting beside her, Selena continued, "He has tried to make conversation with you, Adara, over the years when he's in town and the gangs are meeting. You've always avoided him, or downright ran from him when we've been dragged to family parties or stuff by our parents.

"Last time he looked really, really pissed when you hurried away from him. But now," she looked back then turned around quickly, "he has zero expression, nothing. As usual, his lids are so low over his eyes you can hardly even see them, just spears of frightening blue flints. Like Crystal said, that creepy hawk lying in wait, huh?"

"Yeah," Adara said, crossing her arms over her chest as if to protect herself from something invisible yet palpably evil. "Creepy."

Chapter Two

Vaclav Brașov spat Romanian curses into the phone, then muttered, "On our way, Pietro, hang on." He dialed a number. Keeping his voice modulated, suppressing his rage, he spoke in Romanian, then impatiently shoved the phone into his pocket.

By the time he dressed, raced around gathering more weapons and was out the door, Griffin Gabriēl was pulling up in front.

Dashing out of the house, Vaclav had the door to the SUV open and was sliding into the front seat before it even came to a stop, which it never did. He was closing the passenger door as the SUV kept moving circling back out.

Griffin floored the vehicle, spinning a donut then burned rubber squealing down the driveway and into the street.

Fishtailing into the road, he tore down the asphalt heading to the main highway.

Griffin's slightly satanic appearance unnerved people. Wearing his sleek ebony hair combed straight back from the widow's peak, he had a dark chinstrap beard, and he was as big a menacing man as Vaclav.

The last weak rays of the setting sun lit roofs and treetops, glinting off steel buildings as the crew made their way to the city.

In the back, Kidane Vasillo had hippyish long sandy hair that hung straight to his broad shoulders. He sat crammed thick arm to thick arm with the brooding, black-haired Ivod Dragoș.

No one spoke. Every hard face set grim with tight lips, they stared silently ahead as the SUV slingshot through the city going from the business section, and further where buildings grew more and more dilapidated.

Soon, they passed fewer office buildings, and shops that gave way to seedier bars, and then warehouses. There were no streetlights, and no lights on in any of the old vacant structures they drove by.

"Hit the lights," Vaclav ordered.

Griffin turned off the headlights and they were immersed in twilight dimness. The hum of the car's engine the only sound around them in the dark.

The crumbling warehouses loomed like a nesting tarantula with many wide, ragged legs stretching across the commons. The road had turned into cracked tar with potholes big enough to eat a Hummer.

The SUV slowed, creeping past building after building, until Kidane said, "There," he pointed, "cars."

A hundred yards away, they saw a bunch of vehicles gathered in front of a blocky, bland colored, one-story warehouse. A truck with its headlights on beamed into the open garage door illuminating the inside.

His hand already on the door handle, "Park it," Vaclav said.

Griffin pulled behind a building to block the car from view. As soon as he killed the engine, all the doors opened and the men spilled out.

Vaclav pointed at Kid and Ivod and motioned to the back of the line of warehouses, then nodded at Griffin.

Without a word, Kid and Ivod took off jogging behind the structures, Vaclav and Griffin started down the front.

Clinging to the buildings to stay hidden in the shadows, Vaclav and Griffin hurried silently until they reached the warehouse where the group of cars was parked.

Vaclav trod gingerly to the first window he reached. Soundlessly, he crept to the window, stood on tiptoe and peered in through the grimy window, dusted with age.

Through the blurry glass, he could see a group of men inside. Flashlights placed around and the truck's lights gave harsh illumination to the macabre scene.

Inside, the walls and floor were made of jagged cement and slices of grungy chipped plaster. Wrecked boxes, pallets, some beat-up furniture cluttered the room.

Towards the center, a man was tied to a chair, his face completely bloody, he'd been beaten to a pulp. Even as Vaclav observed, a man stood in front of him and crashed his fist into his face. Blood and sweat spewed as the bound man's head snapped to the right.

Around the room, more than a dozen, by his quick assessment, Vaclav saw rival gang members hovering.

Sitting on the cement floor, their backs against the wall with their hands and ankles cuffed with plasti-cuffs, were three of Vaclav's men. Two more of his men were several feet away. Judging from the way they lay, the ocean of blood on and around them, their faces so bashed in they were no longer recognizable, he assumed they were gone.

Seeing one of them, the blond hair sodden with blood, Vaclav recognized Pietro, the man that had whispered for help into his phone twenty minutes ago.

His eyes flicked to a bat one of the rival guys held. It was red with blood and gunk, Vaclav figured was brain matter. His jaw clenched grimly, he nodded to Griffin then strode with stealth around the side of the building. He pointed up.

Griffin looked to where he indicated. Through the first grimy window, Vaclav had seen another window on the side of the building was broken clear out. Most of the windows were boarded up. But this one was open.

When they neared it, they could hear talking. Standing to the side of the broken window, they paused to listen. A man was yelling, cursing, the smack of a fist could be heard, and the resounding grunt of whomever he struck.

"Now, tell me where the shipment is going out from!" the abusing man shouted, and another strike was heard along with the reactive grunt.

"Fuck you," a groggy voice, gurgling through the blood in his throat said with undaunted contempt.

"Yeah? Fuck me, Vitale?" the man growled. "I got your 'fuck you' right here," the sound of a punch and then the sound of an 'oof' then gagging.

Then, "I've had it," the puncher snarled. "Joey, take the bat to his knees first. Let's see if he talks before his head is a smashed pumpkin like the other two fuckers."

Vaclav and Griffin shared a look. Vaclav jumped up, caught the windowsill and pulled himself inside, Griffin followed him.

They climbed into a vacant room attached to the main area where Vaclav's men were being tortured. Their footsteps silent, when they reached the doorway, they paused.

Vaclav sent a silent text. Several second passed, then he looked at his watch and nodded to Griffin.

Wearing blue jeans, Harley boots, and a black leather jacket, Vaclav swaggered into the main room with calm arrogance. "Delimonte," his deep voice heavily accented, he said coolly, "you want something from me?"

Every eye turned to the young man brazenly strolling into the grisly bullpen of brutality.

The man who was directing the punching, straightened. His eyes narrowed, then he smiled. "Ah, Garatteo sent his toughest enforcer, Vaclav Braşov. Young, but savage as shit, the fucking Russian. You're in charge of these shitheads, am I right?" He jerked his head at the bound men sitting against the cement wall.

Russo Delimonte wore a grey suit coat with a blue tie splattered with blood. His face narrow and gaunt, even with his violent actions, his brown hair was combed to the side, neat as a pin.

With a truculent snarl, he glared at his men. "You stupid fuckers, one of 'em has a phone. You copped their weapons but left one of 'em armed with his cell." His attention turned back to Vaclav and the smile returned.

"No matter. If this shit enforcer called in reinforcements, we'll be long gone before the cavalry arrives. And he will be as dead as his men by the time we're dust."

He turned his back to the man they'd been beating, and fully faced Vaclav. "Only what, eighteen, nineteen? You may be one of the toughest, most vicious fucks in the country, but you can't take on me and my boys alone, you dumb fuck. Why," he made a deal of looking all around Vaclav's body. "You don't even have a weapon, at least not out and ready to use."

He nodded to the man nearest him and ordered him, "Rolf, go check the door to make sure he came alone." To Vaclav, "This is your last stupid day on Earth, my young friend."

He said to the men on his left, "You keep an eye on the prisoners. You," he motioned to those on his right, "get the idiot enforcer."

His men started reaching for their guns, Delimonte halted their action, said, "No."

Chuckling wickedly, he said, "I want him alive. I can beat every one of those assholes' heads into squash for Thanksgiving dinner. When he sees that, knowing he's next, he'll talk." Throwing his arm out in an attack motion, suit coat swinging, he commanded, "Go!"

Delimonte's men roared with bloodthirsty glee and raced to take Vaclav down.

The first thug that reached him had his knife out. Swinging it at Vaclav, in a trick move he also swung his other hand at his head. Vaclav jerked his belly in and ducked his head, both of the man's hands whizzed past him.

As the guy stumbled off-balance, Vaclav grabbed the arm with the knife, and in one smooth motion forced it into a U-turn and stabbed the man in his stomach with his own blade. His eyes wide with surprise, the thug slumped to the floor.

Two other men hesitated in shock at the quick, vicious death, then bellowed and ran at Vaclav.

Jumping from one as he lunged at him, Vaclav slammed his fist into the man's neck, knocking him to the ground, and with the speed of light jabbed his fingers in the other guy's eyes. Slapping his hands over his eyes, the man screamed and dropped to his knees.

Vaclav grabbed him, lifted him to his feet and gripped his thick neck, twisted it with one sharp move, easily breaking it. Dropping the dead man, he started running towards three others that were screaming and rushing straight at him.

It took him seconds to dispatch them all.

As one lay still alive, maimed and flailing in agony on the floor, Vaclav stood over him, and stomped on his head with his rugged Harley Davidson's until he ceased to move.

Muttering, "*Motherfucker,*" seeing the swift carnage, a shade of uneasiness flustered through Delimonte. A slight shake to the end of his words, he ordered, "Kill the fucker, shoot him! Shoot him!" he screamed.

The rest of his men, more than half a dozen reached for their guns. Suddenly, from three corners of the room, a hail of gunfire barraged.

Griffin, Kid and Ivod came out shooting. During Vaclav's distractive, riotous warfare, they were able to get into the building unseen and enter the room with guns blazing.

Screams and cries railed inside the cement block as bodies blew apart, pieces of men showering to the cold hard floor.

A man tried to escape out the front door, Vaclav went after him. He caught him on the threshold- holding the back of his head he bashed his skull into the concrete wall until there was little left of it. Wiping his bloody hands on his jeans, he turned to Delimonte.

His frightened eyes wild with burgeoning panic, gun in his hand, Delimonte pointed it at Vaclav. He was so scared he couldn't hold the gun steady.

His eyes on the trigger, Vaclav marched steadily towards him.

"Get back!" Delimonte screamed. "Get back or I'll shoot! You're letting me walk out of here, or I'll fucking kill you, you psycho maniac!"

Vaclav seldom smiled. When he did, like now, sheer terror curdled every bone in any sane man's body. Vaclav kept moving towards him, his eyes on the trigger.

"You fucker! I'll shoot! Let me outta here or I'll fucking plug you-"

Vaclav closed in on him, he was several feet away when he saw Delimonte's finger start to squeeze the trigger, and he threw himself to the side just as the gun went off. Delimonte kept firing wildly, but Vaclav was on him.

Griffin ran over pulling cuffs from his belt.

Vaclav's face a mass of pitiless fury snarled, "*Na*, even a cockroach has the right to writhe on the ground unbound while being executed."

Slamming his fist into Delimonte's nose, Vaclav turned his own head to avoid the blood gushing and grabbed the hand the thug held the gun in. He forced the hand backwards, ignoring Delimonte's screams of agony, until his wrist-bones snapped and the gun fell with a clatter to the cement floor.

"Oh my God, you Russian bastard, fuck!" Delimonte shrieked. Bending over in pain he held the broken wrist to his chest.

"*Da*, I am a bastard," Vaclav agreed. "But I am Romanian, asshole, not Russian," and he wrapped his hand around Delimonte's neck. "Not that you are going to live long enough to remember."

Lifting the man off his feet with one huge hand, he squeezed fingers of iron around the thug's neck, and seethed, "If I had the time, Delimonte, while you still breathed I would gut you. Then I would cut off your dick and balls and shove them into the open hole. Then I would force your head down so you would have to look at them shriveling inside you while you died. You know I would do it, do you not?"

He dug his thumb like a round bolt of steel into the choking man's throat.

Delimonte's eyes bulged, he tried to nod but Vaclav's fingers were pure iron and they kept squeezing. Gagging, drool running down his long face, Delimonte clawed at his hands, kicked him, punched him in the kidneys, but Vaclav relentlessly squeezed.

Delimonte's body started shuddering, his feet quivered off the ground, the smell of piss permeated the air. A last rattling croak, and he fell completely limp, his neck still clutched in Vaclav's death grip.

Vaclav opened his hands, allowing Delimonte to slide lifeless to the floor.

Without another glance at the dead man at his feet, Vaclav turned and started towards his men tied up by the wall. Griffin was already there.

Together they unbound their men. Ivod and Kid cut the ropes binding the battered Vitale tied to the chair and helped him to his shaking feet.

When they were steady, Vaclav said to one of the captured men, "What the hell happened, Nicky?"

The man he spoke to was a couple years older than Vaclav. His brown hair disheveled, bruises littered his sweaty face, his head lowered in shame. "Ah, *Vâj*, I'm…ah, we're," he glanced around at the other men that had been captured with him.

"We're fucking sorry. They ambushed us. We were on the trucks with the stash. When we went around that hairpin turn at Kaftan Road near the mountainside, we couldn't see them, they had blocked the road ahead on the curve and swarmed us already armed."

Nodding his shamed head, another man spoke, "Yeah, Boss, we didn't have a chance. They brought us here, beat the hell out of us before they took the bat to," his head twitched in the direction of their two deceased compatriots lying in their own blood. His words choked off, tears stinging his eyes, he dropped his head.

The third man mumbled, "They beat Johnboy with that goddamned bat until he was dead then started on Pietro. They wanted to know where our trucks originated from so they could get everything that we stocked, and take out more of our boys."

Looking at their deceased men, Griff muttered, "Their hands aren't tied, must be how Pietro was able to call."

Wiping at his eyes, gruffness clouded Nicky's voice, "Yeah, they were dumping Johnboy and preparing to tie Pietro to the chair, they didn't think he could do anything. You'da been proud, *Vâj*, they died like soldiers, brave men, they never spilled, Boss. Not a word."

"*Bine* boys," Vaclav said, even though he was the youngest of all of them. "Get our guys' bodies and put them Delimonte's trucks, take them home so we can bury them. Grab up anything of value. Ivod," the black-haired man nodded once sharply. Vaclav said, "Burn it."

"Done," Ivod jogged out of the building to go to their vehicle to get the necessary materials to torch the building, and everything, everyone in it.

As the men took to their tasks, Griff said quietly to Vaclav, "At least we cut off the head of the snake. Delimonte is dead. The rest of his crew will scatter. He won't be hurting our people again, or robbing us."

The adrenalin from the fight dissipating, Vaclav dragged his sleeve across his sweating forehead, agreed, "*Da.*"

Starting for the door he said, "Get the word out what happened here. I want all the other gangs, the syndicates, to know whom they are dealing with. The name Viggo Garatteo will chill those thieving hearts and they will back off, leave us alone."

Griff grunted. "Huh. More like Vaclav Braşov will be the name that makes a man shake in his boots, not the head of our local American organization."

The men completed their tasks and proceeded out to the SUV Ivod had brought around.

Using Delimonte's vehicles, they hopped in and were almost out of the warehouse district when they paused to watch the flames reach to the sky.

Then, the cars caravanned from the warehouses, some heading for disposal, some for home.

Chapter Three

Three Years Later

Adara was atwitter with excitement. Mikell Barbosa was going to take her to the school's youth dance. Only thirteen, the teens would be heavily chaperoned. Mikell would meet her there as technically, she was too young to date.

Tomorrow, her Auntie Bianca was taking her to the shops to buy her a dress, and she would be driving Adara to the dance. Adara couldn't wait. Mikell was a gorgeous football player who could have his pick of girls but he'd asked her!

Goodness, he was two years older than Adara; it was so flattering that he wanted to be with the younger teen. Clasping her hands together she swung in a circle with a grin of delight.

"Adara!" Estella Valentina barked at her daughter. The cocktail she held in her hand at two in the afternoon sloshed as she stalked towards her. Her heels clunked on the wood-planked floor until they muffled onto the area rug.

The pale blue walls of the living room were trimmed with white and decked with gilded paintings. Curio cabinets and ostentatious furniture filled the voluminous space.

A white brick fireplace occupied one end of the large room, and the rows of windows covered with vertical white blinds were closed to the sunlight.

The grin and cheer fled from Adara. This was the reason Auntie Bianca was taking her shopping, because her father had taken all the keys to their vehicles away after Estella's fifth DUI.

Keeping her eyes lowered to hide the repugnance she felt for her drunken, abusive mother, Adara murmured, "Yes, Mama?"

Estella stomped to her. "My sister Bianca says she's buying you a dress?"

Adara resembled her mother in her fine bone structure, high cheekbones and plump lips, but Adara's eyes were rich dark brown, and sweetness shone from their chocolate depths,

Estella's were faded, often splintered red from the booze. Adara was quite slender, but her mother tended to be skeletal because the liquor she consumed filled up any hunger pangs that might be in her belly.

Where Adara's face radiated youth and vitality, her skin creamy white, cheeks round with vibrant pink from her English great-grandmother, Estella's skin was darker, Italian olive, her cheeks had sunk in and she was still a fairly young woman.

Estella seethed with resentful jealousy when she regarded her beautiful daughter.

Nodding warily, her voice tiny, Adara said, "Uh, yes, tomorrow, for the spring dance. It's at school; there will be tons of chaperones. Teachers and parents and-"

"Well, little Miss, you will not be the whore in the family that drags our esteemed name through the dirt, ruin our prestigious reputation in this fine city. This community gossips like magpies in flight, for shit's sake. No," she shook her head, blonde hair with dark roots swung back and forth over her bony shoulders.

Holding the glass she pointed her pinky finger at Adara, "You are not going."

"What!" Adara's dark brows shot up. Too late she realized she had spoken out loud.

Estella's olive skin grew as dark as her roots, eyes narrowed to mean slits, she snarled, "You dare talk back to me!" Her palm cracked sudden and hard against her daughter's round cheek. Adara's head flew to the side from the strength of the slap, tears sprung immediately.

Adara wanted to beg, to plead, her shoulders slumped as she held a hand over her stinging cheek, but knew it would be to no avail.

Estella never admitted or took back any wrong she ever said or did. The booze kept her confident she was the prima queen, always right, everyone was placed on the planet to bow to her.

Keeping her head down and eyes lowered, Adara hid her pain. Not the physical pain, she'd grown used to Estella's rampages, her battering hands and kicking feet. Adara grew skilled at dodging flying plates and vases. She still carried a scar behind her ear when she was young and hadn't yet figured out how to get out of the way of dishes flung in a blind rage.

It was the pain of once again not being able to do as the other kids did. She would not be allowed to attend the dance. Her heart twisted, dried up and broke into bitter little pieces.

Once, a long time ago, she had beseeched her father to talk to her mother, get her to change her mind about letting her be a Bluejay. The girls met after school to work on tasks to earn badges for their bright blue sashes.

Salvatore Valentina coldly advised his daughter that he had more important things to do, like head a criminal organization, than to run interference between Adara and Estella. As it was, he was hardly home, preferring to stay at an apartment on the other side of the city away from his shrew of a drunken fishwife.

One of the syndicate's enterprises held several apartments for various reasons, such as for important men coming to town for business to stay at, and for paramour assignations, for illegal card games, and for the occasional drugging, drunken orgy.

Salvatore used it for all of the above as well as other nefarious things. The fancy and expensive apartment had blood on its walls. Painted over of course, but there nonetheless.

At this point, Estella and Salvatore were estranged, and that only kicked up Estella's drinking, and her rage.

Estella screamed at Adara, "I will not have you be your father's daughter, whoring around like he does! You are lucky I let you out to go to school!"

Her bloodshot bleary eyes narrowed further as she considered, "In fact, maybe I should send you away. A good, locked-down girl's boarding school in some third world country will keep you humble and out of trouble, my sassy-mouthed girl."

Pointing again with her pinky, she took a gulp of the vodka she thought she had nicely disguised as water. She smiled with a sneer as she sipped; the lemon was a nice touch.

Thinking about Salvatore's extra-marital adventures always added fuel to Estella's already burning rage. She stomped closer to Adara, glancing around for a weapon.

"I've had it with you, you little slut!" Spying a fireplace poker, she stormed across the room to get it.

"This will knock you down a peg, you fucking little mafia princess!" A murderous gleam glowed in the red-veined eyes bleary with alcohol seepage. Reaching for the poker, she bellowed, "I will show you, you damned-"

A sudden rapping at the arched opening to the living room stopped her. Her head bopped up as a genuine smile showed her yellowing teeth.

Within seconds, a servant ushered Estella's most recent lover into the living room. Estella brightened and rushed to her lover.

"Eduardo!" she shrieked, throwing her arms around his neck. The glass flew out of her hand and cracked against the wall then thumped hitting the floor. The clear liquor poured down the wallpaper like the blood draining from Adara's face.

Eduardo peered over Estella's shoulder at her. He had a rangy narrow face and beady eyes. Those eyes were blatantly devouring Adara while his tongue made lascivious circles around his thin lips.

Grinning at Adara, he winked, reminding her it was only a matter of time before he got her alone.

He had trapped her in the kitchen a few days ago. Adara fought off his octopus hands while he whispered the dirty, kinky things he was going to do to her when no one else was around to stop him. Promises of bondage, whips, cages he could stand under and poke up at her naked body with a-

Blinking the repulsive pictures out of her mind, Adara slid along the wall towards the door.

As Estella pushed Eduardo out of the room, locking lips now, she had one arm wrapped around his neck while she groped at his crotch.

Her mortified face as red as a beet, Adara made a dash around the brazenly grasping, horny couple and darted out the door just barely dodging Eduardo's leeching hand grabbing at her.

Racing down the hall, Adara bolted for the door. Just as she reached out for the knob, one of the servants stopped her.

"Miss Adara." A stiff-faced, grey-haired woman in a grey and white uniform approached from another corridor.

Smoothing her agitated expression of anger and despair, Adara cleared her throat and turned gracefully to the maid. "Yes, Mrs. Gilkes?"

"I just want to make you are aware that I am leaving in five minutes and the others have already gone for the day. As…usual," Gilkes' lips twisted in a disapproving purse, "your mother…"

Sighing heavily, Adara nodded miserably. "Yes. I understand."

The maid was advising her that Estella would be alone, at least once Eduardo had his fill of her which was usually less than an hour and he split. Whenever Estella was alone, she managed to get hurt or in trouble, such as stealing a neighbor's car and getting another DUI.

Estella could not be left alone; therefore, Adara could not make her escape.

Dispensing a sharp nod, the maid turned and trod back down the hall, the rubber soles of her shoes making soft plopping sounds on the thick carpet. In seconds Adara heard the side door close.

Traipsing down the hall, she headed for the staircase, then trudged despondently up the steps to her room, to use a phone. To call Mikell and tell him she couldn't go to the dance.

She swiped angrily at the tears that teemed. Sometimes she just wished her mother was-

BANG!

The blast of a shot ricocheted through the mansion. Adara halted on the steps. Then her mother's blood-chilling screams rent the air.

Spinning around, Adara trampled down the stairs, tripped and caught herself, then continued running along the corridors towards the screaming, her pulse raced faster than her legs could go.

The screams were coming from the den.

Adara burst into the room, then came to such a dead stop she skidded almost falling flat on her face.

In the middle of the room, Eduardo was lying on his stomach. A river of blood saturated the center of his back, and was streaming over his sides forming a gruesome pool around him on the area rug that overlay the varnished hardwood floor.

In the hunter green and dark wood framed room, Estella stood next to him, a gun in her shaking hand, her other hand covered her mouth when she saw Adara standing wide-eyed in the doorway.

"Mother! What happened?" Her face pinched with squeamish dread, Adara made her way to her mother, circumventing Eduardo's prone figure with his blood discoloring the rug and seeping into the varnished wood beneath. "Is- is he-"

Nodding frantically, Estella cried, "Yes!" Then more soberly, she whispered, "Yes, he's dead." Her face softened from the alcohol suddenly hardened. Deep creases ringing her once beautiful mouth, she spat with irate venom, "The bastard."

"What-" Adara slipped around the dead man without looking at him to reach her mother's side. Through a tremor-filled voice she said, "Mother, please, put the gun down and tell me what happened!"

A sigh shuddered from Estella's thin body rattling her bones. Without looking, she set the gun on the nearest table.

"He," sniffing back furious tears, she replied, "the bastard wanted me to get," she paused, her bloodshot accusing eyes lanced furiously at Adara.

"Get? Get what?" Adara's mind was spinning, what should they do? Call her father? The police? She didn't know, she'd only just turned thirteen, a kid, what was she supposed to do?

"You," Estella sneered with a spit of virulence. Her lip curled with hate, she spat, "The bastard wanted you. Said he wanted a threesome."

She snorted. "Me, him, and you. When I told him no fucking way, I mean I'm sure as hell not sharing my man with you." Her sneer grazed down Adara like she was not fit to live.

Snorting a harsh laugh, she shook her head with disbelief. "When I told him no, he said fine, he'd just do you. Can you believe it? Him turning down a real woman for a scrawny teenaged slut." Her snide gaze again tracked over Adara as if she wasn't worth a dime. "You know what he said when I said no way?"

Skin pale as ivory, bewildered and disoriented, Adara shook her head in wretched despair. Her eyes flicked to the man on the floor. It was ghastly, her stomach churned, she was going to lose the salad she had for lunch.

Eduardo's skin drained ashen, the blood completely surrounded him and still kept coming.

Estella looked to where Adara was staring, gave a callous indifferent shrug that the man's lifeblood was leaving his body. "He told me he was only dating me to get near to you. Ha," she snorted rudely. "As if you could call 'slam bam thank you ma'am's dating. The guy shot his load in bare minutes, never cared about getting me off."

She gazed down at him in disgust. "Anyway," her red stained eyes rose with animosity to Adara. "This is your fault. All your fault. If you hadn't led him on, you whore, this never would have happened."

Shaking her head in bizarre incredulity that there was a man dying on the floor of their den, and her mother was talking this way to her, her own young daughter, Adara covered her mouth with a shaking hand. Miserably gulping down her shock, she stuttered, "We- we need to call, uh, the police, maybe Daddy, we-"

"No!" Estella shrieked reaching for the gun. "No, we will do nothing of the kind. We can't let your father know, and I am too beautiful and fragile to go through his punishment."

Struggling to think, she pondered through her alcohol sodden brain, then came up with it. "I know who to call. Where the hell is my-"

Spotting her phone, she stumbled to it, grabbed it up off the floor and started scrolling through her contacts. "That cute guy from the gang I dated last year, Jake or something, let me see, his people will take care of everything. Ah, here it is," she started dialing.

Adara couldn't hear what she said as she mumbled into the cell. The blood was rushing through her head deafening her, scrambling her brains, she couldn't think. Her body shook like she was standing in a blizzard with no jacket.

She could not wrap her mind around what happened. One second, obnoxious Eduardo was with her mother all hot and heavy and the next- her stomach retched, she couldn't look down at the dead man.

Tossing her phone back on the table, for just killing a man Estella spoke quite calmly to her daughter, "I have a cleanup-crew coming. You go to the door, wait for them."

Eyes rounded with shock, Adara muttered, "Huh?"

Taking a threatening step towards her daughter, Estella raised her hand, "You get your slutty, filthy, trouble-causing, man-stealing self to the door and you let them in. Remember, this is all your fault."

When Adara just stood blinking at her in confusion, Estella viciously slapped her and screamed, "Right now! You go there right now! Now! Now!"

Her face all twisted and sallow, she kept screaming until Adara running down the hall with her hands over her ears could no longer hear her.

Chapter Four

It was a short wait before a mind-boggled, distraught Adara heard a car coming up the semi-circle drive. She peeked out the curtain and saw a black SUV, like her father drove, parking right in front of the door.

Her eyes lowered in desperate fear, struggling to hold the panic in, she didn't wait for the person to knock, she opened the door a crack.

Petrified of the entire situation, she stared down at a pair of black dress boots. When the person didn't say anything, she fearfully raised her eyes.

Like a bolt of lightning striking her, a small cry eked out. Adara stepped back so quickly she almost fell, her hand flew to her battering heart slamming at her ribcage, the other clutched madly at the door handle to steady herself.

Terror stealing her voice, she whispered, "It's- you- what are you doing here?"

"Adara," his voice, masculine deep and husky. The heavy guttural accent so unusual, made everything he uttered come out a raw growl, and sound hideously dangerous. Her name said in that dark, foreign baritone sent shivers through her entire body.

Eyes of blue ice burned into her as if he could knife right through her cocoa irises and cut into her soul. The blue ice roved, ever-so-slowly down her body, taking their time rolling over her budding breasts, flat belly, her girlish hips.

When she just stared at him with obvious fear, Vaclav Braşov commanded, "Adara. Let me in."

The brilliant blue eyes half-hidden under his low-ridged brow and hooded lids still pierced at her, they shot down her body again and back up.

Feeling naked under his scalding glower, Adara quickly pushed the door closed, her throat constricting, she stammered, "You- you can't-"

He shoved his huge hand up blocking the door from closing. "*Da*, I can." Her strength was no match for his.

He calmly pushed the door open, she had no choice but to back up or she'd be steamrolled by six plus feet, give or take four or five inches, of sheer, formidable muscle.

Stepping inside, he closed and locked the door behind him, then turned to face her. His hair, darker on the shorter sides, the lighter blond on top was longer than she'd remembered it.

Adara backed away from him, her gaze bouncing everywhere seeking the quickest escape.

"Stop," he commanded. "You take another step and I will grab you and prevent you from moving."

She froze in place. One foot partially behind her ready to take off, she stood still.

His narrowed eyes dared her to run, clearly he would go after her like a voracious tiger and fleeing gazelle and easily take her down.

She prepared for his attack, the way he looked at her, so disturbing, creepy, he was an adult, at least 21, she was just entering her teens.

But Vaclav didn't make another move towards her and kept his eyes on her face. He said, "My...team, received a phone call. From a hysterical woman saying she needed a private...cleanup. I recognized the address; I came to see first what was going on. To understand why Salvatore was not involved. They said that the caller was an adult woman, you are a child. Explain to me."

She couldn't help it; gulping sporadically she couldn't get the words out, "I- I- I-"

He stomped over to her, "Goddammit, Adara, where are your parents? Your brother?" His eyes raked the foyer. "The servants?" Back to her, the blue orbs narrowed, he asked, "Are you here alone?"

She stood with her lips moving and no words coming out.

He grabbed her upper arms and shook her. The heavy accent obscuring his words, he barked, "Goddammit, snap out of it, tell me what the hell is going on! Are you hurt? Do you need to go to the hospital?"

She couldn't make her vocal cords work, she just stared helplessly up at the big bruiser, her abject terror of him radiating from rounded eyes like of melted chocolate.

His strong fingers wrapped around her thin arms, he could feel her shaking so much it was as if her entire body vibrated.

"Adara!" a woman's strident voice shrieked from a hallway. "Where the hell are you, you stupid girl? I see a car out the window, let them in and get in here or I will fucking shoot you next you useless piece of slut shit!"

Adara's eyes dropped in mortification, her pale cheeks flamed in shame. She didn't dare look up at him.

Releasing one of her arms, Vaclav kept his grip on her other arm and dragged her towards her mother's shrill, humiliating shrieks.

Adara dared a quick glance up at the big, fierce Russian. His mouth was set hard as rock as if he grit his teeth. His lids were low over eyes that, to Adara, looked furious, as if he wanted to hurt someone, bad. She didn't want it to be her.

The woman's snarling shouts guiding him, he pulled her down a second hallway that led them to the den.

He stepped into the room keeping ahold of Adara's arm, bringing her with him.

Estella Valentina's mouth was open in mid-shriek, her eyes widened when she saw Vaclav, the red glossy lips slapped closed. She had managed to refresh her lipstick while Adara waited at the front door.

Estella wore a low-cut, white silk dress that had tiny blue flowers woven on it. Her hair was neatly combed, the frizzy ends perched on her narrow shoulders. On her feet were sexy kitten heels.

Her eyes, brown, but not as deep and rich as her daughter's gleamed in carnal interest at him. They raked over his broad thick shoulders, lowering to his powerful chest in the black shirt, lower still to his lean hips clothed in black jeans, where they paused on his fly.

The corner of her mouth lifted, her pointy tongue slid out to lick it. Her alcohol-saturated eyes heated with blatant desire.

"Ah," her seductive smile came with a simper, "Vaclav Braşov, the big man himself." Her eyes still on the bulge behind his zipper, she raised them slowly to his face making no secret of her lewd invitation.

"I hear you're Viggo Garatteo's number one now. And so young," she purred. "They say you were recruited as a very young orphan right off the cold mean streets of Russia to work as one of his runners before being brought here. Now, a ruthless enforcer, your reputation for savagery is legendary." The tongue came back out to swirl around her red lips.

Still holding Adara's arm, Vaclav growled, "Mrs. Valentina, you called…"

Estella stood to the front and to the side of the dead man splayed on the rug.

The den looked comfortable with navy leather and cushioned chairs, bookcases with all the books in tidy, neat rows, two wide bright windows and a huge bricked fireplace. The grisly body seeping blood on the nice blue carpet was grotesquely incongruent with the cozy room.

Her eyes continued raking Vaclav's body while a flush rolled up her face indicating the heat she was feeling between her legs for the Russian brute. "The word is," she said with a lisp of lewdness on her words, "that you killed your first man before you were 12, is that true?" Her eyes glowed with alcohol and bloodthirsty lust.

Vaclav's eyes went from Estella to Eduardo. He trod forward and crouched beside the prone man. Avoiding touching the blood, he reached out a long arm to feel for a pulse, although with the amount of blood loss, it was obvious no one could have survived.

Standing up, he looked at Adara's stricken white face then to the smirk on her mother's hallow-cheeked, yellow-hued face.

To Estella, he demanded, "Tell me."

Estella floated towards him, her kitten heels clacking on the wood panels that encircled the center rug, "Oh," she giggled, then forced her expression into a worried oval. "Adara," she started, shaking her head, she clicked her tongue.

"*Well*," she sighed dramatically, then said, "apparently, Eduardo, being the typical horndog male, fell for my daughter's slutty wiles. When he told her he wasn't serious with her, well," she shrugged negligently. "Poor Adara couldn't take the rejection, and, she, well," she motioned to the dead man.

"Anyway," she sighed as if with mild regret. "We can make an excuse for Adara, like, maybe it was in self-defense, or perhaps she tripped and accidentally shot him. Seriously," she smirked at Vaclav, "my daughter is as graceful as a ballerina, but," the fried blonde hair swished as she shook her head, a disparaging smirk lifted one side of her cracked lips.

"Everyone knows she is clumsy as a new born calf. Keeps her head in the clouds, trips over everything, another scourge to make my poor life harder, you know?"

Vaclav's intense blue eyes narrowed at her, then flicked to Adara who stood frozen in shock, keeping her eyes off Eduardo's body, she swung them in disbelief at her mother.

He could imagine she kept her head in the clouds to stay above the shit that was her life. Vaclav's steely gaze returned to Estella. "Try again."

When Estella snorted affronted and opened her mouth, he snapped, "The truth you old whore or I walk out right now and you are on your own."

Estella's mouth dropped open with her gasp, "How dare you! How dare-" Vaclav turned and started for the door.

"Wait!" she yelled. "Wait, I'll…" taking a deep breath she exhaled loudly, beleaguered. "I will tell you what happened."

Shooting a warning glance at her daughter, Estella told Vaclav, "Eduardo attacked me in a jealous fury for no reason, I was only protecting myself. It was purely self-defense, he had his hands on my throat, I had to stop him," she said with a sharp snap of her head, hard eyes challenging Vaclav to call her a liar.

He had seen the bullet hole in the man's back. *Interesting self-defense*, he thought. He spoke a few brief words into his phone.

When he was done, Vaclav said, "You two leave. Take two, three hours before returning. Anyone else coming here? Servants?"

Wrapping her thin arms around her bony chest, Estella shook her head. "No. I sent them away for the day because I wanted to be alone with," she glanced at Eduardo with no emotion.

"*Bine*. I will wait here, you two leave." He looked at his watch then settled his deadly eyes on Estella and ordered her, "You leave first. I do not want you together. You speak of this to no one. Ever."

"All right," Estella sniffed heading for the door. "I need to grab my purse." Without a word to her daughter, or a sign of concern for what the young teen just experienced, or for her dead lover on the floor, she flounced out of the room.

Her steps small, light, Adara moved gracefully, quietly to the door.

"Adara," Vaclav said.

She stopped and turned to him.

"You have somewhere safe to go? Do you want me to take you?"

Clearing her nervous throat, her shy voice shaking, she said softly, "I can go to Crystal's house, I don't need a ride." Obviously the last thing she wanted to do was be alone in a car with him. "Um," keeping her head down, she said, "I...uh, thank you, Mr. Braşov."

She raised her dark eyes to his glinting blues, then, seeing the enigmatic danger lurking in them, she quickly looked away. She was too young to recognize the banked desire that blazed like wildfire in the pulsing, enlarged pupils, but she did feel uncomfortable from the heat of them.

She murmured, "I, um, owe you, sir."

One dark blond brow arched at her comment, but he said nothing.

When he didn't respond, Adara awkwardly turned and left the room. Feeling the same as when she was a little girl, knowing his eyes bored into her back, she hurried to leave the house before he had second thoughts about letting her leave.

A few weeks later, a tiny blurb in the back of the paper about a man, Eduardo Mejia was reported missing by his roommate when he failed to return home or respond to the roommate's efforts to reach him by phone.

Adara couldn't stand Estella's look of smug satisfaction, like she hadn't murdered a man in cold blood and walked away scott-free.

Adara spent long days in school, staying late in dance class to avoid being home as Estella continued parading men through their home and drinking herself blind every night.

Occasionally her father would show up and the magnitude of the fights was unbearable.

Whenever she saw Salvatore's car pull up, Adara fled out the back door.

Chapter Five

Over the next two years, Adara only saw the mysterious, scary Vaclav Brașov a few times. As before, she avoided him, often turning her back and rushing away as he approached her.

She had been terrified before of him. After he came and, like a ghoul in a cemetery, calmly, easily, expressing zero emotion, inexplicitly had a murdered man picked up and disposed of, and had the rug replaced and the wood floor beneath cleaned of the blood and guts as if no one had ever died there, she was petrified of him now.

Afraid she would be caught alone with him, the second she heard his accented voice, or saw his dark blond head inches above many other men, she ran as fast as she could in the opposite direction.

Adara clamped her hands over her ears. Her mother and her estranged husband, Salvatore, Adara's father, were at it again. She scrambled to the back of her closet and put her earbuds in.

The mansion was enormous but she could still hear the fighting and screaming. Trying to listen to music and do her homework by flashlight, Adara struggled to tune the din out.

Then, in a déjà vu moment, a gunshot boomed.

The deafening retort resonated along the walls, up the staircase and into Adara's hiding place.

At first she tried to pretend it didn't happen, that she didn't really hear it, that it was an anomaly of her earbuds, but, as the quaking in her body started, she couldn't ignore it.

Climbing to shaking legs, she crept out of the closet and hesitated. Standing stock still, she listened. Not a sound. None of the bloodcurdling screams like when Eduardo had died.

Last thing she wanted to do was leave her room, but, her footsteps silent, she moved cautiously down the stairs. At the bottom, she paused again to listen, but there wasn't a sound.

Then, she heard her mother cursing.

Following the ugly coarse sounds, Adara found herself in the foyer. Her breath sucked in loudly at the sight.

As before, Estella was standing calmly over a man lying on the floor. This time it was Adara's father, Salvatore Valentina.

Hearing the sound, Estella swung around. Seeing her daughter's face as pale as a dinner plate, she marched over to her, snatched up Adara's hand, shoved the gun into it, and held her own two hands over Adara's.

"Mama, wha-"

Estella jerked her finger over Adara's forcing her to pull the trigger. The bullet went straight into the wall. Estella let go of Adara's hand.

Her ears ringing, the heavy gun fell from Adara's small shocked hands, clunking to the floor. She gasped, "Mother! What happened?"

Estella hurried out of the room leaving Adara standing bewildered with her father's body already in the blood pool just like Eduardo.

In a minute Estella returned wiping her hands on a towel.

"Mama-"

"For God's sake stop whining you fool," she griped with an irritated exhale. Her gaunt face crinkled with an unsightly smile at her daughter's horrified expression. "Now, my darling daughter, you are in it as much as me."

She trod over to Adara and snaked hard fingers digging her nails around her arm, giving it a nasty shake. "You will get a fucking grip and do as I say."

Tears welling, lips quivering, Adara's eyes hopped to the ghastly sight of her father bleeding out on the floor and back to her. "B- but Mama, an ambulance, Daddy-"

"Shut up!" Estella gave her another callous shake. "Listen to me, the neighbors are around now, unlike before and they've undoubtedly called the cops. I won't have time for the cleanup this time. You will do as I say, you hear me?" Digging her fingers into Adara's skin she shook her viciously.

The big dark eyes blinked with bewilderment and fear, not a word left her frightened lips.

"Good." Taking her silence as acquiescence, Estella told her, "At almost 15, you are still a minor. But me," she managed to make her face sorrowful, miserable. "If I am arrested I will die in jail. You understand me?"

Not really, but still blinking in catatonic horror Adara mutely nodded her head.

Rolling her eyes with an aggrieved sigh, Estella said, "You will tell the police it was you. That you and he had a fight, over a boy, curfew, whatever, and you took his gun from the drawer and shot him."

Her aghast eyes wide with confusion, Adara cried in dismay, "But it was you- Daddy never kept guns here. That's yours..." She motioned to the pistol on the floor near the body.

Shaking her so hard Adara's head whipped back and forth, Estella shouted, "No! You tell them it was his gun, in the drawer, and you shot him. Adara."

Her voice lowered, "You have gunshot residue on your hands. I washed it off mine. They will test you and conclude you shot him anyway."

Confusion wreathing her face white as snow, tears streaming, Adara cried, "But, I didn't, it was you-" Sirens wailed in the distance.

Estella gentled her grasp on Adara's arm, the hard angles of her face softened, she said with sweet coaxing, "Baby, please. You are a juvenile, you will probably only get probation. Do you want to see your mother go to prison and die there, sick and broken?"

She forced a couple of tears to squeeze out, made her expression wretched with fear. "I am your mother, Adara, you would not have life if not for me, you owe me. All I'm asking is that you give a little back to me." She begged, squeezing out another tear, "Please save your dear mama's life, baby, please."

Rough pounding struck the front door. Estella patted her daughter's face with a tender, pleading smile and whispered, "Please baby, I love you," and she headed the opposite way of the front door.

"Mama…" Adara stood watching her mother disappear out to the hall. In seconds she heard one of the back doors close.

The pounding grew louder, harder, voices shouted, "Police! Open the door or we will take it down!"

A few more threats shouted, but Adara could not make her feet move, and the door suddenly burst open crashing against the wall.

Men shouting commands of, "Police! Do not move! Hands above your head!" roiled around Adara.

Her father on the floor, her mother gone, huge officers yelling and rushing at her with weapons out, she couldn't move.

Someone grabbed her, kicked her legs out from under her letting her fall to the floor on her stomach. Her arms were yanked behind her back and she was cuffed. She lay there immobilized while the police searched the house.

When they returned, a big harsh officer roughly lifted her to her feet and held her arm extra forcefully as if the small teen could run away.

He lowered his face to hers, spittle flew as he barked at her, "What did you do? Did you shoot this man? Answer me!"

Her mother's pleading in her ears, Adara's teeth clenched in shock and grief and profound confusion, she said nothing, just dropped her head to stare at the floor.

"Fine, the prosecutor will deal with you, little murderer." Jerking her to the door, the officer read her, her rights as he brought her to a police car and shoved her in.

Adara sat in the back staring out the side window. Several police cars were in the drive, blue lights swirling, officers were shouting and running about the yard and into the house.

Neighbors gathering in curiosity stared wide-eyed at Adara sitting terrified in the back seat of the police car, her white face in shock.

Their nosy gazes immediately turned to accusation. The chatter grew loud enough she could hear, they claimed she wouldn't be under arrest if she was innocent.

An iron grate blocked her from the officers climbing in the front. The leather under her was cold and worn, holes were patched with duct tape.

Her mind a reeling jumble of her father and blood and her mother deserting her, dragged out of her home in cuffs and thrust roughly into the police cad, tears welled then spilled.

As the car pulled from the curb, crying silently for her mama, in her panicking bewilderment, Adara wondered, *would she wake from this nightmare?*

****

A few weeks passed, Adara sat alone in the cell she shared with another inmate also awaiting trial.

At first, she had just waited patiently, confident that her mother would come and get her out. But Estella never came.

Then, she assumed her brother or her uncle, aunts, someone would come. But they didn't. No one came.

It was another couple of weeks before her public defender showed. Accused of killing her father, she could not use any family funds, and none of her relatives offered monetary help, so the judge appointed a PD.

Still in a shocked daze, wearing an orange jumpsuit, Adara was brought out of the cell to an interview room. Her wrists remained cuffed, the guard not gently pushed her to sit in a chair then went to lean against the wall.

The room was ten x ten with only a white plastic table and two matching chairs.

It seemed quite a while before a frazzled young woman lugging a huge bag over her shoulder appeared in the doorway. Heaving burdened sighs, she battled the big bag into the tiny room.

Her pallid face flushed, the woman dropped the bag on the table, noisily rummaged in it then dug out a file. Letting the folder plop down, she sat down herself and shoved her frayed pale red hair out of her pale blue eyes.

Smoothing the rumpled jacket of the unattractive paisley suit, she peered at Adara through oblong glasses with one eye in a squint. "Huh. You don't look like a killer," shrugged, "but then, no one ever really does."

Pushing her glasses up her narrow nose she said with a limp smile, "Except for those guys with tattoos on their faces and necks and whatever, now they truly look like murderers, am I right?"

When Adara just stared at her in confusion, the woman sighed, "Anyhoo." She took a breath. "I am Gilda Wright, your judicially appointed attorney."

She didn't hold out her hand to shake, just peered again over the black-rimmed glasses at a silent, wan Adara, the teen's eyes as big and tired as burnt asteroids.

"So," Wright went on, "the prosecutor is offering a plea. I think it's a good one, I mean, honey, you did mow down your dad in cold blood."

At the flash in Adara's dark eyes the PD shuffled back in her chair. "Anyhoo, if you plead nolo contendere to the charge," she leaned forward and spoke as if teaching a young child.

"That means no contest. It means you don't contest the charges, you're not saying you did it, but you're also not saying you didn't. If you agree, you won't have to go to trial and take a chance on a more stringent sentence.

"Like, heck, this is New York, they could try you as an adult and if you're found guilty, which you clearly are, you can get the death penalty." She paused at the horrified gasp that came from Adara.

Her eyes owlish behind the specs, satisfied she'd frightened the young girl sufficiently, Gilda went on, "Because your father was a well-known, atrocious crime-boss that deserved to die, the prosecutor is offering to charge you as a juvenile, and sentence you to incarceration until you turn nineteen, maybe twenty or so."

The shock was like a slap in the face. Adara's lashes bolted straight up, her mouth dropped open, she choked, "What?"

Gilda draped an arm over the back of her chair, slipped off the glasses and tapped them on the file in front of her.

Then she leaned forward again and oh so seriously said, "Honey, it's a gift. Like I said, if he tries you as an adult you can possibly get the needle, the electric chair, or at best, life in prison if you're lucky." Nodding at Adara's rounded, terrified eyes, she sat back.

"Listen kid, I mean, shit, you killed your own father. They got a solid case against you. You were the only one in the house, the murder weapon was there and had your prints on it, and there was GSR on your hands. It's pretty much a slam dunk, ya know?"

Sitting stunned, her cuffed hands on the plastic table, fingers twined tightly, so bewildered, cauterized with fright, Adara didn't feel the pain as she twisted her fingers so hard in a second they would start breaking. One-by-one. Right now, she felt nothing but fear and hopeless dread.

"I recommend you take the offer, hon. You'll spend a couple years in juvy, what, four, five, maybe six years or so, might be a tad longer, but what's that compared to life or execution?" She stared at Adara waiting for a response, but only received a blank, blinking stare from the pale face.

"Okay, well, I have things to do, other prisoners to see. You think about the plea offer. I submitted a written plea of not guilty, we have a calendar call next week."

Still Adara said nothing.

With an annoyed sigh, Wright stood up. She had never even opened the file. She snatched it up, dropped it in the big bag and hauled the bag over her shoulder. The PD nodded to the guard, the deputy opened the door.

At the door, she turned around.

Adara sat staring blankly.

"You better think long and hard, kid, you got a week, you'd better make a decision. Make the smart one"

The guard let her out then walked Adara back to her cell.

Flopping on the bottom bunk, Adara fell on her back and dropped a forearm over her eyes.

"Hey." A face popped down over the edge from the bunk above. "That was quick. They said you were with your PD. How'd it go?" Curly blonde hair hung over a round, zit-covered face.

When Adara ignored her, she huffed, "Fine, bitch," and heavily dropped her body on the bunk.

The week had almost passed when a guard came to Adara. "You got a visitor, surprisingly. You ain't had one since you got here. Guess no one wants to hang with a murderer, huh?" The paunchy uniformed female snapped gum and twirled keys on a chain.

Swinging her legs down, Adara sat up and asked, "Who is it?"

Snapping noisily, the guard bumped a pudgy shoulder, "How the fuck should I know? What am I, your fucking secretary? It's a guy that's all they told me."

Adara brightened, maybe it was her brother Vincenzo, or her uncle. Finally, they cared, they came for her, they were only letting her stew, teaching her a lesson- she jumped up and hurried to the cell door.

The guard said rudely, "Slow down bitch, you know the drill. Stick your hands through the bars."

When Adara complied, the guard snapped a cuff on one wrist, then pushed her hands back inside before clamping on the other cuff. Then she wrapped a chain around her waist and hooked that to cuffs she snapped onto Adara's ankles.

She was then marched awkwardly down a hall, chains swinging and clinking.

The automatic cell doors clanged open and closed, obnoxious loud bells rang off and on, never ending chatter flowed up and down as they made their way from the cells to the viewing room.

As a murderer awaiting trial, Adara had to meet her visitor through a plate of clear sturdy plastic, using a phone to converse.

When the guard brought her around and she saw who sat there waiting on the other side of the glass, she gasped. Her step faltered, the guard gave her a hard shove.

Vaclav Brașov stood up with a glare at the guard.

Ignoring him, the guard kept shoving Adara until she reached the chair on her side of the glass and she pushed her down onto the chair.

Stomping off, the guard said over her shoulder, "You got ten minutes, the cameras see all," she nodded up a corner of the room. Cameras were perched in all four corners.

Adara sat motionless staring at Vaclav. He picked up the phone on his side and motioned for her to pick up hers.

Staring at him, then the phone, she gingerly lifted the receiver with both cuffed hands and put it to her ear. She said quietly, "What are you doing here? I told the guards before I did not want to see you."

Vaclav had submitted request after request to see her but she had refused them all.

His gaze flowed to her like a dying man in a parched land and she was a cool shimmering brook. "Adara," his thick accent distorted through the phone, iced blue eyes hooded, devoured her.

He said softly, "You look beautiful. Like a mink, huge dark eyes laced with silken lashes, soft dark hair like a luxurious fur coat."

Suddenly he bellowed into the phone, "What the fuck do you think you are doing!"

His voice had lulled her, his shout startled her. Adara's lashed flew up, she jumped back from the window dropping the phone.

"Sir," a guard warned Vaclav.

Without looking at the guard, Vaclav motioned for her to pick the phone back up.

Her eyes wary on him, she lifted it back to her ear.

Taking a huge breath, letting it out, carefully modulating his tone, he said, "What happened? Clearly that whore mother of yours killed Salvatore and you are taking the rap?"

When Adara moved to hang the phone up, he said quickly, "Wait. Listen." He bent his head to the window, she leaned back as if he could reach through the glass and grab her.

"Adara," he sighed. "I can get you out of there."

Her eyes popped wide with fear.

"*Na, na,*" he shook his head. "Legally, *mea* sweet. I will find that bitc- uh, Estella, and make her talk. I can fix this-"

Adara stood up.

Vaclav mirrored her and stood up. "*Na,* Adara wait, listen to me-"

Shaking her head, she moved to hang the phone up.

Vaclav shouted, "*Na,* do not do this, you do not belong here! Let me help you, please, Adara!"

Holding the phone to her mouth, she whispered, "Please don't come back. I will refuse to see you." She hung the phone up and turned and shuffled in her chains to the guard.

She could hear Vaclav bellowing behind the glass, yelling her name. She followed the guard out and back to her cell.

Chapter Six

She took the plea.

A few days later, Adara was transferred to a high security juvenile prison.

Every day was the same in the bleak, miserable place. The girls had to rise at five in the morning, breakfast at 5:25, then they went to classes.

After classes they all had chores. They were rotated between laundry, kitchen duty, mopping, sewing, seldom were they given a moment to themselves.

They worked until 6:00 at night then had dinner followed by two hours of television, then they were put back into their cells.

Within the day they were allowed one hour of time to themselves in the two commons areas, and that was staggered to hopefully keep the gang members associating, and fighting, to a minimum.

Some of the detainees had books, games, iReaders, because people put money in their commissary fund for nonessentials. Adara had to work extra hard to earn points so she could at least borrow a book from the prison library.

When not immersed in a chore with a guard at her back, Adara had to literally watch her back. The prison was rife with gangs. Many girls joined a gang just to have the protection.

But to join a gang entailed initiation. Initiation included but was not inclusive to, the candidate had to allow any other girl to beat her whenever they felt like it, had to steal extra food for the leaders, have willing sex with any girl, or girls, at their choosing, submit to unsanitary jailhouse tats of the gang, and numerous other rites that Adara had no interest in going along with.

She would take her chances, and hell came with those chances.

Later, for the rest of her life the nightmares would butcher her sleep, the times she had been assaulted, beaten, drenched her dreams. Struggling, fighting in her sleep she often woke up screaming. Heart racing, body trembling with fright, so afraid of losing herself in the nightmares, she went long periods without sleep.

Once Adara's brother came to visit her. She was so excited, so thrilled to see him, she wept when she entered the visitors' heavily guarded room.

"Vincenzo!" she shrieked as she ran to throw herself into his arms. But he turned, blocking the contact.

Crestfallen, she stepped back from him. "Vincenzo, what is the matter? I've missed you, I've missed home, I've missed-"

"Father?" his eyes narrowed into mean arrows. So cold, a frosted mist clung to his words, he said cruelly, "Have you missed father? After all, it was you who took him away from us? Huh?" He gripped her arm, then immediately let it go like she was filled with venom and he feared her bite.

Then he grabbed her again with both hands and shook her fiercely, "How about Mother? She apparently fled for her life from you and has been in hiding ever since. Do you miss her too?" His fingers bit furiously into her arms, bruising not only her skin, but her heart as well.

"But," she cried, tears welled blurring her eyes, turning them to dark pudding. She stared at her older brother who glared back at her like she was an ant he wanted to crush beneath the heel of his boot.

He released her arms, throwing them from him as if they fouled his hands.

She reached out to touch him, he flinched away. Brows lowering, she asked quietly, "Why did you come here, Vincenzo?"

He stood just under six feet of lean muscle, dark wavy hair kept short. His legs shorter than his torso, when he grew older he would have the same barrel-chested heft and fuller cheeked face of his father. His sullen, dark brown eyes stared down at her without compassion, no love shone there for his baby sister.

With a shrug, he turned his head from her, then turned back and glared so hard at her she felt the hatred burn in a scalding wave over her skin.

His hands snatched out and gripped her arms again. "I was sent to inform you that when you get out, how it will be. You will be staying at Uncle Massimo's."

Squeezing his rough fingers around her arms he told her with cold hostility, "Understand, he is not doing that out of love. He hates you, he wanted you dead too for killing his brother, *our* father. But, you are blood, and the *familia* honor dictates that he cannot have you murdered for your crime. But you will stay under his thumb for him to do with you as he pleases."

Around them, other prisoners visited in the dour room of grey cement walls, no windows, and the only door to the outside was barred and well-guarded.

There were cheerful hugs and happy smiles, sorrowful faces for the loved one's suffering inside the prison. Some laughter rippled out, loud voices erupted here and there, a couple of lovers tried to steal kisses under the guards' noses.

Adara's mouth opened, the words stammered out almost inaudibly, "And what does he please to do…to me?"

Vincenzo's furious gaze raked over her, surly eyes glowing with his own deep hatred of his little sister. "Once things settle down after you return home, he will," his eyes shifted away with a hint of guilt, then pinged back to hers before lowering so he wasn't looking at her.

"He will loan you out for a while at a price, then he will sell you as a bride. There is a Pakistani king or drug-lord or someshit that has mentioned his desire to have you."

At the look of horror that filled her face and drained it of all color, he let go of her, ducked his head, stuffed his hands in his pockets and hunched his shoulders.

His gaze rose cold to her, he said with zero compassion, "The Pakistani will take you to his desert home so you will be out of our sight, and then we won't have to suffer seeing your fucking betraying face ever again."

"Wha- what do you mean loan me out? For what? As a maid? I don't understand?"

Color stained his thick cheeks. "Come on, Adara, I have to spell it out for you? For sex, you dumb bitch. He will rent you out to whore."

At the tears that sprung loose and overflowed down her soft face, the spots of red darkened on his cheeks. With barely suppressed fury he ground out, "Don't give me that shit, Adara, feeling sorry for yourself. You brought this on yourself, you," he suddenly gripped her arm again pulling her towards him.

Face an inch from hers he snarled, "You killed our dad, you deserved to fry. Instead, you got a cushy cell in a comfy prison that you'll leave when you are of age, get fucking real. You deserve to pay for your crime, Adara. That's all I came to tell you." He threw her arm, releasing her in revulsion.

Vincenzo spun and started to walk to the exit, Adara cried out, "Vincenzo, please, I didn't, it wasn't me-" she broke off, what could she say?

She couldn't deny the deed now, she was convicted and sentenced, no one would ever believe her, not even her own brother. No one except Vaclav Braşov.

A shiver hurtled through her. A mobster. Only an infamous, ruthless, butchering mobster believed her.

Vincenzo paused near the gated exit.

Adara cried, "Vincenzo, please, please don't leave me, please!"

His shoulders stiffened, and her brother strode out without looking back, the bars clanged mercilessly behind him, locking her in.

The only other visitor she'd had was Crystal and Crystal's mother. But the visit was so awkward. Her mother stayed way near the door never once looking at Adara, and Crystal clearly conveyed revulsion and fear of the surroundings, and worse, she was unable to completely hide how afraid, and repulsed she now was of Adara.

So much so that when she thought about it later, Adara figured maybe she had come on a dare. Their other friends, none of whom even wrote her, maybe they wanted to play games, see how the big murderess was holding up.

Maybe Crystal was to go back and report on what it was like to be in a room with a cold blooded killer that they had grown up with. A girl who killed her mobster father.

Didn't matter anyway, Crystal never returned to visit her again, and no one else, not even her Aunt Bianca ever requested to see her.

No one that is, except again, Vaclav Braşov, the last person she wanted to see. His requests to visit her never ceased the entire time she was incarcerated. He wrote her, she had the letters returned unopened, he put money in her commissary account, she had that returned as well.

The only reason she could fathom that he continued to pursue her was that he undoubtedly thought he could recruit her as an assassin for his own deadly organization.

As a young female that already proved how easily she could commit murder, she could sneak around and kill people and no one would suspect the young girl with the big dark eyes. Well, that was not going to happen.

So, she spent her days alone and lonely, dodging lascivious dangerous gang girls, working back-breaking chores, and getting her GED. After that, she started elective college courses.

There were only two people on the inside who seemed to care about her, one of them was Priscilla.

An enormous, young black woman with huge, flowing, tight blonde curls. Priscilla somehow knew when Adara was being assaulted, sexually and otherwise, and came to her rescue. She had girth, but she also had muscle and was head of her own gang.

When Adara tried to talk to her, give her thanks, Priscilla would brush her off and disappear until the next time Adara was in dire danger.

The other person that seemed to care was a guard. In her fifties, round-bellied and grey-haired, Mamie Howell had shown Adara an old harp.

Dusty with nonuse, it was stowed in a storage room with other useless or broken junk. Mamie knew how to play it, but her arthritic fingers wouldn't float over the strings anymore, so she taught a willing Adara to play.

Thus, when she had that daily free hour, Adara spent it alone, or with Mamie, playing tranquilly.

With the dulcet sounds of the heavenly plucked strings, she could mentally transport herself away, out of the dismal, treacherous prison to somewhere sunny, where the sparkling blue ocean crested on soft sand and the breeze tickled her hair.

Her only peace in that dreary dungeon was the time she spent with the harp. The rest of the days were rigorously hard, perilous, grim and lonely.

The days passed one boring, claustrophobic day after the other, never changing except for the rotation of chores, and the assaults.

Until, many months after her 19th birthday, she was informed she was being released.

Chapter Seven

"Come on, son," the normally arrogant, most iniquitous cutthroat mob boss in the country, worked to keep the quiver of fear out of his voice. "I have been like a father to you, Vâj."

Viggo Garatteo warily eyed the young man who stood a few feet away with one hand tucked so casually in a trouser pocket, his grey suit coat pushed back behind his wrist, black tie neatly knotted around his thick throat.

Vaclav Brașov's expression was a smooth mask betraying nothing. He just calmly watched as his boss' eyes twitched back and forth nervously from Vaclav to Griff then Kid, to the door where Ivod lurked, and back to Vaclav.

Head of the crime syndicate, de Comăna, the sixty-seven year old man knew it would be futile to run for the door.

Dark hair salted with grey, he held his imperial Roman nose high even though he was about to die. "Vâj, listen, how can you think such bad things about me? I took you off the squalid, deadly streets of Romania, you would have never even made it to your teens in that indigent city."

At Vaclav's cold, compassionless gaze, he rushed on. "An orphan, barely past a toddler, a street urchin eating out of garbage cans, you were already in training as a cutpurse bandit. Hell, boy, I brought you to my league in Russia when you were what, five? Six? I taught you everything you know, gave you military training to toughen you. I made you my number one, son. At your young age, who has ever held that prestigious title?"

A knife in his hands, Griff leaned against the doorframe of Garatteo's opulent office.

A large room with views of Central Park, flamboyantly decorated with elaborately designed carved desk and chairs bought and flown in from Italy, paintings of his long dead ancestors on the walls.

Griff tossed the knife in the air and caught it on the tip of finger, and did it again. And again.

Scratching his black chinstrap beard with the blade end of the knife, Griff said with a friendly tone, "You gave him that title, Viggo, because you were afraid of him. You sent him in at sixteen as a kamikaze thinking he'd maybe take out one or two of the dozen gang members robbing your drug dealers before he was killed, but," Griff shrugged nonchalantly.

"Instead, he wiped them all out, all on his own. You became more afraid of him then, Boss. You thought if you kept him close, you could control him, rob the business blind, start useless wars with our rivals, and run the child prostitutes."

Leaning against the other side of the door, Ivod watching Griff juggle his knife said coolly, "Yeah, you took him off the streets and brought him to that hovel you kept us all in, in Russia. Fucking frozen wasteland, to make us do your cheapest dirty work. The most dangerous jobs. We were so young and so many, when we were caught and killed, it was a shrug off your shoulder, like mice, there were always more where we came from."

Kid leaned against a wall, one knee bent and his boot braced on the fancy printed wallpaper behind him, he watched Griff as well, but said to Garatteo, "You were the hardest on Vâj because he'd been the youngest, yet the toughest. And," Kid chuckled, shaking his head, the long hippy hair brushed past his shoulders, "you never understood his Romanian. You understood us when we all spoke Russian, you hated that he taught us Romanian and you were shut out."

"Yeah, yeah, listen, boys. I gave you all a home, food, shelter," Garatteo's olive-toned face darkened in anger. "None of you pissants would have survived out there on the streets if it weren't for me. You would have been taken out by other gangs. Vâj," he nodded to the silent, dark blond male standing so still, so passive.

"Brokanoff was on the verge of turning you out for tricks. You were so young, hell, men would have paid big bucks to fuck your little blond ass."

Griff, Kid and Ivod flushed in fury and started towards Garatteo, but Vaclav held up a hand. They all stayed in position, but their expressions boded painful death for their boss' insults.

Tossing the knife again, Griffin followed it up and then down with his ebony eyes. With the black widow's peak and chinstrap, people called him the Vampire. The renowned sadistic skill he had with knives, some of the dumber, weaker men believed he truly was one of the undead.

"Well," Griff said, "you used us, set us up time and again to take your falls. You took the business in the direction we didn't want to go. Children. Just like us, you sold them to brothels, to men to share, little girls, boys. We told you we wanted nothing to do with that shit, but," his sigh annoyed, he glanced at Vaclav who still hadn't moved.

"Ah, fuck you, you bunch of sissies. Who cares, they'll grow up banging like bunnies anyway, what's the difference that they start as children? You guys are just mad I kept most of the profits. Well, listen," Garatteo softened his voice into an amenable cajole.

"I have the money hidden. My vault in my Long Island house. I'll share it with you, just," his dark eyes appealed to Vaclav. But Vaclav's gaze was completely empty. Glacial blue ice stared blankly at him.

Garatteo looked frantically at Griff, "Come on, Griffin, you were one of my favorites, don't let him do this to me-"

Griff's eyes contained the same blank voids as Vaclav's.

Garatteo turned to Kid and hit another vacant wall, then to Ivod who cocked his head at Garatteo, and smiled.

Ivod said, "We already got to your vault, you stupid old bastard. You think you could hide anything from us?" His gaze darted to the several pairs of legs stretched out on the floor outside Garatteo's office. Blood streamed in front of the doorway covering the tan tiles.

Aware now that the four men that had barraged into his office had taken out every one of his guards, his soldiers, hell, there had to be at least 35 men guarding his office building.

"Shit," Garatteo spat his fear, then turned to Vaclav, raising his hands up. "Vâj, son, please, I'm like a father to you, let me go, I'll do what you say, I swear to God. I'll end the child prostitution, share the profits, everything." He was close enough to Vaclav to see the pitiless empty pits of his blue eyes, there was absolutely nothing there.

"Vâj, please, I beg you-" he cried desperately, and Vaclav slashed the blade of his knife across his former boss' neck.

Chapter Eight

Her stomach flipped and flopped, ill with trepidation and excitement. Adara was finally to be released.

The days and weeks and months, the years crawled by like they had been a hundred. To feel the fresh air and the sun on her shoulders again, to walk freely wherever she desired, do what she wanted, eat what she wanted, her heart soared with the thrill of finally being set free.

Vincenzo had sent word he was coming for her and she would be taken to her uncle's house.

Then, horrible fear gripped her heart, squashing the joy of her pending release. Uncle Massimo was a lethal cruel man even in the best of times. Vincenzo had said her uncle hated her and wanted her dead. Worse, he had plans to rent her out to have forced sex with countless men, then eventually sell her to a stranger in Pakistan.

She was totally unable to contemplate this new, hideous horror that awaited her. What was her new life to be like?

She had daily fought off the attacks of sociopathic ferocious girls in prison, was she to do this forever on the outside except now with men? Dread shrouded her from head to toe as a horrible shudder clinched and shook every inch of her body.

After she was given her release papers and her meager belongings in a paper bag, she was brought to the waiting room to wait for her brother to come and take her home.

A fleeting thought of running before he got there assailed her apprehensive brain. But, she had no money, no clothes, she wore a donated outfit. There was no one to turn to, to help her. No shelter, no food, no job. And a criminal record. A convicted murderer.

She had no choice but to wait for Vincenzo. Besides, if she fled, Uncle Massimo would surely send men to find her and drag her back. No, she had no choice but to wait for her future to come for her.

After three hours of waiting, a guard came to her and told her there was a car there to pick her up.

Getting up on trembling legs, she pushed her long dark curls off her shoulders and said bleakly, "Thank you," and forced those shaking legs to transport her to the front exit.

A dozen steps led down to the zone in front of the jail. A parking lot surrounded most of the area.

Her steps faltering, she trod slowly down the stairs to the big black car that sat out front with the engine running.

When she reached it, the driver got out and opened a back door for her.

After she climbed in, the driver went back and slipped behind the wheel, and without a word, drove off.

Perched nervously on the seat, she crossed her legs and folded her hands in her lap. She wore tan slacks and a white blouse the prison had given her. They were big and loose on her frail frame. She'd had no appetite while locked away and fighting daily for her survival.

The clothes she'd worn when she was first incarcerated were long gone. "Uh, sir," her voice tiny, weak, she said, "my brother, I was told Vincenzo would come and pick me up?"

One shoulder shrugged with indifference. In a thick New York, streetwise accent he told her, "I have orders to retrieve yooze and bring yooze to da boss' home. Dat's ouall I know."

She sat back against the luxurious, beige leather seat with a sigh. After almost five years in prison, she wasn't even worth it for her family to come and get her personally.

Swallowing the tears with a grimace, she told herself she was done crying. She would accept her new life, she had no choice anyway, and she would do as she was told without complaint.

The drive took several hours. They turned off the main road. When they reached a tree-dense neighborhood of vast yards and enormous mansions, the driver stopped at a closed gate that blocked the rest of the street.

An armed guard came out. He nodded at the driver and peered in at Adara in the back. His stare cold, he did not acknowledge her. Stepping back, he nodded sharply to the driver to pass through.

Great, Adara thought with bitter misery, *I am to still be under guard, under lock and key.*

The car headed down the street. The lawns were manicured, the homes acres apart from each other.

Finally, the driver pulled through another armed gate and then onto the long driveway that led up to her uncle's estate. Of course Adara had been there frequently as a child.

The building was three stories of austere brick and white columns.

As the driver pulled up out front, two armed guards exited the house, and two more approached from the sides of the house.

One of the guards tromped up to the long, sleek car, he opened Adara's door and stood to the side to allow her to emerge. Her heart in her throat, she slid out to her nervous feet, and stepped from the car.

The guard closed the door and the driver drove around to the twelve-car garage.

Still, no one said a word to her. She felt like a stray cat returned home after wandering off. No, an animal would be treated with more warmth. A rat, she determined, that's what she was, a rat that had escaped and was being brought back to stick in a cage.

The guard walked Adara up the steps to the open front door. Not knowing what to expect, her stomach churned like mad, she clutched her paper bag with both tense hands. The double doors were thick wood reinforced with steel.

When she stepped inside, the chilled, ascetic atmosphere rolled up and covered her like an odious blanket.

She recalled the family parties they had attended in the mansion, music and laughter, drinking and singing had abounded in those days. The servants had gossiped about dark, secretive meetings where unlawful business and pending assassinations were discussed.

Now, her inimical homecoming, she felt the insidious unwelcoming atmosphere, the palpably inhospitable vast foyer of gleaming marble tile spread out, leading to ominous corridors and vindictive rooms.

As she stood like a statue, preparing herself for what lay ahead, she literally felt the forbidding hostility radiating off the antique-white walls.

Her father, Salvatore Valentina had been the head of their crime family, but since his death, his brother Massimo had taken over as boss.

A tinge of sorrow at her father's passing still brought the sting of tears to the backs of her eyes. He hadn't been a warm, loving father, but he still had been her papa. She missed him, and her home, and her friends, her school, her mother, no, she shook her head dismally, not Estella.

Estella had disappeared, not, as Vincenzo had said because she feared for her life from her daughter's murderous rage, but more likely when she found out Salvatore had left her virtually nothing in his will, she had run off with one of her various lovers.

"Miss, you will follow me." A stern voice broke into her musings.

Adara looked up and a woman in a black dress with white trim stood with a harsh face, thin lips pressed in an unwelcome, unfriendly grimace.

Forty-something, her light brown hair was pinned back in a severe bun. Her angular body held few curves, none of them soft or feminine, she had big hands red from housework, they hung at her sides.

Without a greeting or waiting to see if Adara followed her, she turned and trod from the foyer to a hall.

Of course, what else could she do? Adara meekly traipsed after the servant with the guard at her back.

The maid led her down corridor after corridor until she reached Massimo's den. She stood to the side and held her arm out indicating for Adara to enter.

When Adara stepped inside, the maid announced, "She is here," and stepped outside the room and closed the door.

Her fingers clenched the bag tightly in front of her, Adara's gaze lit on the man standing across the room.

He stood facing out the window with one hand in his pocket. He wore a pinstriped suit with a red tie. His still brown hair was lightly laced with silver and combed straight back off his forehead.

With his back to her, she couldn't see his face. Obviously he knew she was there, and deliberately kept her waiting.

Holding her ground, she twisted her fingers over the bag until it nearly tore with her anxiety. Waiting only made her more nervous, more feeling the impending doom that idled across the room from her.

The den was all shades of brown, lush carpet, thick cushioned chairs, full bookcases, pictures on the walls of Italian landscapes. The prerequisite fireplace of brown and beige stones wasn't lit.

The window Massimo stood at was large with mullioned panes, dark brown drapes were held back with gold braided ropes with tassels.

Just when she thought he was going to let her stand there until tomorrow, Massimo turned around. His cheeks were heavier than she remembered. His longer torso, barrel chested as Vincenzo would eventually share was still heavily muscled.

His aquiline nose with the bump at the top had lengthened and thickened as well, but he still carried a debonair stance and suave appearance. His head high with arrogance, he gazed down at his niece with pure loathing in his dark brown eyes.

His profound hatred of her so intensely tangible, Adara felt it strike her in wave after wave of roaring fury.

Smoothing the rage off his florid face, the edge of the side of his mouth nicked up with a mirthless smile. "Ah, my dear niece. My dead brother's daughter, his killer. Convict number AV43563."

His despising gaze was enough to wilt her, his words shriveled what was left of Adara's broken heart, blasting any ego she may have still possessed.

She tried to keep her eyes level, bravely direct at him, but he expressed such malevolent hatred of her, the strength of it forced them to turn down and stare at the beige and tan carpet. Her eyes down she didn't know he'd come near to her.

"Look at me you murdering bitch," he snarled. Staring down at the top of her dark hair, when she didn't move he raged, "Look at me!"

Startled at his shout, her fingers strangling the life out of them, she raised her head, and he hauled off and punched her with his fist.

She stumbled backwards with the power of it then skittered to her knees, her bag flew across the room.

He stomped to her, jammed his fist in her hair and jerked her to her feet.

Her hands came up, tears spurted, "No, please, Uncle, please-" Ignoring her pleas, he backhanded her and she crashed again to the floor.

"You are no niece of mine, Adara. If I could strip the honorable name of Valentina from you, so help me God I would do it, even if it flayed the skin from your body along with it."

Huffing in pain, she climbed to her knees.

Drawing his foot back, Massimo viciously kicked her in the side. With a cry, she fell over, clutching her side.

Kicking her again, he screamed, "You murdered my brother! If you weren't blood you would be rotting under the foundation of a building somewhere!" And he kicked her again.

Adara curled into a ball, wrapping her hands around her body to protect it, but he kicked her in the head, the face, she had to cover her head.

When he kicked her in the ribs the cracking was audible then he went to her belly, hips, back, legs. Her screaming cries for mercy fell on deaf ears.

Beaten almost unconscious, she lay whimpering.

He crouched beside her, grabbed a handful of hair and lifted her head. Tears poured down her face bloodied with cuts, and bruises already swelling. His gaze and voice held no concern, no feelings whatsoever; he glared at her with frigid loathsome eyes.

"When you are healed, I will take you to some parties to meet some men I intend on renting you to. They will fuck you as they desire, maybe pass you around to their soldiers.

"When they tire of you, I have a business acquaintance in Pakistan who will buy you as his bride. He wants the citizenship that will come along with your marriage. He is a brutal warlord that goes through women like army ants through a forest, devouring everything in sight until nothing is left. He had desired you when you were still a child."

His words rolled fuzzily around inside her battered head. She couldn't open her eyes, could scarcely draw a breath through broken ribs.

"But, Salvatore refused to sell you to him then. Now," he said, clutching her hair, he shook her head viciously. "No one cares anymore what happens to you, Adara. No one. The sheik will take you away, out of our sight forever." He shoved her head so hard it slammed on the floor.

Her body burned and screamed in agony, head spinning from the blows, on the verge of puking and blacking out, Adara sobbed, gasping for breath through her bruised lungs.

After more vicious kicks to her back, her head, her legs, when she no longer moved or wept, he left her to lie broken and bleeding on the floor.

Night descended. Adara lay motionless, her arms still wrapped around her body. No one came to the den to check on her, bring her food or medical care.

Occasionally she broke through the subjugating consciousness and could hear the rumblings of people far, sometimes near, but no one came to the den.

Her body burned with excruciating, unbearable pain, she couldn't move a finger. Her tears had dried up, her throat scraped raw from crying and screaming.

When she woke again, she was still curled on the rug and light streamed into the window. She first wriggled her fingers, even those hurt.

It took some effort, holding her breath to keep the cries of pain stifled; she managed to sit up. Every part of her ached and stung, her head pounded with a searing headache, probably concussed.

Her legs crossed, she bent over holding her head waiting for the spinning to stop, the battering at her temples to stop banging, the nausea to recede.

Footsteps approached the doorway.

Slightly raising her pounding head, she cast pained unfocused eyes to the threshold. A pair of black sturdy rubber shoes stood there.

Adara tilted her head back, the dizziness struck with a vengeance. The servant who had brought her to the room was staring with fierce hostility at her.

Her voice held no pity, it was cold and unfriendly, "Mr. Valentina is desiring use of his den, I am to take you to your room."

"Uh." Adara worked weakly to roll to her hands and knees hoping she could stand, but when she tried, her beat-up legs wobbled and she started to crumple.

"Oh for Pete's sake," the woman muttered, stomping over to Adara. Bending with a huff of annoyance, she grasped her thin arm and jerked her to stand unsteadily on her feet.

"Come along you useless bag of shit," she groused, dragging Adara out of the room. Her legs swollen, bruised in pain, moved like wooden sticks as the maid half-carried her along.

The stairs were brutal as the servant practically hauled her up the wide carpeted staircase.

As they trod down the hall, her voice small and shaky, Adara uttered, "Uh, Miss, Ms., um…"

"That's Mrs. Stonefall for your information," she snapped then shut her skinny lips.

She drew Adara into a room then released her. "My orders are to tell you that you will not leave this chamber unless Mr. Valentina himself sends for you. You will take all your meals here; no one wants to see your face. Since he plans to parade you around, there are a few dresses for that," she nodded towards the armoire.

She gestured to the dresser. "There are some clothes one of the fired maids left behind you can wear. There's not much, not that you'll need much," her gaze trailed down Adara's slender form, pausing on her breasts. "Well, the few clothes she left will be big on you, except in the bust area, you have big tits for such a delicate frame."

At Adara's flaming cheeks at her crudeness, the maid cleared her throat. "Anyway, the guards have been instructed to not allow you to leave this room, or this house."

"May I ask, how," Adara gulped, "how long was I…unconscious?"

Stonefall's shrug inconsequential, "Almost three days." She turned and strode from the room, slamming the door behind her.

If possible, Adara's heart plummeted further. They had let her lie in her own blood, severely injured for three days.

She moved painfully to the bed and plopped down with a cry at the pain that radiated from sitting even on the cushioned mattress.

Looking around, she wondered if she would spend the rest of her life in custody. Granted, the room was well above and beyond the cold, gritty grey cell in prison, still.

The room was actually pretty. She remembered it as her cousin Sonia's room before she moved out for college.

The walls were a feminine blush with dark pink and white curtains, matching fluffy comforter and cushioned pink rug. The furniture was mahogany, a desk, vanity, dresser and the armoire. She saw a television, albeit an ancient one, sitting on top of the dresser, with a glass of very needed water.

She looked over, at least she had a window. On the second floor, she knew there would be no escape that way. It was likely locked, and breaking the glass would surely bring guards running. No, she was trapped. Caged again. Soft and comfortable, but a cage nonetheless.

So much for freedom, the breeze in her hair, sun on her shoulders, going where she wanted, do what she wanted, walk in the park, feed the pigeons, eat what she wanted. She doubted her uncle would allow her to get a job so she could earn her own money, or, a heavy sigh expelled, slumping her shoulders, go to college to finish her degree.

The days passed gloomy slow, and lonely.

True to Mrs. Stonefall's words, Adara stayed in her room, even took her meals there. Her body started to heal, she wasn't allowed out but she used the television to find work-out shows to at least keep her muscles toned. The bruises still marred her fair skin.

The door suddenly opened.

Mrs. Stonefall's stern, unpleasant face appeared. "You are to dress, jeans and a blouse will suffice then come downstairs."

"Mrs.-" But the maid was already gone.

"Well," she sighed, "at least I can finally leave this room, maybe see people." The biggest strain, besides the boredom, was not being able to talk to anyone.

Even when her meals were brought, whichever servant took them to her, stared with avid, morbid curiosity at the princess in the cell, but refused to talk to her. They just dropped off a tray and fled.

Or returned later to pick it up and again, to Adara's chagrin, leave wordless.

Chapter Nine

Dressed in crisp, yet a size too big blue jeans, and a pale yellow blouse, Adara warily descended the stairs. When she reached the bottom, a man in a chauffeur's uniform was there.

"Miss," he almost bowed to her but stopped himself. His face settled in a pompous frown. "You are to come with me," he said with flat irreverence.

Aware she had no say in the matter, Adara followed him outside to the long, black car.

He opened the back door and she slid in. In the front seat she saw her uncle. He didn't greet her or acknowledge her presence. The driver climbed in and they were on their way.

Adara wanted to ask where were they were going, what was going to happen, but last thing she wanted was to incur her uncle's wrath. She sat quietly with her hands folded in her lap and watched the town go by out the side window.

It hadn't changed much, of course it had only been five years or so. A sad smile turned her lips up. Everything was relative. Five years seemed a lifetime when she was in prison, but to the rest of the world it probably flew by in a nanosecond.

The car pulled up and parked at a curb. The driver opened the passenger door and Massimo got out, then the driver opened Adara's door. She slid out gracefully to her feet.

Looking around, she felt a comforting peace settle on her in the city. Sky-high buildings, people hustling and bustling along the noisy, busy streets. Horns blew, people shouted, Adara breathed in the familiar sights and sounds, and felt like she was finally home.

"Pull your stupid head out of the clouds, Adara, and come with me," Massimo snapped. Scowling at her, he started for the door to a restaurant.

The chauffeur hurried ahead to hold the door open for them to pass through. Adara followed her uncle inside.

The lighting in the baroque restaurant was low, the air cool. Dark wood paneled the walls with amber lamps and landscape paintings of Italy. Only a few people sat at round tables in a circular dining area.

A melted candle oozed in Chianti wine bottles on each table. Dark burgundy booths lined two walls, and over to one side away from the diners was a bar. Two men sat on stools slumped over drinks at the counter.

Finding her voice, although it was small and nervous, Adara dared to ask, "Uncle Mas, why are we here?" There was no way he was treating her to dinner. He hadn't said a word much less made eye contact with her.

Pausing just inside the entrance, Massimo scanned the room then a hard smile stretched his florid face. To her surprise, he answered her. "It is time to show you off. I want to get the bidding rolling."

He glanced at her with a frown. "You still look like shit." Then he shrugged, "But it's not your face they're going to be interested in."

Seeing her favoring one leg and her hand on her lower ribs that still ached, he snipped crossly, "Dammit. We need to put some weight on you. Stand up straight." He said sarcastically, "And try to look just the slightest bit desirable."

Appalled at his words, after all, it was his fists and feet that caused the damage to her, a terrible foreboding crept with chilly fingertips over Adara's skin, raising goose bumps with every venomous prick.

Straightening her spine, Adara tried to steady her racing heart and at least carry herself with dignity, even if she was being brought to slaughter.

His tone mean and harsh, voice rigid, Massimo glared down at her and said cruelly, "It's time you earned your room and board girl. Today you are meeting Iskander Ali Khan," the side of his mouth lifted with a sneer. "Your future husband."

Her raven brows flew up. She squeaked, "My what?" Her eyes jumped to where her uncle was looking.

Several men sat at a corner table. One of the men, huge, wore a turban but was attired in a suit, his face impassive with a thick beard. Hard, callous eyes, although unreadable, did not disguise the sadistic flecks in them and they were fixed intently on her.

The degenerate orbs slowly, very slowly, traced Adara from the top of her luxurious mane, over her lush breasts visible even in the overlarge blouse, and down to pause at the joining of her legs.

When they rolled back up, a smirk smeared on his cruel face at the color that stained her embarrassed cheeks, and the smirk broadened at the sudden spark of anger in her dark eyes.

"Uncle," Adara whispered, shrinking back.

Massimo nodded at Ali Khan.

The Pakistani drug lord faintly inclined his head in return then his eyes flit back to glower in rapacious interest at Adara.

"Good," Massimo mumbled, restraining his grin, "he's still interested. Come, we can leave." He put his hand on her back turning her towards the door then dropped it like he'd touched nasty poison.

Feeling Ali Khan's odious glare on her back, a shiver twitched through her as she followed her uncle out.

When they stepped outside under a warm sun, Adara breathed deeply, trying to dispel the filth she imagined clinging to her skin from the drug lord's lurid gaze.

His hand on the door handle to the back seat, Massimo stopped when someone said, "Oh my gosh, is that Adara Valentina?"

Both uncle and niece looked over.

Adara's childhood girlfriends, Dominique and Selena stood gawking at her.

Both girls were a few years older than Adara.

Dominique, tall as a child was taller yet. She wore a gabardine suit with a matching skirt and professional heels. Her hair straight-ironed to her shoulders, gone were the pink glasses, she now wore fundamental black rectangles.

She looked like a lawyer in training. Her full lips in the cinnamon colored skin were pinched in revulsion.

Selena, her hair dyed a golden blonde, styled in a flamboyant Farah Fawcett blow-out, contact-enhanced hazel eyes fringed in thick fake lashes, was dressed to the nines in a top of the line, chic designer dress. Her Louboutin's were no less than six-inches high.

Her lips painted ruby red twisted scornfully. "Well, well," she sneered disdainfully with a snooty once over. The end of her long nose had been cosmetically shaved. Her shortened nose wrinkled as if she smelled something bad. "If it isn't the jailbird come home to roost."

Her face stricken with the insult of her once best friend, Adara's face paled with shame and anguish. "Selena," she took a deep breath to steady her roiling stomach. "How- how have you been? And you, Dominique?"

She smiled at the tall woman, "You look so professional."

The two young women looked at each other, rolled their eyes in ridicule then turned back to Adara.

"Yes," Dominique said, deliberately looking down her nose at the shorter Adara. "I am in pre-law, and I'm interning with the most prestigious law firm in town."

"And I," not to be outdone, Selena's mouth curled as she bragged, "married young and rich, of course." She held her hand up wriggling her finger with the enormous diamonds on it. "My days are filled with shopping, spas, tennis. I did very well, didn't I?"

She nudged Dominique with her elbow, and said to Adara, "You remember red-headed Margaret," she waited until Adara nodded with a meek smile.

"Well, if you can believe it, our pudgy, freckled friend is an erotic romance writer, and Crystal is still in prep school and engaged to a senator's son."

Selena sneered down her supercilious nose at Adara. "No need for us to catch up with you," she shared a mean grin with Dominique, "everyone knows where you've been." They snickered shamelessly at Adara's dejected face.

Still trying to be friendly, Adara pushed back the despair that threatened to engulf her, swallowed hard and said, "Uh, so you're married already. Is it Paulie Santone? You always liked him." Wanting to show how happy she was for her friend, she forced a cheerful smile.

The girls shared a look, Selena's was dark and angry. She sniped at Adara, "As a matter of fact, I married his brother, you remember Raimondo."

Now Adara remembered. She had heard the servants gossiping about the hoity-toity Selena Santone. They said her marriage was an empty shell, a sham. She had wanted Paulie but he didn't want her.

When she continued brazenly throwing herself at him, he cruelly and nastily told her to back off in front of a group of their friends. So she did the next best thing and married his brother.

According the tongue-wagging servants, Raimondo wanted heirs and a woman who wouldn't get in the way of his gay philandering and gambling, and Selena wanted to be close to Paulie. They had their separate lovers and lived in barely veiled misery and despising hate.

Nonetheless, not wanting to expose her horrid excuse of a marriage, Selena kept her big, bright white smile aimed at the world, right now she showed it to Adara.

"Unfortunately, you," she said to her petite friend with antipathy, "will never be able to find a man foolish enough to tie himself to a murderess. Heaven's," she said mocking, "a man would never be able to close his eyes at night!" She poked Dominique's arm, "Am I right?"

They snickered like the mean girls in the schoolyard.

Fighting the despair and shame that was swamping her inch by inch, hearing her uncle clear his throat, Adara said quickly, hopefully, "Oh, uh, I would love to catch up more, could we perhaps make plans for lunch one day?" She could only pray Massimo would let her go.

The two girls didn't even try to cover their scornful amusement.

Then sobering, Selena's heavily made-up face distorted with loathing, she replied with heavy derision, "Don't be ridiculous. We certainly would have anything to do with a convicted felon. An ex-con, a killer no less."

Dominique nodded, agreeing, "A murderer." Her body expressed a huge faux shiver. "As if we would ever want to be seen with you, much less be alone with you, talk to you," the shiver rippled over her shoulders again.

Glancing at Selena, she said, "Remember how after they'd locked her up we all talked all the time about how lucky we were that the little assassin had never turned her bloody knife on one of us?"

At her friend's nodding smirk, Dominique said to Adara, "And you think we'd want to spend one second with you? Let you get close enough to- to slaughter one of us? Taint us with your nasty self?"

"Yeah," Selena agreed, "eew." The shaved nose wrinkled in repugnance.

Dominique said to Massimo who had stood there silently with a tight smug smile, "We can't believe you would allow her in your home. Your wife, Tiziana must be beside herself in terror with sleepless nights fearing her niece is going to creep into her room and stab her to death while she sleeps."

"Dominique!" Horrorstruck, Adara stepped back from the spewing venom of her old friends.

Massimo smiled grimly. "Tiziana is spared having to deal with this. We divorced two years ago." Ignoring Adara's shocked expression, secluded in her room she hadn't known about the divorce.

He set a hand to Adara's back and gave her a sharp prod, said coldly, "I have to go back inside and meet with Mr. Ali Khan. You will wait in the car. Ladies," he nodded respectfully to Selena and Dominique and left them to go back into the restaurant.

The driver hurried to get the door and followed him inside.

Selena called out with a jeer, "Watch your back, Mr. Valentina!"

"Uh, well," Adara stammered, wilting under the contemptible glares of her old friends. There was nothing left to say.

It was as if her body was stained with the prison uniform never to be washed away, to cling forever. Ostracizing her as if with felonious leprosy that she will never be able to peel off and be accepted again into society.

"Yes, time to go. I want to go back and see that diamond and emerald necklace in Fabrigio's before we have cocktails before dinner," Selena said, with her nose in the air.

"I really like it and I'm sure-" the young women turned in tandem and walked down the street without another look or word to Adara as if she didn't exist.

Stunned, feeling a dagger twisting in her back, Adara got in the car and slumped in the seat. Fighting tears, she swore she was done trying with the girls. They had all been a close knit group when they were children growing up together.

Adara was the youngest but that had never seemed to matter. But, now, they feared her, reviled her, shunned her, she felt worse than when her uncle beat her, which was weekly.

She laid her head on the back of the seat and closed her eyes to wait for Massimo.

"Adara."

Pins and needles jabbed up and down her arms at the voice. Deep, heavy accent, so chilling, it brought back wretched memories.

Her eyes opened slowly, she turned her head.

Wearing a suit and tie, he was standing by the car, his arms resting in the window, he peered inside.

She suddenly jerked to sit up. "Mr. Braşov," his name slid over the lump in her throat.

"I saw Massimo's car and Dominique and Selena walking away. I thought maybe," the hardness in his face softened, the ice in his blue eyes melted just a hair. "You are out. The prison was supposed to let me know, I planned to pick you up, Adara. I am glad-"

Wearily, she shuffled slightly from the door, cutting him off, "My uncle had me brought home."

His brawny forearms rested in the window. Holding his tie against his chest, Vaclav pushed his rugged face just inside and said, "Now that you are grown, Adara, I would like to take you out. Dinner at Voicioux's on the water is really nice. What do you-"

"I am not allowed to leave the mansion, Mr. Brașov. I don't think my uncle would like it if you were here talking to me. Please, you need to leave."

The frown only made his already hard face harsher. "I do not care what anyone else wants. I only care what you and I want. You refused *mea* help, Adara, while you were locked up. Let me take you out to dinner, give me a chance to let you get to know me a little-"

"No," she said flatly. Her sad eyes speared his artic blues then she looked away with a shudder. "I don't want to get to know you. You are a mobster just like my father, my brother, my uncle. I don't want this life, your life. They say you are no longer an enforcer, that you took over the business from Viggo Garatteo in a bloody war. Mr. Brașov, the last thing I want or need is-"

"I have a first name, Adara," he broke in with that guttural accent, his dark voice sifting over her like an insidious black cloak. "I am not old enough to be your father, call me Vaclav, or Vâj."

"Mr. Brașov," she murmured with a sigh. "Go away. I want nothing to do with you. Please, before my uncle comes back out."

The nervous anxiety in her voice caused Vaclav to lean in further to look closer at her. The smoldering interest in his eyes quickly turned to confusion, then anger.

He reached for her but she shrank from him. Letting his hand drop, he said, "Adara, what the hell happened to your face?"

His eyes narrowed on the bruises still visible under makeup from her uncle's latest beating. When she didn't answer him, he barked, "Did someone hit you? Massimo? I will fucking kill him-"

"Go away, please, I'm begging you, please," big tears rolled and plopped off her cheeks.

Her voice rose with strident panic, "please go away, Mr. Braşov, please."

The fright and panic on her bruised face freaked him out. He wanted to pulverize who would ever dare to strike this beautiful creature. But she was so upset; he couldn't stand to make it worse.

He pulled out of the window and stood back from the car, his ambivalence clear. Last thing he wanted was to leave her now that she was finally free, and all grown up.

When he saw her bend forward with her face in her hands, her shoulders wracking with her sobs, his stomach pitched, he had to leave her. For now.

His hands shoved deep in his pockets, he stalked down the street turning into the first bar he came to.

Chapter Ten

Weeks later, Massimo Valentina dragged his niece to yet another party.

When her face healed, he had started bringing her to parties, to show her off, to get the bidding war rolling. As bored as she was at home, attending events was worse.

The women turned their noses up at her like she was roadkill, rebuffing her efforts at friendly conversation, and the men hit on her relentlessly thinking since she was an ex-con she'd be easy.

Right now, she had tucked herself away in a corner trying to blend in with the wallpaper, the glass of fruit punch chilling her hand.

Taking tiny sips, she caught a glimpse of a plump redhead in the middle of the room. It was one of her besties when she was a little girl, Margaret O'Malley.

Adara threaded carefully through the crowd to approach her old childhood friend.

When she reached her, she saw her friend had tried to tame her red springy hair but to no avail. It was pulled back and up at the sides with barrettes but still fluffed out around her shoulders like orangey moss. She was chatting with a young man who had a cornered grimace on his handsome face, and looked like he was edging away from her.

"Um, Margaret," Adara interrupted softly.

The chubby young woman crooked her head from the man she was hitting on to Adara. Her pale blue eyes widened, mouth dropped, the ruddy freckles that covered half her face stretched over her white skin.

"As I live and breathe," she gushed, "Adara Valentina. I'd heard you were out."

The young man took the opportunity to flee.

Margaret turned and went to say something, but he had already blended into the crowd. Turning her annoyed frown to Adara, she made the effort to plaster on a contrived smile.

"So, Adara dear," she said, appearing to be about to hug her old friend, but then trying to conceal the distaste on her pudgy face, she kept her arm to her side, holding a cocktail with her other hand.

"How does it feel to be on the outside? No iron bars anymore? I have to tell you," she laughed awkwardly, "were we girls shocked when we heard about the murder."

Her disdainful blue eyes swept Adara up and down in skepticism. "I mean, of all people, the gentle fawn of the group. Just goes to show, you never really know a person, huh? True life, that's what makes the best stories I say!" Her voice warmed, and a small smile lifted her thick lips. The pink lipstick clashing with her orange curls.

Covering her wince at the reminder of her incarceration, Adara smiled and said, "It's lovely to be here, Margaret. How have you been?"

Music played from the band at the far end of the room, people mingled, the voices loud over the music. Tables were almost full with those that chose to sit and drink or eat.

Margaret wore a dress in an unfortunate choice of chartreuse. Normally green would be a pretty foil for her hair, but in this case, the shade was just a bit…off.

The material was clingy; it stretched snuggly over her plump belly and large butt, yet gapped slightly loosely in the bust. The bodice was quite low exposing pushed-up snow-white breasts and bigger freckles.

"I've been great, Adara," she crowed, gold hoops swung under her oddly tiny ears. "With the help of my uncle who's a publisher, at my young age I have been published under the penname Meggie Madison."

Her proud grin wide, she expounded, "Romance novels. Actually," she said, leaning into Adara, her pale eyes darting around the room. "I write erotic romance. Tons of bitchin' sex, BDSM, some rape fantasies, you know, that titillating sadism stuff. Have you heard of me?"

Taken aback at Margaret's dissertation, Adara didn't know what to say. "Uh, no, I can't say I've read any of your...books." Incarcerated, they weren't allowed that type of reading material.

Margaret laughed. Her teeth had a beige tint from heavy cigarette smoking. "Oh child, you must! Fucking, sucking, tied up and ass smacked, vibrating butt plugs and nipple clamps, gang rape, honey, you would love it. A lot of it is autobiographical, I write what I've lived, you know?"

Adara had never even had a boyfriend; she had no way to relate to Margaret's world. She was speechless. Her little pudgy friend had certainly grown up, at least had grown older.

Margaret uttered, "So, uh, anyway," her whitish lids half-mast, she sidled closer to Adara.

Not like being crowded since that was the dangerous life in prison, Adara schooled herself not to step back from her old friend.

Margaret gushed, "You must have amazing tales to tell. I can get such juicy new crap from you. We will have to meet so you can tell me all the gory details of prison. Cor, girl, the way you look, the guards probably raped you relentlessly.

"Did they put you in restraints, or just have the guys hold you down while they took turns? Did they fuck you all at once or one at a time? Did they whip you with their belts and stuff, what about sodomy? I bet that was insane with all those men! I love it up the ass!"

Ignoring Adara's horrified appalled face, without taking a breath she rushed on, "And the girls, I hear the lesbian activity is out of this world on the inside. The dildos, tell me," she leaned and whispered, "did they just do it to you, or did you reciprocate? Tell me-"

"Margaret!" Adara yelped wanting to slap her hand over her old friend's mouth. Her voice firm, hard, she said, "I- I don't want to talk about that time in my life, ever. It's over, done. I'm moving on. I do not want to relive it."

Margaret's pink lips pursed, she crossed her chubby arms deliberately pushing her small bosom up and out. "Well, Miss High and Mighty, listen to you!"

The pink gloss twisted with her sneer, "Who the hell do you think you are? You think anyone will give you the time of day?

"The only interest any of us have in you is hearing your juicy stories. Rape sells hon, so does torture and BDSM. We can make a fortune. Just jot down some of the more lurid stories and I can string them together. Hell, with the true life bio aspect the books will sell like hotcakes!"

Shaking her head vigorously, Adara said, "No, no, no. I will not tell you, or anyone what went on in there. I said it's over. I will never talk about it, especially to have it written in a perverted book and plastered in the tabloids. Please, can't we just go for coffee or something someday? Get caught up?"

Her face turned ruddy and warped, Margaret said callously, "You need to get over yourself sweetheart, like I said, no one gives a shit about you. Those that aren't repulsed by you, are afraid you will shoot them if you get mad or something. You don't wanna give me a story, fine, fuck you."

She pivoted and trod away from the stunned Adara, her fat ass sashaying in the clingy chartreuse dress like two beach balls bouncing down the beach.

Adara stood there for a second, her mind lurching with the vitriol Margaret had spewed at her. She unobtrusively shifted her eyes scanning the area to see if anyone had heard them. Thankfully, no one was paying her any attention.

She slowly slunk back to the corner of the room and melted into the wall. She couldn't leave until Massimo came to get her. The shame scorching her face, she kept her eyes downcast, she didn't know if she could endure running into any more old friends.

Only seconds passed and a male voice said, "Hey pretty girl, how come you're hanging here all alone?"

She was hurting, but her manners prevailed. She raised her head and gave the young man a tremulous yet not inviting smile. "I am waiting for my uncle, and, not to be rude, I would like to be alone," she wanted to make it clear she was done with people. Men, women, family, old friends.

"Ah, a pretty babe like you doesn't want to be alone. How about a dance?" He set his hand on her arm.

She tugged, pulling from his grasp.

His voice dropped to a sexy purr, "Come on honey, how about I buy you a drink?" He nodded at the glass in her hand that was now empty except for a couple of ice cubes.

"No," she declined, shaking her head. "I don't care for anything, I just want to be left alone. I don't mean to be rude, but…"

The cajoling sexy voice became nasty. His sociable smile turned fetid, he said in a low belligerent voice, "Listen babe, everyone knows who you are. You're a felon, a killer. I bet," his eyes tracked up and down her body settling on her breasts.

"You learned some hot racy shit in the joint. Come with me and show me something new, babe." He gripped her arm pulling her close then drifted a hand behind her to drop on her ass.

"Mister, please," she protested, putting her small palm on his chest and pushed at him.

"Don, baby, hotstuff, Don Baker. We can go to my place, there's no one there right now. I'm dying for you to show me what you got. Even in that ugly dress a blind guy can see you got it goin' on!"

Her shame was complete. Her family disowned her, her old friends had disparaged her, everyone knew who she was and had not one good thing to say to her.

Men thought she was easy and raunchy, and except when her uncle was parading her in front of specific males he planned to 'rent' her to, he made her wear frumpy outfits.

The dress she wore tonight, light yellow hung shapeless and went just past her knees, and the ballet shoes gave her petite frame no extra height. Not that she cared, the last thing she wanted was to draw any attention to herself.

Wrenching at her arm, she whispered, "Please, don't make a scene, just let go of me and go away."

Don moved his arm to slide it around her slender shoulders, the hand still on her butt squeezed.

Laughing at her futile struggles, pulling her closer, he said, "No way, babe. I can take you down the hall to one of the rooms and we can screw our brains out. Now, if you don't want to cause a scene you will come along peacefully."

He started maneuvering her to leave the room when a burly hand came down heavy on his shoulder.

"She said let go. Do it now or I will break that hand that is on her ass." Vaclav Brașov wrapped long, very hard fingers over Don's shoulder and dug them in.

Shooting him an irritated glare, Don said, "Get your hand the fuck off me, dude, the lady and I have plans." He chuckled at Adara's consternation, "And we all know I use the term lady loosely!"

Vaclav's fist smashed into Don's nose- he grabbed his collar, holding onto it, shifting him to the wall as Don slumped to the floor out cold.

Staring wide-eyed at Don crumpled against the wall, Adara clapped her hands over her mouth.

The big dark eyes popped up to Vaclav, and she turned to hurry away, but he moved with her, fingers of steel wound around her forearm holding her until they were away from the unconscious man.

He stopped her, then forced her to turn and face him. "Adara," he said, frowning down at her.

Adara remembered that Vaclav didn't look like his other Russian compatriots, because he wasn't Russian.

He was from near Romania but spent most of his life on and off between Russia, Romania and the US. His hair, still blond on top yet a shade darker than years before, he kept the top longer and the lower, darker blond at the sides shaved closer.

The icy blue eyes were the same as the ones that glowered at her weeks ago when she was in her uncle's car. They were still partially hidden under hooded lids yet still generated cold ruthless aggression.

To Adara he was pure and utter violence on two legs. She looked at his hand gripping her, deliberately keeping her from leaving, then to the exit.

He ignored her glance to the doorway. "You always run, girl, when you see me. Anyone ever tell you that is rude?"

She tugged at her arm, he firmed his grip. "Mr. Brașov, anyone ever tell you it's rude to hold someone against their will? Let go of me."

With despair she thought, *was she put on this earth to be manhandled forever*? Enormous dark eyes like hot cocoa, still round yet now slightly tilting exotically, heavily fringed with long curled lashes, glared up at the tall, overbearing man.

Now that he had her attention and she couldn't flee, his hard face relaxed into a semi-smile. Vaclav's face was pure manly tough with sharp angles, low ridged masculine brow, and a strong jaw always covered with a slight scruff even when he'd just shaved.

His beard, brows, and the chest hair that showed under his shirt with a button open, was contrasting dark compared to the lighter hair on his head. He wore slacks, white shirt and a suit jacket but no tie.

As far as Adara understood, he had been an enforcer in the Russian mob, and was now a mob-boss, head of the crime syndicate de Comăna, and it showed in the aggression of his stance, the pitiless empty eyes, and the danger that tightened his full harsh lips.

Scars crossing over one temple almost to his cheek, only made him appear more dangerous, more lethal, more scary. Ink traveled up his neck, when he moved, the long sleeves revealed tats.

He was everything Adara did not want in her life. Her father had been connected, her brother and uncle were connected, and she hated every single bit of the life. The secrecy, treachery, sexism, bloodlust, violence. Especially the violence, and it radiated out of Vaclav's vivid blue, enigmatic eyes.

He loosened his grip but continued to hold her from leaving. "You can spare a moment of conversation with me, Adara," his voice lowered, "after all, you owe me. Remember?"

Her shiny dark eyes popped brilliant against the rich creaminess of her skin, she stuttered, "You- you, that was a long time ago-"

A slow smirk shifted the side of his tough face up, the hooded lids lowered even further. "*Da*. But a blood debt never goes away, it is forever."

He lifted a dark glossy curl, watching it spiral around his thick finger, murmured, "Mink richness, Adara, so fucking soft and beautiful like the rest of you."

Adara yanked at her arm, her stomach churned with growing panic. "You- would hold me to something that happened when I was a- a child? That I had no control over?" At least a foot shorter than him, she had to tilt her head back to look up at him.

The smirk hardened into a riled scowl. "If you did not run from me every time I was in the vicinity, if you spared me the slightest of polite conversation, I would not dwell on it…maybe. But," his sigh growled as his thick fingers squeezed her arm, and he pulled her closer to him, frowning at the fright that widened her eyes.

Blinking rapidly at him, trying to control her fear, she whispered, "Mr. Brașov, what do you want from me?" She jerked at her arm attempting to push back from him, wincing at the pain in her side from her uncle's latest beating.

He gave her a sharp little shake with a glare. "That, right there, calling me Mister like I am a stranger. Although we have only seen each other sporadically over the years, nonetheless, we have known each other most of your life.

"You do not show me respect. You see me coming and you push your little nose up in the air and turn your back to me." His gaze traveled to where she held her side for the second time. He had manhandled her but not enough to cause her pain. "Adara, what is wrong with your-"

"Mist- uh, what, I mean, I'll talk to you, if that's what you-want. But, you can't make me pay back this…blood debt, I mean, you can't make me!"

Forgetting she favored her side, his voice roughened as he pulled her closer until their faces were only inches apart.

His breath with a hint of whisky and cigar misted her lips when he snarled, "I have helped you, and kept your secrets, Adara Valentina, both of them, and now tis too late for talk. I will now take what I want from you, and I will not be polite about it, just as you are discourteous with me."

The barely suppressed lust smoldering in his eyes iced into glacial blankness. There was no longer any emotion showing, he had tucked back the rage that simmered, burning hotter over the years of her incarceration, and her continuous ignoring him.

Stuffing down her fear, Adara let her anger out, "Mr. Brașov, I insist you release me this instant! If you do not I will call…" Who could she call for help? She thought of Vincenzo, but her brother wasn't there and she wouldn't want him involved if he was.

This Russian, or whatever he was, had a deadly reputation and she feared what would happen if Vincenzo interfered. Not that he would, he was clear that he hated the sight of her. And she'd heard Vaclav owned half the police department.

He gave her a sharper shake, glowering as the rage boiled back up to the surface. A lock of blond hair dashed down over one brow, he snarled, "You will call no one for help, little girl, because no one can help you."

"My uncle will stop you. Besides, you can't tell me what to do," she whispered furiously not desiring anyone to overhear their conversation. "You can't make me do anything."

Leaning into her, calmly but with a commanding tone, his accent obscuring some of his words, he said, "I will tell you what you will do. You will calm down. Tomorrow night I will come and get you, take you out to dinner. We can get to know one another. *Na* strings, I swear I will not make any moves on you."

Rounding closer to her, he frowned.

Catching her chin with tough fingers, he lifted and tilted her face to the side. "What the hell is that, Adara?"

Peering closer, the frown darkened. Mouth pressing into a hard line, he said, "Another damn bruise under your eye? The makeup ain't hiding it girl. I can tell a bruise from a hit, what the hell happened? And you keep wincing and holding your side, who-"

Twisting her head, straining to break free of his strong fingers, but he wasn't a man to let go unless he wanted to, she cried, "Can't you all leave me alone? I don't want to date anyone. Ever. Leave me alone!"

"Goddammit Adara, you tell me right this damned second who the hell hit you, *na* fucking way anyone is going to-"

"Vâj you old bastard!" A cheerful voice interrupted them.

A young man around Vaclav's age strode up and slammed a hand on Vaclav's broad shoulder. "Vâjâi, Vâj," he called Vaclav by the Romanian nickname that had become attached to him. "How the hell have you been? I didn't know you were in town, we need to hit the bars, bro, the strip clubs, the whores, uh-" he glanced sheepishly at Adara.

His gaze widened in astonishment at her soft beauty, "Uh, sorry, Miss." Heat lit the eyes that traveled from her lustrous hair down her body hidden under loose clothes but the curves still evident.

At Vaclav's warning growl, he blinked, said, "Yeah, uh, anyway," then he grinned at Vaclav. "Come on, lose that dour look that always blackens that tough face of yours and let's have some drinks."

"Collier," Vaclav said, turning to his friend with a frown, and his grip on Adara slackened enough she wrenched her arm free and rushed away before he could stop her.

A huge grin smirked across Collier's face as the two men watched Adara hurry across the floor. Even in the loose skirt, her bottom was round and shapely, her small hips snapped back and forth hypnotically as she scurried away.

Collier grinned, "Hey, sorry bro, I didn't mean to bust up your date? Or were you vying for one? I've seen that little honey around, she is one cold fish, regular snow queen. Gorgeous and scorching hot as all fuck-get-out, but she won't even look a guy in the eye when she blows 'em off. I've never been this close to her, her beauty is breathtaking, eh?" He said slyly to his friend, "So, how were you doing?"

Vaclav stuck his hands in his pockets and glared at the disappearing Adara. "She is a work in progress."

His dark brows slated down between his angry eyes. "I have waited a long time for her to damned grow up, but I will have her. Trust me. She wants nothing to do with any man, so I have a level playing field."

A few beats of silence then he turned to Collier with a half-smile that didn't reach his eyes. "*Da*, let us hit the clubs, we can grab up the boys on the way."

Chapter Eleven

Several weeks later, Mrs. Stonefall opened Adara's door.

Sitting by the window reading a book, Adara looked up at the sudden intrusion. She had given up on asking the servant to please knock first before entering.

It was only polite, but, her shoulders drooped with a resigned sigh, it was not just Mrs. Stonefall, everyone in the mansion treated her with disrespect during the infrequent times she was allowed out of her room.

Her bony chin up, voice condescending, the maid announced, "Mr. Valentina orders that you put on the black dress and heels. I will do your hair and makeup."

Another fight she had given up. She hated wearing makeup, it made her feel sticky and her skin tight. Her uncle enforced it to make her look more sophisticated.

She also knew it would do no good to resist wearing the sleazy dress and going downstairs. Her hand went to her stomach, it revolted with her nerves.

It meant that her uncle had produced another man to look her over. He was intent on renting, pimping her out, as a whore to men before selling her to the Pakistani warlord.

An hour later, her heels in her hand, Adara trod down the stairs in bare feet with heavy reluctance.

When she reached the bottom, she slipped on the high heels. Vampy black stilettoes with bows on the heels, so high she walked awkwardly, she had to work to not trip in them or twist an ankle.

Her uncle laughed at the awkward way she walked, he told her it was sexy. He said it was kittenish sexy tripping with her ass and tits bobbing while she tried to keep in a straight line and upright.

A butler waited for her at the staircase to escort her to her uncle's den.

She fought back the cringe as she entered the room. A dread memory of the first vicious beating he had given her as a welcome home wound in her mind, writhing with the ever present anguish that was her existence.

He had hit her since, but not like that day. He had realized he had almost killed her and backed off…a bit.

"Ah, there she is." Her uncle beckoned to her to come in.

Brows down at her hesitation, he snapped roughly, "Don't hover in the doorway, niece, get your ass in here. I want you to meet Raffaele Fiorenzo." He cocked his head to smile at the man standing beside him.

To Adara, the smile gone, he said, "Raffaele is the head of the Brinvendetto Organization. Come in and say hello." His face was impassive, but the threat was clear in his dark eyes.

She was to behave, act polite, do as he said without hesitation or argument. She would be sorry later if she didn't, very sorry.

Adara tripped gracefully into the room, both men watched her breasts bounce in the extremely low-cut dress.

Massimo did not allow her to wear a bra when she was at one of her 'showings.' The bodice was tight down her ribs to her bottom, then flared into a tiny skirt that fluttered around her thighs.

"So," Massimo said with a grin. "She what I said? Check out those tits, nice, huh? Turn around Adara, give him a view of the back."

Standing half-naked like a piece of meat being selected for a meal, the man's lewd eyes shining at her like a wolf hovering over an injured prey, Adara froze.

Massimo's brows drew back down with an angry frown. "Adara," he snapped, the warning of a stringent beating blared in his annoyed eyes.

Taking a deep breath, Adara slowly turned around so they could stare at her behind.

At their silence, knowing she was being visually raped, Adara held in the shudder that wanted to shake her body into oblivion. The back of the dress was cut all the way down past her tiny waist to the curve of her bottom where a bow matching those on her shoes sat right on the swell of her butt.

"Fucking ass," Fiorenzo groaned, "those legs, so girlish, so young, fuck me, Massimo." His breathing heavy, voice hoarse with lust, he said, "I want her now. Right now." His hands twitched towards his crotch.

Adara swung around in fright.

Massimo grinned like a fox with a canary in his teeth, and held the other man back with a grasp of his arm. "Not yet, Raffaele, I have others to show her to, you know that. When the bids are in, I give her to the top five, starting with the highest bid and then down, each to have one week with her." Adara's gasp only widened his grin.

Fiorenzo's eyes gleamed debauched lust at her. "Come on, Massimo, a taste. I want a taste to hold me. Let me feel a tit, pull the top down, I bet there's no bra under that thing." His eyes lit brighter, mouth wet from his tongue licking at it, his gaze stripping her.

With a sharp inhale, Adara crossed her arms over her chest and stepped back.

Massimo still held Fiorenzo's arm, holding him back as the man was about to pounce on Adara.

"Mas," Fiorenzo huffed, his face turning red, "just yank the top down. I just want to see those naked tits, lemme cop a couple of feels, my bid will be higher, I swear. Come on, man."

Massimo chuckled, keeping a grip on the mobster.

"Patience my man. Cough up your bid and you win, then you can touch her, bang her all you want, her cunt, her ass, her mouth, whatever, to your heart's delight. Until then," he nodded to the butler who stood like a statue by the door.

The butler came forward, cupped Adara's elbow and drew her out of the room.

Her breath expelled with a soft cry, her legs shaking like leaves in a brutal wind, Adara would have toppled over if the butler wasn't holding onto her so hard.

Without a word he walked her back up the stairs to her room.

****

Thank goodness Massimo had left town for several weeks, giving Adara peace and a temporary feeling of safety. He hadn't started the bidding on her yet, to her relief.

She got up and stood at the window. Setting her palms on the sill, she sighed and looked out. It was as she'd known, too high to attempt to climb down. There was nothing for her to hold onto, she would plunge to her death if she tried. And she had still considered it, daily.

At this point, living wasn't high on her list. The angst of her uncle's plans for her hung over her head like a lead cloud. There was no escape for her. She had no friends, no relatives to help her, half the police were in the gangster's pocket. There was just nowhere to turn.

The door opened, Mrs. Stonefall's hawkish unsmiling face appeared. "Your uncle has returned. Wear the purple one, he is bringing you to the Mercers' 50th anniversary party at the Cascades. I will do your hair."

Staring down at the hard ground below, Adara wondered if she could throw a chair through the glass and jump out the window before the maid could reach her.

At the maid's steeled look, she knew she'd read her mind. Massimo would have Stonefall exterminated if she allowed anything to happen to Adara.

Her body sagged, there was not a chance of getting away. As horrid as the maid was to her, Adara still did not wish the torturous death that Massimo would prevail upon her if she let anything happen to his niece before he could sell her.

Sighing in resignation, her shoulders rounded as she went to prepare for tonight's exhibition.

When they entered the grand ballroom of the lavish Cascades, they were met with a boisterous crowd. A band played loud joyful music, people danced and laughed.

Leaving their jackets at the coat check, uncle and niece moved into the white and gold room with dangling chandeliers and golden drapes and matching tablecloths.

"Behave yourself, I need a drink," Massimo said tersely to Adara then left her standing there. His men melted into the background to guard Massimo, and prevent Adara from leaving.

Feeling like a piece of sugar on an anthill in the sleazy outfit he'd made her wear, keeping her head down, Adara made her way through the crowd to where she knew there was a balcony.

It was on the chilly side, maybe there would not be anyone out there. The back of the room was all glass French doors. They opened to a long, wide balcony. The doors were unlocked, Adara turned a knob and stepped outside.

She wore a form-fitting purple suit with big, purple material-covered buttons down the front of the top, waist-fitted jacket. The short, tulip-shaped skirt had the same big buttons down the back, and she wore matching purple heels. A tiny purse containing only a brush and lip-gloss hung on a strap over her shoulder.

It was cool outside, but as she hoped, the balcony was vacant. She trod to the railing to look out over the inky sky. Cloudless, a million stars twinkled in the heavens above.

Breathing in a rare deep breath of cool, fresh air, Adara let it out slowly.

Out on the lawn in the shadows, she noticed a couple embrace, then move to the trees where things got hot and heavy. Blushing, she averted her attention to the other side of the grounds where the swimming pool was secured behind a fence.

Hearing the door open and close, she groaned, another kissing couple no doubt. Her life was hell enough without having to see young couples in love. Something she knew she would never experience herself.

No, she was to be whored out then sold to a cruel and fierce warlord to live imprisoned on the other side of the world, a world of searing heat and dusty sand.

She felt warmth at her back, breath wisped the top of her hair. She smelled his cologne. He always wore Mandrake, a subtle masculine scent of musk and something like allspice. It smelled as virile as the man himself.

"Adara," that one word said in his deep, accented baritone always raced shivers up her spine and clamped her stomach tight with nerves.

She turned and made to push past him without a word.

He took a step to block her way. She could have easier moved aside a mountain.

Hard face, harsh with the dangerous life he led, the strapping man would move when he wanted to. He said, "We need to finish the conversation we were having at the last party."

Standing still, she averted her head slightly from him, her gaze not connecting with his and stated, "Mr. Braşov, I have told you again and again that I am not interested in you. I am not interested in anyone. If I could drop down into the middle of the Amazon and be left alone, with no company except lions and snakes, I would be thrilled. Now, let me pass."

He wore a long-sleeved white shirt and dark blue slacks and suit jacket with dress boots. A turquoise stone hung in a leather tie around his thick neck.

Raising her eyes, she forced herself to look him squarely in those artic blues.

As usual, they were hooded, only a bit of icy blue glinted out. His dark blond hair was combed neatly, although he had shaved, there was a dark shadow on the clenched jaw.

She blinked and stepped quickly to the side, but not fast enough.

He stepped in front of her, a mountain of a stone wall. "Adara, you will talk with me. I have never harmed you, you owe it to me to give me some of your time."

"Mr. Braşov," she saw his teeth grit at the title. "We have nothing to discuss. I have asked you to leave me alone. It's not just you," she sighed her suffering. "I've told you, even if my uncle would allow it, which he wouldn't, I have no interest in being with anyone." *Especially a mobster.*

He bent and whispered in her ear, "But I am not just anyone, Adara, I insist you-"

She suddenly darted to the side and made to race past him- but he snaked his hand out and snatched her arm. He grabbed her other arm and brought her to face him.

"*Basta*, enough of this shit, you will give me a minute." He held her regardless of her furious face and agitated struggles.

"Let go of me, Mr. Braşov, right now. I will not be manhandled by every man in town, let go," she wrenched to the side.

Lowering his head, gripping her arms, he growled, "I fucking told you to call me Vâj. I have had it, Adara, you will-" she suddenly twisted hard and threw herself, almost slipping from his grasp. Expelling a grunt, he jerked her back in front of him.

With their wrestling, the buttons on her top popped apart and the bodice fell wide open. Vaclav's angry eyes dropped to the swells of her breasts mounding over the black lace bra. As his eyes widened, the pupils dilated to obsidian nickels.

He prattled off a torrid string of foreign words before switching back to English. "*Niaba*, damn, Adara, you have the tits of a goddess." The heat in his eyes could have scalded her fair skin.

"Stop it!" Adara shook her body to break free. "Stop looking at me!" Her struggles only made her plump breasts joggle in the black lace and turn his temperature up ten more degrees.

He stared unblinking, his lips parted and more Romanian muttered out.

She jerked as hard as she could, and he had to let her go or risk her hurting herself. She raised her hand and slapped him.

He didn't even flinch at the slap. Blinking back his desire, he stood without moving, watching her button her top with shaking fingers.

"Braşov," her uncle's cold voice snapped from the open glass door. He stepped out onto the balcony. "Why the hell are you sniffing around my niece? She has no interest in a bloody fucking Russian. Foreign bastard, get the hell away from her."

Using his body to block her from her uncle's view, Vaclav calmly turned to face Massimo, he nodded with a muttered, "Valentina. We were having a conversation that I desire to finish. Give us a moment-"

Cutting him off, Massimo marched forward, glaring his fury. "No. I have plans for her and they don't include being with a goddamned Russian. You know damned well we are rivals, I will see her dead before I see her with you." And he meant it.

One brow cocked, his tone and stance calm, Vaclav asked coolly, "And what are these plans of yours?" His eyes flicked to Adara.

Her skin had drained of color and her eyes slid down to stare at the floor. Seeing her abject fear of her uncle, the blue eyes narrowed back at Massimo.

"None of your bloody business, you *scopano* Russkie, commie shit. Now, I am taking my niece. You stay the hell away from her, you hear me?"

A crooked grin tugged up one side of Vaclav's harsh mouth, his eyes stone cold dead, he said calmly, "I am Romanian, and this is not over."

"*Fanculo*, you asshole," Massimo snagged Adara's wrist and hauled her bodily past the brooding mobster, leaving him standing on the balcony, his face blank, fists clenched at his side.

Chapter Twelve

Her legs persistently ached, her back still stung from her uncle's lashing belt.

Massimo had been out of control livid when they returned to the mansion after the anniversary party. Seeing her with one of his stiffest rivals stabbed a knife in his gut and slashed it with invidious fury.

Vaclav's syndicate was a constant burr under his vest. Vaclav owned the best restaurants, had the banks that laundered his money in his back pocket, the authorities with the most power bowed down to the Romanian mobster. The only things he didn't control were the drugs and the girls.

Vaclav Braşov, one of the youngest bosses of a made syndicate, stayed away from prostitution and drugs. He had let it be known only bottom-feeding scum got their money from the exploitation of victims weaker than them.

The people he did business with were willing participants well aware of what they were getting into. If they betrayed him or cheated him, or hurt any of his men, he went after them with savage vengeance.

His reputation was vicious and fierce, and he held a grudge. No one got away with doing him wrong for long. Due to his ruthless rep, most people, even the toughest thugs on the street steered clear of pissing him off.

His soldiers were loyal and ruthless warriors, and his closest friends were as barbarous as Vaclav, and would mercilessly avenge him if anyone dared attack or kill him.

Massimo Valentina acquired most of his money from the desperate junkies that bought his poison, and off the backs of young girls taken in sex slavery and forced into brothels, or to work on the streets.

He had fairly recently gotten involved in gun trafficking. It was worth the danger from the lowlife smugglers he dealt with, and from the law. His wealth already immense, soared into the billions.

Yet Vaclav Brașov still niggled him; a pesky, powerful gnat in the peripheral of his crime world. He was jealous of Vaclav that he made his money in a more sophisticated way.

The Romanian didn't get his hands dirty with human trafficking, drugs, and selling protection to the mom and pop stores. Protection from Valentina himself. Controlling the drug traffic was difficult and dirty work. People overdosed and that kept the news in the paper, and families after the law to clean it up. Vaclav steered clear of any of that kind of mess.

So, when Massimo saw his niece cozying up to his hated rival, he blew a blood vessel of blind rage and beat Adara so badly his major domo pestered him to take her to the hospital. Instead, he had a doctor that was on his payroll brought to the mansion.

That was almost a month ago and the pain still lingered. She needed to get away. But she had no money, nothing. Adara thought back to the rides home from various events her uncle took her for viewing so he could put her on the cyber auction block. He dressed her in skimpy scandalous outfits and paraded her in front of the wealthiest of fellow gangsters to get their blood boiling so their bids would go sky high.

There was a diner they had passed several times and it always had a help wanted sign in the window. Surely she was capable of learning to be a waitress? Or even bus tables, dishwash, whatever, she would do it.

The problem was how to get there. They were miles from the city, too far to walk. She was going to need help.

Her dream was that someday if she earned enough money, she could finish her college degree, get a job somewhere far away from people, work out of a cute little bungalow near the sea, maybe even get a dog.

A rare smile curved up Adara's solemn face. She needed to have a goal, maintain hope. If she earned money, she would be independent and could hide from her uncle and the men he wanted to sell her to.

A soft knock at the door brought her from her musings. Looking up, she saw one of the younger part-time servants, Lucia, poke her head in the door.

Lucia had only been working there three or four months, and still shy, she didn't treat Adara with contempt. Yet.

So lonely, Adara was thrilled to see anyone, and the sweet maid was uplifting. "Hi, Lucia, come in," she said with a warm smile.

Carrying a tray, the girl shyly entered the room and set it on the desk. Around 22, her chestnut hair was tied back in a pert ponytail and she had blunt bangs. Big blue eyes twinkled with mischief. The twinkle dimmed, she said with uncomfortable sympathy, "It's just some oatmeal and orange juice, you uncle's orders-"

Cutting her off, Adara stood up and said, "Uh, it's okay, I know." Oatmeal for breakfast and lunch, and whatever was left over from the evening's dinner. If nothing was left, it was more oatmeal.

It was humiliating, if she were a dog she'd be treated better. "Thanks, Lucia." She smiled kindly, nonetheless grateful for the food and the company.

The young maid bowed her head and started for the door.

Adara took a few steps towards her, "Lucia, wait." The girl paused and turned around with a quizzical smile.

"Um." Adara moved closer to the older girl. "I was wondering, I..." Well, should she tell the truth, or make up a lie that would probably sound worse.

"Listen, Lucia. My uncle sort of keeps me...secluded here. I would dearly love to get a job. There's a diner in town that's hiring. I'm sure if I can get there I could, you know, get hired."

The smile still there, yet puzzled, Lucia nodded. "Yes?"

Twining her fingers, Adara stepped closer and lowered her voice. "The thing is, I have no money. I was wondering, I mean I could take the bus there, I've seen a bus stop on the main road a mile from here, but…"

The question left Lucia's smile, she nodded with understanding. "You're wondering if you can borrow some money for a bus ticket."

Sighing her relief, Adara grinned apologetically. "Yes. It shouldn't cost too much, and as soon as I earn my first check or tips I would pay you back with interest. Do you think you could help me?"

"Sure, Miss, it's only a couple of dollars. I can even tell you which bus to take."

"Oh, Lucia, that would be so terrific, I would be forever in your debt. Right now would sort of be…" She trailed off awkwardly.

Comprehending Adara's being uncomfortable with asking for money and wanting it now, Lucia shared her very toothy grin revealing her prominent two front teeth. "Of course. Here, I always keep cash in my bra in case I want to buy some cookies when caterers are here."

She dug her hand into the top of her grey and white uniform and pulled out a small wad of cash. She counted out how much a bus to the diner and back would be and handed it to Adara.

Accepting the bills, Adara crushed them to her chest, exclaiming, "Lucia, I can't tell you how much I appreciate this. I will be eternally grateful." At first her face was glowing with hope, then it fell.

Seeing her crestfallen, her brows inverted in question, Lucia asked gently, "What is it, what's wrong, Miss?"

Staring down at the crumpled bills in her hand, Adara's shoulders slumped. "Even with the money, I could never get out of here unseen. Here, thanks for the loan, you are a wonderful generous person," sighing dismally, "but it won't do me any good. I still appreciate it though," she held the bills out to the maid.

"Miss," Lucia said sternly, "don't be silly. I can get you out. I will go down the stairs and when the coast is clear I can wave you down. I can sneak down the back halls ahead of you and keep an eye out for anyone coming."

Her lips pulled in, face stiff in trepidation, she so dearly wanted to go, but she couldn't put someone else in peril for her.

Shaking her head, Adara said softly, "No, seriously, I appreciate it but I can't put you in danger. I should have thought before I spoke, before I asked you to borrow money. I'm sorry, I never should have asked you, involved you. You don't know my uncle. If he thought you helped me," her shoulders shuddered with the thought of what he would do to the young maid. She shook her head again, "No, but thanks anyway." She pressed the bills into the maid's hands.

"Oh don't be ridiculous," Lucia grinned and grabbed Adara's wrist. "Come on, let's do this while you still have the nerve," she tugged her to the door, then paused and stuck her head out.

Looking around, she whispered, "The coast is clear. Let's run for the stairs, then I'll go down first and if it's clear, I'll wave to you to come. Got it?"

"No, Lucia, listen, this isn't-"

"Come on," Lucia pulled her out of the room and the girls hurried down the hall.

At the staircase, Lucia shoved the money back into Adara's hand and whispered, "Wait here until I give the all clear," and she rushed to the stairs before Adara could object.

****

It worked. Adara got out of the house unseen. Lucia showed her an opening in the gate a few yards from the guardhouse hidden in the thicket of garden bushes.

Adara hadn't even thought about how she would get past the guards at the gate. The little maid seemed to know every sneaky thing that went on around the mansion.

Adara had almost run down the street in her nervous eagerness to get away.

She was now on the bus Lucia had told her to take. Breathing in deeply to quell her nerves, a soft smile spread over her face. She did it. She was out. She would get this job. By the time she was hired, Massimo would see the practicality of her helping to pay for her keep while nesting away some of her money for college. And hopefully, she dreamed, her own place one day.

The bus jostled and rocked, the brakes squealed every time it slowed. A man sat beside her on the red vinyl seat reading a newspaper.

Excitement bubbled up her throat as she watched the world go by out the smudged window. Freedom. She was finally free. It felt amazing, no bars, no walls, no guards, no abusive uncle. Free.

The bus stopped twenty times in the forty minutes it took to reach her destination. When it came to a squeaking, bouncing halt at her stop off, Adara stood up. She was so anxious and so excited she could hardly breathe.

Smoothing down the skirt that thankfully she was wearing when Lucia had come into her room, it would be perfect for her interview; she followed several other people down the rubber-ridged aisle.

Her feet felt so light as she danced down the steps on her way to freedom. The cool breeze ruffled her hair and the skirt; she tugged her jacket more tightly to her body.

She stared down at the steps being extra careful, her mother had always said she was clumsy, and it was true. She didn't need to fall and show up at her interview with a dirty torn skirt.

When her foot reached the bottom step, she paused and looked up with glee to see the whole wide world stretched out in front of her. Then, she saw the long black car at the curb. The exhaust that poured out the pipe in the back showed the engine was running.

A quiver struck Adara's belly, the hairs on her arms rose, her pulse started to hammer.

Three men exited the car and started straight for the bus, their eyes on her. She recognized them; they were her uncle's men. *Oh my God*, her skin shriveled as her legs shook.

The men stalked to her and stood to the side of the steps.

When her feet hit the ground, one man set a hand lightly on her back and wordlessly ushered her to the car. He opened the door and waited for her to get in.

Her heart pounding, mind grinding with fear, she got in and slid over as he climbed in next to her. The other men got in the front and the car took off.

No one said a word. Adara sat motionless, swallowing hard and squeezing her stomach internally to keep from retching in the terrible fear that gripped her. Her uncle knew of her escape. *Oh no*, that had to mean he knew about Lucia's helping her.

Adara needed to somehow convince her uncle Lucia had nothing to do with it. She would say she stole the money for the bus, sure, he'd beat her, but he was going to anyway.

She would tell him…her mind raced with her pulse, her breath just froze in her lungs, her brain scrambled with panicked thoughts. She needed to think, come up with a plausible story to keep Lucia out of it.

The bus had taken forty minutes to get to town, the car only twenty to get home.

The long car rocked as the two men exited the front. The one sitting next to her got out and stood aside to wait for her to exit.

The other two stayed by the car, and the first one walked her up the drive and up the steps and opened the door.

They passed through the vestibule and started for the hall that led to her uncle's den. Someone was coming towards them. Two someones, and they carried something between them. A black bag.

Adara's heart thumped so hard against her ribs she thought the man beside her could hear it, her breakfast was climbing up her throat. He nudged her to stand closer to the wall as the two man trod past.

They each carried an end of the bag, as it went by. Adara saw it was zipped up, but part of one end was open. A perky chestnut ponytail bobbed out. One of the men grasped it and shoved it back inside the bag and they kept on down the hall.

Adara's brain quailed dizzy with dread and terrible hopelessness. Grief and guilt for the young maid spun madly inside her. She should never have involved Lucia. Never asked to borrow money, never should have even talked to her, looked in her direction. Poor Lucia.

94

Adara choked back the tears and swallowed the sobs that regurgitated up her throat with her oatmeal.

With a bump of his hand on her arm, the man started her walking again. She wondered if she was heading to her own black bag.

When they reached the den, the man opened the door, he waited for her to step inside before closing her in with her uncle.

Massimo stood in the center of the room. As usual, he wore a suit. This one was black with a red and white striped silk tie and a red handkerchief in the breast pocket. His dark hair combed back stiff as a board, his hands clasped behind his back, feet spread slightly, his eyes held no hint of his wrath.

Adara hovered by the door. Massimo stared at her for so long she thought she would pass out from the nerves waiting for what he would do.

Finally, he said, "Come here."

She forced her legs to move. She trod silently across the room to stand before him.

Now that she was within arm's reach, he allowed the malevolent virulence scourge his features. Lids drew dangerously low over seething murderous eyes, through clenched teeth he snarled, "You *fottuto* dare to disobey my orders you worthless bitch?" His big hand swung out and backhanded her.

Though she knew it was coming and tried to prepare, she still stumbled backwards.

It didn't matter how hard she tried to stay strong, he hit her again snapping her head so hard to the side her hair flew across her face.

He shouted, "I told you, you do not leave this house, you do not work, no school. I will not have the murderer of my brother on the streets dishonoring the good Valentina name."

"Huh," she snorted having enough of his bullying her into silence. He was going to beat her regardless. Maybe this time he'd beat her to death and end her miserable life.

Resisting the urge to cup her stinging cheek, she sneered, "Good name? It is the heritage of a mob, an immoral syndicate, a criminal organiza-"

Whack! Slapping her again, he grabbed her collar. Dragging her to him and up on her toes, he shouted into her face, "You bitch, you disobey me and sneak out of this house, and now you backtalk me after I brought you into my home after what you did, and you dare insult our name?"

Balling his hand into a fist he slammed it into her jaw and cursed her.

"You don't know how much I wish I could suck the Valentina blood right outta your ungrateful murderous veins, just cut them open and let you fucking bleed our DNA out. But I can't. It would be dishonorable on my own *famiglia* blood to kill you." His fist wrapped in her shirt he pulled her right up close and spat in her face.

Shaking her so hard her hair swatted back and forth he screamed, "I have started the bidding, and soon you will be out of my hair."

His grin a tragedy of sick glee, he said, "On your back, or like a dog on all fours, with dozens of men fucking you until you are nothing but a tortured, used up gnarl of blood and guts. Then that bastard Ali Khan will take you to that godforsaken desert and you will burn in hell until you die. And I will have avenged my brother."

Adara fought not to cry, show her pain, her fear, but the tears rolled relentless. Sobs cluttered in her throat blocking her airwaves, her lungs shuddered with agony. The words, 'Mama did it, not me!' crawled up her gullet, she swallowed them down.

He punched her again, his face a twisted blight of hate and cruelty. "That desert rat will marry you, put his spawn in you, along with his harem of a thousand women. You will never get away, you bitch, never. You will finally pay for what you did to my brother."

Hitting her until she collapsed to her knees, he bent over her and still pummeled her, cursing her, "I am done with you, done with having to look at you," his hate filled, abusive voice grew fainter and fainter as she went under.

Chapter Thirteen

After suffering through more weeks of healing, Adara lay in her bed too depressed to get up and dress.

She didn't look up when someone came into her room, now only once a day to bring her food. They would set the oatmeal and a glass of water on the table by her bed and leave without a word.

The servants knew what happened to Lucia, none of them wanted the duty of bringing her food, but Massimo screamed at the housekeeper and shouted, "Make it happen or there will be more Lucias!"

He needed Adara healthy enough for the bidders. He had one more gangster he wanted to take her to.

When the bruises had almost faded completely, Mrs. Stonefall barged into the room. Adara didn't bat an eye. The maid said coldly, "The fuchsia dress, I will do your hair and makeup. We have one hour."

An hour later Adara was getting into the black car, Massimo climbed in the front. Normally he would have sat in the back while being transported, but he did not want to sit near Adara. He didn't even want to look at her, and he was quite adept at avoiding it. When she was in his direct line of vision, he just looked through her like she wasn't there.

Her back slumped hopelessly against the backseat; Adara didn't have the energy to smooth the flouncy skirt. Like the other dresses, it was tight and hugged her curves.

Silky, the top tied halter-style behind her neck and dipped low enough to show a generous amount of cleavage, the skirt barely covered her tush. At least Stonefall had provided a silk halter-bra, last time she wasn't allowed a bra. Massimo was getting bolder with showing her ample wares.

The car parked in front of an elegant restaurant.

Without looking at or touching her, Massimo brought Adara inside. The place teemed with boisterous people. The owner was throwing an engagement party for his son.

Not seeing the owner, Gregorio Vega, head of the main Latino organization on the other side of the city, Massimo told Adara to go sit somewhere, and he went to find Vega.

Adara glanced at the door, several of Massimo's soldiers loomed, their eyes constantly scanning the room for possible danger for their boss. There was no way she could get past them.

Didn't matter, she no longer had the energy or the will to try to escape again. It had already cost an innocent girl her life. Adara had finally given up. She would face her destiny with dignity and peace.

Men tried to catch her attention as she wandered through the room like a phantom. She was already dead inside, she didn't notice their attempts.

She went to the bar and although underage, got a glass of white wine, then strolled through the happy crowd to find a place where there were less people and less happiness.

Leaving the main restaurant, she found a hall and trod down it looking for some privacy. A door was ajar near the end of the hall, she peered inside. Boxes and chairs, a few tables filled the room. It was a storeroom, and what she wanted, it was empty of people.

Slipping inside, she thought she could sit for a minute, drink her wine, get up some liquid courage before she was put back up on the metaphorical auction block for Gregorio Vega's lascivious viewing.

The door she had carefully closed behind her creaked.

She turned to see Vaclav Braşov stepping into the room. Instantly she stiffened and held the wine glass in front of her as if it could protect her.

"Hello, Adara," he said quietly. Artic eyes glittering, he prowled through the room to her.

"Leave me alone, Mr. Braşov," she sighed wearily. "Why do you persist in harassing me?"

His gaze stroked over her like a starving bear and a honeycomb, admiring the perfect wasp shape of her slender, yet strikingly curvy body. The way the fuchsia halter cupped her plump breasts, the seductive swing of them when she moved, her legs, shapely yet quite slim from being just a shade from her teen years and allowed little food.

Heat coiled in the cold blue eyes. "I have told you, Adara, I want us to get to know each other. I want you to go on a date with me."

"Why? Why would you want to date me, get to know me, be seen in public with me?" Of course he was a murderer as well so it wouldn't faze him. "I can't imagine you are attracted to me," her deprecating snort drew his brows down.

She was constantly told she was too skinny, too delicate, fragile, her eyes too large for her head, lips too swollen like a permanent pout.

She said, "I am only desired as my uncle's niece. Men want me so they can be attached to him, and," one small shoulder shrugged, "the forced sex of course is an inducement." Her words, her harsh laugh sarcastic, set his mouth hard, his jaw flexed.

She went on, the painful desolation threading her soft voice. "Apparently men are eager to pay for a captive slave, a sex toy they can do anything they want with, regardless of the desires of the female."

Her gaze slipped away from his blue irises that darkened with sudden fury. "But you, my uncle won't sell me to you, and you have no interest in allying with him, so I don't understand why you keep after me. Is it because you want to punish me? My uncle? Or is it because you want to entice me to work for you?"

Before he could respond, her pretty eyes thinned and she declared, "Well I won't, ever, so move on, please."

Shaking his head with an eye-roll, frustration groaned from his thick chest. "Adara, if you would only listen to me, give me a chance." His big hands were out and up in entreaty, head cocked in boyish sincerity, eyes half-lidded in hunger for her, and in supplication for her acquiescence to his request.

Forehead furrowed in curious contemplation, she studied his harsh face with the strong jaw, the cruel full lips, the cold menace that always lurked in his frightening eyes. Even now as he attempted to get her to do as he asked, the danger was always there.

"I don't understand your relentless interest, I don't get it. When I was younger, they always said that you were a pervert for chasing after me, a little girl."

She sipped her wine, then took a big gulp as he stalked closer to her. "I am an adult now, your sick interest should have waned long ago."

Angry, he snapped, "Fuck that shit, I never lusted after you when you were a child, Adara." He cooled the irritation in his deep voice, heavy with his unusual accent.

"But there was…something, that held me even then. However, now that we are both adults, the age difference is not that big a deal. If you were 40 and I was 50 no one would say a thing about it."

He moved closer to her, his eyes sweeping down her figure and up again. "Go to dinner with me, Adara," it was more a command than a request.

She didn't want to show her fear, but still she took a step back from him.

He was a big, hard muscled man; tattoos peeked from under his shirt sleeves and on his neck. He was a notorious gangster that didn't hesitate to eliminate anyone who got in his way. Scars on his face showed he feared no one and nothing.

His warrior years were carved in the iron hardness of his face. The only reason he hadn't come after her recently was because he knew her uncle would refuse him. He had to wait and get word of when she would be at an event and then show up.

She took another step back. "No. I will not go out with you. As I've told you, even if I wanted to, which I don't, my uncle would never allow it." Her head tilted to look bravely up at him.

His face was razor hard, the scars making him look even more brutal, hooded eyes as scary as always, yet, there was a bestial sensuality to his mouth. The way he stood, broad shoulders back with confidence, powerful chest puffed out arrogantly. Even with all the hardness and scariness, he was handsome, in a menacing kind of way.

His one step covered the two steps she took backwards. His jaw clenched and a vein pumped the scar at his temple with its irritated beats. "Dammit, Adara, stop fucking moving away from me, and stop turning me down. I want you for you. You are a woman now, not a little girl anymore." His accent made woman sound like *voman*.

"You can go on one damned date with me. I will not fucking beat you or rape you for God's sake." He didn't say he wouldn't keep her once he had possession of her.

He stood more than a foot taller than her, his shoulders alone likely weighed more than her entire body.

She held a dainty hand up to ward him off. "Last time I saw you, you threatened to take me, take what you wanted," her cheeks tinted pink with embarrassment at the tremble in her voice. "Is that supposed to make me feel…safe?"

His scowl only made him a more fearsome hulk. He growled, "I have asked like a gentleman, politely for you to go out with me, yet you turn your back and show me that fine little ass as you walk away from me. I will have you, *mândră, mea* beauty."

His tone softened to sultry velvet, lifting his hand he stroked the backs of his fingers down her cheek. "Come with me now, *mea* beautiful girl."

Adara felt herself slipping into those artic eyes that had coalesced into hot springs of desire. They beckoned with silken promises of nights of unbridled passion.

She tilted her face into the seducing caresses of his gentle, beguiling fingers. Her lids lowered, tongue faintly flecked her lips, his gaze lowered to her mouth. The heat flamed, fire flashed in his hooded eyes.

She blinked, stepped back from his touch and shook her head. Setting her wine glass on a table she said, "No. Leave me alone. Even if I wanted to go with you, and as I said, I don't," not seeing his frown she went on.

"My uncle would never tolerate my being with you. He has plans for me, and they don't include you." She started to walk by him. "Now, I am leave-"

Vaclav grabbed her, one hand at her back, the other clinching the back of her head. He jerked her to him, her breasts crashed into his hard chest, and his mouth set upon hers.

Her protest disappeared into his mouth as he assaulted her lips. Crushing their mouths together, he bit and lapped at her lips before forcing them open and plowed his tongue inside, invading, despoiling the tenderness of her mouth, harvesting every vestige of her innocence.

Her hands came up between them to push at his chest, but he roughly pulled her closer, so hard and tight her hands were shoved aside.

She gripped his bulging biceps to force him away, but she hadn't a thread of his strength. He was big and hard and manly, a powerful gangster that took what he wanted, and he had wanted her as long as he's known her.

He had been drawn, mesmerized by her as a child, his inexplicable, irresistible attraction pure, not pedophilic, but now he was mindlessly captivated by her as a grown woman.

His mouth roguishly massaging hers, corrupting that wholesome innocence, he sucked at her plush lips, her tongue, his own probing deep and aggressive and urgent.

He worked her until she grew boneless in his arms and her own body responded. Her little fingers dug into his biceps, she moaned when he rubbed his granite chest against her soft breasts. His hand moved down her back to cup her bottom and he pulled her pelvis against his, she could feel the hard thick club of his desire pressing into her woman's cleft, and her panties grew damp.

Adara was dizzy with arousal and confusion, he was so quickly stimulating her, her mind was swimming with new, unfamiliar carrousels of sensations. He was skillfully, deliberately charging her body, making it feel strange things until a thick fog of pure pleasure flooded her.

Vaclav kissed her, his mouth sucked at her lips then he kissed down to her chin, licking her neck, he bit her soft flesh quickly bringing a red mark to her creamy skin.

Kissing his way back up, he besieged her mouth again, pursued her tongue and sucked it so hard she whimpered before he shoved his tongue halfway down her throat. His gravelly moans vibrated against her mouth.

Adara was taken in a whirlwind, he was whipping her body into a frenzy, she panted against his mouth. He gripped both of her butt cheeks, fondled them roughly then squeezed. It hurt, but felt oddly pleasurable, her curvy body squirmed against his rocky male frame.

Releasing her bottom, he stroked his big hands up and covered her supple breasts. "Ah, fuck, Adara," he groaned as he kneaded her plump flesh and his mouth groped hers.

Suddenly afraid, Adara shoved him, breaking away, her chest heaving with panting breaths.

In a confused daze, she slapped him. That was twice she had done that, she didn't know where the violent bravery came from, she would never even swat a fly.

Her hit didn't even make him blink. His eyes cut from her furious face to her heaving breasts.

Seeing the fire ignite fiercely in those frosty blues, Adara quickly strode towards the door, but he swung his hand out and caught her arm.

Hauling her back up to his face he said softly, "Last slap, sweetheart. I am taking them because I deserve them, but *na* more. I want your body under mine, not your palm striking my face."

Twisting to get out of his grasp she demanded, "Get your hands off of me."

The rest of his body unmoving, his eyes flit down her body then back up to the dark rich chocolate of her angry orbs. A slow smile crept over his rough face. "*Da*, baby, for now. But I warn you," the smile gritted with a grim intent.

"Next time we meet, you will be mine. I promise you. I am not afraid of your uncle, *mândră*, *mea* beauty, or your own fears." His gaze set on the mark he had deliberately left on her neck.

When she looked in the mirror later she would think of him, his kiss, remember how his hands brought her body to singing rapture. He unwound his fingers from her slender arm.

Rubbing her arm where he had gripped it in his amorous anger, watching him, she backed away until her back hit the door. Her hands behind her, she fumbled for the knob.

He stood calmly observing her, his face a scored stone, expressionless. He watched her get the door open, her eyes never leaving him until she was out and running from the room.

She didn't see him again that night. Later, her uncle brought her to Gregorio Vega. The three stood at the bar. Massimo chatted while Vega ate up Adara with his eyes.

This time when he demanded to touch her, Massimo nodded a slight incline of his head.

When Vega suddenly gripped Adara's breast with painful greedy violence, a smile curved up one side of Massimo's face.

Adara thrust from Vega's groping pawing hand, spun from the men and stormed to the door. She ran right past her uncle's guards to the car.

****

A few days later, early in the morning, when she was still drowsy with sleep, Massimo stood, a dark shadow in her bedroom doorway.

Her eyes flew open with a start. Heart slamming against her chest, she half sat up, hair draping over one eye. He had never come to her room before. The only time she saw him was when they were in the car on the way to a party or exhibition for her auction.

"Tomorrow is the day, Adara," he said with a sly biting smile.

At her bewildered expression, the smile deepened. "The bidding is done, Raffaele Fiorenzo won the first week. Tomorrow I will personally be delivering you to him. Gregorio won the second week. I bet you can't wait, huh?"

A hateful gleam lit his vile eyes, he said, "Aren't you glad now that I made you keep up with those electrolysis treatments? Your gentlemen lovers will be pleased to find not a hair on your luscious body except for those lovely long lashes, those sable brows, and that gorgeous mane on your pretty little head. Ah, but they are not gentlemen, are they?"

With a malicious grin, he bowed his head, ticked two fingers off it in salute, and left.

Adara turned towards the window. This was it. She will shower, dress, fix her hair, then fling herself out that window to her death.

A sound at the door made her look to it.

Mrs. Stonefall stood there with a knowing grunt. "Don't even think about it, Missy, I am to stay glued to your side until the boss takes you. Then it'll be good riddance to your murderous self. Now get ready, I have to pack a bag for you."

Chapter Fourteen

Vaclav of all people, knows how vulnerable Adara is. He has broken into her home several times. Her uncle thinks he's so fucking sly and smart, thinks he has them locked up like Fort Knox.

Vaclav could break into anywhere; they should have called him The Ghost instead of Raging Storm. Of course both were true. He had even watched Adara sleep one night.

Stood right there in her bedroom, the house surrounded by guards and alarms, and he stood there peacefully watching his beautiful girl sleeping.

Someone was beating her and she had refused to tell him who it was. It was undoubtedly either her brother or her uncle. When he finds out who the fuck was laying hands on her he was going to-

Shaking his head, he should have taken her then, but he had forced himself not to. He had still harbored hope of her coming willingly to him. But now, he didn't have the luxury of time, he needed to get her away from whoever was striking her.

So, he put in bugs, miniature GPS's in her belongings. Her purse, her shoes, clothes, hair accessories, the meager jewelry she owned.

He had looked at her vanity in disgust. Her brother and uncle were as rich as Croesus, and they bought her shit. Didn't think she was worthy of it. If- when, she was his, he would drape her in jewels. Gems that could never rival her exquisite beauty.

The help talked to each other. Gossip always got back to Vaclav. Massimo kept Adara isolated. He wouldn't allow her to leave the mansion, to work or have a car, to keep her dependent on him for when he was ready to sell her off.

With a criminal history, a conviction for murder no less, she wasn't about to get hired anywhere anyway.

Massimo couldn't put her to work for the family crime business, their personal organization, because she was too moral, too good, she would never do anything illegal, and she would undoubtedly turn them in if she saw the true depths of their depraved evilness.

Even the story of Adara's one aborted attempt at escape got back to him. No one said positively, but the word was that a young maid who had helped her, forfeited her life when Massimo found out about it, and had Adara dragged back home. That made Vaclav even more intent on taking her from him.

Vaclav had guiltlessly rummaged through Adara's things. One day she would be his, he felt he had the right to inspect any and all of her secrets.

One of the servants was taking their life in their hands to smuggle mail in and out for her. He found her applications to universities, and the rejections that came back to her. Again, due to her history.

Each time he had come and explored her personal space, he saw the applications returned from lesser and lesser accredited schools. She was waiting to hear back from an online university. Dammit, he could get her in anywhere she wanted to go.

But she would never come to him, and her relatives would never help her. No wonder she was cold, somber as shit all the time. She had never truly left the prison.

Since he kept trackers on her all the time, had men keeping an eye on her as well, he was aware when she'd been brought to the big mobster don, Raffaele Fiorenzo.

He chastised himself, he had waited too long to take her, and now Vaclav was beyond enraged. The bastard dared to take what belonged to him!

But, Vaclav had to get her out carefully; the don could go nuts and kill her before he could extricate her with the least bit of violence. It was imperative that he gets to Adara before that goon harms her.

He paid off the guards to get him and his men peacefully in the door.

Vaclav entered the room to see a group of men gathered in a circle. In the center of the circle was Adara.

On her knees with her hands tied behind her back. She looked like the lamb on a platter with salivating wolves stalking around her licking their chops and sharpening their teeth.

Motherfucker, he should have moved faster, gotten there sooner. Hell, he should have just taken her from her bed when he was in her room instead of granting her, allowing her to retain her free will, hoping she would eventually come to him.

Her lush hair was a tousled cloud around her beautiful face. She was wearing shorts and a white blouse with buttons, she was barefoot, and trying so hard not to cry, and failing.

As Vaclav walked in, Raffaele Fiorenzo bent over, gripped Adara's blouse and tore it open. "Oh yeah baby, I knew those tits were fucking sweet. What'dya say boys?"

Raffaele e glanced around to see his men grinning their approval at her full breasts almost falling out of the lacey bra.

The shirt slipped off her shoulders exposing her even more, her slim shoulders, more of her rounded flesh. The men smacked their lips like she was a juicy dinner straight out of the oven.

His leering snarls spitting all over her, Fiorenzo commanded, "Come, girl, I want my new prize to blow me, suck me off. Show my men who owns you!"

Little whimpers escaped her trembling lips as she tried to back away from him on her knees. He shoved his fist in her hair, grabbed a handful and forced her head towards his pants that he was awkwardly opening with one hand.

Adara struggled, tears flowing. Fiorenzo gripped her hair so hard he about scalped her. Yanking her head back, her neck and spine arched, pushing her breasts out further.

He forced her face up, ready to take his cock in her mouth. In shorts, her knees were red and scraped from him shoving her around on the rough carpet.

Using every inch of willpower he had, Vaclav restrained himself to casually approach the don. He said calmly, "You owe me, Fiorenzo, I will take her as payment."

Vaclav's hard eyes slanted to Adara, who kept her head still. He knew she recognized his voice, he'd seen her shoulders stiffen even more than the terrified rigidness they already were. Vaclav said coolly, "She can suck *mea* dick, Fiorenzo."

Fiorenzo scowled at Vaclav. "Where the fuck did you come from?"

Pissed at the interruption, Fiorenzo glared at Adara. "I am renting her from her uncle, and I want her. I plan on fucking her until there is nothing left of that beautiful skin, like satin it is, huh? I hope to get my babe on her before I have to return her, force Valentina to give her back to me." Shaking his head he smiled, "No, I want her-"

Vaclav's hooded lids lowered in threat. Not backing down, his accent thick and gravely with his fury, said unyielding, "I said, you owe me."

"But her uncle sold her to me, man." Fiorenzo's eyes rolled up and down Adara's body, latching onto her breasts mounding over the tiny bra. Sucking back saliva that slid down his throat from drool, he said, "And I do very much want her."

Raffaele Fiorenzo was big like Vaclav and strongly built, but much older at 44. He had started his early days as an enforcer too. If you wanted to stay alive in their world, you had to be tougher, quicker, stronger, more violent and ruthless than the next guy. Tough workouts along with boxing and marital arts was mandatory.

With dark eyes and short, wavy dark hair, Fiorenzo still maintained his physique. Olive-skinned, he had the Patrician nose of his ancestors, and right now it was flaring in annoyance at Vaclav.

He twisted Adara's hair around his fist; her cry of pain brought a sadistic smile to his classically handsome face.

Vaclav's severe gaze stayed on Fiorenzo. The don had her in a vulnerable position. If he got mad or reckless he could break her neck.

Vaclav said, "I will buy her from you. You owe me, you bastard, for letting you take that protection money from the hotel without annihilating you and your gang. I am taking her."

Fiorenzo saw the determined set to Vaclav's jaw. Scowling, he said sulkily, "Later, I'll let you borrow her later after I've had my fill." He winked at Adara, "That may be a long time though, huh little lass?"

Gripping her hair painfully, he jerked her head up harder. Yanking his pants open, he reached in and fisted his dick, taking it out.

A vulgar grin uglied up his handsome face. "Oh," he said, "and the other guys. I promised them they could all take a taste of her too. When they're done, I'll give her to you for a night, son, but you need to be patient," he laughed. "It'll be a while. C'mere bitch," her jerked her forward.

He grinned down at her and said, "Open that gorgeous mouth for my big dick. I want to feel those lush petals around my cock before I shove you on your back and spread those pretty legs of yours for me and my men."

Without appearing to move, Vaclav had slipped close to them. He said quietly, "Adara, do you want to come with me? You will only have to fuck me, at *mea* will, instead of all of these motherfuckers, and the rest of the bastards your uncle has lined up."

Everyone gawked at him in shock. The don's rough fist held Adara so tightly, her mouth an inch from the hard penis, she couldn't look at Vaclav. Her lips quivered, tears poured.

"Well?" Vaclav demanded at her silence. "Choose. Right now. You come willingly with me, do what I say and give me what I want, when I want it, and I will take you out of here." Not that he wasn't going to anyway, but he wanted her to say it.

Barely audible she whispered, "Yes."

He stepped closer. "Yes what, Adara?"

Her hair ripping out of her scalp, Fiorenzo's cock rubbing against her lips, her sob choked, "Yes, I want to go with you."

"You will do anything I say, willingly give me anything I want?"

She tried to nod but Fiorenzo held her immobile. Her throat so slogged with tears and terror, her whisper fell out in a hushed, "*Yes*."

He needed her to be fully aware of what she was saying, agreeing to, he said, "*Da*? Yes, what? Say it." She was his regardless if she said it or not, yet he wanted her to agree, wanted her to know she said it.

Shaking out of his stupefied distraction, rapidly becoming aware he was losing control of the situation, Fiorenzo cussed, "Fuck, Brașov-"

Vaclav ignored him. "Adara?"

"Yes Mr. Brașov," she sobbed. "I…will do anything you say."

"You will stay with me, be mine, in every concept of the word? Obey me?"

Blinking uncomfortably, she couldn't move her trapped head, her eyes shifted around the room at all the horrid men staring like hungry lions over fresh kill at her exposed chest, impatiently waiting their turn to take her.

When she was first brought in and they were binding her wrists, some of them had tried to get their hands up her shorts, prying at her sex with their filthy greedy fingers.

Her gaze returned to Vaclav's; his was cold, void of emotion, hard blue ice stared back at her, mouth a gashed line, he obviously had his own miscreant plans for her. But there was only one of him. At least that was what he said. She could only hope he didn't plan on sharing her.

She sighed, "Yes."

Watching the interplay, at first thinking Vaclav was just bullshitting around, Fiorenzo grew angry. "What the fuck is all this chatter, Brașov, I told you she's mine. Now, get the hell out of here, I got a blow job coming from what I hear are virgin lips. I got a lot to teach her."

His lewd grin aimed smugly down at Adara, Fiorenzo said, "Am I right, honey? I'm gonna get to break your cherry, huh, girl? Are you as excited as me?"

Gripping her hair, he shook her head, his voice lowered, "I hope you get off on pain, gorgeous, 'cause I love giving it. Of course I don't give a shit if you don't, I-"

"Release her." A gun suddenly appeared in Vaclav's hand.

Everyone froze in shock, then Fiorenzo's soldiers went for their weapons. But Vaclav had brought his own men. Their weapons were already raised.

Fiorenzo's men threw their hands up to show they weren't reaching for a gun.

"You gotta be fucking kidding me Braşov, if you think I'm letting this prize get away." Fiorenzo released Adara's hair to tuck his now limp dick back in his pants. He stood with his fists at his side impotent to stop the abduction.

Ignoring him, Vaclav trod to Adara, bent, grasped her arm and pulled her to her shaking feet. Keeping his gun aimed at Fiorenzo, holding her arm, Vaclav walked her to the door.

He wanted to cover her tits but didn't dare take the time to stop and do it. Fiorenzo had a troop in the back that if Vaclav took too long or tried to take out the don like he wanted to, for laying his filthy hands on Adara, there were enough men on the property and the chances of Vaclav getting her out safely would be tricky. That chance he wasn't prepared to take.

Seeing a small suitcase near the door, he said, "Is that yours?" Hell, the asshole hadn't even let her settle in before assaulting her?

At Adara's nod, he said, "Grab it, Griff," and he took her out. His men stayed to ensure they weren't stopped or followed.

Outside, Vaclav hustled her to his waiting SUV. Popping the passenger door open, her wrists still bound behind her, he put his hands around her tiny waist, lifted her and set her inside.

Slamming her door closed, he jogged around to the driver's side and got in.

A moment later Griff tossed her suitcase in the back seat. Keeping his eyes above her chest, he gave Adara a friendly wink and went back to support the rest of Vaclav's team until everyone was clear.

Vaclav leaned over Adara. With a frightened gasp she shrank from him.

His brow twitched along with the beating vein at his temple. His eyes went to her open blouse hanging half off her shoulders, the heat flared in his pupils.

But he just reached for her seatbelt and clinched it then moved back to his seat and did the same and started the engine. In moments they were gone from Fiorenzo's compound.

Vaclav, struggling to control his rage at the way he'd found her, half naked, beyond terrified, surrounded by brutalizing animals, and Adara in harrowing shock, neither said a word as he drove through the black night.

Her sniffs and shuddering breaths hitching with tearful hiccups filled the compartment, mangling his heart.

Vaclav glanced over at her periodically, his gaze stroked down her exposed breasts bouncing gently over the bra then up to her face. Her skin, still tracked with tears, was stricken white from her ordeal, and her eyes stark with desperate apprehension of whatever was going to happen next.

Her trembling lips pressed hard together, she stared straight ahead, chest heaving with suppressed sobs.

He'd wanted to get as far away from Fiorenzo and his soldiers as fast as possible; he hadn't stopped to take the time to unbind her. Her hands still tied behind her back, Adara was as vulnerable and defenseless as she'd been at Fiorenzo's.

After many miles, he pulled over to get gas.

When he stopped the car, he leaned over and unlatched her seatbelt, grasped her shoulders and turned her to face away. He slipped a knife from a sheath on his belt, and slit the ropes that bound her.

Her moan of mixed pain and relief made his stomach pinch. He waited while she slowly turned around, rubbing her arms from the strain of being restrained, but not making eye contact with him.

"Stay here, I will be right back," he ordered brusquely and left the car to pump the gas.

When he was done, he went inside to pay cash and buy a pack of European thin cigars.

Tucking the cigars in his breast pocket, he headed back to the car and frowned when he saw the car door open. He sprinted to the car, glanced inside, and scowled when he saw she was gone.

She couldn't have gotten far; he looked around and saw her glossy locks flapping behind her as she ran towards the woods. "Goddammit," muttering curses, he raced after her.

He was on her before she even got out of the parking lot.

She cried out when he grabbed her, halting her. Caught escaping him, and fearful of his wrathful retribution, her head fell in resignation.

Vaclav knew she was in shock and terrified so he let her escape attempt go, although he was pissed she ran from him. Neither said a word as he gripped her arm and walked her back to the car.

Lifting her onto the seat, the step was high and wide and she was petite. In his ire, he slammed her door with more strength than the last time, then strode around the front of the SUV and got back behind the wheel.

Hearing her still frantic, rapid breathing, the tears continued rolling, he said quietly, "Adara, you need to chill, relax." He glanced at her, his mouth bunched.

Face stiff with fear and trauma and hopelessness, she stared hard out the window blinking away tears, mouth clenched to stall the trembling, her fingers twisted and wrung each other in her lap.

Vaclav clamped down his temper, hell, he'd just plucked her at gunpoint from certain savage gang-rape and torture, tossed her in his car and driven away with her to who knows where. She had every right to be distressed.

There was nothing he could say that would convince her she was safe with him, so it was another hour of silence before they reached his place.

He had several homes in America; he took her to the one in the Hamptons. Instead of pulling right into the three-car garage, he slowed by the mailbox out front and stopped the car.

The fool mailman had left envelopes sticking out the top. He got out to get the mail, and heard her open her door.

Sighing with aggravation, Vaclav tossed the mail on the car seat and jogged after her. Shit, why she thought she could outrun him, and where did she think she could go? Shaking his head he ran up and snatched her wrist.

"Goddammit, Adara. *Basta*, enough of this shit. You try to run again and I will fucking discipline you. You agreed to this, now do not fight me on it." He gave her a little shake, but she refused to look at him.

"*Bine*, okay, we go in." He let go of her to retrieve his mail and lock up the car, and damned if she didn't take off again. "You got to be fucking kidding me, girl," he growled, and with his long legs he was upon her in a second.

He snagged her so quick and sharp her body flew up in the air. Held up with her feet off the ground, her back to his chest, she kicked her legs, flailed her arms and screamed.

"Dammit," he muttered, slapping his hand over her mouth. "I have neighbors for fuck's sake. You want the cops here, they'll take you back to Massimo and right back to Fiorenzo."

Carrying her to his house, she bucked and threw her head back trying to make him release his hand over her mouth, he said in her ear, "Cut the shit, Adara, I have had enough of this crap, I told you to stop fighting me."

She still kicked and flailed, struggling to make him drop her. "Goddammit Adara," he cursed in Romanian, "you will fucking listen to me. Wait until I get you inside, you will regret this resistance. Tis time for you to accept me."

Chapter Fifteen

He hauled her into his house.

"Stop! Stop! Let me go!" Adara shrieked.

Vaclav held her off her feet while he rummaged for some rope.

Finding it, he dropped her on a chair and held her down while he tied her up. Positioning her forearms flat on the arms of the chair, he tied her wrists to the ends.

She screamed the entire time he knelt down, grasped one ankle and bound it to a chair leg. Her legs short, her tiptoes touched the floor. He bound the other ankle to the other chair leg. This forced her legs to spread wide, he'd made it impossible for her to escape or hurt herself trying.

Bound the way she was, she could barely move, only her hips slightly and her torso. Tossing her head violently back and forth she screamed, "Let me go! Let me go! Let me go!"

Vaclav picked up a chair and set it down in front of her and plopped down on it. When he set his big formidable body a few intimidating inches from her, Adara cowered, her small body pressed back against the chair.

Leaning forward with his elbows on his knees, he silently studied her so intensely she squirmed uncomfortably and jerked at her bindings.

She whispered in desperation, "Why are you doing this to me?"

He sat back in his chair, crossed his muscled arms over his bulky chest, stuck his long legs out slightly to the side of her chair and crossed his ankles, and continued perusing her.

Her arms immobilized, legs spread, ankles restrained and toes gracefully pointed on the tile, her blouse was still wide open and half down her back from Fiorenzo's attack.

Vaclav's heated gaze rolled down her, pausing on the mounding breasts that jiggled with her every thrust to get free.

"Mr. Braşov, quit that, quit looking at my…please, I need to button my blouse," her fretful whine made him grin.

"Ah, finally, I can look at you as long as I desire without you turning your back and running from me." His gaze swept all over her, pausing here and there for so long her face heated from the graphic flames in his eyes tactilely licking out at her.

"We can do this again later, sweet, when you are naked." Lids heavy with desire lowered, covering the fervor in his eyes.

The longer he stared, the more she squirmed under his blatant perusal, the redder her cheeks grew. "Please, Mr. Braşov, untie me, let me go. I- I will sit and not move, I promise." Her dark eyes begged plaintively, she had no idea how her plump lips pouted, making him die to bite them.

"*Na*," he said, shaking his head. "You will not sit as I desire, motionless and spread out for my pleasure, it has to be this way. This is a lesson, Adara, *mea* sweet girl, so pay attention." His grin grew at her raised brows.

"*Da*. I hate to bind you *mândră*." The grin curled with deliberate eroticism as his gaze swept back down to ogle her breasts, lower to between her spread legs. His fingers tapped then gripped the ends of the chair arms.

"At least not when we are not having sex games." The grin curved into a side smirk at her hateful glare that glimmered with fright.

Sobering, he said, "But if you disobey me, run from me, I will discipline you, and restrain you for your own good."

Struggling, Adara threw her body back and forth trying to get free. "You have no right to do this, let me go right now!"

His hair was blond but his brows were dark, they arched. "*Na right,* ah you say I have no right? *Da,* I have all rights when you agreed for me to take you from that bastard."

He stood up, moved to stand beside her chair, and frowned at her shrinking back from him in fear, her chest heaving with frightened breaths.

He sifted a hand against the side of her neck, his thumb caressing her skin. "Calm down, Adara," he ordered quietly.

"You," her cry seethed, bosom hitching with frantic breaths, "you are treating me just like that man, that pig. Tying me up-"

Shaking his head at her, he said gently yet with a no-nonsense tone, "You ran, Adara, we had a deal and you ran. Even after I warned you, you did it again. I had to bind you to keep you still to listen to me, and to show you what happens when you flee from me. You have always avoided me, run from me, so now you cannot. This is what will happen every time if you attempt to run again."

Her fair skin darkened with fear and anger, throwing herself again she wailed, "You can't make me, you can't do this to me!"

He bent and kissed the top of her head, said softly, "You said *da,* ah, that is yes, Adara. Yes you agreed you would do anything, everything I say. You are an innocent, but you knew what that would entail."

His fingers trailed down her throat to trace lightly over the top swells of her breasts mounding over the bra, ignoring her sharp intake of breath, her body going rigid, as still as an alabaster sculpture.

He dipped a thick finger gently, so lightly like a mere brush stroke into her cleavage, between the valley of her breasts, and smiled at her nipples hardening into little beads in the lace bra.

Adara held her breath, then she struggled again, fighting at her restraints, it only jostled her breasts against his hand.

He moved from her and sat back down, shifting the chair forward so his knees were between her open legs.

Her chest huffed and pitched with her panicking gasps, cheeks red with fury but the rest of her face was pale as snow from her escalating terror of him.

His voice autocratic, he said quietly, "You are mine, Adara, finally, you are mine. Tell me you have not always known, felt it, that we would be together."

Rolling his sleeves up his rocky tattooed forearms, he bent towards her and set his large hard hands on her knees. Her skin quivered under his intimate touch.

Slowly, drawing his palms up her thighs, he said, "You have nothing to say, Adara? Are you a coward? A dishonorable woman who does not keep her word? You know we made a deal, are you reneging on our deal?"

His hands kept moving up, his biceps bulged, the etched tattoos under the dark hair on his arms flexed.

Her eyes glued to them, her entire body stiff, she tried to move her legs from his grasp but she was securely bound.

His hands slid under her shorts, he stopped just as his fingers reached the juncture of her thighs. His thumbs brushed back and forth over the tender inside skin of her thighs. "Well?"

Hair a tousled chocolate curtain behind her, gulping air, she stammered, "I…uh, I was trapped, you know that."

A shrug pumped his wide shoulders. "Does not matter. You said you would do whatever I want. You want me to take you back?"

Dark lashes flew up. The Godiva-dark eyes struck with terror, her face drained of the last of its color. She looked at the big man in his snug black jeans, dark blue button-down shirt straining over his broad shoulders, boots planted stubbornly on the floor.

A cry broke from her quivering lips, "No- no, oh God, you wouldn't, please-"

He said coldly, "Then you stick with our agreement. Whatever I want." He stood up; she cringed, bringing a scowl to his hard, scarred face.

Standing between her legs, leaning towards her, he put his hands on her arms and moved his palms up until they were under the short sleeves of the blouse.

His thumbs pressed between her bound arms and her breasts making it clear what she had agreed to. She swallowed heavily, the pulse at her neck beat like mad.

"Well, Adara? Tell me right now," he insisted, his gaze dipped to her breasts swelling over the lace trimmed bra.

She looked down the front of him, his lean hips to his fly, to his erection.

A big erection. His manhood was straining against his jeans, long, thick, hard as steel, and he scared the life out of her. It was like being cornered in a cave with a horny, hungry, grizzly with no way out.

"I- I- don't-"

"Now!" he bellowed so loud she jumped. "I am done with this flighty frightened shit of yours. Do you not get it? You are not safe out there. There is only way to protect you from that fucking uncle of yours. From whoever the hell is beating you. When I find out who it is, they are dead, Adara."

He dipped his head to make sure their eyes stayed connected. "In the meantime, you will marry me."

Dark brown eyes popping, her lips fell open with her gasp, "You can't be serious."

"Oh but I am, *mea* sweet." He moved his hands from her arms to cup her face, and just barely touched her lips with his.

He said, "You have proved you are incapable of taking care of yourself, keeping yourself safe. First your shitty mother, then that damned prison, and now…You say *da* right the hell now or I take you back to Fiorenzo right now, bound, barefoot, torn blouse and all. Is that what you want?"

He stood back, his hands on his hips, face impassive, mouth flattened, eyes hard and cold as blue icebergs. "

Answer me, say *da*. Last chance." Like he would ever in a million years bring her back to that despicable hood.

The tears she struggled to hold back flung out and ran down her cheeks. She pinned her lips together to keep from sobbing out loud. The stiffness left her shoulders in her submission as they slumped slightly.

Her mumble almost inaudible, it came out in a hitching sob, "*Yes*." Whatever brutal evilness he was, he couldn't be as bad as her vicious uncle or the sadistic Italian he sold her to, or ultimately the sheik.

"Swear, Adara. Swear you will marry me without a fight, say it."

Letting out a huge laboring breath, without raising her head to look at him she said in a small voice, "Yes, Mr. Braşov, I swear I will marry you without a fight."

He stood silently watching her for a moment. Tears streamed over her pale round cheeks, quivering sad mouth turned down, eyes downcast, shoulders slumped in surrender.

"*Na* going back, Adara, swear to me."

Shaking her lowered head she murmured, "I swear, no going back." Then she lamented with a grievous cry, "Why can't I have a normal life? Freedom to do as I please, school, work, have a family," her voice hitched with her tears. "Why must I always be under lock and key? This is as bad as the prison."

Satisfied he finally got what he wanted, but at her dejection, he sat back down and stated dispassionately, "Baby, you were unfortunate to be born into that shitty family. A heartless whoring mother, and a murdering sociopathic father, same as your brother and uncle. You never had a chance."

Bending forward, he set his hand on her knee. "I tried to protect you, help you, but you refused to let me. I would have done anything for you, *mea* sweet beautiful Adara, anything. You know how it killed me to see you go off to fucking prison?

"*Mea Zue*, my God, Adara, I almost died that day they told me you accepted the plea bargain. I could not stand to envision the pain that you would be enduring, suffering. The abandonment, the loneliness…abuse, rape, molestation. So many tormented years I would have to bear without seeing that breathtaking face. You even refused to see me, it destroyed me, Adara."

Shaking his head with the devastating memories still haunting him, his voice dropped, "I went nuts with *mea* fear for you, got *mă,* that is to say myself in some bad situations." She didn't need to know about the heavy drinking and brawls where he beat men to death, and it still had not taken the anguish of her loss, or his fear for her away.

Sniffing back tears, she said softly, "It wasn't your fault."

Brows down over his eyes fierce with both of their pain he said grimly, "I should have been able to do something, regardless of you shoving me away." Standing up in agitation, he let out a heavy sigh with a mirthless chuckle, his face glum.

"The story of you and me. After your release, now an adult, I tried to win you over, Adara. I asked you out, you still shoved me away, avoided me, said *na* again and again.

"I tried to be with you, let us get to know one another normally. But you refused. Would not even give me a chance. Now," he scrubbed his broad fingertips down over his face, scratched at the scruff on his square jaw. "Your refusal forced me to have to do it this way."

The sadness churned in his eyes then slipped away leaving the glacial, hard blue marbles. "You have little choice, sweet. You cannot go anywhere that your uncle or brother will not find you, and this whole thing will happen all over again. You have *na* friends, *na* relatives that will help you, you have *na* money, *na* ID."

Shaking his head, incredulous at her naiveté. "I do not know how you thought you would get a job without identification. So, you have *na* way of supporting yourself. He killed, baby, Massimo killed that young girl for helping you, you think he would not do it to anyone else that helps you?"

He shook his head with a melancholy smile. "You would never be able to hide from him or the fuckers he tried to sell you to. Or me." His mouth twitched at her eyes flicking up to him.

He said, "You can go back to your uncle and then he would send you back to a very furious and very vengeful Raffaele Fiorenzo, and his men, and then what was left of you would get passed on to the next batch of men that won their time with you.

"Then, and lastly, from what I understand, you would be married off to that scum drug lord, warlord, Iskander Ali Khan." He paused, watched her sitting slumped, her entire face and body a picture of desolate misery.

"Or," Vaclav said coolly, "you marry me, Adara. You know that I am the only one that can protect you. Now, you will do as I tell you. I want you to repeat it, say it again right now, and no more reneging."

She glared at him, he glared at her. His lips bunching at the new crop of tears that fell blurring her sad, despairing eyes.

She cried, "But who will protect me from you?"

Grating exhale indicating his anger, Vaclav sighed, "Adara, say it."

Her gaze fell to stare nervously at the jeans in front of her that still bulged with his obvious arousal. "All right." She sighed in resignation. "As you say, I have no choice. I will…" she sucked in a long hard breath, expelled it and finished, "marry you."

He let out his own held breath, and sat down. He was pissed she sounded so depressed at the idea, but, she would come around in time. "*Bine*. Now we discuss the rest."

Her brows rose in question.

He said nonchalantly, "You have agreed, I am giving you terms." A dark scowl marring his face was the only indication of the anger that brewed in him that she had to even *think* about whether to face the hell of her uncle and Fiorenzo, or fucking marry him. *Da*, he was a monster too, but still…

"But-"

"Number one is, you will address me by *mea* given name, or *mea* nickname which is easier for you English-speaking people to pronounce. Or you will call me Husband, or an endearment.

"I hear Mr. Braşov out of those pretty lips again and you will feel *mea* wrath go from *mea* hand to your bare ass. You understand me? I want *na* doubts, *na* confusion, *na* you saying you did not know. Answer me."

Another labored sigh. "Okay."

"Okay, what?"

The sigh turned irritated, she snapped, "Okay, uh, Vâj," she stressed his name with unsuppressed anger like a snared animal.

Ignoring her resentment, he continued, "Now, second, you will obey me. You have been so locked away from the world you do not

123

understand the workings, the evil, the danger out there." He motioned towards a window.

She said with sarcasm, "I was in prison, that was pretty dangerous."

"Ah. A juvenile federal prison where they worked you to death every day so you girls could get into little trouble. *Yah*, I know there was still horror you bore, but you have *na* experience with the sharks of this world we are in now. I do. There is much more danger out here than there was locked in there with you. You will always do as I say so I can keep you safe."

"Who keeps me safe from you? Are you not a stalking, preying, lethal shark yourself?"

The edge of his mouth quirked. "A smart mouth will get you discipline, Adara. Third," he said ticking off a finger, "you go *nawhere* without me, ever. Unless I know and is with *mea* permission."

Incredulous at his dictatorship, she said, "What? I am not a child, as you keep pointing out, I am an adult. I should be free to go about as I please."

"It tis a hard limit I will not bend on. You may be an adult, but you are childlike in your view of the world due to your being in seclusion in the formative years of your life. As your husband, I know best, it tis *mea* duty to protect you.

"As I said, you are not safe. There are people out there that would hurt you alone just for being Salvatore Valentina's daughter. Your uncle, Fiorenzo, they will certainly going to want revenge. You will never go anywhere without me."

Her brows daggered down in vexation. "Listen, this is not the dark ages for Pete's sake, I can take care of myself, and I am not a child-"

"Ah," he pondered, innocently gazing at her. "How did you get convicted of a murder you did not commit? How did you get sold to that fucking Italian fiend?"

Annoyance ringing impatiently in her tone, she explained, "Those were things I could not have prevented. The prison, you know I -" she stalled at the smug, knowing smirk filling his face.

"*Yah.* Any modern day female knows to tell her attorney the full truth, to not let the law, or her waste of a mother railroad her into taking the rap. Or at the very least allow someone, like me, to help you. You," enraged that she had put herself in that horrible danger, he pointed an angry finger at her, "did not. That bitch never even came to see you after you took the rap for her, and yet you would not let me get you out of there."

"Because you would have only taken me to use me, like as a-an assassin to do your own dirty deeds!"

He was so taken aback, his spine slapped back against the chair, his mouth dropped open. "What? What the fuck are you talking about?"

"Why else would you have wanted to try to get me out? I could only figure that as a young woman that apparently has killed already, that you wanted me to do it for you. I wouldn't be noticeable as an assassin. You've said I owe you."

Aghast, he was dumbfounded at the way her mind worked. "Fucking A. Adara, why do you always think the very worst of me?"

"Huh," she snorted, nodding to her bound wrists. "You have stalked me, molested me, tied me helpless to this chair and informed me that I will be held captive by you, and have to marry you and obey your every command, Your Highness. You wonder why I think so highly of you?"

She glared at him. He glared back.

Tossing her long waves back, she snipped curtly, "Is there anything else, Boss? Any more of your *demands*?" Her snippy attitude sending the message she wasn't about to follow his rules.

He leaned towards her with his brows slashed down in fury. "You think to defy me, and you will find yourself over *mea* knee. I do not think Fiorenzo would tolerate your resistance, and his punishments, trust me, would be a hundred times harsher than mine. Now, I am done debating this shit, unless you want me to return you to him, repeat *mea* terms and tell me you will follow them."

Last thing he would ever do, would be to take her back to Fiorenzo or her uncle, but she didn't need to know that.

He was met with silence and huge gorgeous eyes filling with tears. She lowered her head, the tears spilled on her thighs.

Choking back a distraught breath, in a tiny voice, she murmured, "Yes, I will marry you, and- and," she made a grainy sound in her throat, "obey you." Her bleak, angry eyes flicked up to him. "There. We done?"

He noticed she didn't agree that she would not go out without him, but it didn't matter. He'd told her, it was enough. She had the warning. Besides, he wasn't letting her get away from him. Ever.

"*Da*, another term. You will never be with another man. *Na* flirting, *na* touching, *na* fucking, nothing. You do, and he will disappear."

Her face stricken white, she whispered, "And me? What would happen to me?"

Scowling, he said, "Why would you even ask, we are not even married yet and you are planning to deceive me? Betray me?"

Her emotions on a roller coaster of powerlessness, fear, anger, she shouted, "Oh geeze, Mist- uh Vâj, get over yourself. You spring this bonanza on me, I need time to digest all this crap you are throwing out." The way her legs were bound there was no wriggle room.

She twisted and yanked at her wrists but the way he had tied them she couldn't really move enough to even scrape her skin on the ropes. And every time she struggled, her breasts jiggled drawing his attention, so she stopped moving.

His brows lowered, but the corner of his mouth nicked up slightly amused, then he sobered. "Also," at her rolled eyes he frowned, "you will show me respect, *na* insolence like that rolling of the eyes, if so, there will be-"

Sighing, "I know." She mimicked him, "There will be discipline."

Peeved eyes narrowed, mouth pursed in a frown, he said roughly, "You think I am not serious about what I say? I will take you right now girl, strip those shorts and panties right the hell off you, and wail on that gorgeous ass until you cannot sit for a month."

Lids crushed down in a mean squint, he sneered in a dare, "Go on, test me, I dare you to."

Her lips pressed together, eyes lowered, she said nothing.

With a growl of annoyance, he said, "Another thing," the frosty blues narrowed more as she was about to roll her eyes again, she didn't. "You will dress with *mea* approval. I will not have other men gawking at and ogling *mea* wife."

Her mouth dropped, affronted she retorted, "But that's ridiculous! I ask again, seriously, are we in the Dark Ages? You want to control my coming and going, you want to submit me to corporal punishment just because you're a bossy male and bigger than me, it's- it's bullshit.

"Now you want to control what I wear? Outrageously absurd!" She couldn't move her bound body but she snapped her head with her indignation.

He stood up, leaned over setting his hands on the back of her chair bringing his face close in on her.

She cringed back, turning her head from the fury crackling in his eyes. Worse, now she was facing those huge muscled arms covered with dark hair and tattoos that she knew could break her in half if he chose.

He tapped her lightly on the tip of her nose. "Watch your mouth when you speak to me."

"What? You curse all the time, filthy, vulgar words come out of your mouth all the time!"

He said matter-of-factly, "I am a man, you are a woman. I will not tolerate a trashy wife."

She sputtered again, "What?" Then she burst in anger, "The women you hang out with, you think I've never seen you with them, but I have. They curse like truckers, they-"

He held up his hand at her protest. "*Na*, those women are trash. You are a lady, swear words come awkwardly from your beautiful lips, and everything is negated when you blush like a naughty child." His smug smile broadened at the red that crept into her cheeks even now.

When he sat back down, sarcasm emphasizing her tone, she asked him, "Is that it? Or do you have a hundred more things to add to my imprisonment? You have me bound, restricted, just like that horrible man did but you think it's okay for you to do it. You are as vile a beast as he was."

Sitting back against his chair, face implacable, Vaclav considered her words. "Hmm, so you think sitting there in a chair, tied loosely enough you are not in pain but cannot wriggle free, is *na* better than Fiorenzo stripping you in front of his men?

"Jabbing his fist in your hair, not caring if he is hurting you, while he shoves his dick down your throat until you gag? Then raping you and then passing you to his men as they all get to have their fun with you too? You think this is the same as that?"

Her face turning redder, she stayed quiet. Eyes closed, they opened to him in pique. "You have molested me too. At that party. And just now, your hands were all over me."

"Hmmm. They were. You know why?"

She shook her head wordlessly.

"Because..." His voice lowered husky, his words steaming with sultry desire, lids draped low, he said, "I have ached for a long damned time to touch you. Just, touch you. Not sexually, just," his gaze rolled down her body slowly, then made its way back up to her face. His complexion darkened as his annoyance returned.

"But, again, you have always refused me the slightest touch even of your arm, your hand, your shoulder."

"Humph," she sniffed. "I have that right to not be touched if I don't want to be."

Bending at the waist, he leaned towards her, his hands clasped over his slightly spread knees. "Not anymore. You belong to me now and I have the right to touch you. And, Adara," he shifted to the edge of the chair, bringing his knees right up to her chair, between her legs.

"I plan on touching you. A lot. All the time. And you will not fight me, nor refuse me. I will be your husband, you will give me that right."

"But, you don't have the right-"

"*Da*, I do. Again, you agreed to anything, and that is part of the anything. It tis another reason why I bound you. I wanted to look at you, touch you and I knew you would fight me. So," he leaned further and set his palms back on her thighs.

She turned rigid at his touch, her legs quivered. His husky voice steeped in lust, he told her, "Now I am free to see what that creamy skin of yours feels like."

He slowly stroked his hands up and down her thighs ignoring her struggles to avoid him.

When his hands moved under her shorts again, he said, "If I was Fiorenzo, I would not stop right now. I would rip those shorts apart, tear off your panties and stick my hungry fingers right up that tender, fresh little cunt of yours."

A shocked gasp spouted from her as red flooded her face. As his hands moved slightly closer, his thumbs on the inside of her thighs almost touching her sex, she held her breath, pressing her back so hard against the chair she was almost part of the wood.

His lids lowered almost covering the craving eyes that stared so hungrily at her as if he wanted to start chowing down on every inch of her body.

After a long hesitation, while his chest rose and fell heavily with his lusting breaths, and Adara sat frozen in panic, he pulled his hands back, and stood up so quickly she almost got whiplash looking up at him.

Bending to her, he slid a hand around her head, cradling the side of it and said with dark sensual intent, "I am going to kiss you now, Adara, and you are going to let me. You will participate in the kiss." His thumb rubbed over her jaw,

"You resist or bite me and after I thrash your bare ass you will stay tied in that chair until tomorrow. Every time you move on that seat your blistered bottom will remind you what happens if you defy me."

Like Crystal had once said when they were children, he was staring down at her under the low lids that made him look like that hawk in the tree hunting, watching the sparrow he was going to snatch and gobble.

Cupping both sides of her head, he slowly lowered his head to hers, and lightly touched their lips. Feeling them quiver on his mouth, he just pulsed his lips against hers for a second. When she started to relax, he pushed at her lips until she opened them, then he sank his tongue inside.

His moan against her mouth vibrated in his chest as he took her. Harshly exploring every inch inside her velvet lusciousness, he bit at her tongue, pulling it inside his mouth where he viciously sucked on it like a feral animal.

Her hands tied, she was helpless, forced to submit to his siege. At her whimper, he released her tongue, then fondled it with his. Slanting his head to cinch their mouths as tight as possible, he went at her until they were both breathless and trembling.

Lifting his head, he stood back gazing down at Adara. Her doe eyes were glazed chocolate, and dazed. Soft, damp lips parted, she blinked vaguely at him.

A small chuckle, he said silkily, "I bet if I put *mea* hand back under those shorts and felt you, your little pussy would be soaking wet."

At her shocked look that quickly turned to an embarrassed, furious glare, the passion rapidly vacating her eyes, his smug smile broadened with satisfaction.

He of course had a boner that could smash brick buildings. His palm slid over it and he squeezed the giant organ, smiling at her mortified face.

"You- you-" she sputtered furiously, "how dare you-"

Sighing big, he said, "Again, *mea* dear fiancée," a smile lit and sharpened at her swift scowl. "As I just got done saying, our agreement is that you will allow me to touch you, whenever I want, without fussing. And," the smile turned into a leer, he said silkily, "I repeat, I will be doing a lot of it, so get used to it."

Huffing furiously, her words blew out in a snit, "Me, me, me, it's all about you. Do I get any terms?"

Vaclav's dark brows, such a contrast to his light hair arched. "Other than anything that would negate *mea* terms, what would you like? I will shelter you, clothe you, protect you, give you anything you desire, what else could you possibly want?"

She cried bitterly, "Freedom, to go where I please, to go to school, work, choose a man of my own-"

"*Basta*, enough!" he shouted, slashing his hand down, she jumped. Anger tightening his voice, he said, "We are done discussing this shit. I am your man, and you will do as I say, you have been warned." *Why can't she be satisfied with me*? He bent over to her wrist and untied it, and moved to the other.

Under her breath Adara mumbled, "Chauvinist, misogynistic bully, freaking caveman."

His body stiffened, but he made no response as he unbound her ankles.

Chapter Sixteen

Buttoning his sleeves, Vaclav answered the door.

"Griff, bro," he greeted his friend, opening the door wide for him to come in.

As tall and with the same muscular build as Vaclav, Griffin Gabriēl tromped in, they fist bumped.

"So," following Vaclav into the kitchen, Griff said, "you did it."

"*Da*," Vaclav replied, opening the refrigerator door. He took out two beers and handed one to Griff. They both twisted the tops off and clinked bottles before swigging.

Wiping his mouth, Vaclav's smile was a short hard twitch. "*Yah*, you know I have always told you what I planned. That fucker Fiorenzo," his head shook back and forth in his disgust.

"I took her and *yah*, we are going to marry. Tis the only way to keep her safe from that scurvy uncle of hers. No man, no matter how scurrilous, cannot buy or sell another man's bride."

"Yeah." Griff grinned. "Especially yours. It would be a death sentence, and they would know it."

Vaclav grunted.

"Well, you finally got what you've wanted for half your life. No one ever understood this…unbreakable enchantment, this obsession you've always had with her."

Vaclav shrugged. "You, *mea* friends, I never said anything but you guys always knew."

"Knew?" Griff burst a laugh. "Shit, bro, anyone with eyes could see as far as you were concerned, even as a child, the sun rose and set on her."

Vaclav arched one eye at his friend, then both eyes narrowed. "You know there was *na* sexual attraction for her when she was young, just…an irresistible fascination for her. I always knew one day she would be mine. I would place *meaself* between her and a bullet. I have always felt protective, possessive of her. She is now mine to fully protect, take care of."

Griff nodded thoughtfully as Vaclav spoke. "How does she feel about all this? I mean, hell, Vâj, she was half-naked, on her knees in a room full of rapacious thugs, even then you had to basically force her to agree to be with you. Plus, you know she has always been afraid of you."

Vaclav shrugged again, "Makes *na* matter. The abusive way she has been brought up, she does not know how to care for herself, she does not know normal relationships. *Da*, I had to force her hand, but she will see, I will be the best thing that ever happened to her. She will need a little training."

He recalled kissing her while he had her tied to the chair. Blouse open, tits blown up over the tiny lacy bra, gorgeous legs open for him, he could finally touch her without her balking and running from him.

His brows rose then lowered in question, Griff asked, "Train her? What do you mean?"

Rubbing the back of his neck, Vaclav bumped one shoulder. "Ah, as yet she does not realize that I only want what is best for her, and above all to keep her safe. She will fight me, I think," he grinned crookedly, "for a while." The grin flattened, he frowned.

"I need to teach her to listen to me, always do as I say without hesitation or argument. I know this motherfucking world, but Adara, as horrible as her life has been, she had really been sheltered. She is as trusting as a lamb being led to slaughter." Then the grin was back,

"But," he said, "as petite and fragile as she is, that girl has a spine, she is bloody stubborn. You know our old school training, our upbringing. I will need to use this," he raised his hand, "on that hot little ass of hers until she learns. I will not let anyone, including Adara herself, bring her harm."

Griff watched his friend talk about the girl he'd always wanted, saw the icy blue eyes turn warm, his harsh mouth soften.

"But, Vâj, what about this marriage of yours you told us about? You planning on tying this girl to you forever? What if it's not what she wants, what if she wants something different, what-"

Vaclav swung on him, fury blazing from his defiant eyes, fists clenched under his bowed shoulders. "*Na*," he snapped, slamming his hand down in fury. He said fiercely, with pure confidence, "I will teach her to want me. She will never want another man but me."

"Uh huh," Griff mumbled with a bit of doubt. "Vâj, think about it, you are this big rough, hard, brutal mobster, Adara is," his lips pulled in. "Well, she's like a delicate angel. Soft, sweet, I mean, Vâj, you've had women, more than your share," he chuckled, then sobered at the scowl his friend shot him.

"Anyway, Adara is a virgin, as innocent as the un-driven snow. I mean, she's a gentle, lovely child, hell bro, you gotta outweigh her by a hundred pounds of sheer muscle, you aren't worried you," he paused. Then ignoring Vaclav's scowl, he went on, "You aren't worried you're too big, too rough for her? You don't think you might hurt her?"

"Ah, *basta*, Griff." Vaclav swept his palm in front of him to end the discussion. "She," he swiped his hand over the top of his hair with a sigh, and said, "is, was, made for me. And I for her. *Yah*, it will be rough at first. I will have to go slow, careful, but, Griff," his hands on his hips he shook his head.

"I will teach her to want me, want sex with me, to listen to me, come to me, only me. Tis normal, Griff, for the older husband to teach the younger inexperienced wife. You will see, it will be *bine*, fine."

"Okay." Griff smiled at his friend's absolute confidence, and old-fashioned ideas. "So, what now?"

Forking his fingers through his hair, Vaclav calmed down. "She has *na* relatives or friends that give a shit about her, I am taking her to France. We will marry there, give us some space from the fuckers here, some time to get to know one another without the threat of Massimo or anyone else looming over us."

"Uh huh." Griff nodded, taking a swig. "And since there will be no one else around, she will be forced to depend solely on you. You will be her only company. Clever, and sneaky, my brother, she will automatically come to lean on you, trust you, and-"

"*Da*," Vaclav agreed, taking a long swallow, "care for me."

"Where is she now?" Griff finished his beer, set it on the counter and got both of them another.

Accepting the bottle, Vaclav said, "She is getting fitted for clothes in a room that I have ensured she cannot escape from." His annoyance lifted one side of his mouth.

"*Da*. Although we have an agreement, I can see it in her eyes. She is scared right now, although she has nowhere to go, she still wants to run. I have explained to her that I will give her everything she needs, but still," he shrugged with a weary sigh, "she still seeks total freedom."

"Ah, doesn't she have it in that gorgeous head of hers yet that she is in danger every time she leaves your protection? Her uncle has got to be mindless with rage, and Fiorenzo too." Griff shook his head.

"They are too smart to try to take you out, but they will still go after her. And at that point, rape and beatings may no longer be on their menus, but total revenge. They get their hands on her, and they will leave nothing left for you to save."

Ash silting his skin, with a worried furrowed brow, Vaclav drank silently for a minute. He blinked out the gruesome images of Adara's death after heinous torture that Griff's words brought to mind.

"I will never allow that to happen."

Finishing the second beer almost all at once, Vaclav grunted. "Anyway, her putrid uncle gave her little to wear other than the slutty shit he took her out in to get his bidders' blood boiling. I have a woman in there from a salon measuring her. The woman will purchase clothes, styles that I have indicated to her I want, and a gown for her to marry in. The gown will be here by the day after tomorrow. The rest will have to come to us by mail."

"You're leaving on Thursday?"

Nodding, he said, "*Da*. That is why I asked you here now. I have to get a license, and airmail paperwork to France for the marriage. I do not dare leave Adara alone. She is too wily for that woman in there." He chuckled. "Maybe for you too." He gave his friend a mocking smile. "At least you are aware of her possible shenanigans."

A laugh barked out of Griff as he slammed his bottle on the counter. "Shenanigans? Where the hell do you get these words?" The men shared a laugh.

A little more soberly, Griff said, "You will be a lucky man, Vâj, if she ever comes around. Feisty, brave, smart, damned sweet, and one of the most beautiful, sexy women to walk God's green earth, she is the whole package."

His expression growing solemn, Vaclav's smile was weak. "*When* she comes around. Right now I am the top man of the totem pole that she fears and despises."

"Shit, Vâj, you told me on the phone that you tied her up, and you are forcing her to marry you, you wonder why she is somewhat reluctant?"

"Somewhat reluctant?" Vaclav snorted with a wry grin, "That is an understatement, brother."

They laughed and joked until Vaclav left for his errands.

****

For the next few days, Vaclav slept in one room and had Adara stay in the secure one he could lock from the outside.

He had food brought into the house, but did his best to avoid her, knowing she was angry and resentful, and unfortunately, afraid of him.

On Thursday, he had a limo take them to the airport where they took a private jet to France.

She still stewed, shooting him angry glares, so he let her sit apart from him to read quietly, and doze.

There was a bed in the back of the aircraft he really wanted to introduce her to, instead, Vaclav hung around up front with the pilots for part of the trip to give her space. Otherwise, he did business on his laptop.

They took another limo to the hotel resort where he had made reservations. A few items had arrived that Vaclav had ordered from the tailor for Adara, but she would be limited for the time being to the clothes she'd gone to Fiorenzo with.

The driver brought their luggage in, and an attendant took them to their suite. He opened the door with a keycard and ushered the couple inside.

"Sir, I will show you the rooms," the attendant said with stiff politeness. He kept his eyes on Vaclav. The few times he had glanced at Adara with an approving gaze he heard a grunt and looked back at Vaclav, the threat of death radiated clearly from the mobster's frosty eyes.

The big tough man didn't need to say, 'hands off' it was there in every fiber of his being.

Speaking English with a heavy French accent, the attendant took them to the kitchenette, and then showed them the huge marble bathroom with bidet and hot tub, describing how everything worked.

Then on to the bedroom, where he showed them where the television remote, closets, vault and other amenities were.

The walls of the bedroom were ivory, the duvet scarlet as was the furniture with hints of reds and yellows. The crimson floor-to-ceiling drapes covered a huge window as well as a balcony, and a cushy white rug covered the floor. It was erotic and romantic in spades.

Adara stood in the threshold, she didn't take one step inside.

Curious at her reaction, she seemed anxious, unenthusiastic at the beautiful room, but the attendant didn't dare look in her direction with the hulking beast nearby. He gazed nervously at Vaclav's big fists, scarred from a lot of use, shivered and hurried out to the hall.

"Sir," he said when they re-entered the living room. "Here are your cardkeys," he set two on the desk and said nothing when Vaclav picked them both up and pocketed them.

Adara stood staring blankly, unsurprised at his action.

Vaclav walked him to the door and handed him some bills.

The attendant asked, "Can I get you or the missus anything else?" He mistakenly glanced at Adara. Her pretty face was a pale heart-shape, huge eyes glowing rich and dark.

His eyes lowered to those plush lips, and he heard a dangerous growl. Not daring to look up, he opened the door, said, "Ring if you need anything," and dashed down the hall.

Seeing that the door was locked, Vaclav turned to Adara. She stood warily watching him, appearing on the edge to bolt like a startled mare.

He closed the distance between them but didn't move too close to her. She had grown tenser every mile they flew from the U.S. Her arms were stiff at her sides, but he could tell she wanted to wrap them protectively around herself.

"Adara," he sighed when he saw her flinch. Softening his hard voice, he said gently, "I need to go complete the arrangements for our…wedding. I am going to leave you here."

He wanted to scope out the hotel, the area, see if anyone had followed them. He had vacillated between staying at the hotel under aliases, but his name alone inspired terror in most. If he determined there was danger, he would move them to a different city and then go underground.

Her expression hadn't changed; she just stared tight-lipped at him with her fear of him clear as shit in those big dark eyes.

"Ah," he instructed, "you are not to leave this room, Adara, do you understand me?"

At her frown, his voice darkened, "You promised, Adara, you swore to marry me and obey *mea* orders. If you leave this room without me I will tan that round hide of yours. Are we clear?"

She had no money, no passport, she was in a foreign country and didn't speak the language, but he had no doubt if she thought she could get away from him she wouldn't hesitate to run. Foolish, reckless female. The girl had to be protected from herself.

Brows like furious sable slats pushed out some of her fear, her mouth pursed mutinous, she nodded with an angry shrug.

"Out loud, Adara, *na* mistakes, *na* misunderstandings."

Rolling her eyes she said, "Yes, Dictator Braşov, I understand, I will not leave this room."

His mouth quirked at her sarcasm and rolling eyes, she'll pay for that, but right now he had things to do. "*Bine*."

He moved to the door and opened it. "And, do not open the door to anyone. Not even the attendant, a maid, the manager, *na* one but me. Clear?"

Rolling her eyes again with an exasperated huff, she said with laborious patience, "Yes, my Lordship, I understand."

His ominous gaze flowed up and down her, she quailed at the look on his face. The brazen sarcasm disappeared from her suddenly dry lips.

At that, his mouth nicked up in a smile. "I will be back in a couple of hours. You can shower, take a nap, we will go to dinner when I return. *Bine*?"

Her face had returned to its nervous stiffness. "Yes."

He gave her a long hard look before he left her alone.

****

During the next few days, they toured the quaint city with ancient and modern structures in their unique blend. Enjoyed meals sitting at outdoor cafés watching the colorful people pass by with brisk gallant strides.

They shopped. He bought her outfits, shoes, a diamond bracelet, gold watch with diamonds around the face, diamond earrings, necklaces. A diamond engagement ring they had argued about. She claimed she didn't see the need for such financial waste.

Actually she was trying to avoid his branding her as his. Although, the brief thought of how much bigger it was than Selena's did sweep through her mind. She tried to refuse everything he bought her.

He ignored her protests. At night, Vaclav had Adara sleep in the bedroom. He took the guestroom that was closer to the living room, that she'd have to get past if she tried to leave the guestroom.

Saturday arrived and Vaclav opened the door to room service.

The attendant's tray contained fruit, eggs, bacon, flaky croissants loaded with butter, juice, coffee, he set it on the balcony.

When Adara left the shower, she found Vaclav sitting outside, sipping his coffee. She strung the fluffy terrycloth robe around her, secured the belt, and went out to the balcony.

"*Mândră,*" he smiled, set his coffee cup down and stood up and pulled out the other chair. Indicating for her to sit, he said, "You are beautiful, even in a bulky plain robe."

When he pushed her chair in, he bent, gently cupped her chin. Lifting it, he kissed her softly, almost chastely, then returned to his seat.

"So, uh," Adara turned her attention from him to the view that overlooked the city. "Today…are we still going through with it?" She cut off a piece of egg, stuck it with her fork and tasted it.

His lips pulled in, the irritation in his voice coming out acrid, he said harshly, "Adara," then he paused at the flicker of nerves that rolled into her eyes, pressing her lips together.

He reached across the table and took her hand. More softly, he said, "*Da.* We are marrying today. I have made arrangements with a pretty chapel in a charming town with the turquoise seas rippling below."

"Vâj," she said softly, tears gleamed in her dark eyes, "isn't there another way-"

His scowl tightened his mouth, brows a low hard ridge he started to speak, then, he took a deep breath and squeezed her hand. "Adara, we are moving forward. We are not going back to what your hell was. Resign yourself to your new life. I promise," he squeezed her hand again.

"I will do everything in *mea* power to make you happy. Just," he sighed at the tenseness in her face, "go with it, baby. Be open, give us a chance."

Her eyes on the table, she blinked the tears back, tried to smile at him and failed.

"Baby, eat your breakfast. You will enjoy the ride to the chapel. The town is green and hilly, the homes ancient but pretty and interesting." He drained his coffee and lifted the carafe to pour her a cup then added more to his.

Picking up a croissant, Adara put a dollop of grape jelly on it. While she smoothed the jelly with a knife, she watched Vaclav pour their coffee.

He automatically pushed the cream and sugar that he didn't use, but she did, across to her, and then salted his eggs.

At the moment, he didn't look like the vicious mobster he was purported to be. He appeared tranquil, calm, he looked like a country gentlemen in a sweater over a tie and shirt, black slacks and dress boots.

She figured out why he always wore boots, a variety of weapons could be stashed in them.

Not that she saw many of his weapons, he was very careful to keep them out of her sight, and reach.

Chapter Seventeen

Adara had been too anxious to enjoy the picturesque countryside. In the back of the limo, she sat mute with her fingers clenched tightly in her lap.

Vaclav was quiet as well. Appearing to be reflective, he only occasionally turned his stern face towards her.

Their wedding clothes had been carefully laid in the trunk. She hadn't seen the dress he picked out for her to wear. She withdrew every time he tried to ask her opinion on anything to do with the wedding.

Everything had a surreal quality to it, she couldn't believe she was in France and about to be wedded to one of the most notorious gangsters known to man.

The day was blue and softly sunny, she felt as if wrapped in cotton wool. Her wedding day. It wasn't what she had always pictured, at least when she was a little girl and still had fanciful dreams before life catastrophically assaulted her.

Since going to prison, and living with, then being sold by her abusive uncle, she never fantasized about a wedding again. It seemed beyond the realm of her life. Having a normal husband and a family and a normal life seemed to be forever out of her reach.

And now? With this outlaw who was forcing her to marry him under the guise that he was protecting her? It was clear he wanted her for sex.

What happens when he takes what he wants and then becomes bored with her? Would he dump her back with her monstrous uncle so he could carry on with his original heinous plans? Adara sighed. Normal was never going to be life.

Her eyes flipped to Vaclav, her stomach twittered. He was staring at her. The wintry blues unfathomable, his expression inscrutable. She wondered what he was thinking. Was he already regretting forcing her into this sham of a marriage?

Or was he thinking about tonight when he would ravage her, with or without her consent, claiming his husbandly rights. She was tying herself, body and soul, to a vicious, murderous mobster. His brows arched at the shiver that rolled through her.

She averted her gaze to the window, and gushed with a surprised smile, "Oh my goodness, Vâj, you're right, it's exquisite."

The chapel was pretty and quaint like he'd described. It sat on a grassy knoll overlooking the shimmering Mediterranean.

He smiled warmly at her. "*Da, mândră,* it had to be perfect to showcase your beauty."

A woman hurried out of the chapel to greet them. In her fifties, her grey hair wound in a twist around her head. A friendly smile brightened her plain face. She wore a blue dress and heels. "Welcome, welcome, I am Francine Anglo," she said in fractured English.

The driver brought their clothes inside. Francine showed Vaclav where he could change, then brought Adara to a dressing room.

The older woman helped Adara dress.

Vaclav had chosen an elegant satin gown. Lace cap sleeves, it skimmed her curves down to her heels. Just a hint of cleavage showed under the beautifully scalloped lace bodice. It was soft and ivory and shimmery.

Francine fixed her long rich curls on top of her head and placed a lacy veil over them, pulling the front of the veil down to cover her face to her chin. The pumps had higher heels than Adara normally wore so she would be a tad closer to his height.

"Ah, mademoiselle," Francine gushed in delight when she pulled Adara to stand in front of the full-length mirror. "You are a fairy princess. Your fiancé will die on the spot when he sees you!"

Adara stared at her reflection. The surreal-dreamy state still cocooned her. It all felt not real, hazy, she was almost lightheaded with it. Was this really happening?

"Smile, honey," Francine told her. Sighing happily, she clasped her hands in front of her flowered midriff. "I have never seen a more breathtaking bride. Your husband-to-be is a lucky man!"

With a wink Francine grinned and said cheekily, "And he, honey, what a, what do you Americans say…ah, a hunk. When he is not brooding so dourly, he is quite devastatingly handsome, eh? You are lucky as well."

Adara tried to push her lips up in a smile, but she couldn't do it. Vaclav was forcing her to marry him, for her own good he said. For her own safety.

Humph. She'd seen the way he'd looked at her all her life. With excruciating coveting. When she was young, he had just…watched her, as if spellbound. Since she'd left prison, grown up, a searing heat had entered his eyes whenever he gazed at her, and it never leaves.

"Come along, dear, shall we go meet your fiancé?" The older woman smiled kindly.

Adara's eyes were on her reflection. What was she waiting for? Something to miraculously pop out and save her from...what? Vaclav had taken her from Fiorenzo by gunpoint. Fiorenzo and his men had planned to…horrendously violate her over and over.

After, she would have been sold to the next man until eventually sent off to her doom with the desert warlord.

Could Vaclav be worse? So far, other than tying her, and feeling her up that day at the party, he had treated her kindly, gently, respectfully.

Remembering his hands all over her, a smile ticked at the corner. Those huge hands had created arousing heat and tingles all over her body. His kiss…

"Dear?" Francine waited by the door.

Blinking rapidly, Adara shook the enchantment away and tore herself away from the mirror.

Francine brought her through a carpeted corridor to an arched doorway. Inside, a small cathedral ceiling, stained glass windows strung along the sides of the domed chapel made up of light wood panels.

Darker wood pews led up to the altar. Jesus on the cross hung on the wall behind the altar. White calla lilies and pink camellias were in pretty bunches on either side of the dais.

At the top of the few steps to the raised platform, Vaclav stood with a minister, both men's eyes on her.

The room became a blurry peripheral. Adara's gaze froze on Vaclav.

He didn't smile. Nothing unusual there. He wore a dark suit with a vest, powder blue tie and matching handkerchief. His expression hidden under hooded blue eyes glimmered at her as he watched her walk towards him.

When she reached the altar, he came down the steps, took her hand, and led her back up to the minister who smiled broadly at the pair.

Francine stood off to the side, a man, her husband, joined her, they were to witness the union, both beamed joyful smiles at the couple.

The minister's words flowed strong yet gentle. Finishing his speech, he had them take their vows.

His face rocky and angled, Vaclav still didn't smile. His unreadable eyes never leaving hers, he held Adara's hand and murmured his vows with sure confidence yet quietly, in his guttural accented voice.

When it was Adara's turn, her skin paled and she wavered.

He squeezed her hand and his lips firmed; he gave her an encouraging nod.

Yes, she had agreed to this, she couldn't run from it, or him. Adara knew he would chase her to the ends of the world if she fled. If he gave up easily on something he wanted he wouldn't be the powerful man he was today.

Sucking in a deep stabilizing breath, she let it out slowly, and cleared her throat.

Their eyes joined, and she said her vows in a halting whisper.

She balked at the word obey. Adara almost rolled her eyes. In the modern world that word was usually left out of the ceremonial vows. Vaclav had to have deliberately told the minister to include it.

When she paused, he squeezed her hand with a bit of hard, prompting pressure, reminding her that she had promised to obey him.

She wanted desperately to refuse to utter it, his eyes narrowed. Adara had the feeling he wouldn't hesitate to put her over his knee right in front of everyone to give her a reminder of their conversation when he'd laid down his terms for their relationship. She pushed the word out, her cheeks turning bright pink with the effort.

She was rewarded with a faint smile from Vaclav for her acquiescence, and a happy nod from the minister.

Vaclav produced two gold rings. He said quietly, "Take off your engagement ring."

Puzzlement pulling her brows down, Adara did as he said. Then he pressed the small gold ring on her finger, took the engagement ring from her and slid it on to join the band.

She stared at the shiny gold band as if in a trance. He handed her his ring and held his hand out. She stared at it but didn't move. He lifted her hand and helped her push it on his finger.

The minister pronounced them man and wife. Vaclav lifted her veil. Her eyes already huge, glowing in apprehensive ebony, her pupils enlarged in her uncertainty, fear of the future, of him.

He held her face with both hands, thumbs brushing her cheeks, bent his head and they kissed lightly.

His lips against hers, he whispered with rough affection, "It will all be *bine*, it will be fine, sweetheart, I promise." At the panicked catch in her inhale, he kissed her again, still soft, light, like she was as delicate and fragile as one of the pink camellias.

After completing the paperwork, they took a few pictures, then, receiving the minister's, and Francine and her husband's good wishes and blessings.

With the marriage license and certificate in hand, Vaclav bundled Adara into the waiting limo and they drove back through the soft winding hills.

He took her to a fancy, lavish restaurant for dinner. The gorgeous couple, obviously just married, drew constant attention. They drank champagne, enjoyed authentic French cuisine, and talked about the country, the city they were in, the resort, nothing personal.

Back at their suite, Vaclav brought her to the bedroom, and kissed her gently. Her soft body trembled stiffly in his arms, she kept her eyes lowered, he couldn't look into them.

"*Bine*, baby. Goodnight Wife. For tonight, I will leave you in peace. Let you absorb the notion of us, married," he stroked her hair back off her face, kissed her forehead then left her alone.

As before, Vaclav bunked down in the guest room.

In the morning, they took turns in the bathroom then shared breakfast. The suite was large and extravagantly lush.

Like the pool out back, it was decorated in turquoise with splashes of cherry red and bright yellows. In the bedroom, the carpet was pure white, the bedspread, drapes and pillows erogenous ruby red.

"Baby," he took her hand, gave it a gentle squeeze and said, "I have to make some phone calls. I will go in the bedroom so I do not disturb you. When I am done, I noticed people gathering around a pool in the back, maybe we could go on the patio, soak up some sun, have a few mimosas?"

He finally smiled genuinely, it was so deep, a dimple in his left cheek emerged and his eyes twinkled. The ruthless violence that always lurked there vanished...for the moment. He asked, "Would you like that?"

She had never seen him smile like that before. Real, broad, happy, she'd never seen the dimple before either. Adara's face melted into a reciprocating soft smile, she nodded. "Yes, that would be nice."

Even with the slight smile, tension still wound around her eyes. He hadn't claimed his husband's rights last night. He hadn't forced her to consummate their marriage as she'd expected.

She'd lain awake most of the night, preparing, waiting for him to come in and basically rape her because, though she had agreed to be willing, she knew full well she was terrified of sex, of men, mostly of him, and deal or no, she wouldn't be able to help herself, she would fight him.

But, he had done as he said, stayed away, slept in the separate bedroom.

Maybe he really had married her only to protect her. Maybe she had imagined his sexual interest in her. The tension reduced until she remembered the way he always stared at her, undressing her with his eyes, touching her whenever he could. Kissing her.

What game was he playing with her? Getting her to let her guard down then he'd pounce? But why wait? He could overpower her easily and take anything he wanted even if she refused. Shaking her head, she smiled weakly at him hoping to disarm whatever he was up to.

"*Bine.*" He got up, bent and gave her a gentle kiss on the side of her head. A frown wrinkled his forehead, he said, "As long as you are inside with me, you can wear anything you want, but you know I would not want you to go out in public wearing that."

His eyes tapered as he took in her tight shirt with the top buttons undone, and the shorts, her feet were bare. He remonstrated, "Tis too revealing, I have *na* desire to get into brawls with men who would flirt with you or try to take liberties. You dress like that and it looks like you want attention from men. Right?"

Her lids lurched up and down in puzzlement. "What?" She looked down at her outfit. She didn't have much to wear, only the few things Mrs. Stonefall had tossed in the small case, and some items he bought her that were mostly for going out on the town.

Most of her clothes were too small for her, as her uncle didn't think she needed much except for the slinky gowns he bought and forced her to wear when he was dragging her around to meet men that would be bidding on her.

Otherwise, she was still wearing the same clothes a maid that had gotten fired left behind.

"Adara," he said, then swallowed his natural gruffness. "I have never in *mea* life been a jealous man. I could have cared less if the woman I just fucked left *mea* bed to jump into another man's. But," he sighed, long ago he had at first been surprised at his own reactions involving Adara, he had learned to accept them.

A crooked smile rose with the softening of his eyes. "You are different. I find it almost impossible to control *mă- măself*," he shook his head, he was still saying it wrong. "I mean myself when men fawn all over you."

After a deep breath he said, "You are mine now, I am asking you to help keep things smooth with us, and do as I say."

Adara thought, *you say ask, then you say do as I say, he wasn't really asking, he was dictating.* Seeing the hard set of his jaw she knew there would no arguing with him. Bossy jerk. Treating her as a possession, not an equal person. Stifling her sigh of irritation she mumbled, "Okay."

His smile brightened. Vaclav kissed her lightly again then headed for the bedroom dialing his cell. His muffled voice started in English then switched to Russian.

Adara gathered up the plates and coffee cups and set them on the silver tray. Thinking she would be helping the room attendant, she picked up the tray and carried it to the door.

Opening the door, she stepped outside, crouched and set the tray on the floor next to the wall.

A familiar sound, one she thought she'd never hear again, at least in person, wafted up the stairs.

A tinkling of a stringed instrument, except, it plunked harshly in the inexperienced hands that dissonantly strummed it. Nonetheless, she was drawn to the sound.

Without thinking, as if beguiled from its spell, she descended the carpeted stairs in her bare feet, following the discordant sounds.

The bottom of the wide staircase opened to a large room. An octagon, with windows at every juncture, morning sun shone through the sheer drapes pulled aside.

There was a large sitting area set aside from the front desk, numerous corridors led out from the lobby. Gold cushioned chairs clustered around glass tables and sofas.

People had gathered in the room after breakfast. Laughter rang out as they visited. A few were tucked away in knots of more private seating reading the newspaper or looking at their phones.

Then Adara spotted what she'd heard.

A glistening harp stood nestled in a corner. A little boy was the one noisily plunking at it, annoying everyone else around. His harried mother was dragging him away from it as quickly as she could.

Adara hadn't noticed it way off in the corner before, her attention had always been on Vaclav and what they were there for.

She walked slowly up to the harp, her eyes on it, relishing the sight of the magnificent instrument. She had never thought she'd ever get to see one again. Her eyes glued to the harp, she didn't see the sign that said 'Please do not play, for decoration only,' and picked up a stool nearby, brought it to the harp and sat down.

No one paid any attention to her; they were involved with their friends and families. Until.

She drew her fingers across the strings, and again. Then she angelically strummed a song she had learned in prison.

People stilled, the room grew quiet, and she played.

Upstairs, Vaclav finished his phone calls. Freshly shaved and dressed in black jeans and a long-sleeved white shirt, he was combing his hair when he came out of the bedroom.

"Baby," he said as he entered the living room, then broke off when he saw it was empty. He thought, she must be on the balcony, and headed to it.

Before he reached the glassed balcony he could see she wasn't there. He checked both bedrooms. Nothing. Panic started crawling up his spine, his stomach clenched, she was gone. "Fuck!" he cursed and ran to the door.

Flinging it open, he rushed out- and stopped at the top of the stairs.

There was not another sound but music playing.

From above, Vaclav could see the entire area below.

Everyone, including the clerks at the front desk, the bellhops, guests, all stared enthralled at Adara sitting at a harp, her small fingers streaming over and plucking the strings.

Her eyes closed, head bent, hair a dark glossy cloud sweeping across her back as she swayed with her strumming, completely oblivious to the crowd watching her, listening spellbound to her mystical music and her soft singing.

The music and her voice as beautiful and ethereal as she was, so moving, even the children stood quietly entranced.

The song ended, and she took a breath.

And the room blew up with cheers and clapping. People yelled out, "Bravo! More! Play more!"

Stunned at the attention, her face a crimson blush, Adara rose awkwardly to her feet.

Vaclav was there, next to her. He put his hand on her lower back and said to the audience, in his best English, "My wife thanks you for your kind interest but she is done playing for the day."

His hand at her back, he guided her up the staircase. In their wake people exclaimed how wonderful her music was while clamoring for more.

Plodding on each step, he asked quietly, "Where did you learn to play the harp?"

Adara shrugged, unsure if he was mad or not. "There was an old one in one of the storerooms at the prison. Apparently one of the wardens from long ago had played and wanted one there. She died, so the harp just stayed in storage.

"One of the guards had some rudimental idea how to play and she taught me the little she knew. The rest I just learned from the songbooks we found stuffed in a drawer."

She glanced longingly back at the harp with a bittersweet sigh. "I never thought I would ever see one again."

Their steps matching on the stair steps, Vaclav said with frank awe, "It was beautiful. The way you played, sang, it was heartbreaking, haunting." But his voice quickly turned cold as ice,

151

"You left our suite without me. I warned you about that. You could have been abducted-"

She scoffed, "In the middle of the hotel lobby with a million people around?"

They kept moving up, he said, "A man comes up behind you, has a gun hidden under a jacket, sticks it in your back, you would have no choice but to go with him." Hell, he'd done it himself enough times to know how easy it was.

"You're being ridiculous."

They reached their suite; he unlocked the door and held it open for her to enter first. Following her in, the door closed automatically behind them, but he checked to ensure it was locked, the bolt connected.

His jaw working, brows low with anger, he said, "Adara, I refuse to allow you to put yourself in danger again. I suffered while you were being harmed in that abominable prison, and while your uncle, or brother or both abused you, and when I took you from Fiorenzo."

Sucking in a harrowed breath, he went on, "How do you think I felt seeing you that day," his hand splayed on his stomach as if holding his breakfast down, the iron-hard face paled. "On your knees, bound, half-stripped and that bastard shoving his dick in your mouth, and knowing what horrors would follow?"

He was scaring her. His face darkened with the recalled terror of a few minutes ago when he had realized she wasn't in the room with him, safe and sound, the lid had blown off his dire fright.

Now, a vein pounded at his scarred temple, his features contorted in impotent fury. The buff broad shoulders hunched as his arms bowed with clenched fists. The scar at his temple beat more fiercely staccato as his rage rose.

Holding her hands up in front of her she backed away from him. "Vâj, please, I wasn't in danger, I swear, listen, please-"

Face like thunder, coarse voice very low, hushed, he murmured, "You would not know danger if it came up and hit you in the back of the head. And your clothes, I just got done telling you not to go out dressed like that. I will show you, Adara, what happens when you disobey me." He moved purposefully towards her.

"No, wait, please, Mr. Braşov, stop, I never left the hotel-"

One brow arched as he paused, rage shaking his voice, "*Mândră,* still? I am your husband and you call me that?"

Her hands up in a useless attempt to hold him off, her increasing anxiety made her speak brashly, "Would you prefer Master?"

A humorless laugh coughed out. "Seriously? You know I am livid and still you taunt me with your fresh mouth?" He stalked to her and scooped her up in his arms.

She screamed and pounded his chest, kicked her legs to no avail. He marched into the bedroom and sat on the bed. He set her on her feet and pulled her to stand between his legs.

Trying to step back she cried, "Vâj, please, you can't do this, think, you said you would never hurt me!"

He unbuttoned the cuffs of his long sleeves then rolled them up to his elbows exposing his brawny, tattooed forearms.

"No!" she cried and tried to move but he pinched her still with his knees.

Snatching at the button on her shorts he said calmly, "This will cause *na* damage, it will not hurt that badly, but it will show you *mea* wrath when you disobey me and put yourself at risk." Popping open the button, he yanked the zipper down.

Lifting her, he laid her across his lap and jerked her shorts and panties down exposing her bare butt.

"Stop!" she shouted, kicking like crazy. "Are you crazy? Don't, Vâj, please! Oh!" His hand smacked her bottom. The shock of the sudden sting made her scream and try to flail herself off his lap.

His big hand set on her back keeping her from moving as he smacked her ass again and again and again.

"Vâj!" she wailed, and he spanked her. "Stop! You said I was grown up, you can't treat me like I'm a-" Whack!

Her round butt jiggled with his spanks, red prints marred her fair skin, and Vaclav was entranced by her sexy bottom. Spreading his hand over one cheek, he squeezed, then caressed it.

She stilled. He kneaded it, running his fingertips down the crease until they reached her sex. He pushed her thighs apart.

"No!" she shrieked, thrashing under his firm hand holding her in place.

"Baby," Vaclav murmured hoarsely, forcing her thighs wider. His fingers stroked her nether lips, up her slit, and down. She stopped moving, he heard her hold her breath.

He drew his fingers back up the crease of her butt, and back down to her sex and he fondled her folds, drawing the silk that was easing from her body over her slit and up to her clitoris.

She lay across his thighs restrained by his hand; he moved it to reach under her to cup her breast. Kneading it over her blouse, at the same time he skillfully fingered her sex.

A moan slipped from her, her hips squirmed against his hand. His fingers moved to her entrance, started to invade her woman's sheath, and she froze. Her legs clamped together, a sob tumbled out, "Please, "Vâj, no."

Vaclav pulled his hand from her sex and spread his fingers over her red bottom. Stroking her back with his other hand, his deep voice low, pleased with her initial reaction to his fondling, he said calmly, "You are angry and humiliated, baby, but the spanking turned you on, *na*? It did not actually hurt too badly, did it?"

He knew she wouldn't answer him, and she didn't. The long hard ridge throbbing against her belly showed it had turned him on too. He didn't move the hand on her ass but he continued stroking his palm soothingly up and down her back.

"*Mândră,* please, let me show you the pleasures of a husband and wife."

When she said nothing, didn't move, he cupped her bottom, squeezed, relishing the smoothness of her supple flesh between his long fingers then slid them back down between her legs.

"Vâj, no, don't," her cry rasped.

A growling groan grumbled in his chest, he grasped her waist and lifted her off his lap to her feet, and jerked her shorts up. He waited while she fixed them with trembling fingers as tears dripped over her round, pink-tinged cheeks.

Lines appeared around his eyes and mouth in his consternation. He asked, "Adara, why did you make me stop? You were so damned wet, you wanted it. I was-"

"Going to rape me," she cried in a hoarse exhale, buttoning her shorts.

Setting his hands on his knees, he said with frustration and aggravation, "Sex between husband and wife is not rape."

With a sniff she responded, "It is if one of the parties is not willing."

"Adara, you are just afraid-"

"Of you." Wiping at her damp eyes she sniffed, "Shouldn't I be?" She moved from the cage of his knees and trod across the room. He got up and followed her.

Chapter Eighteen

When he didn't answer her, Adara spun around and saw him moving menacingly towards her.

One hand out with her palm up warding him off, she wrapped an arm around her chest and said, "You stay away from me, I mean it, do not touch me."

Moving closer to her he said coolly, "*Na*. You are *mea* wife, you agreed. Enough of this being afraid of me shit. I want a real marriage with you, Adara. I want everything, that includes," his eyes glazed with fiery lust, "the marriage bed. Now, I will pleasure you, teach you, show you the shooting stars, come here."

But Adara continued to back away inching to the door.

The calm in his bearing disintegrated, irritation replaced it. Glowering, he snapped, "Stop moving away from me!"

She turned and ran to the door to escape out to the hall. Her bare feet peddled along the carpet as she raced to the front door.

"Goddammit, Adara!" he shouted, growing angrier that she would fucking run from him, again. And to think she would actually attempt to leave the suite after what he just did, rancor rose steaming his head as he went after her.

He caught her at the door. Picking her up, disregarding her squeals for him to release her, he carried her a few steps, set her down, grabbed her blouse, tore it open and wrenched it off her.

"Vâj!" she shrieked, pushing at him but he was like a gorilla on a rampage.

"I am going to help you get past your unnatural fear of sex," he growled. Throwing her blouse to the floor with a grunt, "And you will not be wearing that shit again."

Behind his mouth of a flattened blade, his teeth ground, his concealed eyes so slit they were nothing but angry spurs. He shoved everything off the desk with his forearm; it all went clattering to the carpet.

He turned back to her, gripped her shorts, ripped them open and shoved them down her thighs. Slinging his arm around her waist, he lifted her over his shoulder and pulled the pants off.

He was moving so fast, so purposefully, his strength beyond measure, she could only cling to him as he worked like an unstoppable typhoon stripping her.

Down to her bra and panties, he set her down hard on the desk.

Shocked at his marauding attack, Adara froze.

Vaclav leaned in close, grasped her nape pulling her to him and kissed her brutally hard, ravaging long, stripping her mind of sense and protest along with her clothes.

When he released her, she blinked, stunned. His scorching kiss left her head whirling, if she wasn't sitting down, her knees so weak, she would have fallen.

Vaclav wasn't done. Lids low and heavy over his smoldering eyes, he took a moment to enjoy the dazed, slightly euphoric look on her beautiful face. He had waited a long damned time to see it and he wanted to savor it.

But, this was only the beginning. He wouldn't be satisfied, wouldn't stop until she was clawing his back, shrieking his name as her exploding orgasm seized her. The orgasm he was going to bring her to. It was time they were true husband and wife in every sense of the word.

Reaching behind her, he unclasped her bra and jerked it off her before she could put up resistance.

Feeling the cool air on her bare skin brought Adara around quick. She covered her bare breasts with her arms and started to protest again when he just stuck his fingers in her panties and ripped them right off her body.

She was naked, and his unrelenting aggression and fierceness was scaring the begeezus out of her. He was a big tough man and she'd never been with any man naked like this before, much less a brutal enraged mobster.

"Please," she cried, "please don't hurt me, Vâj." Tears streamed as he tossed her torn panties to the floor.

Vaclav was mindless with hunger, he had craved her for so long, and she had continuously denied him, rejected him. His primordial brain was nothing but a blizzard of burning desire to fuck his wife.

Now that he'd stripped her, his marauding hunting male's instinct was to push her down and drive into her. Screw the getting her ready, the fucking foreplay, he'd waited too long; he needed desperately to be in her right now. He grasped his belt, then the terror in her voice reached his buzzing brain.

He dropped his head, dragged in deep breaths to get control of his bursting hunger, calm his raging erection. Scrunching his eyes closed to not look at her, if he saw her in all her glorious nudity, that succulent body he dreamt about every night, shaking his head, he shoved the dark blond locks back off his forehead.

Dragging a shaky hand across his eyes, wiping his mouth, Vaclav looked at her. Keeping his gaze on her face, seeing her fear of him, he wondered if it was all men or just him that terrified her.

"Adara," knowing his deep, hard, accented voice made him sound darker, more dangerous; he stopped to clear his throat of the husky growl clotting it from desire so thick it choked him.

More softly he said, "Why are you so afraid? Tis just sex, normal, a natural act between two people, there is nothing to be afraid of."

Her lids covering her thoughts, she bit her bottom lip to fight the tears.

It broke his heart to see her so afraid, so unnerved. "But, someone made you afraid, baby, who?"

Pulling her knees up, she wrapped her arms around them. Her head down, refusing to look at him, she struggled to keep the tears at bay.

He didn't touch her, just stood patiently studying her broken face, so in pain he would give anything to fix whatever hell had put it there.

"*Mândră, mea* sweet beauty, tell me, tell me what happened to make you so afraid of being with a man, with me."

Vaclav gently combed her hair back off her face but kept his eyes up and hands off her body. He stood fully clothed, she was naked.

He should give her his shirt or something, but hell, he'd waited so long to see her like this, and the more she was naked in front of him the more acclimatized she would become with it. Besides, he was not going backwards, he would have killed to see her nude, and now, he was finally there.

As she stayed silent, he softened his voice as best he could, but he was a harsh man, it took effort. "I am your husband now, Adara, that means you trust me. You trust me in everything, to take care of you, help you, listen to your most terrible secrets and work through them with you. Was it prison?"

At her silence, laboring to keep his cool, he murmured through his tight throat, "Your uncle? Did, he," he broke off to steady his rising fury, if Massimo touched her-

"Ah, *mea* sweet, tell me what happened. Whatever it was, I am here now, to help you," *avenge you*, "not judge you, ever. We are a team now, we work out things together."

Sniffing, she tightened her arms around her knees.

He sighed, "Sweetheart, we are not leaving here, right here, until you tell me. I want a real marriage with you and that cannot happen until you trust me with your pain and your horrible secrets." Stroking her hair he murmured, "Tell me baby, trust me."

Adara raised her head slightly to look at him.

His iron-rough face was nonjudgmental, icy eyes abnormally warm and caring, he wasn't smiling, this was too serious for that, but his mouth was as gentle as she'd ever seen it.

A shuddering sigh shook her entire body. Her voice barely above a whisper, she said, "It happened the first week I got there," sobs gurgled up her throat and she dropped her head.

Vaclav waited patiently stroking her hair. "*Da*, baby, tell me what happened." He had to steel his heart and body to hear what she had to say.

Another deep breath and a long shuddering sigh, she wiped at her eyes with both hands and looked at him briefly before edging her arms back down to cover herself.

"There was this girl; she was one of the oldest ones there, Lucretia. I think she was Russian." Her gaze flashed at him and away.

Vaclav grabbed up some tissue from a box he'd knocked to the floor and handed them to her.

Dabbing at her wet eyes, she said, "That first week, Lucretia and some other girls, five or six, I don't know how many. Anyway, they cornered me in the back of the kitchen area where there were no guards because there was no way to get out of the building from there."

When she paused, he encouraged her softly, "*Da*, baby, go on." His hand so big, so strong, he could crack her head in his palm, gently, soothingly stroked her hair.

"Uh, this Lucretia, the ringleader, had the girls gang up on me. I fought them, but they knocked me down and pinned me to the floor. Lucretia, uh, shoved up my blouse, and my bra, exposed my breasts to everyone, and," her voice hitched, shoulders rocked with sobs.

Vaclav waited. The rage of what they'd done to her climbed up from his gut to claw at the inside of his chest and bite at his throat. His Adara. While he was safe on the outside, she was greeting hell in prison. He had been helpless to protect her.

He wanted to gather her in his arms and make her feel safe, but he knew it would shut her down, so he waited. A minute or so passed and she started again.

Her eyes shut tight, she said, "Um, so they all grabbed at me, groped me, hit me, pinched me, twisting my skin as hard as they could, slapped my face, my breasts, they did what they could to hurt me. Then," she took a breath, "they got my pants off and that girl," her lips knotted with the horrid memory.

"Lucretia, huh," she snorted, her shoulders rippled with a shudder of the remembered nightmare. "She had the most malevolent grin, Vâj. It would have scared even you."

She stole a glance at him with a paltry smile, but his face was too distorted in pain for her torment he didn't return it.

"Yeah, so, she held up this thing for me to see, I didn't know what it was. Long, hard metal." Her lashes lowered to cover her shame. "She showed me and told me what she was going to do with it. First my…uh vagina, and then she said they would turn me over, and um, do the other side, you know."

Her eyes went blank as the memory flooded bringing the terror and anguish, and terrible defenseless and hopelessness, fear of what they would do. Maybe even kill her when they were done torturing her.

Staked to the ground by a gang of vicious tormenting girls, laughing coarsely, making raunchy frightening jokes of what they wanted to do to her while punching, groping, squeezing every body part so hard her sobs were just gasps of air. Adara had been in the deepest despair of her life at that time.

"They held me down and covered my mouth so I couldn't scream." Sucking in a tremulous breath she said, "She jammed it in me. Oh God," she wailed, "it hurt, Vâj, it hurt, she viciously tore my- my hymen, such agony!" Adara broke down in sobs, her shoulders jerking with the wrenching cries.

Now he did put his arms around her, held her to the strong safety of his powerful chest. Embracing her tight to him, his own strong body quaking with her nightmare story, her endless, permanent suffering. His heart, his gut, his brain, ached, screamed in anguish at what his precious Adara had to endure, alone.

When she calmed somewhat, his lips against her hair he murmured, "Was there not a…someone who helped you? Protected you at some point?"

Her body stiffened, she leaned back from him, wiping at her eyes. Brows down in suspicion, she asked, "How did you know?"

Saying nothing, he peered at her with a sad, lopsided smile.

She stammered with growing comprehension, she said, "You, you got Priscilla…"

"*Da,*" he admitted. "I knew her, knew she was there. I visited her and paid her to protect you. Tell me, did she not help you?"

His anger ignited like a stick of dynamite about to blast but she said, "Yes, yes she did. She came, Vâj."

A brief frail smile, she said, "While Lucretia was getting rougher, more and more violent with that…thing, and hitting me, kicking me," her eyes closed as she struggled to get a grip.

Letting out a heavy breath, she smiled through the tears up at him. "I was bleeding, and screaming against their hands. Lucretia was getting so violent when one of the girls said it was time to turn me over, do my other side. Lucretia said 'just a little bit more, I want to make sure she can never have children' and suddenly- she was gone.

"My eyes were closed, but suddenly I was free, the thing was gone. I heard cries and screams, thumps and scuffling, when I opened my swollen, bruised eyes, this girl, Priscilla she told me after, was crouched beside me and pulling my clothes on. She and a couple of her gang friends had beaten Lucretia, pretty badly I heard, and the others that had held me down. Priscilla helped me get dressed, took me to the infirmary."

With a curled lip Adara said bitterly, "The doctor never even asked me what happened. Anyway, after that, I was still occasionally groped and hit and stuff, but whenever they got me alone, somehow word got to Priscilla and she came to my rescue. She was big, like over six feet, had to be over 200 pounds." A soft smiled eased some of the torment that had gripped Adara's face.

"A black girl with the craziest curly blonde hair, and a bunch of tattoos right on her face. She was the toughest woman I have ever seen. You," the smile turned puzzled, shy. Her head tilted to the side as she looked up at him, "You paid her to protect me even after I refused to see you?"

Nodding his head, he dabbed the pads of his thumbs over the tears that still clung to her cheeks, feeling the sting of his own pressing the backs of his eyes.

"*Da*, it was the only thing I could do. I could not get you out without your cooperation. I tried to hire you a better lawyer but you shut that down too. I had to do something, Adara, I was going bananas with you inside and not knowing what they were doing to you."

Her palm rested on the side of his rough face, her smile sweet and grateful. "Thank you Vâj. You saved my life, truly. That Lucretia, I don't know, some of the girls said she was jealous of me and she planned to burn me, cut me, mutilate me-"

"Fuck stop," he held a hand up with a gutted sound. "I cannot bear it, please," his agonized voice tight, the backs of his eyes stung fiercely with threatening tears. He had never cried, even as a child starving on the streets of Romania and beaten within an inch of his life whenever he got caught stealing food.

But this was Adara, a delicate angel, with her soft sweet doe eyes he had always fallen helplessly into. He could not bear to think of what more could have happened to her.

She kept her palm on the side of his face; he covered it with one of his own. His eyes scrunched again to push out the images of what she was saying.

"Anyway, Vâj, you did protect me, you did save me, and I am so grateful." Her knees were still up, one arm wrapped around them, her hair a wavy varnished cloak around her.

"You tied *mea* hands, baby, to do anything else. What about," he needed to know it all, what he was up against. "Males? Guards, did they," he couldn't say it, couldn't say the word rape.

She shook her head. "No. That is, I mean, when we were transported sometimes, our hands cuffed behind us made us defenseless, those times they would uh, grope us. Everyone. It was almost like they did it just because they could."

"*Zue*," Vaclav's tortured sigh was a tiny indication of what was going to haunt him for the rest of his life. His sweet, precious Adara in the hands of monsters. If he could find out every person who ever harmed her, he would wipe them from the universe without a thought.

"Vâj, I…" Her rich chocolate eyes rose to his blues darkened with his symbiotic pain. "I have never been…intimate with a man. After all that, and my uncle selling me for sex, I," she exhaled her grief.

"I don't want to, I can't be with…anyone, in that way. I am sorry, I accepted your aid with dishonesty. I agreed to this…marriage, because I was hysterical with terror that day in Mr. Fiorenzo's clutches. I- I would have agreed to anything to get out of there in one piece. I should have bucked up and accepted my destiny, not drag you into it with me." Her exhaled breath ached with remorse and sorrow.

He started to say something, she went on, "We can get the marriage dissolved as soon as you want. I'm sure after what I just told you, the last thing you would want would be to touch my tainted, soiled body. And, I could never get…um passionate. I would be incapable of satisfying you as a wife should. So," her breath hitched.

"If you take me back to my uncle, or…him, I will understand and not fight you." Big globs of tears rolled down, plopping on her arms that hugged her knees.

"Ha!" his wretched barked laugh made her jump.

"Ah, sweetness," he stroked her hair. "I just treated you as badly as Fiorenzo, and those bitches in prison did, ripping off your clothes like that. I am the one that needs your forgiveness." The spanking she deserved, and needed, to keep her out of danger, he was not apologizing for that.

Her head dropped, shaking back and forth. "Vâj, I am giving you an out. Now that you see that I can never be a wife, a true wife. Especially to a man like you. You need someone who is…strong, wild, lusty, can give you what you are…" her voice trailed off in confusion.

She wasn't sure how to put it. "I mean, you are so virile, so- so aggressive, you would require a robust woman to satisfy your rough, uh…" Wringing her hands, she raised then lowered her shoulders. "You don't want a- a damaged woman, a convicted felon who can feel no passion."

Vaclav stuck his hands in his jean's pockets to keep them off her. He said, "You are not getting rid of me so easily, Wife. It was hard as hell to get you here and I am not letting you go. As far as tainted, fuck babe, what a few sick bitches did to you in no way despoils your perfection. Even if, *Zue* forbid, guards had or Fiorenzo and his men had...assaulted you, I would still fight heaven and earth to get you and keep you.

"You are mine, always have been, and we are done with any talk about dissolving our marriage. *I* am your destiny, Adara. You are stuck, babe, you aren't going anywhere without me, ever again."

He cupped her face with both hands and kissed her softly. "Baby, just having you by *mea* side tis satisfaction enough. But," he sifted his fingers through her thick waves.

"You do not know your own body. You are more than capable of being passionate. You are inexperienced, but hell, the way you respond to *mea* kisses, shit, girl, I about shot *mea* load with just our lips touching. And," he kissed her quickly as she started to speak, "I have made you wet," his brows wriggled wickedly with a cagey grin.

"So I know I can make you come, baby. Maybe even another spanking? It turned you on..."

She returned her arms to wrap around her knees. "Vâj, wait, you don't want to be saddled with an inexperienced woman, I know you need more than what I can give you. Maybe if I had time, to learn, be with other men-"

His face closed in instant fury. "Fuck that shit, Adara. You are not going to be with any other men. I will teach you all you need to know. And," he forked his fingers through his hair in consternation, "I do not need anything, anyone, but you." He settled his hands on her bare shoulders.

She flinched, awkwardly moving her shoulders so he would drop his hands. He stroked his palms down her bare arms then dropped them to his sides.

Wrapping her arms tighter around her knees she said, "But, of course you do, you need more, much more than me. All those women you've been with, I can't compete with that, with them. You can't want to be with just one, frigid and inexperienced woman when you can have your pick of any gorgeous girl you want.

"I see the way they look at you, you don't even have to ask, they would follow you." She said it all with a light uncaring manner, but a twinge of jealousy, or was it inadequacy, invaded her tone. Vaclav hoped it was jealousy.

His eyes wandered over her sad face, the huge doe eyes so dark and warm, puffy lips turned down, damn he wanted this woman with his every breath, always had.

He informed her, "I was with those women because I could not have you. If you had been of age, *mea* age, trust me, there would never have been any other women. I have only ever wanted you, the others were only biding *mea* time while you grew up.

"*Da*, sweet, when you were a child *mea* interest was not sexual, but, hell, Adara, I have just always felt this compelling internal pull to you. *Mea* instincts have been like a wolf to its mate, possession and protection at all costs." A lusty smile drew his full lips up.

"And now that you are grown up, and we are man and wife, tis time for us to learn about each other, learn everything. Become as one. The time is now, baby, come, let me show you, teach you."

"No!" she squeaked and held a hand out to stop him when he reached for her.

Chapter Nineteen

His large strong hands massaging her slender bare shoulders, voice deep and sultry, his smile sensual, Vaclav cooed, "Have you ever had an orgasm, Adara?"

Cheeks blossoming bright bubblegum, she shook her head. "No, I don't like it. I mean, I don't like touching myself."

"Ah, tis because you do not know how to do it. How to relax and enjoy your own body. We are going to change that right now." The erotic spark in his eyes swaggered with his grin.

Flushing darker with her embarrassment at his sexual words, Adara said adamantly, "No, I can't. Really. Can I put my clothes on now?" She squirmed to the edge to get down while still trying to keep her body covered with her arms.

Blocking her way, he said, "*Na*, sweetheart. I will teach you. When you learn how to please yourself, you will then let me do it, *da*?"

Vehemently shaking her head, the lustrous locks flying back and forth, she said, "No, I can't, I won't, let me down." She indicated for him to move back so she could get off the desk, but he stayed near, close enough to prevent her from getting down but not so close he was in her personal space.

He lowered his voice to a hush, "Sweetheart, you trusted me with your terrible secrets, trust me with this. I have not hurt you yet, and I never will, ah, stop-" he brought his hand up.

"The spanking did not hurt. And once we are comfortable with our sex life, I will show you how to really enjoy a spanking, with restraints, but for now, just do what I tell you, *bine*?"

Face wrinkled, lips pursed in worry, tension filled her voice, "I can't Vâj, please don't make me." The big round eyes begged him to let her go.

"Tsk, I will not make you do anything, sweet, you are going to do it." His voice flush with passion and soft caring, he said, "Lesson number one, baby. Use your little hands, cup those tits I am fucking dying to see."

Her brow furrowed sharply. "What!" Shaking her head fiercely, she stated categorically, "No, I can't-"

"*Da,* you can. Put your legs down," he ordered and gently gripped her knees and pushed them down so her legs were dangling off the edge of the desk, then he held them there.

"Now, put your hands over your tits, like this, hold them." He let go of her legs to show her. He spread his huge hands over his masculine chest and made like he was cupping his muscular pecs.

Giggles trickled out seeing the big man cupping his own hard pectorals like he had breasts. "You're silly," she chided.

Smiling at her giggles, he ordered with a pretend frown, "Now, sweetheart, you do it, just like I am doing." He looked ridiculous cupping his nonexistent breasts over his shirt.

Realizing he was not going to let her go until she did as he said, she muttered, "Um, like this?" She lifted her hands and held them over her breasts, cheeks burgeoning from pink to red as she did it.

His eyes hooked on her hands covering her full breasts. She had no idea what this was costing him, the strain of watching her fondle her naked tits, *fuck me*. He nodded with a tight, "*Da*, baby, now, squeeze them, like this." He showed her knowing he looked foolish but didn't give a shit.

Her face bursting to scarlet she dropped her hands, she protested, "I can't, Vâj, l can't."

"I will help you, baby." He moved closer to her and reached for her hands. He brought them up and held them over her breasts and gently squeezed them. "There, like that, baby. Ahh," he groaned. Almost, he was almost where he wanted to be.

His hands over hers, he had her cup and knead her breasts, keeping his eyes on hers, she closed hers. The rigid set of her jaw lightened, her pressed lips softened as her nerves lessened.

Molding his hands over hers, he kneaded her plump flesh then lightly maneuvered her fingers to pinch her nipples, she giggled again then shivered.

"Ah, you like that, *mea* sweet?" he asked with a smile. Then he made her pinch and pull and tweak her own nipples until he saw goose bumps rolling up her arms and her nipples were hard little peaks. Damn, it was hot as shit watching her play with her breasts.

They needed to do this later when he could sit back and watch while pumping his cock. Feeling the blood rushing to his already engorged penis, he gulped hard, then calmly said, "Good girl." Resisting the urge to take his dick out right now and grip it with his fist, he said. "Now, next lesson."

Her eyes popped open. "Next?" she parroted weakly, her hands clutching her breasts.

"*Da.*" He let go of her hands and grasped her thighs pulling them apart. She resisted, to no avail. He took one of her hands and brought it down to between her thighs.

She tightened her hand into a fist. "Vâj," uncertainty rang in her soft voice.

A coaxing smile shaved off some of the hard edges to his face, he said, "Shh, just do it, I will show you what to do." He pulled her fingers open and placed them on her woman's mound. He held them still for a second to get her used to it.

Her eyes hopped up to his then quickly lowered in embarrassment, "Vâj, I've never-"

"I know, sweet, but tis *bine*, that is okay, normal, everyone loves themselves. You have to know what you like so you can show me. I am your husband, Adara, tis *mea* job to teach you these things, right?" *And what a fucking great job.*

Keeping his eyes on her face, he started moving her fingers over her tender lips, directing her how to stroke, pinch her nub.

His hips were between her knees, his boner almost leaning against the desk. He knew if he touched it he was so bloody hard he would blow off like a rocket. He watched her, her eyes closed tight, then relaxed some as she got used to touching herself.

Heavy-lidded, his tongue wetting his lips he swallowed hard and whispered, "How is that, baby, how does that feel?" His head bowed over hers, he inhaled the fresh natural scent of her. Damn he wanted to grab handfuls of her hair and rub them over his naked chest, his dick, his balls, *shit*.

"Um," her cheeks still flaming now, she murmured, "it's okay I guess."

He chuckled. "*Da*, well when you let me do it, it will be more than just okay." While they talked, he moved a hand up to gently clasp her breast. When he did, she stopped moving her fingers on her cleft.

"*Na*, sweet, let me feel you, keep going." It was a chore to stifle the groan that roared deep inside of him as he finally handled her bare tit. Hell, he'd been with more women than he could count, he'd never had to do anything, they practically had their clothes off before they got in the door.

But this was Adara, his Adara he'd waited a lifetime for. He would do whatever it took to be with her as man and wife. Finally touching her so intimately was damned heaven. He'd dreamed a thousand nights of this.

Her body stiffened all over again at his rough palm covering her breast. First he just held it there to get her used to the idea of it.

When she started to relax again, he moved his hard hand, massaging her plump flesh, netting his long fingers over the full, soft as a pillow globe, swallowing his moans with each squeeze.

Last thing he wanted was for her to hear him growling like a vulturous canine waiting to attack and rut her, even if he was. Dragging his thumb over her nipple he was rewarded with a little quiver that wriggled through her body.

He lowered his head; cupping her breast he sucked her nipple into his carnivorous mouth.

"Oh, Vâj," a tiny sound reverberated from her, but she didn't push him away.

Her saying his name with a sensual moan was music to his ears, only thing better would be her screaming it at the top of her lungs as she came with him inside her.

His mouth tasting, gnawing, tongue teasing her nipple, he moved to suck marks all over her breast then back to bite her nipple, tugging at it with his teeth before sucking it back into his mouth. "You like that, babe?" Kissing her silken skin, he moved to tend to the other breast.

"Um, yeah," she smiled. He kept her fingers working at her vaginal lips while he suckled her like a starving infant.

He moved her fingers to slip over her opening, and feel how wet she was. His voice a low moaning rumble, he hissed, "See that, baby, wet, I told you, you are made for loving, for *mea* loving."

His dick screeched at him to take her, his swollen balls aching, bursting through their sack, he was so fucking hot, his mind was blanking, all the blood rushed to his dick.

Letting go of her fingers, he cupped both her breasts hard, wringing them in in his highly aroused, big hard hands, her fingers stalled at her pussy.

Gripping her full globes with his strength, he crushed her supple flesh in his iron fingers and they both moaned.

Vaclav whispered, "*Da, mea* sweet, see, see how good it feels?" Kneading them roughly with his hunger, he murmured, "So fine, baby, so fucking fine, you have the most beautiful tits I have ever seen, felt," he nipped at her mounded skin and licked her pebbled nipples, "tasted."

He leaned back for a moment to look at her. "Does it feel good, baby, *mea* hands on you? *Mea* mouth on you?"

She nodded silently, her eyes still closed.

His smile growing, he released her breasts and pushed her thighs apart and moved her hands away. He cupped her sex, his thumb on her clit, groaned with exultant need and desire and ignored her trying to close her legs.

"Put your hands behind your back," he ordered. When she didn't, he grabbed her wrists and placed her arms behind her with her hands braced on the desk.

"Do not move them," he frowned his directive.

She resisted. "But-"

He said simply, "You move them and I will tie them back, *bine?* You understand?"

"Um." She bit her lower lip, eyes heavy, growing low-lidded and sultry.

He told her with a grin, "Say *da*, ah, I mean, say 'yes Vâj.'"

She said through a giggle, "Yes, Vâj."

"Good," he replied and he stared at her.

Her eyes closed, she was sitting completely nude with her slender legs spread exposing her exquisite womanhood, her hands behind her back caused her gorgeous tits to thrust out and up, *fuck me*, his mouth watered. If only he had a camera, his phone, anything to capture this moment.

But he didn't dare stop, he might never get her back to this position. But he would sure love to preserve the sight.

"Ah, all right sweet, keep your hands back," he said, and he stroked her slit. Drawing her silk out, he spread it over her woman's bud already hard with his ministrations.

He swirled her natural lube, raking his broad fingers up and down her clit, pinching her folds, tugging, circling her bud and then, she moaned, her little hips wiggled.

"Ah, good baby?"

Murmuring, "Hmm," she nodded and squirmed her hips, lifting them slightly for him to press harder on her.

"Ah, *na*, sweet, I am in charge now, hold still, I will let you come when I am ready," and he slid a finger slightly inside her and right back out before she even registered what he'd done.

He played with her clit and then pushed his finger back inside, deeper. She squirmed, but didn't protest.

"Good girl," he praised, and moved his finger deeper. She was as small as a doll, so tight he would have to work to get her able to take his girth without pain. He was a big man all over.

Women extolled the huge size of his cock, but she was petite, never had a man inside her before, thank *Zue*. He would be the only one to ever enjoy that sweet little honeypot of hers.

His powerful body bowed over her, shoulders rounded like a protective wall, his nose in her hair. Inhaling the floral scent of her locks, he lifted them and let them tumble down her back so they couldn't cover any of her flawless beauty.

He fingered her, curling his thick digit inside her soft depth, searching for her hot spots, then thrusting his finger in and out until her moans were coming with huffing little breaths then he bent over, spread her legs further and put his mouth on her pussy.

She sat up straight and put her hands on his shoulders, "No, Vâj, what are you *doing*?"

Lifting his head, he pushed her to lie down on her back. "Hands down, sweet, do as I say. I am your husband, this is what husbands do to their wives. You taste as sweet as fucking ice cream baby, share your body willingly with me. Let me enjoy you baby, all of you. Now, hold those gorgeous hips still, and keep your hands down or I will tie them. *Bine*?"

He had tied her once before, the day he took her from Fiorenzo, she knew he was fully capable of following through, still, "Vâj…" her chest lifted high in anxiousness then fell with her resigned exhale.

Smiling at her giving in, he lowered to his knees, pushed her thighs wide, and went to work on her pussy with his mouth.

He ate at her, chewed her lady parts, reached up to grab a tit for a grasping squeeze then put his hands on her thighs to keep them down and apart. Sucking her bud deep into his mouth, he flicked it with his tongue, gave it a little bite and thrust a thick finger inside her.

She made a tiny sound, her legs went rigid, then he gently moved his finger in and out and sucked her clit and she relaxed. When he had to hold her hips down forcefully because they were bucking at his mouth in her increasing excitement, he added another finger, stretching her.

Moaning, her head flopped back and forth, Adara cried, "*Vâj,*" gasping as he thrust his fingers harder and he chewed and nipped and sucked so hard, her spine arched and she about came off the desk.

Her knees rose to press her thighs against his head as her hips lifted to his mouth. Wheezing sounded through her clenching chest, "It- it feels, help me," she whimpered.

Pressing her legs back down, his voice vibrating against her sex, Vaclav smiled. "*Da,* sweet, I will. Just relax and let your body go, I have you, I have you, do not fight it. You are feeling it build up, baby, just let it build, do not resist the feeling. You are burning inside, *na?*"

Grunting with the force of his plunging fingers, her hips twisting to make him do it harder, faster, she cried, "Yes, oh," sucking in a short breath. "It- I- I'm burning, it- tingles, prickles, oh, Vâj I feel like I'm going to- to- like burst," another breath sucked in, caving in her already flat belly.

Aggressively shoving his fingers inside her, he sucked her hard on the edge of violent. Cutting gasps ripped up her throat, her pelvis sucked in, her pussy gripped his fingers.

"Go baby, let it go, come for me," he growled against her flesh, moving his fingers so fast her body shuddered against them. A low keening wail started, her neck and back arched, thighs clenched and her back came up off the desk.

She cried his name as her body convulsed around his fingers, hips banging against his mouth. He lapped her faster, plunged his fingers harder, pulling her orgasm from her, prolonging it.

Adara sat bolt upright with a breathy scream and the spasms wracked her, grabbing her body, they shook her until all the screams, every breath was wrung out of her.

Heaving, she fell over with a harsh whimper. Vaclav moved his forearms onto the desk to pull her in and cradle her against him.

She wept into his hair. He held her until the spasms lessened leaving little convulsing trembles, she hung limp, her head on his shoulder. He sifted his hands under her, lifting her up into his arms and carried her into the bedroom and laid her on the bed.

Eyes fluttering in her hazed brain clouded with ongoing stinging sensations, tiny after-shocks shook her body, Adara gazed up at him with glassy eyes, still panting.

"Vâj…"

Still fully clothed, he sat down on the mattress beside her. It was so thick it barely shifted with his weight. Staring down at her in pleased wonder, blue eyes fluxing like burning sunspots, he brushed her hair off her damp face.

Petting her arm, he slid his palms down the soft limbs, then he cupped her breasts enjoying their weighty feel for a bit before stroking her thighs. He moved on to savor the smoothness of her flat belly, and then shifted his hand briefly between her legs to stroke her soaking pussy.

"I am going to get a cloth and clean you up, sweet. Then you are getting under the covers and taking a nap, and then we are taking a shower, together. And we will do this all over again. What do you think about that?" He thrust his long finger inside her and grinned at her hips squirming in anticipation at more.

With his hands all over her, in her, Adara forgot she was buck naked lying splayed out on the bed like a starfish while he sat in shirt and pants touching her everywhere.

She said shyly, "I, uh, think that sounds…nice."

So pleased, so happy he could soar like he had wings, blue eyes stroking over, all around her body, her beautiful face, his dark blond brows crinkled with humor. "Nice? So bland, baby. After your nap I will show you fucking nice."

Smiling, her lids flickered a few times before they stayed shut.

As she dozed off, Vaclav took out his cell. Traipsing down the hall while dialing, when it was answered, he said into the phone, "Griff, I need you to find some people. *Da*," he replied nodding, heading for the balcony so Adara couldn't hear him.

"A Lucretia, and-" he closed the door behind him as he stepped out onto the balcony.

Chapter Twenty

Later in the evening, the couple went outside to the courtyard. The patio, made up of blue and green glossy tiles seemed like an oceanic extension of the shimmering turquoise pool.

Near the back of the deck, people were bouncing and tapping to calypso music played by a live, colorful band.

To one side of the patio a smoking grill permeated the air, and along the other side the lively bar was hopping. A boisterous crowd hovered around the bar, and a few people were lined up at the grill for burgers or dogs, pizza or barbeque. A handful of people splashed laughing and playing in the pool.

Vaclav held Adara's hand, and as usual, his expression was shut in, hard. But the atmosphere was so gay and lively it brought a smile to Adara's tense face.

Finding herself whisked to another country and suddenly married to a man she had always been afraid of kept her constantly on pins and needles.

Granted, Vaclav treated her well. He wined her and dined her, bought her jewelry, took her sightseeing wherever she wanted to go. And today, he absorbed her devastating secrets with nothing but caring support, and…he gave her, her first orgasm.

Still, he tended to bully her, and because he was of old world thinking and a male, and older than her, he felt he had the right to spank her, discipline her as if she was a child.

His mentality of men and women was terribly archaic; she figured it was his upbringing. He had been basically raised in an all-male Russian gang, by cutthroat gang members, and in a patriarchal society that severely controlled their women, and was also known for its spectacularly dark and brutal way of life.

Vaclav had never known a soft touch, kind word, any sort of benevolence. He grew up being beaten, and beating. Killing, and avoiding being killed. The only people he was ever able to trust, to count on, to care for, were his close friends.

He had never learned how to treat women past screwing them, and commanding them, and felt it was his duty to direct them and discipline them if necessary. For their own good.

Recalling the incident of his punishing her, her hand unconsciously went to her behind. True, he had held back the brunt of his strength so it had stung only a bit, but it was why he did it, to force her to obey him. Darned caveman.

Then again, rosy heat burned her cheeks, when his hand smacked her bare bottom, it caused her lady parts to bounce against his muscular thigh and it had brought heat and tingles to those…womanly bits.

And then when he had stroked her at the same time, *oh dear*, she covered her flushing cheeks with her palms.

The things he had done to her, on the desk, in the shower, his mouth on her most private parts, his long thick fingers inside her, uh oh, the tingles were back and she felt her panties grow damp.

He had said he would pleasure her, and boy did he! If his growls and groans and fearsomely hard erection were any judge, he was enjoying it as much as she. Adara had thought at the time that he would want it all, that he would force himself, in her.

But, instead, she had watched him with awe and embarrassment, and interest, after he washed every inch of her with his soapy hands, he jacked off in the shower

Holding her hand now, Vaclav felt the sudden tension in her hand. He bent to look at her. "What is it, baby? You *bine*?" Then he noticed her flaming cheeks, and the hard face shifted into a knowing smirk.

Bending closer to whisper in her ear he said, "Ah *mea* sweet wife, you keep blushing like that and I will have to swoop you back inside and do more wicked things to you."

Her hands covered her flushed face, she couldn't look at him. His evil, sensual chuckle made her whole body heat.

He told her, "We have yet to make love you know…we can go remedy that right now, what do you say?" Squeezing her hand, his smile rose higher as her blush blazed scarlet at his words. If she said yes, he would have her in their suite and naked in a heartbeat.

As it was, even after relieving himself in the shower, he had the blue balls of the century. But, he wanted her willing and wanting him, and finally, thankfully, it seems his plan to seduce her was going well.

"Vâj!" she chirped embarrassed. "Shh, someone could hear you!"

A laugh chortled from the tough man. "Baby, they would only be jealous of our fun, *da*?"

"Stop," she scolded with a mortified expression. "Let's get something to eat." Tugging on his hand, she dragged the grinning big man after her towards the grill.

She could hear him snickering and pictured the sensual softening of his sharply hewn mouth, and she didn't need to look at him to know the blue in his eyes was smoldering, and a huge erection was swelling in his jeans.

They grabbed burgers and sodas and when they saw no empty tables, Vaclav asked a group of people at a table if they could join them. There were two vacant chairs.

The group appeared to be in their mid-twenties to mid-thirties. One of the men nodded with a grin and gestured to the seats. "Sure," he said in unaccented English, "please join us."

Vaclav pulled a chair out for Adara then sat beside her.

"You are American?" he asked the man as his hooded gaze traveled the table.

Adara kept her smile on her face although she knew he was studying everyone there for possible threats. It was him, it was as natural as breathing to Vaclav, the life he led, it gave her the willies.

"Yep." The man grinned more. "But you aren't. That's an unusual accent, sounds kind of…Russian?" he asked with one eye squinting at Vaclav. He had tousled blond hair and brown friendly eyes.

Before answering, Vaclav's harsh gaze swept the man, letting him know he wasn't a man to be fucked with. Then he nodded sharply, stiffly said only, "*Na*, I am not American raised."

The man, somewhere in his late twenties was a bit taken aback. His brown eyes flit from Vaclav to Adara and back. "Oo-kay," he replied, keeping the friendly grin in place.

"Uh, I'm Brad and this is my wife Madeline." He motioned to a pretty blonde next to him. Brad's hair looked natural, hers with the glinting highlights did not.

Brad appeared tall as did Madeline. She looked like the model type to Adara. Long and willowy, the opposite of Adara's petite, curvy frame. Those types of girls always made her feel plain and dumpy.

Brad gestured to a second couple at the table. "That is Tim and his wife Gloria." Tim's hair was thin and straight and he had freckles but a handsome grin. Gloria's brunette locks waved to her shoulders, her nose and chin slightly too long making her just shy of beautiful. Both had friendly smiles, in unison they said, "Nice to meet you."

Brad motioned to a third couple, "Jason and his girl Jasmina." They both greeted Vaclav and Adara with nods and polite smiles. They appeared to be the oldest and the more serious couple of the group.

Both had black hair, Jason's cut short, neat and trimmed, Jasmina's hung straight as a black arrow down her back. She had sleek blunt cut bangs that just about hung in her brown eyes. When she blinked, the bangs flickered.

They all stared at Vaclav and Adara with friendly questioning gazes.

"Ah," Vaclav muttered with a frown. His accent made his voice harsher as he replied, "I am Vaclav and this is *mea* wife, Adara." When he introduced them he placed his hand over Adara's on the table, not so subtly indicating ownership.

"Welcome guys," Brad said cheerfully. "We didn't know each other before we got here, so we're happy to meet more people. We are all visiting from the States. Most everyone else at the resort is French and we pretty much lack in the language department," he chuckled. "So we kind of are hanging with each other, ya know? Where are you from?" He looked expectantly from one to the other.

Hating to be so painfully shy, Adara forced herself to speak. She said softly, "We are from America, my..." She swallowed back the unfamiliar word, and felt Vaclav squeeze her hand and knew he was frowning at her for pausing at the word.

Pushing her lips up, she made herself say it. "Uh, my husband was born elsewhere, we live in New York."

Vaclav gave her another squeeze, sharper this time and his frown stiffened in place telling her she was giving too much personal information.

A server came by and asked if anyone wanted any drinks. Everyone but Adara and Vaclav ordered beer or harder alcoholic drinks.

"Oh, how interesting," Madeline drawled, sultry hazel eyes leveled boldly at Vaclav, the edges of her wide mouth painted deep red curved up. Her gaze audaciously roamed over his broad shoulders and thick chest. "What a unique accent. Where are you from originally?"

For the first time ever, Adara felt a pinprick of jealousy. The woman was flirting with...her husband. There. She'd said it twice. In her mind anyway.

Madeline slung her eyes to Adara. They skated briefly down her curves, then with a dismissive sniff, swerved right back to Vaclav, her smile indicating she was pleased with what she was looking at.

Silent at first, under his hooded lids, Vaclav just stared at Madeline. For so long the rest of the table, except for Madeline, seemed to grow jumpy. Then, his mouth a harsh line as always, he said abruptly, "Eastern Europe."

Madeline's smile rose higher on one side and her own lids slid down with an enticing blatant invitation. "Ah, quite a broad answer, um, Vaclav did you say? Can you be more spec-"

While she was speaking, Vaclav turned to Adara, cupped her chin with his fingers, gave her a kiss and in a hushed dulcet tone asked her, "*Mândră*, would you like another soda?"

Blinking at his sudden attention she stammered, "Uh, I, sure, okay."

He kissed her again, then moving his hand from her face he said, "I will get it, eat your hamburger before it gets cold." Then he stood up and without a word to anyone else at the table, trod away to the bar.

Everyone gawked at him then at Adara. She gave a little shrug and explained, "He's, uh, I mean he can be a bit abrupt, he doesn't mean to be rude." *Actually he undoubtedly does*, she thought wryly.

"So, A-" Gloria grinned sheepishly. "I'm sorry, what was your name? It's unusual."

"Adara," she replied with a smile, self-consciously pushing her long wavy locks back off her shoulders. "I know it's different, please don't be embarrassed. It's an old family name."

Glorie returned her friendly smile. "Okay, Adara. It really is very pretty."

"Like you," Jasmina said to Adara. "My eyes are brown, but I had always wished they were that deep rich color of yours. And they're so big, gorgeous, really, like dark moons," she complimented.

Adara felt her cheeks heat up, she never handled compliments well. She always felt people were being disingenuous. The few times she said thank you when she was in prison, the person would turn on her and sneer sarcastically, "Conceited much, mud eyes?"

If she said nothing she was being accused of being stuck up. So she lowered her lashes and mumbled a response, her words deliberately unintelligible.

Having been in prison, Adara never felt on an even footing with others. People in her town had treated her so shabbily, like she was criminal filth beneath their shoes, that she was dirty, not equal to them, she just habitually avoided eye contact or conversation.

Now that she was rudderless for the first time in, well, forever, she glanced around for Vaclav, he was still at the bar. Forcing her

181

shyness aside, she said, "You have lovely shiny black hair, um, Jasamina."

The other woman laughed. "Thanks. That's Jasmina, no extra a." Her laughter eased the tension at the table and everyone started chatting at once.

The men talked to each other about football. Gloria and Jasmina discussed the difference they found in the French fashion. Adara pleaded in her mind for Vaclav to return. Madeline stared off in his direction, her face a thoughtful blank.

Adara was taken by surprise when she spoke to her.

"So," Madeline didn't say her name. Adara didn't know if she already forgot it or did it on purpose to make her feel less than.

"Tomorrow they're having a big pool party here. Will you and your…" Her eyes slid off to where Vaclav was turning from the bar carrying two sodas.

"Husband," Madeline said the word as if she didn't believe the delicate young woman was really married to the big brute of a man, who was obviously older than her, "be joining us?" she asked, her gaze under shifty lids watched Vaclav approaching.

"Um, well, I don't know. I," searching for a reason to say no, Adara said, "I didn't bring a swimsuit, so." She bumped a shoulder. "I guess not."

Madeline looked down her aquiline nose at the younger woman. "Oh? You travel to the south of France and don't bring a suit?"

"Uh…" Feeling on the spot, Adara blinked rapidly. She sure couldn't tell this obnoxious stranger the story of how she got there.

After being released from prison for murdering her father, her lifelong stalker had stolen her by gunpoint from the man that bought her from her mobster uncle planning to sexually abuse her, and said stalker forced her to marry him, and therefore she lacked a wardrobe.

No, that wouldn't carry over so well. Shrugging again, she simply said, "I guess I forgot."

"Forgot what, *mândră*?" Vaclav asked, sitting back down and setting the colas on the table.

"That I-" Adara started to answer him but Madeline spoke over her. "She was telling us how she didn't bring a bathing suit, and I was telling her how much I would love to loan her one of mine so you both can join the pool party tomorrow."

Vaclav took his time looking from her face, down over her small, obviously braless breasts. Her taut nipples were poked through the very tight, almost see-through, cropped white t-shirt. His gaze traveled down further to her long legs streaming out of obscenely short shorts, and back up.

He said, coolly, "I do not think *mea* young wife would fit in anything of yours, madam."

A blasé chuckle showed she wasn't offended at his intentional rudeness. He was a fascinating, foreign, virile male challenge.

Her red lips curved alluringly, she said, "Oh, but I have a suit that unfortunately the stupid help here shrunk, I mean, the incompetent dolts don't know how to wash silk, right?"

She looked over at the other women who pursed their lips and nodded in commiseration with her. "I'm sure it will fit your," she swept down Adara's delicate figure with a slight curl to the one side of her mouth, and said with an offensive tone, "*tiny woman.*"

His lids couldn't get any lower, ice freezing his words, Vaclav replied intractably, "Adara is *mea* wife. She does not wear anything unsuitable. I will not have her dressing as a slut."

Gasps rang around the table at his coarse words.

Adara's cheeks reddened, lashes quickly covered her discomfited eyes.

Brad's brows drew down, he said with a cold edge, "Are you calling my wife a slut?"

Vaclav's expression said 'if the shoe fits' but he voiced, "*Na.* I was just being clear that if Adara borrows anything it must be…" He glanced at his wife who was rigid with mortification. "Presentable. I do not want her tits and ass flaunted."

"Vâj!" Horrified, Adara stared in shamed shock at him.

One of his wide shoulders shrugged dismissively. He didn't care what anyone thought of him or his language. "I am just being clear, *mândră*, that you will be dressed appropriately, as the lady that you are."

His gaze cut to Tim whose eyes were settled on Adara's chest. Feeling the heat of his silent wrath, Tim jerked his attention away and pretended to be looking at a girl strolling by in a bikini.

Everyone shifted uncomfortably at Vaclav's vulgarity and rudeness, that is, everyone except for Madeline. Her sultry invitational gaze stayed directly on the big bruiser. In fact, a smirk tugged the corner of her mouth as if she found his uncouth crudeness to be amusing, and titillating.

Vaclav's hooded eyes slid to her, and moved disparaging down her long body and up.

Her eyes gleamed brazenly lascivious at him, his were contemptuous, and he turned his back to face his wife.

Madeline's smile didn't lessen, she clearly loved a challenge, a hot male challenge.

"That sounds lovely," Gloria commented, distracting everyone, "what you call your wife. Like Mahndrra, you trill your r's. What does it mean?"

Vaclav pushed his glare from Madeline to Gloria. He clasped Adara's hand. His face softened when he looked at her. He said tenderly, "It means 'my beauty.' "

"Wow, that is so romantic," Gloria sighed then dug her elbow in her husband's ribs. "How come you never call me pretty stuff like that?"

Tim jumped, flushed, blurted, "Huh?" He blinked at the girl passing in the bikini.

"You see," Gloria complained, "always gawking at other women instead of gazing at me like he does her." She nodded her head slightly to Vaclav and Adara.

"Like he can't wait to drag her away, toss her over his shoulder like a caveman and take her back to their room. I mean," she sighed, "he hasn't stopped undressing her with his eyes since they sat down here."

Everyone chuckled awkwardly. Madeline pouted.

Adara's cheeks kept flaming. Vaclav shrugged, it was true.

Rubbing his arm where she jabbed him, Tim scowled, "Yeah, well, maybe she doesn't nag him day and night."

Upping his voice a few octaves, he mimicked Gloria's girlish voice, "Do this, don't do that, buy me this, why do you always have to watch football, take me shopping, I'm not sucking on that-"

"Okay, okay, let's all have another drink and we'll be looser for dancing later." Brad broke up the friction between the bickering couple.

At that moment Vaclav stood up and pulled out Adara's chair.

"Tis been a long day, *mea* wife and I are weary. Come, sweet," he helped her to her feet. Without saying goodbye, he set his arm around her shoulders and started to turn her.

Embarrassed again at his rudeness, Adara pushed slightly apart from him and turned around. Smiling at everyone at the table she said cheerfully, "So nice to meet you all, please have a lovely evening."

Her words slinking out like snake, Madeline said silkily, "Yes, you as well."

Then she said louder as Vaclav prodded Adara to head towards the hotel, "Don't forget the party tomorrow, kids. I will bring the suit by for you, Adelaide." "I can also bring a pair of Brad's trunks for you, Vaclav," his name slippery on her tongue, her gaze skewed deeply to Vaclav.

He said over his shoulder, "*Na*, I wear *na* other man's underwear, I have shorts." And he moved Adara to walk more quickly to the hotel.

When they reached their suite, Vaclav opened the door and ushered her inside.

Annoyed with his boorish and dominating behavior, in irritation she frowned, "Vâj, why can't I have a keycard?"

He stuffed the key in his pants pocket. "You have *na* need of one." Kicking off his boots, unbuttoning his shirt, he yawned while heading for the bedroom to change his clothes.

She traipsed after him, consternated with his macho attitude. "Wait, but I might not always be with you, what if I go-"

He swung around so fast she almost plowed into him.

His face dark with anger, he said, "We have discussed this ad nauseam, Adara. You will not be outside this room without me. Do not make me implant *mea* orders on your ass again with *mea* hand."

Her fists lodged on her hips she said, "You need to stop threatening me all the time with spanking if I don't do as you say, I'm not-"

He snatched her upper arms and yanked her to him. Breathing roughly, brows low over his furiously darkening face, rattling off a horde of Romanian curses he said, "You are the one that needs to stop, Adara. Stop arguing with me. Tis not safe out there for you alone. That is it. I have told you again and again I will not allow you to put yourself in peril again."

Digging his fingers into her arms he repeated firmly, "I will not. If I have to beat your little ass to make you understand, then, I will." He let go of her and stood back to cool his fury. The thought of Adara being in the slightest danger just made his heart about jump out of his chest.

To release some of the anger in the room, Adara quickly changed the subject. "What, ah, did you think of those, people, um…"

Blinking rapidly, he shook his head to attend to her abrupt change in conversation. Frowning, he dragged a hand across the top of his hair. "What?"

"That, um, Madeline. She is quite beautiful, isn't she, like a model. She um, seemed to really…like you." Adara hoped she hid the hint of jealousy in her voice.

Scrubbing his fingers over his eyes he looked at Adara in exasperation. Squinting in annoyance, he said curtly, "She is a whore."

"Vâj!" Adara blurted, "that's a terrible thing to say!"

He shrugged a broad shoulder. "Tis the truth. Sitting beside her own husband with a sexual gleam in her heavy-lidded eyes, the curved leer of her lips clearly invited me to take what I wanted. She is a whore."

He lowered his head to look at his wife. Seeing her blushing at his words, a small smile erased his anger. "Ah, is *mea* little wife jealous?"

Angry that he could read her so well, Adara shook her head. "Of course not. But," she sighed. "She is beautiful, tall and willowy, not," she looked down at her figure, "squat and frail like me."

His brows rose to his hairline, then lowered in anger. "Sweetheart," he gripped her arms again but gently this time.

"First of all, she is not beautiful, she is barely pretty. Second, *na* one holds a candle to you, *na* one. You are petite, delicate, fine-boned, feminine as shit, not frail. Fragile maybe, but it only makes me want to protect you all the more."

At her frown, he said, "And third, she tis flat as a board. She looks like a tall gangly boy. I like curves on *mea* women. Your curves," and he let go of her arms to grope her breasts.

"*Da*, sweet," he kneaded them roughly, "so fucking fine, these are what I dream of at night, *mândră*. Not some flat-chested, cheating whore." He muttered, "Her husband should have been disciplining his woman from the beginning and she wouldn't be a skanky adulteress."

His erection was clawing at his pants in seconds. He knew if he kept it up she would be laid out on her back on the carpet and he would be driving brutally into her without getting her virgin's body ready to take the width and iron span of his cock.

He would hurt her badly, and she would never forgive him. If he wanted her hot and willing, he had to slow it down.

Now," he exhaled, unwinding his fingers from feeling up his wife's gorgeous breasts. "I am tired. I am going to change, then crash in the extra bedroom. I will see you in the morning."

He gave her a quick, rough, kiss, then released her with a bearish grunt and stalked to the bathroom.

Chapter Twenty-One

The next morning, Adara woke to his lips on her forehead as he gave her a gentle kiss. "Baby, I have to go meet with Griff and the guys. I will be back in a few hours. I have already ordered room service. Your breakfast is on the counter in the nook. Shall I bring you anything?"

Rubbing the sleep from her eyes, she blinked to bring him into focus. "I…don't think I need anything. I have books and the iPad you bought me. Maybe I could go out by the pool-"

His brows dropped down in a swift scowl. "Adara, do not start with me." His sigh loud and cross, he said, "You are not to leave the suite, you know that. Stop trying *mea* patience."

Straightening, he glared down at her. "Nor are you to answer the door, as I have previously instructed you. Not to anyone, the room attendant, maids, manager, *na* one. One heart attack finding this room empty and you out there not under *mea* protection is enough. Tell me you understand this, Adara," his voice hard and gritting stern.

Rolling her eyes, she sniffed, "Yes, yes, oh God yes, Your Highness, I hear you."

Suppressing a grin, he tapped the end of her nose affectionately. "*Bine,* you sassy little upstart." He bent and kissed her again. Straightening, he said, "If you are good while I am gone, when I return, we can go swimming if you would like. *Bine*?"

Lips shoved out in chagrin, rolling her eyes again, she sighed. "Yes, overbearing husband."

The grin broke through at his proud smile. "Ah, finally, you call me husband. For that I will bring you diamonds."

"Vâj, don't be silly, I don't need more jewelry, don't-"

He bent and gave her a quick kiss before striding towards the bedroom door then he turned and said with all seriousness, "You should have been draped in jewels from birth, baby, I have a lot of lost time to make up for," and he was gone.

Just as she heard the front door close she remembered, "Oh, wait, Vâj, the party," oh dear. He had forgotten that Madeline might be bringing her a suit. Well, he would just have to get over it if the woman meant what she said and stopped by.

Adara spent a couple of hours online researching universities. Vaclav had told her to choose what she wanted and he would ensure she would gain entrance.

She would be doing her studies online but when she took her exams he told her she would have to have him or his guards accompany her.

At least she could get her education and that was what she wanted. She was still trolling when there was a knock at the door.

Vaclav's warning ringing in her ears, she peeked out the peephole. Madeline with her snobby face was staring off to the side with a look of boredom.

Adara quickly opened the door. "Madeline, hi, you remembered." She stood aside so the older woman could enter the suite.

"Of course," she retorted. With her snooty, ski-slope nose in the air, she tromped past Adara in six-inch wedges. Already tall, the heels put her in the six-foot mark. Still, she would have to look up to Vaclav.

Madeline wore a tiny skirt that showed off her long legs and another cropped top. Her blonde hair was in a tight fashionable ponytail. Her head swiveled as she glanced around. "So," she said, tucking an errant hair back in place, "where is that hunk of man you claimed to be married to?"

Adara's mouth pinched at the audacity of the woman. "My *husband*," she stressed the word, "is out on business." She looked at the bag in Madeline's hand and her expression lightened. "You brought me a suit to borrow?"

"Hmm?" Madeline was tugged back from scanning the room, obviously not believing Adara that Vaclav wasn't in the suite. "Oh, yes, here." She abruptly handed the bag to her.

Adara accepted it gratefully. Pulling the suit out, she grinned, "Thank you so much, Madeline, I can't tell you how much I-" She broke off at the two miniscule swatches of silk in her hand.

Face falling, she said, "Oh, I'm sorry, you said it was…I mean, my…husband," now she faltered over the word, "would never allow me to wear that." She put it back in the bag and handed it back to Madeline.

Immaculate winged brows arched, Madeline refused to take the bag. "Seriously, hon? You let your husband dictate what you can and cannot wear?"

Her chin up she rolled her eyes with a haughty huff. "That would be the day Brad or any other man would tell me what I can wear. This is the 21st century darling, you know."

"But, you don't know Vaclav, he-"

A sly smile drew up the long face. "Darling, I know he's a man. You brandish a bare tit or pussy in his face and he'll do anything you say. Trust me," she said with a saucy wink. "It is really the woman that wears the pants in the family."

Adara felt her face flushing at Madeline's crassness. She wanted to tell her she didn't know Vaclav. That he was domineering and would punish her if she disregarded his dictates. But, she didn't want to look like a wuss in front of the sophisticated woman. So sure of herself, Madeline wore her confidence like a fur coat.

Of course, Madeline didn't have a criminal past and a mobster for a husband. She had that nice, congenial Brad. Nice and boring Brad, Adara giggled to herself. She wouldn't trade her big, bold, rude and crude, harsh husband for anything, much less a guy like boring handsome Brad.

The realization slapped her in the face. When had that brute slithered his way under her skin? And into her heart? Her heart? Had he truly insinuated himself into her heart?

"Well?" Madeline demanded, bringing Adara out of her ruminations.

"Um, well, I…"

"Oh stop twittering. Be a grown woman, for fuck's sake, girl. Just do it. Once he sees you in this bikini, trust me hon, he will forget his anger. He will just want to take you back to your room and fuck the daylights out of you." Her smug smile wavered a bit, her envy of Adara's tough and rough, obviously dangerous husband was clear on her face.

"Anyway," she said, "keep it. If you don't wear it, just give it back to me tomorrow or whatever. Or keep it permanently. Like I said, the stupid help shrunk it, I can't wear it anyway. So," she tripped to the door in her heels, "see you later at the pool, darling, ta ta," and she swooped out the door.

Adara stared at the bag in her hand. What to do, what to do, she pondered. Then a mischievous smile rolled up her face, yeah, she's gonna do it. She's gonna be as hot and confident as Madeline. Maybe not as good looking, but still, Adara was gonna wear it, own it, strut it.

She hurried into the bedroom to try the suit on before her courage left her. Or Vaclav returned, or both.

Two hours later he returned. "Baby!" he called out as soon as he was in the door.

Hearing him, she strolled in from the balcony and went right to him. He lavished a long, scorching kiss on her.

After a few minutes, they both leaned back to breathe.

Smiling at her, Vaclav said, "Ah, I missed you, sweet, I could not wait to come back home to you. What do you say we," he wiggled his blond brows towards the bedroom.

"But, Vâj, the party at the pool has been going on for over an hour already and you promised we could go."

He chucked her chin. "Who could resist that pretty pout? But, your swimsuit-"

Clearing her throat and averting her guilty eyes, she said, "Madeline brought it by."

His smile morphed instantly into a frown. "She came here? And you opened the fucking door? Adara-"

Pursing her lips she snapped, "Oh come on, Vaclav, I saw it was her. It was perfectly safe. You knew she said she would be coming by. Please," she softened her tone and stroked his angry face, "you promised we could go."

His mouth bumped, pushed in and out, he struggled to restrain his anger.

With a hard exhale he said, "*Bine*. But, never again, do you hear me, Adara? I fucking mean it. Never again do you open that door unless is me or one of *mea* men. I swear, you do it again and I will-"

"Yes, yes, I know, tan my hide into next year. Come on, let's get ready."

"*Zue* you test me girl. *Bine*," he grunted reluctantly, stuffing his ire.

He was ready way before Adara as she had waited to take a shower. "Baby, come on, I am ready to go," he called, the sooner they went and played a bit, the sooner he could drag her back here and they could play alone.

She called out from the bathroom, "You go on ahead, I'll be right there. I'll meet you at the pool."

"Adara, *na*."

"Geez," she grumbled, "you will be right outside in the courtyard, I think I can get from here to there safely in a few minutes. Go on."

He hesitated. He didn't like to always be a bully to her, but she was too precious, her safety too important. Yet, she was right. He would only be downstairs and a few steps away.

He gave in grudgingly. "*Bine*. Just this once, Adara, this will not lead to a habit. I will meet you at the pool. You have ten minutes and I will come looking for you."

Hearing the door close, she came out of the bathroom. The real reason she wanted him to leave without her was because if he saw the bathing suit he would never let her out of the suite and they'd have a big fight. Because she was going.

She stood in front of the full-length mirror and blanched. She had never ever worn such a…revealing outfit. Sapphire blue silk with red swirls barely covered her nipples. Geesh, her bra covered more.

Looking down, she quailed, the bottom was worse. Just a slash of blue and red across her sex. Twisting to the side she got a shot of the back, and groaned, half her butt was hanging out. Oh dear, Vaclav was going to have a heart attack when he sees her. Her bravery was flagging.

No, she shook her head with resolve, she needed to show him he couldn't boss her around. This would show him she was not the child he treated her as, and had a mind and a will of her own.

Slipping on the kitten sandals Madeline had included, Adara wondered where she'd found them. Madeline's feet were twice the size of hers. But they fit pretty well.

When she opened the door, she almost lost her nerve. Then, taking a big strong emboldened breath, she strutted out the door and down the stairs and along the back corridor to the courtyard.

Stepping out to the patio, she almost lost her nerve again. Straightening her spine, lifting her chin, she strode onto the sea-green and blue tiles.

As soon as she felt the warmth of the sun on her shoulders, she glanced around. The place was teeming with people. Drinks flowed, the pool was filled with bouncing boobs, spray and laughter.

Tables were crowded with food and conversation. Feeling eyes on her, staring at her barely dressed form, she hurried to the side and searched for Vaclav.

Easily spotting him, he was so tall, the dark blond hair heads above most the men there. He was smoking a thin cigar and talking to Brad and Tim from last night.

She saw his head continuously twitching from the men to the patio door, obviously looking for her. She saw his frown deepen as he glanced at his watch and back to the door.

"Hey hotstuff, shit, aren't you gorgeous!" A man standing right next to her whistled. His gaze rolled up and down and up and down her body lingering on her breasts.

She jumped startled when a man on the other side of her drew his finger down her arm and said, "You need a drink, honey, what can I get you?"

"Uh- uh, I don't need anything." Feeling exposed and awkward, Adara crossed her arms and took an imperceptible step back from both men.

At that moment, Vaclav turned in her direction. He started to smile when he saw her face, then, he saw what she was wearing and his eyes popped, he looked like he swallowed his tongue.

Then he noticed the men flanking her, gawking at her breasts and his skin slowly darkened, the square jaw gritted. Tossing the cigar to the ground, he immediately stomped across the patio to her.

By the time he reached her, goose bumps of fear spiraled up her arms and across her shoulders. The rage boiled so strongly from Vaclav, the two men took one look, mumbled nothing, and hurried away.

Face clenched like an angry fist, he barked, "What the fuck are you wearing?"

"Hey, Vâj, uh honey." She fought to sound calm and confident, tossing in the unfamiliar endearment and giving him what she thought was a sexy smile. "I-"

He grabbed her arm and instantly started ushering her back to the entrance of the hotel.

Adara snatched her arm from his grasp. Because she did it suddenly and unexpectedly, she was able to get free of him. "I am staying out here, Vaclav Brașov, you said we could do this party and you are being unreasonably prehistoric about my-"

"Goddammit Adara, you heard what I said about putting your tits on display. You know I do not want the other fuckers to see that bitchin' body, it belongs only to me. Your ass, your cunt, your mouth, everything, it all belongs to me. Now, get your ass inside, right the fuck now." Maneuvering so he blocked her from view of the rest of the crowd, he pointed to the door.

Cheeks flaming, Adara planted her hands on her hips. Dark brows drawn down in pique, she said, "No. I am not doing what you say. I have every right to be out here. Stop ordering me around, telling me what to wear, what to-"

Muttering foreign curses under his breath, he suddenly snatched up her arm and hauled her across the few feet of the patio and back inside the hotel.

He half-dragged her down one hall after another and up the stairs until they reached their suite.

Chapter Twenty-Two

Pulling her into the room, then, still holding her arm, Vaclav stepped back and glowered fearsomely at her.

His eyes traveled over her breasts spilling out of the skimpy bikini, and down her concave stomach, and lower to where her sex was barely covered by a swath of sapphire material.

Teeth clenching, a vein hopped a furious beat at his temple while his pupils grew to large blue moons of desire.

"Damn, Adara," in a flash he had his hand on the back of her neck, and pulled her to him. "Baby," he growled, covering her mouth with his with a shuddering groan, and drew her to press against his instantly hot, hard body.

He wore a long-sleeved dress shirt and slacks; he hadn't dressed in pool party attire. Her rounded, half-naked breasts wedged against his huge rocky chest, molding up on the verge of escaping the scanty bikini top.

So hungry for her, his anger gone for the moment, Vaclav chomped at her mouth, sucking her lips in hard, biting nips at the tender plump petals, before burrowing his tongue in and taking control of his bride's young mouth.

Cradling the back of her head, he turned it and slanted his head to get as tight to her as he could and roughly shoved his tongue down her throat.

Vaclav fought to control himself, his head was combusting in a bonfire of grueling lust. He was quickly losing it, the leash on his control weakening with every harsh breath that left him.

Then, a whimper pulsed against his lips, and her small hands slipped up his bulging biceps to circle behind his neck.

Grating moans rumbled in his chest, scraped up his throat, he lowered his hands to grip her ass and jerked her hips against his raging erection. His slacks and her slinky bikini offered little protection from the dry humping thrusts of his bombarding cock.

Feeling the iron club of his desire lodging into her cleft, doused some of Adara's passion. Nerves moved her hands from his neck to his enormous chest.

Vaclav's eyes lowered to see her dainty hands pressed to the muscles flexing under his shirt.

Dipping his head, he whispered, "Baby," his breath cooed against her ear, kneading her plump bottom in his big hands. "Do not shut it down, shut me down. I have you, sweetheart, trust me to take care of you."

Lashes of sable covered her eyes, then raised slowly to look up at him. "I…" Her eyes fell to the huge hard lump straining at his slacks and pressing into her sex.

She uttered, "You," her small fingers splayed on his shirt, "you're so big, Vâj, I don't think…" The lashes lowered again to cover the fear, and arousal in her dark virgin's eyes.

With a tremble on her plush lips, she said, "What that girl did in prison, it hurt. I'm afraid, Vâj."

Vaclav wound his thick fingers around her upper arms, he said with loving tenderness, "Baby, I am not some psycho cretin in prison, I am your husband. I would never hurt you, you must know that by now."

Still uneasy, she nonetheless snorted. Glib eyes rolled up, she murmured with mild flippancy, "You call spanking not hurting?"

The smirk lifting his lips went with the lewd glint in his horny blues. "Come on, Adara, you cannot tell me the tiny slaps from *mea* hand on your bare ass hurt. You would have enjoyed them if you were not allowing yourself to feel humiliated, and had *mea* exploring fingers bringing you thrilling delight."

Without waiting for her to comment, he lowered his head and captured her mouth again, bringing her with him in a body-shaking, mind-screaming kiss.

When she softened in his embrace, Vaclav released her arms and cupped her breasts so full and firm and supple, cradled in the silken bikini top.

She stiffened, resisted his touch, but when his thumbs rubbed over her nipples bringing them to hard peaks, the shudder racing through her body showed him she wasn't immune to his touch.

Sexy groans exuding from his lips, Vaclav gripped her plump flesh and moaned. "Damn, Adara, you are so fine, so worth the wait, I could never stop touching you, ever, not in a thousand lifetimes. Please baby, relax, let me feel your treasures." His mouth ravaged her lips already swelling with his vigorous kisses.

When she softened against him again, he grinned against her mouth, and webbed his long strong fingers over her breasts, clutching, kneading the full flesh until he heated up too much, too fast, crushing them too hard in his over-excited hands, and she cried out.

Breaths hard and heavy rushing from his heaving chest, Vaclav forced himself to release her. He tipped a finger under her chin and raised it so their eyes connected.

"I am sorry, baby. I do not know *mea* own strength sometimes, and you just drive me fucking crazy, take all *mea* control and rip it from me. If I hurt you, tell me, I will stop immediately. *Bine*?" The Icelandic blue eyes melted into warm lagoons pulling her in, begging her to give him a chance.

The anxiousness dissipated from her dark liquid eyes and she nodded with a tiny smile. Whispering, "Okay," she set her hands on his arms, clutching his bulging biceps.

His grin took over his hard face. "Thank you, baby." Reaching behind her neck, he untied the thin string of the top of her bikini and pulled it down. His eyes dropped to stare at the chubby creamy globes.

"You are so goddamned beautiful, Adara, you make *mea* heart beat like a hard-rock drum so damned vicious I fear it will implode. Only you have ever made me feel this way."

When he untied the back of the suit and it started to fall, Adara self-consciously held it in place.

"*Na*, baby, I have waited a lifetime to fully enjoy your beauty; do not deny your husband the pleasure of looking at you." He tugged the top from her hands and tossed it.

Leaning back to take in the view, he stared at her for so long she started to stiffen in her shyness.

He covered her plump breasts with his big hands. Feeling the firm plushness of them, their weight in his palms, his fingers rode over her taut nipples, pulling, pinching them.

For a minute he just stood and watched his hard, calloused scarred hands fondling, clutching her soft feminine flesh, at long last he was living his dream. He lowered his head to suck a pink nipple into his mouth.

Vaclav made love to her breasts. Suckling, squeezing until her whimpers made him lighten his grip. Leaning back again, he enjoyed seeing his hard, tanned hands crush the satiny globes.

He traced his fingertips over the dark red marks he'd made with his tough sucking. He smiled when he glanced up and saw her watching him playing with her tits.

Slowly, he released a breast, stroked his palm down her side and between her legs. She stiffened, he whispered, "Shh," and cupped her sex.

"*Zue*, baby, I need to feel you now, right the hell now." He gripped the bikini bottom and was about to rip it off her when she cried, "Vâj," the worry in her voice made him force himself to slow down.

There would be time later for him to add some aggressive roughness to their playing. For now, he wanted her to be happy, feel safe, relish their coupling.

He slipped his fingers in the waistband of her bikini bottoms and, crouching, slowly drew them down her slender legs. Lifting each leg, he pulled the wisp of cloth off and dropped it, leaving her wearing only the strappy sandals.

Almost eye-level with her naked sex, "Oh, baby," he murmured with awe. He moved his hand to mold his palm over it.

She made a tiny sound and stiffened again. He drew a finger up her slit, then pressed her plump folds together and the sound turned to a soft moan, her legs lost some of their stiffness.

"Good girl," he praised. Stroking her sex, pressing down with his thumb, he plucked at every part of her folds, slick slit, tender clitoris. Her little clit tightened to a bud and he felt her wetness ooze out. *Fuck, da*, he thought to himself, he knew she would be responsive and so amazingly hot.

"*Da*, baby, your body, you, you were made for love, for sex, for me." He lowered his head and clamped his mouth over her entire mound and she yelped. Her silk poured into his mouth, he shoved his tongue up inside her.

"Vâj!"

Chuckling, he said with blissful desire, "*Da*, sweet, we have done this before, nothing to be afraid of. Now tis time to consummate our marriage. Please trust me to make this pure heaven for you."

Licking her slit, he bit her clit, drew her silk on his fingers, and swirled them over her sex. Her round hips moved with his strokes, tiny moans eased from her parted lips.

Vaclav gazed up at her, his heart melted like snow in a desert. Her naked breasts were full and round and high, her head was tilted back, mouth open slightly, eyes closed, long feathered lashes curled on her pink cheeks.

Her shoulders shivered and a sultry sound came out and went straight to Vaclav's burning dick.

"My shoes, Vâj," she gasped a breath. "I need to take off the sandals, ahh," the moan eased out.

His mouth on her sex he muttered, "Uh huh. Too sexy you naked in heels, leave them on." When his fingers and lips started a disjointed rhythm, her hips rolled with them.

200

Still sucking at her, biting the tender flesh between her thighs, he nudged her feet wider apart, spread his hand over her bottom to steady her in the heels, and slowly inserted his hard finger into her tender channel. Her hips went still.

"Baby, put your hands on *mea* shoulders to hold your balance, I have you. You liked this before, right?"

She settled her hands on his thick shoulders. Her hushed nod encouraged him.

One of his big hands splayed, holding her bottom like a bowl with fingers, the other continued moving, pushing his finger up her further and further, then pulled it out then back in, and did it again, and again, curling and prodding his fingertip until the high pitched sound gushing from her lips told him he'd found her hotspots.

She moved her hands to twine her fingers in his locks and gripped them then twisted the strands fiercely hard as her channel slickened and her insides thrummed with licking flames.

It was like she was riding a wild horse, humping it while clinging feverishly to its mane. Her head arched back and a buttery, utterly feminine sound seethed from her parted lips.

"Uhh," her moans deepened, grew louder, harsher, her hips writhed against his mouth, and he plunged a second finger inside her tight sheath and smiled at her surging gasps and breathy hitches, her fingers twisting his hair more tightly, more urgently.

It stung but in a pleasurable way, made him so incredibly hot. Feeling her sex clench his fingers harder and harder, the silk poured out, he moved his hand from her butt to reach up and grip her breast, he palmed it and squeezed.

Her breaths rapid and heaving, little whimpers huffed and her hips bucked at his mouth, her hands clenched his hair, Vaclav knew she was on the edge.

"Let go, baby, let go, give it to me, trust me to take care of you," he murmured, mixing words of his language with English, the throaty, dark velvet voice bringing tremors to her legs.

"Vâj!" she gasped, pulling his hair and shoving her sex at him.

He plunged his fingers nonstop, licked her, then, as he felt her right on the precipice, he bit her bud alternating thrusting his fingers, crushed her breast in his hand, and pinched her nipple hard, and her legs started shaking.

The climax raced through her body, lighting fire everywhere, it raked raw, hemorrhaging sensation so biting, screams roiled up her throat erupting with his name as her body undulated wildly in his hands.

His fingers still pumping, Vaclav held her bottom tightly while the orgasm tore through her, wringing her, shaking her so hard she almost wrenched from his hands.

Hissing air rasped from her throat, her chest heaving, hitching with hiccupped breaths, the orgasm shook her until her knees buckled.

She had heard a few of the girls in prison talk about such intense orgasmic sensations, the other women said those few women were greatly embellishing. They weren't.

They must have lucked out being with the same type of man as Vaclav. She felt sorry for the rest of womanhood that would never experience such exquisite agony.

"Baby," he murmured. Standing up, he lifted her, holding her to his chest, he moved her legs to wrap around his waist and held her as her body trembled with jerking aftershocks. The sandals slipped off landing silently on the carpet.

When she quieted, wheezing to catch her breath and slow her hammering heart, Adara tilted her head back to look at him. Apple cheeks red with her climax and embarrassment, she stammered, "Vâj, I…" her eyes dropped from his.

"Adara, baby," he held her with his forearm under her bottom, and curled a finger under her jaw and lifted it, forcing her shy gaze to meet his heated one.

"That was insanely fantastic. So fucking hot I almost blew *mea* shit right then and there along with you. Do not ever be embarrassed or shy with me, sweetheart. Few men are blessed with a woman like you, one who comes that marvelously hard, it is major extraordinary. You are magical to me, you always have been," he kissed the tip of her nose.

"You take *mea* damned breath away. I can't wait to see you orgasm again. I could watch that shit for a million years."

Her lashes fluttered over shy eyes, her hands on his shoulders, she said quietly, "But, Vâj, again, I am," she looked down at her bare breasts, still heaving with her racing pulse pressing against his shirt. "Um, naked, and you," her gaze flit to his shirt, "are still fully dressed."

"Hmm, sweetheart, there could not be anything better in this universe. A man's sexual fantasy, tis highly erotic to hold a naked woman in a man's arms while he is still clothed." His gentle smile touched her lips with a soft kiss.

"Hmm," she mimicked against his mouth. "That's nice for you, but for me, uh, it's kind of…awkward."

As they moved, her breasts rubbed against his cotton shirt making her shiver and turn her nipples into tight little beads begging to be sucked.

His smile broad and pleased, Vaclav held her nude body and shamelessly gazed all over it from her shy smile to her naked breasts to her sweet pussy pressing against his abs of ridged stone. He had an armful of softness and graceful femininity, his Adara, finally. Her cheeks reddened to beets at his nonbreaking perusal.

Chuckling, he carried her to the bed and set her on it.

When she started to pull her knees up to hide her nudity, he frowned, bent and caught her ankles. "*Na*, I have told you before, I am your husband, you never keep your beauty from me. Lay down, sweet." He gave her shoulder a push, and when she gently fell on her back, he held her legs, pulling them apart.

Her hands up by her head, legs spread, hair like a long mink stole waving around her head, his groan was palpable.

"*Da*, oh fucking *da,* baby, perfect. You have always been perfect and you have only grown more so every year."

Gazing adoringly at her, Vaclav unbuttoned a few buttons before reaching over his head to grip his shirt and pulled it off, dropping it without care. His hands went to his belt. Never moving his eyes from her, he unbuckled it.

Her huge dark eyes glowing lazy with satiation followed his every move.

Crouching, he undid his boots, kicked them off and removed his socks. Opening his slacks, he pushed them and his briefs down, and stepped out of them.

If possible, her eyes grew wider and rounder at his thronging manhood. Hard and heavy, thick and long, it hung almost straight out shouting its hunger for her.

She quailed, the red cheeks blanched, her legs pulled together and she leaned up on her elbows as if about to flee.

"*Na, na*, baby, do not be afraid of me, I swear, Adara, I will not hurt you. You feel any pain, you tell me to stop and I will, I promise. But tis time to make you *mea* wife."

The past few days he had primed her, playing with her, conditioned her body to automatically turn on at his touch even against her will.

She was so petite and delicate, he big and brawny, a tough man, he had to be cognizant of his strength. Too rough and she would call a halt.

He had prepared her to take him, her tender virginity. The fiends in prison had destroyed her hymen, but she was a virgin. He had carefully stretched her with his big fingers to be able to accept his girth, take in the thick width of his pounding, raging hard cock.

His arms, shoulders, were covered with tattoos, but his strapping chest was matted with dark hair. Adara had told him he was a contrast with his blond hair but everything else on him was dark. His brows, lashes, hair on his arms, chest, legs, and his nether parts as well.

When they had showered, she had asked what the foreign words and pictures detailed that were painted on his body were, but he just shrugged without telling her. She didn't need to know what the coarse, deadly, Romanian and Russian gangster signs meant.

Vaclav climbed on the bed, the firm mattress barely sinking under his muscular weight. Kneeling over Adara, making sure their eyes joined, he pushed her legs apart and moved between them.

He wrapped his fist around his shaft and saw her gaze fall to it, her pupils enlarged and not due to passion.

"Baby, Adara, look at me," he instructed and waited.

A second or two passed before she forced her gaze back to him.

"Just keep looking into *mea* eyes, sweetheart."

He shifted his body lower, nudging her thighs wider, and put his shaft at her opening. Their eyes still connected, hers huge and so doe-like, his heart quivered with overwhelming adoration. *Mea wife*.

Slowly, he pushed the head of his cock, breaching her tight little womb. Her legs stiffened.

Vaclav moved his head down to hers, the longer top of his hair brushing her forehead, and whispered words in his language.

She didn't understand them, but she felt the gentle sultriness of his husky voice, saw the tenderness, and striking need for her in his piercing blues.

Inch by slow inch he nudged inside and couldn't stop the groan that razed from the depths of his groin to rumble in his chest.

"Baby," the groan roughened, "I have waited forever to be here, inside your beautiful body, and, uhh," the groan ground in his throat, cracking his voice.

"We are finally one. You are more magnificent than I ever imagined. *Mea* dreams of you," he pushed deeper and moaned, "do not come near the true extraordinary feel of you. Your soft, firm body, gripping me, *mea Zue*, Adara, I have come home. I will never have enough of you," he swore, "fucking never."

Sweat trickled at his temples, dark blond hair fell over his eyes as he paused to look at her. Her eyes were closed, mouth tight, her face scrunched in pain.

"*Zue*, baby," he stopped moving. "You were to tell me if it hurt."

Her eyes fluttered then opened to him. "I- I'm okay, Vâj."

The air gushed from his lungs in a vexed sigh. "Sweetheart," he said and cupped under her jaw with his big calloused hand.

"I do not want okay. I want you to soar with pleasure, mindless bliss, passion for me. *Fuck*," a string of foreign curses fled his harsh lips. Without penetrating deeper into her, he dipped his head to kiss her. He stroked the side of her face as their lips meshed.

Bussing her lips, chasing her tongue, when he seized it he sucked on it, hard. While plundering her mouth, Vaclav skimmed his hand down her body, stroking over her collarbone to capture a plump breast.

Against her mouth, he murmured, "I love your tits, baby, I will never tire of touching them. Even when they are ripe with milk for our child, or drooping with age, they will always delight me."

Adara smiled while their tongues pursued and mouths rollicked in sync. Pulling back slightly she said, "Who knew the big Romanian mobster could be so poetic, so romantic."

Her breast filling his hand, he kneaded it with hard fingers then pinched her nipple. At her gasp he whispered wickedly, "That is for calling me those the sissy things." His hand softened, then again caressed her robustly.

"I am romantic only with you, never with any other." He glided his palm down over her smooth belly to just barely touch her clitoris. Her hips jumped with a startled sound.

Vaclav murmured with sensuous urging, "Just feel, baby, just feel me." His fingers trickled lightly over her sex.

When a mew simpered from her, and her hips responded by writhing against his hand, he applied more pressure, more dominance and started to push his shaft deeper into her as her silk oozed to lubricate them both.

It became slightly easier to penetrate her now, her hips rippled sinuously under his skillful manipulating fingers.

She sighed when he reached the end of her. "Vâj," her voice a soft rasp.

"Hmm?" He slowly pulled back out while still playing with her clitoris, then pushed carefully all the way back into the very depths of her. "I love when you say *mea* name."

"I, uh…" her body loosened as waves of sensation effervesced over her, every cell tingling. "I can feel you, your, uh, manhood inside me, it's like…throbbing."

"*Da.*" He smiled. "How does it feel?" He pulled almost all the way out again then shoved back inside with more force, a shade faster.

"It- *uhnn...*" his sudden thrust pushed a grunt from her. Her bosom rose to press up against his masculine chest, brushing the dark hair covering the rock-hard slabs of muscles. Feeling it, Vaclav lowered his chest to brush against her pointed little nipples, squash her swollen breasts.

"*Yah?*' Vaclav asked, and thrust harder in her. He felt ready to burst, explode with the amazing feel of her, more amazing than he ever conceived in his mind or invoked in his fantasies of her.

"Oh, Vâj, it's, good, it feels," she grunted with his sudden deep thrust, her body quivered under and around him.

He increased his rhythm, dragging out slow then plunging in faster. He moved both hands to curl around her shoulders holding her as he thrust.

The muscles of his chest flexed, his biceps already huge turned to iron as they braced him on the mattress, he grit his teeth to control himself from driving into her with such powerful force he would hurt her.

Yet, her groans deepened, her gasps sharper as he lunged harder, he began pumping faster. The thick, hard length of him pummeled into her soft dainty body eliciting tiny squeaks and squeals that made the blood rush faster to his dick swelling it impossibly even bigger.

His hand stroked down her body and under her to clutch her bottom, lifting it to meet his plunges, and he had to wrap his arm around her shoulders to hold her from being shoved away from him with his strong rapid thrusts.

Adara writhed beneath him, their bodies coating and rubbing, the friction of their skin meshing with the friction of his shaft plunging in and out of her, slow then fast again.

Releasing her bottom, he reached between them, his expert fingers stroked, pulled and squeezed her enflamed nub. Tiny wheezing screams started peaking in her chest, hitching up her taut throat.

Without pausing his increasingly faster thrusts, Vaclav looked down at her. "Baby," he rasped, the incredible feel of her, the wonderment of finally having her, taking her, making her his, he was holding back as long as he could to savor the feel of her, for as long as possible, he never wanted it to end.

She struggled to lift her heavy lids. Midnight eyes glazed with cloudy desire stared up at him. Damn he wished he could swim naked in their velvety pools. Feel the soft, warm, dark liquid sinuous against his bare skin.

Her plush lips parted with her arduous panting as her orgasm continued climbing, rising, ready to take hold of her, split her body apart.

"That is it, *mea* sweet," he panted, the air in his lungs tight with his body's strain. "Look at me, I have to watch you come. Have you know whom your husband is, who is bringing you to full ripe womanhood. Keep your eyes on me, baby," and he thrust so hard she cried out.

With her cry, he watched her eyes tremble, a pretty pink blush rose over her creamy skin, and her body shimmied in his hands.

His shoulders hunched, one arm around her, the other strumming her sweet sex, Vaclav could see her climax hitting her.

Her eyes blanked and rolled back in her head, her lips fluttered with his name on them.

He moved his fingers faster, rougher, her breasts bounced with his every hard drive deep into her, he'd never seen anything so breathtaking, so damned mesmerizing as Adara in the midst of orgasm.

"Vâj!" she cried, her fingers digging into his broad shoulders, her nails raking his skin, it was great, he loved the pain of her pleasure. And she rocketed over the moon.

Her hips bucked wildly at him, her body thrashing on the sheet, hitting him with its unbridled exuberance. Her breasts now mashing into his chest as he lowered it, pressing harder against her lissome flesh. Her legs lifted to wind around his hips bringing him deeper and deeper inside her clenching silken chasm.

Adara's torso arched to him as the convulsions grabbed her body and racked the living hell out of it. Shrieks exploded from her throat as she cried his name and the scalding spasms took her over, the mad zinging rush of sensation railing uncontrollably through her body.

"Oh *yah* baby," Vaclav growled watching her. "*Da*, fuck me, baby, fuck me with those little hips of yours, *Zue*, so fucking amazing," he spouted a flood of his native words as he felt his dick swell to the bursting point, and his balls burned on fire.

He couldn't hold back anymore. Gripping her ass with his large hands, he lifted her up off the bed and pummeled her like a jackhammer until he was blind and deaf to anything but her and the fire raging inside him.

Fire exploded from his dick, his seed blew up his balls, and they ruptured from him, spewing into her.

Clenching her bottom, Vaclav moved it like it was an extension of his fist, savagely masturbating with her body, he brought her ass up to slam into each of his wild, manic thrusts until he paused deep inside her. His mouth clamped onto her neck, fiercely sucking her flesh as if he could eat her, absorb her, swallow her to possess her completely.

Feeling his seed undulating from his body, he held Adara so tightly to him it was unlikely she could draw a breath. Seizures wracking his body, wringing him inside out, he hissed her name, then roared it, "Oh *mea* fucking *Zue*, Adara!"

He slammed into her, his mind a spinning kaleidoscope, all coherent thought gone. One last violent plunge, and he shuddered as he emptied his all.

He managed to move his bulk slightly to the side so he didn't collapse on her, crush her with his weight as he endured the spasms until they decreased, his breaths rapid and shallow, sweat dripped from his hair, and his hips stabbed into her again until every bit of strength and seed left his body.

Feeling like he'd run a mile flat out, his chest pumping with buffeting inhalations, Vaclav's eyes were shut tight, sweat dripping on the sheet beside Adara. He felt her soft and squirmy, curvy and so amazingly responsive body tucked under him.

Her breathy purls mewed near his ear. So fucking feminine he couldn't stand it.

He pushed his lids up and gazed at her. Those large doe eyes laced with chinchilla lashes, ivory skin framed by luxurious dark waves like spilled roasted coffee. She had grown into the woman he had known she would. Even after her horrendous ordeals, she remained sweet, kind, compassionate, everything that he wasn't.

He rolled more onto his side. Still panting, pulse racing, still semi-hard inside her, he was loathe to leave her warm luscious body. Brushing his fingertips over the stray hair that clung to her damp face, Vaclav smiled at his wife. Her lids were heavy, revealing only dark tones peering blurrily at him.

He murmured, "Baby," and a gentle smile curved her plush lips. Still huffing, he panted, "You *bine*, ah, all right?"

Adara stretched beside him like a resplendent, contented kitten, then curled into his rugged body, facing him. She caressed the side of his face grown scruffy since the morning.

"It was…" The smile broadened. "Wonderful, Vâj. More, unbelievably more mind-blowing than I'd ever heard." The pads of her fingers dusted over his solid jaw, sharp cheekbone.

"For such a…strong aggressive man, you were gentle with me," a giggle rippled from her pretty lips. "At least until towards the end. I think I'll be sore for a while."

His frown expressed anger with himself. "I tried, baby, so hard to not hurt you. You took *mea* breath, *mea* control away; you wiped out *mea* brain so I could scarcely draw a thought. You, ah," his lips pulled in with hope on his face, he asked, "will you want to do it again? I mean, when the soreness leaves?"

His arm rolled for her to lay her head on it then he settled his hand on her hip, his big fingers curled around her plump bottom.

Her head brushed against his arm with her nod, then the smile turned serious. "Vâj, we need to talk."

His body bristled. That always boded ill when a female said they needed to talk.

Vaclav wriggled to sit up and he pulled her up with him to lean against the headboard. His gaze went immediately to her naked breasts and his hand reached out like Pavlov's dog.

Adara brought her arms up to cover her chest. "Wait, please. We need to talk about things, this…marriage."

Skin darkening with his frown that sunk lower with displeasure when she blocked him from touching her, a growl rumbled. She had enjoyed his touch, went up in flames in his arms,

"Adara, why are you preventing me from touching you?" As if she could really stop him if he didn't want to.

She drew her knees up and wrapped her arms around them.

His frown hardened to a scowl. Accent coarse with his ire, he said, "Baby, you are shutting down, shutting me out. Do not do this, please."

Chapter Twenty-Three

Her slight smile warm, eyes caring, Adara said, "I am not shutting down. I want to be with you, 100% fully as your wife, but," her gaze cast down.

Vaclav couldn't help himself, he had to touch her. He twined his fingers around her ankle. Rubbing his thumb on her skin, he caressed her lower leg. "But what? Tell me, anything, is yours, everything I have. Everything I am, baby, is yours."

"I don't want things, Vâj, I want to be treated with respect. Your jealousy is insane; you're going to hurt someone badly someday. A man just looks at me and you go berserk. I won't live like that.

"Instead of hauling me bodily out of a room because you don't like the way I'm dressed, just tell me quietly how you feel and I will oblige your feelings, your objections. I don't want you to feel uncomfortable, but I will not be treated as chattel, your possession to be dragged around or carried off if I refuse to obey."

He said nothing, lips thinned to a tight line, he only watched her as she spoke.

Not encouraged by his silence, she sighed, took a breath and said, "You married me, Vâj, for whatever the reason. I want the respect and trust that goes along with that. I am not your child to jump to do what you say. I expect to be your partner."

Seeing his brows slash down and his mouth open, she said quickly, "Not in your business. However, I am hoping we can talk, some day, about the type of…work that you do."

His brows arched with a slight curve to the side of his mouth. But he said nothing.

"What I mean is," she continued, "I want to be treated as your equal, your life partner. If you can't do that, then," her shoulder lifted in resignation, "I will do everything in my power to dissolve our relationship, deal or no."

The dark brows popped then lowered in anger and worry over eyes that had instantly turned to blue ice. "Adara, you will not leave me. Ever. I-"

She snapped, "Don't you dare say you own me. You do not. And you will find that out quick enough if you say that. Vâj," she stroked the arm that was still holding her leg but had stopped caressing it. His fingers tightened around her calf.

Her soft face gentled. "I loved what we...uh, just did." Her cheeks pinked in remembrance of her wantonness at his touch. "I wish to do it again, the feel of you on me, in me, touching me," her gaze slid from his eyes to his mouth.

Full rugged lips that tantalized her mouth and her sex, driving her into delirium. "I want more of it, Vâj, but not to the detriment of my life, my pride, my freedom."

His face lightened, a smile lifted his dour expression, his hand resumed caressing her leg.

"I mean it, Vâj, I mean what I'm saying. If you think you can bully me and humiliate me, then what we just shared, enjoyed, won't happen again. You would have to force me and then it would be fast, straight sex. Rape. Nothing more. And, I repeat, no matter how much I am starting to care for you, I will find a way to leave you if you bully me."

The blue eyes brightened at her words. She had never expressed any feelings of interest in him before. In fact, he had been pretty sure she didn't even like him much.

"You care for me?" he asked, his voice hushed. The heavy masculine brow lifted, sharp cheekbones softened, the tense jaw loosened. His big hand wrapped around her leg stroked up and down.

"Vâj, please. This isn't about whether or not I care for you; it's about your treatment of me. Not giving me the freedom to come and go as I please."

"Ah, sweetheart," he gathered her against him. Wrapping his burly arms around her, he kissed her gently, her lips then her forehead, the top of her hair. "I will do as you ask. I have never had a serious relationship, never been with a woman I wanted to keep. The fact that I would ever marry would have brought hilarious laughter from everyone that knows me."

Shaking his head, he cuddled her chin raising it so they were looking at each other. "I am unpracticed with this gentleman behavior shit. I am a tough, viol- ah, aggressive man, tis unlikely that I could change who I am. But," she started to turn her head away, sadness subduing her beauty.

"Adara." He held onto her jaw, keeping her from moving from him. "I am a brute, but I would never hurt you. I will do *mea* best not to bully you, and," his smile came with a wince.

"The uh, jealousy. Tis not something I have ever experienced before and it just grabs me and takes me over. I see a guy leering, ogling you, *touching* you, I," shaking his head, he dragged a hand down his face. "I just go crackers. I see red, a blind rage takes me over. But-"

She cut him off, "I, um, appreciate you at least talking about this with me. Telling me the truth, that you can't change-"

"Baby," he gave her jaw a little shake. "It chills *mea* blood to the bone to think of you leaving me. And, hell," his chest barreled with a deep inhale, he expelled it slowly, regret crunching his face.

"I cannot stand it if I hurt you, your feelings I mean. You mean everything to me, you are *mea* whole world. Last thing I want to do is humiliate you, shame you, treat you like a possession, a child, a broad, a whore."

He pulled her face closer to his and said softly, "You deserve the best of everything, baby, I will do everything I can to make you happy. I swear to *Zue*, on *mea* honor, babe, I will work to do as you ask."

The doe eyes widened, her mouth dropped open in surprise. "You mean that, Vâj?"

Vaclav wrapped her in his strong arms holding her tightly against the warm strength of his powerful chest. He stroked her back, caressing her soft skin, loving her. His hands stroked up her arms, he held her away slightly.

"Adara, you are *mea* wife. I want you to be happy. I do not want to lose you, I cannot lose you. I will do all I can to prevent you from wanting to leave me. However," placing his finger under her chin he tipped it up.

His tone turned serious, "I am sorry. You are Salvatore Valentina's daughter, and *mea* wife. You know damned well is not safe for you out there on your own. I cannot allow it. I would rather lose your affection than your life." He would chain her to their bed if he thought she would try to go out on her own, even if it made her hate him.

Her head dropped, the long dark hair covering her like a sable cloak. Her resigned sigh sad and laborious, she raised her head to him. "I know."

"I cannot let you out there," he gestured with his hand, "without *mea* protection."

"But school, Vâj, you promised," she tried to smooth out the whine in her voice.

"Adara," he murmured again, brushing her hair back then let the lux locks slide through his fingers before sifting free.

"You have been searching the online colleges. I told you that you can enroll and do your studies online. Perhaps," he said, his wide shoulders bumped in a shrug, "by the time you get your degree maybe things will have changed and it will be safer to be out there on your own." She would always be protected, whether she knew it or not.

"I would have to take the tests in person," she reminded him, her head drooped sadly again.

"Then I will drive you there."

"What if you aren't around? I would flunk out because you couldn't take me to school?" her head shook in exasperation. "You treat me like a child."

His smile cleared the worry and anger from his stone chiseled face, then his expression hardened.

"*Da*, I know, I do. Tis because I watched you grow up. Waited in hell while you did. Those years when you were in prison? I thought I would lose *mea* mind. I could not see you, talk to you, touch you. I fretted every single day if you were all right, if you were being…abused."

An unsteady breath shook out. Inhaling relief that she was there with him, safe and sound and bloody naked in his arms, the rare smile took over his harsh face. "I knew from day one that you would one day be mine, but I could not claim you until you became an adult."

Her nose wrinkled, mouth curdled, "So you did lust after me when I was a child? That's totally perverted, Vâj."

"Huh. *Mea* friends always accused me of the same thing. *Na*, *mea* sweet. When you were little, it was your eyes. Such unearthly beauty, those huge dark wells of chocolate, so mesmerizing, I fell right in, I was instantly possessed. You were so fucking precious. I felt," he thought about it.

"I felt the desire to be near you, to see you, protect you. You were always so delicate, so fragile, I constantly feared for your safety. That wretched family you came from," he shook his head again.

"Tis hard to explain. I had *na* sexual desire for you when you were a child, that would be fucking sick. But, I was drawn to you like a tide sucking me out to sea, I couldn't fight it. I just knew, like I said, that when you grew up you would be mine. As you matured, *mea* sexual feelings for you developed, and girl," he shook his head with a wry smile, "they hit me hard."

Her eyes flit over his face in confusion. "But, that's…bizarre."

He shrugged. "Maybe. But *mea* attraction to you now is purely adult for adult. Hell babe, those tits, you did not have them as a child and I cannot keep *mea* eyes off them, *mea* hands off them." As he said the words his palms closed over her breasts, and he caressed them, a groan ground out with his hiss of extreme pleasure.

"Vâj," she protested and pushed at him until he released her.

He leaned back, his heavily hooded eyes filled with his hunger for her torched with passion.

"You see?" he smiled. "I want to fuck and fondle and kiss the adult woman, not the child. I was captivated by the child, those eyes, I understand now when they say 'she has haunting eyes.'" He closed his own blue orbs and shook his head. Opening them, his smile curved bigger.

"You bought me with those fucking doe eyes, baby, and your sweetness, *Zue*, so sweet, Adara, I could barely stand it, and I wanted it. I wanted to possess your sweetness, suck it in, drink it in." His eyes closed again, then they rose to hers.

"And now, *mea* precious wife, I have the hots so bad for you, there are days I think I will blow apart from the hunger, the need for you, for that damned righteous body." He grasped her arms to tug her back against the shelter of his big body.

Sighing, her resistance flowed out taking the tension with it. Her shoulders relaxed as did the strain in her face, her jaw unclenched.

Curling up to him, she asked, "Did you mean it about what you said, you would not bully me, not behave like a jealous buffoon and brawl with every man who looks my way, and not drag me off like a misbehaving child?"

"*Da*, I will try my damndest." Nodding, his mouth descended to hers. "Ah, you are the sweetest, juiciest, hottest little gumdrop in the world."

As their lips touched, cuddling her in his stalwart arms, he exclaimed, "And you are mine, baby, all mine." *And we are gonna fuck like bunnies.*

Chapter Twenty-Four

They showered together, soaped each other endlessly until he lifted her and took her against the wall. Then they showered again and now were in separate rooms dressing.

Wearing cargo shorts and deck shoes, Vaclav was just pulling a t-shirt over his muscled chest, when she came out of the other room wearing a little sundress and heeled sandals.

Tossing a short-sleeved unbuttoned shirt over the T to hide the gun in a holster at the back of his shorts, his brows jerked up, lips pushed out. Failing at tempering his voice, he said querulously, "You really thinking about wearing that shit outside?"

A piqued frown pressed her mouth down. "Please remember that I did not purchase these clothes, your shopper did. I normally wouldn't wear this in public, but, this is a test, to see if you meant what you said. We will go out and join the party, and you will control your jealousy. You think you can do that?"

"But- but, baby, you are half-naked, you are not even wearing a bra, your fucking tits are bouncing the hell all over," his anger was heating up, red crept up his neck, he rubbed agitated at the tip of an ear.

The lightweight red sundress with tiny yellow flowers was a halter that cradled her breasts while showing how perfect and plump they were, and it tied snugly around her tiny waist. The flouncy skirt drifted around the tops of her thighs, the sexy heeled sandals made even her toes look seductive.

His cock was already swelling and he'd be damned if he wanted every other Tom, Dick and horndog getting hard over his wife's body.

Pulling her petite frame up as tall as she could, glaring at him in the eye, her hands curled on her hips, she said with crisp rebuke, "Are you saying everything you said to me when we were in bed was a lie?"

His jaw jutted, bottom lip pushed out further, brows daggered down between his eyes he was keeping hooded so she couldn't see them. "Baby, you do not see what you look like. Go, look in the mirror. You are a walking wet-dream. You cannot-"

"No," she snapped. "You either come out with me peacefully," she held a hand up. "No, I can see the look of intention on your face, you want to strip this off me and dress me up in loose clothes."

Her voice softened, "Vâj, you know that's how I normally choose to dress. I don't flaunt my body, I don't want the attention, but," she stroked his tattooed arm, "I want you to prove to me you meant what you said. This will be a test."

Growling under his breath, he muttered, "Some fucking test. Wants to parade herself half-naked in front of other men and she wants me to stuff *mea* alpha feelings. Sure." Foul curses thankfully in his own language streamed out as he scraped his fingers in his hair then down his face.

A frustrated brooding sigh groused out. "*Bine*. Fine. We better go now before I change *mea* mind." He'd waited so long for her he didn't want to share her with the world. Why can't she be satisfied staying in their suite, with him?

He sure as hell didn't need anyone else around but her. Sure, he had friends that he enjoyed their company, but right now, she was his world and he wanted to savor her.

Adara slid her arm through his and gushed, "Oh Vâj, thank you. You can do it, you'll see." She admired his own body. "You look fabulous in those shorts, they show off your strong legs and how muscular your chest is, and those huge manly biceps in that T."

His neck heating in embarrassment at her compliment, he nodded and said grumpily, "Let's go," and opened the door. They trod out the door, his feet plodding and heavy, hers light and floaty.

Just as they left their chambers, her heel caught and she tumbled forward. Vaclav threw out his hand to catch her.

When he steadied her, she smoothed her dress. He said smugly, "You cannot even walk without tripping and you expect me to let you run around out there alone? Unprotected? You're outta your mind," he shook his head with condescension. "Your ma said you were as graceful as a butterfly but clumsy as shit."

Her lips pursed in a frown, "I don't think those were her exact words."

"Whatever, gives me a reason to hold on tightly to you." He smiled, caught her chin and lifted it to kiss her.

After a deep smoldering kiss, she bent back from his face and said, "You will not keep me glued to your side. You need to trust me to handle myself. I can't have you looming over me everywhere I go."

His lips pushed out again with his scowl. They left the hotel to join the people out on the patio mingling around the pool.

Tucking her hand in his arm, they wandered, mingled with the few people they had met.

Brad and Madeline, Tim and Gloria, Jason and Jasmina had pulled lawn chairs into a cluster. They all held drinks, everyone was laughing at something Brad had just said when Vaclav and Adara joined them.

Vaclav picked up two chairs from around a table and brought them to the group. But Adara didn't sit down.

"I'm going to go get us something to drink. I want a piña colada, Jasmina said they're refreshing. What would you like, Vâj?" Holding her hand out for money, she smiled mildly at the thunder that was storming his face.

The pair glared at each other with the group snickering around them. Finally, with a pissed huff, Vaclav pulled out his wallet and handed some bills to her, said gruffly, "Get me a Coors."

Her grin bright, she said gaily, "Thanks, honey, I'll be right back!" Her skirt twirled as she spun to go to the bar. Vaclav stood scowling at her back.

"Hey, Vaclav, bro, she'll be fine, sit down." Brad grinned at him and nudged Madeline who twisted a lip and turned her head from her husband with an unladylike snort.

Grunting his displeasure, Vaclav flopped heavily into a chair keeping an eye on the flouncy red dress.

Brad snickered, "I told you guys they were going to go at it." Everyone in the circle chuckled.

Vaclav tipped his eyes at Brad, not smiling. "What?"

"Hell bro." Brad grinned at Vaclav then the rest of the group. "Before, the way that girl looked in that skimpy suit, the way *you* looked at her in that suit," everyone laughed except Madeline.

"Then the way you hauled her ass inside, in cave-dwelling days it would have been by the hair or over your shoulder. Shit, we knew you were going to go at it like minks." Everyone broke into louder laughter.

Vaclav's temple pulsed, the tips of his ears tinted slightly red.

"And," Brad wasn't done, "you two come skipping out now. Her cheeks are rosy as hell and she's radiant and smiling so shyly, and you have that satisfied smirk on your face, you glow like a light bulb when you look at her, man, yeah you guys did the tango. Didn't I tell ya, Mad?" He nudged his unsmiling wife again.

Tim scowled a little. "Lucky you, bro." Glaring at Gloria he snarked, "I asked for a little afternoon delight and what'd I get? Shit. That's what."

Gloria gave him the dirtiest look. She said, "I had a headache," and snapped her head from him.

Vaclav could care less what was going on with them. His attention was on his wife across the patio. Men stared at her, Vaclav wanted to go and punch out every one of them.

He pulled out his pack of European cigars, angrily tapped one out, fished a lighter out of his shorts and lit it. Puffing fiercely on it, he glowered at the men that lusted after his bride.

While men eyed Adara like she was the lone piece of candy in the dish, women hanging around the courtyard had no compunction in giving Vaclav the once, and twice over and smiling their clear invitations to him.

He looked past them as if they were invisible. They wore make-up painted on with a trowel, hair teased all over their heads and wore extremely provocative clothes. Shit, they would be more covered up if they were in their underwear.

He didn't hear a word anyone at their group said, his attention never diverted from his wife, not even aware he was holding his breath.

Da, he knew he was obsessed with her, had been for over fifteen years. He'd fought it, but couldn't stop it, so he had learned to accept it. His fear for her safety was way over the top, a constant worry for him. But then he knew that was a very real concern.

Her Uncle Massimo, Fiorenzo, the fucking Pakistani drug lord, there were others that would snatch her in a heartbeat if he looked the other way for a split second.

He felt relatively safe here, halfway across the world from home with his core team nearby. One of his employees had searched the travel nets and found the place.

His gaze left Adara for a second and trickled around the hotel, he unwound a hair. It was beautiful, serene with sunny blue skies, the ritzy hotel, balmy air, *da*, it was nice. His eyes traveled back to the red dress and a faint smile touched his lips. At long last, after all this time, he had her, she was his. For good.

Finally, Adara turned from the bar with her white frothy drink and his beer and started back to the table. With her every move, her breasts jiggled in the tight, light material, the skirt flipped around her thighs with teasing peeps of tantalizing flesh with her every graceful step. Eyes flicked to her like bugs to a lamp.

Vaclav forced himself to stay seated until she arrived, then he stood up and held her chair out for her.

She set their drinks on a small, beige rattan glass table then sat down. "Hi everyone," Adara shyly greeted the group.

They responded with their own smiles and greetings, except Madeline, who kept her cool gaze latched onto Vaclav, her gaze strolling up and down his burly tattooed arms. The foreign words inked on his body kept her attention.

The group sipped their drinks as people took turns chatting, offering pieces of their lives to their new friends.

A trio of men sauntered over, Brad greeted them. "Hey bros, glad you could make it. Let me introduce you. This is Bruce, Glenn and Dale," he made the introductions.

"We met in a bar the other night. This bastard," he grinned at Bruce, "beat the pants off me at billiards. I owe him a drink." The men fist-bumped and they all settled into the group.

Under the low hooded lids, Vaclav watched men passing by and also the men present checking out the women in their throng, then their attention loitered on an unaware Adara.

Seeing Vaclav's scathing glower, most gawkers walking by scurried on, but in their own group, Tim stared unblinking at Adara. Brad's eyes bounced back to her often even when she wasn't talking. The new males stared unabashedly at her.

Fuck me, Vaclav seethed silently, the wedding band wasn't doing it. He pulled Adara's chair closer to his, then very deliberately, he slowly lifted the hair on the far side of her neck and nestled it over one shoulder.

Casually, he curled his big hand around her slender neck, and stroked his fingers over the dark hickey he had put on her pearly skin. His movements were discreet, subtle, Adara was oblivious to his displaying his brand on her.

It was his way of staking his claim, his ownership, showing the other men she was his. She would be embarrassed and furious if she knew what he was doing. Hell, he was practically pissing on her.

Bending to her, he delicately set his mouth on her skin, kissing her softly. While appearing to just be nuzzling with his wife, Vaclav was making a statement. Mine, back off. Licking her flesh, he took little nips and nibbles, she stretched her neck like a purling kitten, her smile soft, eyes closed.

223

His gaze trundled to each male, stared them in the eye until each one looked away. Then he realized, the shade of a smile lifted the side of his mouth, every man had a hard-on, and the women looked visibly heated. Half of them were squirming in their seats and licking their lips.

Hell, he had turned the lot of them on just by kissing his wife's neck. *Freaking hot.*

Adara pushed her chair back. Vaclav's arm tightened around her. She pushed harder. "Vâj, I need to go to the powder room."

His mouth at her ear, his breath wisped her hair, he murmured, "*Bine*, I will take you." He went to move his chair back but her hand came up to press on his bicep.

She whispered, "No. I am perfectly capable of going to the restroom on my own. I will go to the one right inside the door there." Before he could respond, she shoved her chair back and jumped up and was moving off.

"Adara," he growled, his ridged brow hard over his annoyed eyes, but she was already gone. Frustrated air growled noisily from his lungs. All the men in their crowd stared at her skirt flouncing around her little round bum as she strolled off.

"Shit, bro, you have it bad," one of the new guys, Bruce, chuckled next to him.

Vaclav forced his eyes away from Adara to glare at the man, grunted, "Whatever."

Swiping a hand over his slick black hair, one of the other men, Dale, took a sip of his drink and grinned. "You, my large friend, are pussy-whipped."

"You want to shut up right now, bro," Vaclav warned, his eyes flitting back to follow Adara's path. His brows slanted over his narrowed eyes.

Two men had stopped her near the door and were each vying for her attention. Vaclav's hands rolled into tight fists, his teeth clenched. The vein at his temple batted like mad.

"Yeah, there it is, bro," Bruce laughed, "you got fucking pussy written all over your possessive face."

Without looking at him, Vaclav's voice dropped to a low growl, "I said shut the fuck up, asshole."

Bruce and Dale were still standing. Glenn dragged a chair over and made himself comfortable. He and Madeline were soon in a flirtatious conversation. Brad didn't seem to mind.

Across the patio, the two men with Adara were imperceptibly moving closer and closer to her. Both had their eyes glued to her breasts. She was trying to dodge them without causing a scene. Vaclav tried to force the heat, the rage down, tried to swallow the urge to go over and flatten both the fuckers.

"She is one hot piece of ass, I'll tell ya, dude," Bruce remarked, watching Adara across the piazza. "I wouldn't kick that bitch out of my bed for sure. Hell," a smirk puckered his lips, "I'd even eat that cunt, and bro, I don't do that very often, but shit," he stared hard at her. "I would want a taste of that."

Growls deep down in his chest, about to erupt like roaring lava from a volcano, getting to his feet, his voice filled with warning, Vaclav said, "That is *mea* wife you are talking about, fucker, shut the hell up before I shut you up."

Bruce chuckled, ignoring the seething Romanian's warning. Not listening, he kept on, "Damn nice titties, bro. I wouldn't mind getting my hands on those. Firm and high and round, yeah," he sighed.

Then he foolishly continued, "Makes a man's hands itch to grab those babies and squeeze the shit out of them, right? Maybe get off stroking my cock through her fucking bountiful cleavage. Those tits are out of town, dude, wish youd'a untied that halter and let it fall, shown us those bare babies while you were sucking on her neck. I think I'm gonna try to hit that. I bet her snatch is tight, I could finger it-"

Blam!

Vaclav punched him in the face.

Bruce was out cold before he hit the ground. Vaclav stepped from him just as Adara turned around to look for him with a silent plea to come to her. She couldn't ditch the two men; they weren't leaving her alone as she asked.

He hurried over to her. "Hey, baby," he said, smiling at the two men who looked up at the fiercely dangerous man, and promptly turned and left them.

He walked her to the ladies room, and waited for her to come out. Then they started back outside.

A happy smile drew up her face. "I'm proud of you, Vâj. You didn't cause a scene with those men that were hassling me."

"*Da.*" He shrugged coolly. "I told you I could control mă, that is myself," he said with a sniff. "I am not a barbarian, you know. Come, let's get something to eat." He smiled down at her pretty face and dropped his arm around her shoulders.

As they started for the food tables, he glanced back and saw the group they had been hanging with gawking at the ground then up at him in horrified dismay. Several men lifted the unconscious Bruce up and toted him inside the hotel.

Adara and Vaclav filled plates from the food on the buffet table. It overflowed with chicken wings, potato salad, macaroni salad, and tons of other picnic food with gooey things like brownies for dessert.

The couple stood leisurely near a plastic palm tree nibbling at their food chatting comfortably. Nearby, a man kept staring at Adara.

Not noticing the warning glares Vaclav sent him, his eyes narrowed as he studied her. Vaclav was just about to say something to him when the man's eyes widened and he snapped his fingers.

"Yeah," he said as he moved to them staring oddly at Adara. Then he smiled. "I have it. You remind me so much of someone. The same big eyes only yours are much darker. You have the same full rosebud-like lips, the high curving cheekbones, except she has blonde hair but her brows are dark. You look so much like her, a younger, fresher, prettier version, but still…"

The handsome guy, maybe mid-thirties with wavy dark brown hair and twinkling blue eyes smiled at her but held his hand out for Vaclav to shake. The big bruiser's expression made it clear he would not tolerate anyone touching the stunning woman beside him. "I'm Forrester."

Vaclav glared at his outstretched hand for a few beats, then grudgingly shook it using all his self-control not to break it.

Adara blinked at him several times, then her face whitened. "What is her name? This woman you described?"

Vaclav's glare turned to a frown.

"Uh, Este, Este Darceaux." Seeing the color drain from Adara's face, his brow furrowed. He asked, "Do you know her?"

Her throat too tight to let out much sound, she whispered, "She is my mother."

Vaclav rolled his arm around Adara and pulled her close to him, he said, "Babe, that is highly unlikely." His glare darkened at the man, "Forrester, you are-"

But Forrester was nodding emphatically. "Yeah, yeah, that's it, mother and daughter. You look like you could be her twin, her daughter." He squinted at her like he was looking through a camera lens. Said with his head shaking in astonishment, "The resemblance is freaky."

"Oh my gosh," Adara cried, her hand on her chest. She looked up at Vaclav. "Vâj, it's her. Este is Estella, Darceaux was her mother's maiden name. My mother moved here to France, to her family's home, that's why they could never find her. Oh, Vâj …"

Vaclav aimed a scowl through angry slit eyes that could scare the dead. Smoothing the violence from his face, he pasted on a smile and petted Adara's hair. "Baby, tis not possible. The private investigators would have found her. I am sorry, I never wanted to say this to you, but she is likely dead."

He had hired investigators right off the bat to find Estella and force her to admit her guilt and get Adara out of prison. But when they turned up empty he presumed one of Salvatore's men had somehow learned, or guessed the truth and took her out.

Her head shaking adamantly back and forth, the velvety waves swishing across her back, she exclaimed, "No, Vaclav, it's her, I know it is." She moved to stand closer to Forrester. "Sir, please, tell me where-"

"Adara." Vaclav stepped in front of her. He said firmly, "I will look into this. You-"

Anger flashed from her dark eyes. "No. I am her daughter, you'll hurt her. I will find her. I need to talk to her, see her," she stepped aside so Vaclav wasn't blocking her and said to Forrester, "Please, where can I find her?"

"Adara," Vaclav's voice turned hard as concrete. He said uncompromisingly, "I will investigate this. I do not want you involved."

Chocolate brows arched with irritation. Squaring her shoulders, Adara turned to face him. "How dare you? This is my business, not yours, Vaclav."

He also turned to fully face her, face dark, implacable. The warm, gentle, lusting Vâj of earlier was gone. The ex-enforcer, the mobster Vaclav Braşov was back.

All hard angles and hunched broad shoulders, his voice dark and low, he said painstakingly slowly, "I said I will deal with this, Adara. Your business *is mea* business. You do not know this man here, you do not know if tis a trick, if tis a setup to con you, lure you out in the open, *na*," he shook his head coldly at her. "I am your husband, this is *mea* business, and you will do as I say-"

"Oh!" Lashes flying up over furious eyes, she snapped, "How long did that last? You said you wouldn't order me around, bully me-"

Vaclav worked to backtrack, smooth the frigid hardness he knew was on his face, loosen the muscles in his body that were taut, ready to fight anything that could, would, harm her.

"Ah, baby," he tried to smile, soften his expression, lighten his voice. "I told you, your safety is all that matters. I will do anything I have to, to protect you. Now, let me ask him some questions-"

Turning from Vaclav, seeing no one there, "It's too late," she said in dismay, "he's gone." While the couple had been arguing, Forrester disappeared.

"What?" Vaclav spun around, scanning the area looking for the man with short brown hair, but he was gone. "Aw damn," he muttered, stabbing his fingers through his hair in ire at the man taking off before Vaclav could get information from him.

The man suddenly disappearing like that clearly showed he was up to no good.

Vaclav turned to Adara. She was stalking towards the patio door back into the hotel.

"Shit," he spat and jogged after her.

Chapter Twenty-Five

After a long hot-tempered argument, Vaclav stood near the door to their suite. "*Bine*, baby, I have to go."

He needed to meet with his men and had previously scheduled a meeting in thirty minutes otherwise he would never consider leaving her.

Even though he was on his honeymoon and out of the country, he still had a business to run.

Adara stood a few feet away, arms crossed over her chest, mouth bunched up expressing her anger with him.

Vaclav's chest rose in a deep breath as he fought for his patience.

Heaving a sigh, keeping his voice moderate and his face as smoothed of aggression as he could get it, he said, "Sweetheart. We have been over it. I already called Tito and Kid to canvass the people here, the staff, see if anyone knew this Forrest guy. Ivod will have the cameras pulled, inside and out."

Seeing the distraught look creasing her smooth brow, he said softly, "Baby, I promise, we will find this Forrester, and if it really is your mother," his voice indicating he not for a moment believed it was, "then we will also find her. Now," he cocked his head and gave her a little pout. "Do not make me leave without a kiss, get your ass over here."

Her lips twitched as she tried to stifle the smile that threatened. The huge, tough, ex-enforcer looked silly, but so cute with his pout, she couldn't resist him. Adara strolled over stopping a few feet from him.

He snatched out his hand, grabbed her arm and pulled her to him. Hauling her into his arms, he growled, "When I say get your ass over here, that means all the way, babe."

Tilting her head up she said with sassy boldness, "I do not answer to a potty-mouthed dictator."

The strain of their argument and him having to leave her flowed from his tight expression. A sly smile crooked up his rugged face. "Ah, this tells me a little girl needs some discipline, some punishment for her fresh mouth. What do you think?" He slid his hand under her hair to palm her nape, the other hand skimmed down to the inner curve of her lower back.

Now she pouted with a frown. "Are you threatening to spank me again, Vâj? We talked about this, you promised you wouldn't bully me."

"Ah, sweet." He clipped the end of her chin with two fingers lifting it. His smile sexy-evil, he said silkily, "A husband disciplining his smart-mouthed wife is not bullying, tis teaching."

He spoke before she could, "Now, you promise me you will not leave this room. *Mea* guys are all over the place, you need anything, you get scared, whatever, you call *mea* cell and I will have someone here in the blink of an eye. You got that?"

Adara dragged her fingers through the sides of his hair to pull his head down. She planted her lips on his effectively distracting him from his never-ending issuing orders to her. The kiss heated them both instantly.

Vaclav put both hands on her bottom and tugged her in. Grinding their hips together, his bulging cock pushed hard against his slacks to get at her sex, he groaned into her mouth then moved a hand to clutch a breast. He squeezed too hard and she pulled back with a little moue of protest.

His chest rising and falling with heavy breaths, a guilty grin nicked sheepishly up the side of his mouth. "Sorry, babe, you just get me so damned hot. Ah," he combed his hands through his hair that she had so amorously mussed.

"When I come back, sweet, you better be naked lying spread-eagle on our bed waiting for me. I would prefer you on your back so I can see those tits and pretty pussy, but," he lifted a shoulder. "I will not complain if tis your fine ass that greets me. Just make sure those legs are spread wide. I want to see it all the second I enter the bedroom."

A laugh burbled out of her lush lips, "Ha! Giving me orders again! What if I'm not naked, not on the bed?"

His eyes narrowed in lewd threat at her, his mouth curved up in a sinful smile. "Hmm, then we will see how long and hard your punishment will be. I think you will not be able to sit for a week-" and he smacked her butt so hard she jumped with a squeak.

"Hey," she muttered, frowning while rubbing her bottom. "That wasn't nice."

"Just a preview, *mea* sweet wife of what will happen if I come back and you are not buck naked lying on our bed with your arms out waiting to welcome me, and those gorgeous gams of yours spread as wide as you can get them. I plan to get *mea* fill of you, tonight. All night."

His voice husky, he said, "I plan on putting more of these," he ran his fingertips over the hickey on her neck, "all over your beautiful body. And I want to eat that sweet pussy into tomorrow then we-"

"Vaclav Braşov!" she gasped his full name, slapping his arm, red flew up her face.

His laugh barked out a thundering clap. He gave her another quick kiss and said, "Just warning you, babe. You are so adorable when you are embarrassed over sex, when I talk dirty. Now, be good," and he kissed her again, smacked her hard on the tush and fled out the door laughing when he heard a pillow hit the door behind him.

Adara flit around picking up their clothes strewn about from their love-making earlier and his getting dressed for his meeting. She took a shower and dressed in white jeans and a white frilly blouse and dried her hair.

She was heading to the kitchenette to fix something to eat when she noticed something lying on the floor in front of the door. Brows lowered quizzically, she went over and picked it up.

Her name was scrawled across the folded paper. She opened it, and her hand clapped over her mouth.

The note said:

'Adara Valentina, this is your mother. A lovely young man told me you were here. I am alive and well and I am dying to see you. Leave immediately, I have a taxi waiting for you. Tell no one, especially Vaclav, it would put me in grave danger. I have so little time, please come, please hurry. I can't wait to see you, my darling daughter.

All my love, your mother, Estella Valentina.'

She stared at it, read it again and again in astonished disbelief. "Oh my gosh, Mama!"

All the hell Estella had begotten on her vanished from Adara's mind. All she could think about was the years without her mother, and thinking she was likely dead since no one has heard from her since that fateful day she killed her husband and left her child to suffer for her wicked deed.

Adara whispered, "I have to go…"

She glanced over at the landline. Since she rarely left the hotel, and never without Vaclav, she didn't have a cell. She contemplated, should she call him? He would only yell at her and tell her to stay there, wait for him. But if she did, it might be too late.

The car waiting downstairs was the only link to her mother, she couldn't take the chance in losing it. Besides, the letter said 'don't tell Vaclav' as it could put Estella in danger.

Making up her mind, Adara dropped the letter on a table and ran to put her shoes on.

Grabbing a jacket, the temperature had suddenly dropped the last hour or so from an early autumn cold front pushing through.

She peered out the door, looking for any of Vaclav's men. The hallway was vacant. She hurried to the back stairwell. Rushing down the steps, when she emerged from the staircase she scurried for the main entrance to the hotel.

When she reached it, one of the doormen held the door open for her.

His uniform was tan with black trim on the sleeves, the buttons were gold and a black bowtie was in place under his starched white collar neat as a pin.

His slightly flaccid face jiggled as he bowed. In highly accented English, he said with stiff friendliness, "Mrs. Brașov." About twenty pounds overweight, his hairline was receding, little of the light brown hair was left but he had wings over his ears.

Adara blinked, it will take a while for her to get used to hearing her called that. She still couldn't believe she'd married a mobster, former number one enforcer, Vaclav Brașov.

A shiver ran through her at the thought. He will certainly spank her bottom red as a tomato when he finds out she left without him.

The doorman glanced around, brows lowered in a frown. "Madam, where is Mr. Brașov?"

The help had been heavily versed in the demands of the dangerous man. No one was to get near his wife. Absolutely no one touched her, no strangers were allowed to speak to her, and the staff was to keep conversation with her at a minimum.

The mobster had insisted on meeting any attendants that would be coming to the room so he knew who was knocking on the door so they wouldn't get a nice bullet hole between their eyes. Goose bumps rolled up the doorman's arms at the thought.

"I, uh, he's uh, meeting me. Told me to wait outside for him. He has a taxi, see, it's right there, Mr. Streeves," she told him, pointing to the yellow taxicab idling right out front.

"Ah." The doorman looked all around; there was no sign of Brașov or one of his men. The big man never let her out of his sight. Something was wrong. "Madam, perhaps you should-"

She said quickly, "Yes, he will be right down, thank you so much," and she hurried out the door and ran to the taxi before Streeves could make a ruckus.

Opening the door, she hopped in the back and said urgently, "If you are waiting for Adara Valentina, that's me and you should really floor it out of here."

The man was already staring at her for the way she suddenly jumped into the car. He nodded, and seeing the doorman blowing a whistle and waving, he punched the gas pedal and the taxi tore off around the circular entranceway, down the drive, and out to the street.

Adara sat back and let out her held breath. She turned around and looked out the back window and sighed in relief when she saw that they weren't being followed.

"You're taking me to my mother?" she asked when she calmed some. Butterflies were flapping up a storm in her belly, Vaclav was going to kill her.

The driver lifted a shoulder in a half-shrug. "I don't know, Miss. My instructions are to take you to a building at Fontainebleau and Douglas, that's all I know, hon." He turned his attention to his driving. There was a slight hint of a Spanish accent in the twenty-something driver's voice.

Adara settled herself, crossing her legs and folding her hands in her lap. She was nervous. Anxious and apprehensive to see her mother. The abuse she'd suffered at her mother's hands was starting to filter back. The abusive beatings, the ugly verbal whippings.

And of course, Estella had her daughter take the rap for the murder of Salvatore, sending her to prison and turning her into a pariah. Then she had disappeared, apparently not caring what happened to Adara. Without even a letter or phone call, she left her to suffer at the hands of her monstrous uncle.

Adara had survived everything, but at what a price. Her relatives, old friends want nothing to do with her thinking she'd killed her own father out of spite or anger. She couldn't get a job as a convicted murderer.

Her gangster uncle had viciously beaten her, rented her out, was going to sell her, and then she had been taken- and ultimately to save her life, was forced to marry Vaclav Brașov, a man she had feared since a small child,.

Her cheeks heated with a smile. Recalling their vigorous, passionate love-making, she was starting to think it was all worth it to be with Vaclav.

Her heart fluttered, then the butterflies tumbled as she thought again how livid he would be, and what he might do to her when he got his hands on her. Well, no point in thinking about that now.

She would just clear her head of everything, and wait until she spoke with her mother. Maybe Estella was going to beg for her forgiveness; maybe she had matured into a better woman. Maybe. But if she had, wouldn't she have contacted her only daughter before now?

Maybe she didn't know Adara was out of prison. Maybe she hadn't been able to try to reach her, she said she was in danger and hadn't much time.

The taxi stopped in front of a café. The entire front was glass. Adara sat frozen. Her mother was there. Right inside.

She could see her through the glass, sitting at a table staring off into space.

Adara sat stunned. Deep down she hadn't actually believed her mother would be there. And here she was, alive, apparently well, and waiting for her.

A gulp caught in her throat, she struggled to swallow it, she couldn't make herself move. What should she say to her mother? What will her mother say to her? What if-

"We're here, Miss," The cab driver said. When Adara didn't move, he got out of the taxi and went around and opened her door.

Holding his hand out for her to take, he said, "Miss? We're here."

Blinking rapidly, her lashes flapped up and down, her heart clogged in her throat. Adara took the driver's hand and allowed him to help her out. When she was on the walk, the driver headed back to his cab.

Adara never saw him leave; her eyes were trained on the woman behind the glass.

Taking a huge breath and letting it out slowly, Adara made her feet move, forced herself to walk to the door of the café.

When she entered, a hostess came over to her with a smile. But Adara's eyes had never left Estella. She murmured, "I'm meeting someone," and like a moving statue, she threaded through the tables until she reached Estella. Adara stood at the table, Estella didn't look up.

"Mama," her voice soft, hushed with hammering nerves.

Estella calmly raised her head to look at her daughter. Nothing changed in her face. Not a flicker of emotion, no interest in the changes in Adara over the years. She appeared calm, almost…indifferent. She held a teacup in her hand; she set it down with a light clink. "Adara," her flat greeting was chaste, without inflection.

"Um." Adara shifted from one foot to the other. "Do- uh, don't you want to…hug me?"

Estella's dark brows lowered with slight disdain. "Really, Adara," her voice haughty, she reprimanded her, "have you not learned any manners or decorum in all these years? One does not have public displays of affection in public."

The older woman was still blonde but now hints of grey showed in her brunette roots. Her eyes brown but were still as bloodshot as they had been throughout Adara's childhood. There were lines on her face now, her papery skin ashen, making her appear gaunt, aged. Apparently she had been living very hard.

The creamy skin of Adara's face paled then turned red at the rebuke. But still… "Um, shall I sit?"

One shoulder hitched with disinterest. "Probably not. You won't be here long."

Confusion spread over Adara's face that turned redder. "I…don't understand."

When Estella wasn't forthcoming, Adara said, "Are you…did you ask me to come and see you so you could come home with us? I married Vaclav Brașov. You can come with-" She broke off at the sneer on her mother's ashen face.

"Yes. I had heard you wedded that Russian gangster." She tossed her head slightly to the side and tucked some hair behind her ear. "You always went after the older men. My God, Adara, he's a fucking pedophile. He's had his eye on you since you were five years old and he was in his teens. Of course," she sniffed and tilted her chin up.

"It shouldn't have surprised me you went after him. The way you went after my boyfriends, the little slut that you were. Ugh," she grunted, her eyes raking up and down her daughter, and as she always had, found her lacking.

"I wanted that Russian, you know. Sure, he was half my age," she shrugged a thin shoulder. "But, damn, so fucking hot. Big, brawny, such a dangerous man, even when he was barely twenty I wanted him between my legs. Tell me," she leaned towards Adara, one forearm on the table, finally some interest sparked her deadened eyes.

The color once again drained from Adara's face, appalled, shocked at the filth that came out of her wanton mother's mouth. "T-tell you what?" she stammered. Stunned, her heart hurt at her mother's cavalier, slutty attitude.

Estella leaned over further as if they were going to whisper in conspiracy together. "Is he as big as they say? I mean," she shook her head and sat back. "That bulge alone was big enough but I never saw him hard. I've heard he's like a nuclear warhead in bed. Crazy rough, violent even. So, is he-"

"Mother!" Shock felled Adara, her mouth dropped, eyes pained in disbelief. "What is wrong with you? He is my husband; you are my mother for heaven's sake. Why are you acting like this? Please," she softened her voice, imploring, "come home with me. We can-"

"*Fuck*," Estella exhaled with disgust, dropped her arm over the back of her chair, and regarded her daughter with all the interest of an animal that eats its young.

Then she leaned forward again. "I never wanted children. I married Salvatore because he was wealthy and powerful. But," she sighed and sat back again.

"He quickly lost interest in me. Got me with you and that idiot brother of yours so he could have heirs, carry on his name. Then you turn out so…" She paused, her despising gaze again rolling up and down Adara.

"Huh," she grunted again. "You turn out looking like an angel, gorgeous, no, not just gorgeous, breathtaking, yeah," she snorted. "After you hit puberty if you were in the room I couldn't get the attention of any male. If you weren't so," she sneered, "sweet. That sweetness just shined off you making that beauty ethereal, fucking angelic they'd say. Who could compete with that?"

She could see the red eyes, Estella's skin was grey. Adara's gaze fell to the marks on her mother's arms. Her brows inverted, rose to her hairline. "Mama, those aren't, you're not-"

Estella snorted, "A junkie?" A sick mocking smile showed her yellowing teeth. Some were chipped, a few were missing. "Actually," she said, lifted her hand and studied her nails. "That's why you are here, my dear."

Her legs shaking from the effort to keep her shocked body up and still, Adara whispered, "Why?"

"Hmmm." Estella raised her bloodshot eyes to her daughter, then shrugged. "I have a sugar daddy, I take care of him, and he takes care of me." A leer pricked her dry cracked lips, she said, "If you know what I mean," and wiggled her brows.

"Granted, he's no Salvatore Valentina or Vaclav Brașov for that matter. He's pushing 80. Kinda gross, ya know?" Her nose wrinkled, then the sick smile returned. "Thank God he can only get it up on occasion. My mouth used to be able to get him off quick, but now he-"

"Mother," no longer hiding her dismay and disgust, Adara cut her off. "You said the reason why I am here?"

Estella had the needle-thin grace to look vaguely guilty. "Well, Astaire takes care of most of my needs, but he can be stingy as shit. Never gives me extra to get my hair, my nails done, and the drugs, I have to steal from him to get the money for them. That's why when I was given this offer, I just could not refuse."

"Offer?" Adara asked with sudden unease.

A male voice behind Adara startled her when he spoke, "The offer to entice you away from Brașov. The only thing that could ever do that would be your loving mother."

Skin crawling as if ants wriggled all over it, the hairs on her neck stood up one by one. She hated to look, praying with every fiber it wasn't him.

But, she slowly turned around, and faced Raffaele Fiorenzo. If she had an ounce of blood left in her trembling body, it was quickly seeping away.

"Ah, I see you remember me, darling." His smile as lewd and sadistic as ever, his oily gaze dragged down her body like palpable fingers, pinching and groping as they slid over her curves. A pointed tongue emerged and he blatantly slicked it over his lips.

Adara tore her eyes from him and begged her mother, "Mama, what have you done? Please, don't do this to me! You don't know what he will do to me! Mama, please!"

Her desperate pleas didn't faze Estella. Her mother's eyes were lighting up at the cash one of the men with Fiorenzo was handing her. Stuffing it in her purse, Estella shoved her chair back and got to her feet.

With a faintly guilty glance at Adara, Estella ducked her head, muttered, "Sorry kid," and fled the café.

Stomach in knots, Adara stared after her, watching her hurry out the door and disappear into the pedestrians that flocked the cobblestone street.

"I hope we will have no trouble with you, Adara," Fiorenzo's slinky voice ran a chilling finger down her spine.

Without looking at him or the two men with him, Adara suddenly made a run for it. She hit the door so hard she crashed into it as it opened in, not out.

Scrabbling at the doorknob, she frantically twisted it, pulled the door open and raced out of the building.

She had no idea where to go, she didn't know where she was. Adara just blindly ran down the street.

Taking a breath to scream for help as she ran, she passed an alley and suddenly a hand clapped over her mouth from behind and she was lifted off her feet.

One of Fiorenzo's men, a big beefy soldier held her clamped against his huge oxen chest. His hand on her mouth, the other arm wrapped around her, over her arms to restrain her, he held her up in the air with just one arm.

"Very nice, Rudolph," Fiorenzo praised him, striding down the street to them. He snapped to the other man, "Get the car before someone sees us."

He stepped up to Adara and gripped her jaw. Mercilessly digging his fingers into it, he pressed hard enough there would be bruises.

"You bitch. I let you run, you stupid female. I couldn't take you inside, there would have been witnesses. You helped me out by fleeing so I could nab you out here. Priceless, huh?" and he punched her, and Adara's world went black.

Chapter Twenty-Six

Vaclav rushed from the car through the lobby and up the stairs. He hadn't the patience to wait for the elevator.

His legs biting long strides down the corridor, he forced himself to slow down. His heart was racing, he tried to calm down. Damn, he wanted Adara so badly.

The picture of her naked and spread eagle waiting for him taunted him the entire meeting. It was agony to sit there with a boner and try to concentrate on what was being said, and to give orders.

He was so aroused, so damned excited, he fumbled the keycard in the door and had to do it several times before he could get it open.

Thrusting the door open, he let it close behind him and stalked with fast steps to the bedroom while peeling off his long, black trench coat. Under it he still wore his suit.

Jerking at his tie he, walked faster, but, then, before he even reached it he felt funny. The suite felt too…empty, cold. A chill ran up his spine.

He strode faster and stopped dead in the doorway of their bedroom. It was empty. The bed still made.

He raced around checking the bathroom, but as the bad feeling had told him, she was gone.

Fishing his phone out of his pocket, he raged to the room, "Fuck, Adara! What the fuck have you done now?"

Stalking to the door and dialing Griffin, a white piece of paper on the table caught his eye. Hurrying to it, he picked it up, and his stomach dropped like lead in a pool when he read it.

"*Yah! Yah?*" Griffin's questioning voice broke Vaclav's stupor.

"Ah, hell, Griff. Tis Adara, she has been tricked to leave, lured out with a letter from her mother. Call the others and meet me downstairs."

Throwing the letter down, he ran back into the bedroom and to the safe where he retrieved more guns.

Stuffing the weapons around his body, he grabbed up his coat and raced to the door wishing he had been able to bring his shotguns but they would have been impossible to sneak into the hotel and there was nowhere to securely hide them.

His dress boots clomping down the stairs, he hurried to meet his men. They were already congregating at the entrance.

Each man wore a long black trench coat, if they'd had fedoras and Tommy guns they would look like a picture right out of the Untouchables from Prohibition times.

"Mr. Brașov!" the doorman called out, rushing over to Vaclav.

Vaclav could tell by his expression, he barked, "What happened to her?"

"Sir." He nodded at the phone in his hand. "I was starting to call you. It wasn't a few minutes ago that she left. I had to go find your number or I would have seen you come in."

Gasping for breath, the doorman had been torn between calling the mobster and telling him his wife was gone, or minding his own business. After all, she might not have been lying, her husband may have told her to go down ahead of him and wait- no.

Streeves shook his head at the look on Brașov's hard face. Streeves was a tall man but he still had to look up at Vaclav which only added to his anxiety. His small pot belly jiggled as he swiped at the sweat beading across his high forehead.

Every angle of Vaclav's face was sharp and grim, and livid with rage. Except for the fear that bloomed clearly in his cold blue eyes. "Tell me," he commanded.

243

Streeve's accented English was as precise as his French, he said, "Sir, she came down and said you knew she was down here without you, that you were right behind-"

At Vaclav's impatiently narrowing eyes he hurried on, "So, so she said a taxi was waiting for you, and before I could stop her, she ran out and jumped right in. It was like it really was there waiting for you guys."

"Ivod," Vaclav said to the black-haired, grim man standing beside him with his lips pressed together. "Trace the phone in our room, see if she called a taxi." Ivod nodded and turned away from the group.

Vaclav asked Streeves, "What kind of cab was it?"

"Uh," he mumbled, his legs quivering, heavy cheeks joggled when he swallowed hard. Tugging at the black bowtie at his neck, a quiver shook through his French accented voice, he said, "It was yellow, sir, the yellow service."

"Get me the number."

"Yes sir." With a huff of relief to get away from the frightening man, Streeves made fast work of his long legs hurrying to the front desk to get the information.

To Kidane, Vaclav ordered, "Check security tapes."

Kid spun on his heels, his long sandy hair flapping over his shoulders as he hustled off to do as tasked.

"Griff," Vaclav said, "get the car."

Griffin's face mirrored Vaclav's concern. He knew what the woman meant to him, he grasped his shoulder briefly to center his friend.

Obsidian eyes glittering with menace, Griff said, "Vâj, we'll get her and eliminate every threat to her. Hang in there." The widow's peak gleamed in his slicked back, black hair as he nodded with the avowal then took off to do as instructed.

Streeves rushed over and told Vaclav the number to the taxi service.

While his men took care of his orders, Vaclav dialed on his phone. He said to the doorman, "Did you get a look at the plate or the driver?"

The doorman's flaccid face was streaked with white and red as his emotions rippled over it, fear, terror, fear, *why the hell had he been the one at the door the day this deadly mobster's wife goes missing*?

The sweat beading over his forehead, and at his temples started sliding down his thick face. He wiped at his damp upper lip and cleared his throat a few times. Gulping his nerves down, he pressed his thighs together hoping to hold back the piss that was threatening to escape from his fright of the big intimidating bruiser.

A grimace spread Vaclav's lips in a hard straight line, hooded eyes narrowed to bare slits, the violence in his low voice on the edge of volatile, he growled with impatience, "Do not fucking make me repeat *meaself*."

Even as he barked at the doorman, Vaclav spoke into the phone, "Hello, I want the name of the driver and destination that just picked up a fare at the Grandrove Hotel. *Da*, I will wait." The phone to his ear, he looked at Streeves.

"Sir, no sir, I mean yes sir, that is," Streeves sucked in a breath that fluffed his chest out. "I didn't get the plate number, I only got a brief glance at the driver." He pulled out a white handkerchief and scrubbed it over his sweating face.

"Goddammit!" Vaclav bellowed, uncaring that everyone in the lobby jumped at the chilling sound. Barely holding his temper in check, Vaclav said through clenched teeth, "What the fuck did he look like?"

Streeves appeared about to pass out, he got a grip and said, "Young, uh, guy, maybe mid-twenties, short, curly brown hair, his skin was darker."

"Darker than what? Like he was tanned or black or what?" Into his phone he said, "Repeat the name?" Nodding as he memorized the driver's name. "Tell me where he took her and where he is right now."

Vaclav's brows drew into deadly daggers, his voice as enraged as his face, he threatened, "You will tell me or I will come to you and make you tell me, you understand?"

The person must have acquiesced because Vaclav was nodding again.

Streeve's babbled, "Uh, I'd say more Hispanic. His coloring seemed Latin. Uh, that's it sir, all I really noticed. I ran after her, sir, tried to stop them-"

"*Da*, good," Vaclav muttered, and started for the front door. Griffin was right out front of the circular drive, parked on the mosaic of red and brown pavers.

As Vaclav reached the door, Ivod and Kid were rushing to him from different directions of the lobby.

The trio strode through the glass doors a different doorman held open for them. Streeves was walking in the opposite direction on jelly legs to go have a heart attack in private.

The new doorman kept his gaze lowered, he had no desire to make eye contact with the fierce men striding past.

In their black coats that fell to their ankles, the doorman figured they were chock-a-block filled with weapons. He exhaled a sigh of relief when he let the door close behind them.

Griff drove the big SUV, Vaclav sat shotgun, with Ivod and Kid in the back.

Vaclav reached to the GPS and plugged in 1245 Fontainebleau Street. He said, "We are going to the Châles Café."

Griff said nothing, just drove following the directions of the GPS.

Ivod spoke first, "Adara didn't call the taxi. According to the Front Desk, there were no outgoing phone calls from any of the rooms in the hotel in the time that you were out of your suite."

Vaclav merely nodded, his eyes unmoving out the front windshield. She had clearly been lured out. He had to work to keep his mind from going to whatever was happening to his wife.

His head down, Kid was viewing his phone. "Here," he said passing the cell to Vaclav. Vaclav took it and watched the video stream of Adara hurrying out of the hotel while looking back over her shoulder.

"*Da*," he muttered under his breath, "you were looking for me. Wait until I get *mea* hands on that round ass of yours, Wife." And he would punish her because he would get her back. In what condition, that was the worry.

After a short, racing drive, Griff parked the SUV right in front of the café. "Kid, you come with me," Vaclav said as he exited the vehicle.

He strode quickly to the small eatery and jerked the door open and charged right inside.

Immediately scanning the room, he saw right away Adara wasn't there, neither was Estella. Vaclav trod to the hostess who was speaking with a server.

Vaclav impatiently interrupted her. "Do you speak English?"

"Yes," the young woman answered, smiling politely at him.

"I am looking for *mea* wife. She was to meet me here, but she is not in the restaurant. She is this tall," he held his palm below his shoulder. "She is very beautiful, long dark wavy hair and big dark eyes, delicate, fair-skinned."

The hostess was nodding with a smile, a blonde braid twitched across her back. "Yes, sir. She was here. She was sitting, no," the girl frowned, "she never did sit down. She stood talking to a woman who was seated at that table."

She pointed to a table near the front picture window. "I think they were related, like maybe mother and daughter, they looked quite a bit alike."

"*Bine*. Where is the young woman?"

The frown deepened as the hostess recalled the episode. "Well, they seemed to be having a…I wouldn't say argument, but, neither looked happy. Then, three men came up behind the girl, your wife. I have to admit," a guilty expression passed over her face, "she looked a bit upset when she saw them, uh, actually, I would say she looked scared. She seemed to get more afraid when this one man spoke to her."

Her eyes flicked from Vaclav to Kid who stood stone-faced, but their eyes never stopped canvassing the restaurant and out the window and back inside.

"Then what happened?" His impatience mixed with his fear for Adara's safety made Vaclav's brusque voice coarse, his accent overwhelming.

Sensing the menace exuding from Vaclav, the hostess took a step back from the tough looking males. "Uh well, when the men came, one of them gave the older woman some cash and she left." She paused as she tried to recall what had happened.

"Um, then your wife suddenly ran out the door. All of the men quickly left the restaurant. I think they went in the same direction as your wife," she gestured her head to the right. "That way, east."

"Did you see exactly where they all went?" His stomach churned with the fear that ate at his gut every second Adara was missing. Now hearing three men chased after her drove his brain insane.

The hostess shook her head, the braid bounced. "No. Just saw them through the window go that way. Uh, anything else, sir? I really must uh…" She wanted to get away from the two obviously dangerous, angry men.

"One more thing," Vaclav said, his eyes boring into hers. "This fuck- uh, man, the one who talked to her, what did he look like?"

"Oh." Her eyes flicked to the left as she thought back. "He looked to be like in his forties, big, tall and built like you," her smile went from nervous to coy as her gaze rolled over Vaclav's body.

"And?" Vaclav's bark shoved the smile right off her face.

"Uh, yeah, he had short dark hair, handsome with like a Roman kind of nose, I would say he was Italian. He was dressed in a designer suit, very expensive, he-"

Without a word, Vaclav turned from her and strode out the door with Kid right behind him, leaving the girl with a flabbergasted look on her face, her mouth still open.

His mind racing, Vaclav yanked the car door open and climbed inside. Grimly he muttered, "Fiorenzo has her."

Silence met his words; his friends knew what that meant.

His throat closing with emotion, Vaclav said gruffly, "He and two others followed her out of the restaurant heading east, the hostess did not see where they went."

Silence fell again.

His eyes out the window, Vaclav pulled out his cell and dialed a number. "*Yah,* this is Vaclav Braşov again. Has that driver checked in yet? Have you reached him?" Vaclav had told the dispatcher to contact the driver and then let him know where he was.

His face was set in such granite it didn't fall at the negative response, but the lines around his eyes crunched.

"*Bine,*" he said miserably, "have him call me when you reach him." His hand holding the phone just fell on his thigh.

The men sat contemplating what to do next, when Griff's eyes widened. "Hey, Vâj, fuck, look over there," he motioned across the street.

Down a few yards, a yellow cab was parked along the curb.

Without a word, Vaclav hopped out of the car and jogged over to the taxi, the unbuttoned, long black coat flapping at his ankles. When he reached it, he started pounding on the hood. Ivod was jogging to him.

"Hey! You!" A man hurtled out of a diner cursing in Spanish. In a mix of English and Spanish he shouted, "What the fuck are you doing? That's my car!"

Vaclav swung on him so fast the man stopped short, his shoulders pulled up.

"The fare, the girl you brought to that café," Vaclav motioned with his head. "Where the fuck is she? Who hired you-"

"Who the fuck do you think you are, man," the driver scowled. "Get the fuck away from-"

Whack!

Vaclav slapped him hard, very hard across the face. "I will not ask again, next hit will put you in the ground. Now, who hired you?"

Stunned, his palm on his face, the man stuttered, "Uh- uh- uh, dunno. Dispatch just got a call to pick up a fare, a woman, I think her name was Valentine or something, at the Grandrove Hotel and bring her here. It was just an order. They paid with a card over the phone."

Vaclav already knew the caller was anonymous and didn't leave a good contact number, the credit card likely fraudulent. He was hoping the driver might still be involved somehow. "Where did she go? Your fare?"

The driver shrugged crossly, "How the hell would I know, it's none of my-"

Whack!

Vaclav hauled off and slapped him again, harder. So hard the guy's eyes wobbled as he staggered, trying to keep from falling down.

"Okay, okay, fuck, quit hitting me!" He held his hands up protectively in front of his face as Vaclav raised his hand again, this time it was a fist, not an open palm. "I parked over here to get a burger. I happened to look out the window and saw the girl go hurrying out of the café and three guys followed her."

Vaclav pressed, his voice so dark and low he could barely be heard, "Where? Where did they go?"

"I uh, they kinda all disappeared in that alley there," told him, nodding down the street a block away.

They had passed the empty alley on the way to the café.

Like a claw was digging into his heart, crushing it, stealing his breath, Vaclav didn't know what else to do.

What could he do next? She had vanished with Fiorenzo and they were in fucking France. It would be time consuming and difficult to find them.

"Uh," sweating bullets the driver said, "I didn't see where she went, but I did see where the woman she was talking to inside the restaurant went."

Vaclav snatched the driver's collar hauling him up on his toes. "What? Where?" He gave him a rough shake.

His mouth opened and closed a few times before he spat the words out, "I saw her go down there, down the street there's a drug dealer. Everyone knows. She went there."

Holding the driver's shirt in his fist, Vaclav started dragging him down the street. "Show me."

By the time they reached the apartment complex the driver's body was shaking and sweating like he had the flu.

He pointed with a quivering finger, said with the words trembling out of his mouth stiff with fear, "There, that one. She went in there. I noticed 'cause it's not usual to have an older female down here buying drugs. She-"

As he spoke, the door opened and Estella emerged.

Coming down the steps, her head was down, concentrating on the bag she held in her hands. An eager, dissolute smile lifted the corners of her mouth as she peered at the drugs she'd just purchased.

Her skirt was crooked and there was a run in her stocking. Her blonde fuzz was unruly and her blouse half-unbuttoned. It looked like she did a little more than just buy drugs. She didn't see Vaclav until it was too late.

He shoved the driver at Ivod and grabbed her arm and dragged her the rest of the way down the steps.

"Hey! What the fuck-" she barked, quickly slamming the drugs to her chest to protect them.

When she saw who held her, her eyes grew to terrified saucers, cracked dry lips fell open. His name scraped from her throat tight with fear, she whispered, "Braşov…"

Snatching the drugs out of her hands, he squeezed her arm so hard she yelped. "*Da*, Estella, you fucking whore, tis me. Where the hell is Adara? Answer me or I will shove these drugs down your throat, bag and needle and all. Answer me."

Scared, but Estella sniffed with smug haughtiness. "You are too late, they are gone. Long gone. Now give me my drugs!" She threw out a hand to grab the bag but Vaclav stuffed it in his pocket.

Clutching her arm, he dragged her down a few feet and shoved her into the alley. Not letting go of her, he slammed her back up against the wall and wrapped his big hand around her throat.

"You know me, Estella, I do not make empty threats. If you do not tell me where Fiorenzo has Adara I will drop you right now. I will fucking snap your neck, you bitch and stomp on your putrid face until you die. You have one second," his hand tightened around her throat.

Gagging, Estella tried to fight him, it was futile, she was only hurting her fists pounding on his chest and arms.

Finally, she sagged, and Vaclav lightened his hold a hair. "He-he," gasps hitched up her roughened throat. "He has an enclave a few miles out of the city. Here," she rummaged in her pocket and pulled out her cell.

Scrolling through her contacts, she stopped at one and turned it so Vaclav could read it.

He swiped it out of her hand. "Hey!" she objected, then shut her mouth at the glower he shot her.

"Tell me the password."

She glared at him. He lifted his hand towards her, she muttered it out.

He stuffed the phone in his pocket and gave her a shove.

She stumbled, her back scraping on the brick wall.

Without a look back, Vaclav sprinted down the street with Ivod at his heels, to his waiting car.

"Hey!" Estella yelled, "Give me my phone!" He didn't look back.

"My drugs you bastard, at least give me my drugs!"

Chapter Twenty-Seven

Vaclav jumped in the car and said, "Hit it," and pounded coordinates into the GPS.

"You just gonna leave her there?" Griff asked as he drove the car. "She can clear Adara's name."

His gaze hot and intent out the window Vaclav replied, "I can find her when I want to. She has a nasty habit, I have contacts here. Just go, fucking speed, I will pay the ticket if you are stopped."

A chuckle tippling from him, Griff grinned and floored it.

It was a lengthy, agitating drive on the highway until they put the city behind them.

The men were silent as the car left the asphalt and followed a dirt road into the dark herringbone maze of the Harzbergite Forest. Rocking and bumping, it was a rough ride for miles before they reached the enclave.

Cloaked amid knotty oaks and tall beeches, the two-story French manor comprised of stucco and stone would have blended into the dark umber if not for the lights glowing golden behind antique mullioned windows.

There was no garage, just a wide flat parking area fifty or so yards from the main house.

Stopping just inside the covey of trees, Griff murmured, "We've passed no patrols, there are no guards."

Vaclav nodded, scrutinizing the area, searching for any concealed danger. "Fiorenzo has grown complacent thinking he is safely hidden in this country, that his enemies would be looking for him in the U.S. He does not think I can find him. He would have stayed hidden, and alive, if he had not taken what is mine."

"Vâj," Kid commented, "he came to France for Adara. He likely thought he could position himself here tucked in the woods until he created the opportunity to snatch her. He probably has his own jet on the ready to fly out of here once he figures it's safe, after you've given up looking for her and return home."

"He should know that would never happen. I will go first." Shoving his door open, Vaclav slid out, and staying as close to autumn trees dropping their colorful leaves, he made his way to the building.

Behind him, at a ten-second count, Griff came, then Kid then Ivod.

They scoured the outside of the structure and all around the back, surprised they still didn't encounter any resistance.

"Fool," Griff spat under his breath.

"*Da*," Vaclav agreed as they met back around the front. "His last mistake unless he fucks with Satan in hell."

All the doors they came across were securely locked. Not that they couldn't break in, but they wanted stealth.

"*Bine*," Vaclav said quietly. "Kid, you are the most innocuous looking of us, at least when you want to be. Knock on the door, tell them," he pondered for a moment. "Tell them you have word, that Estella…ah, what the fuck was it? Some French shit…"

His face scrunched as he tried to pull in the name Adara had said. Mar- Dar- what the hell was it? Fishing her phone out of his pocket, he scrolled through it.

Then his creased face smoothed back into an implacable mask, he said, "Tell whoever answers the door that Estella, No, Este Darceaux is trying to send Fiorenzo a warning."

Using the alias Estella was using would seem less suspicious than her married name since she was going by Darceaux while in France.

254

Fiorenzo must have found her at some point, at a saloon, through mutual low-life scummy acquaintances. Probably picked her up when Estella was out hunting down her drugs.

Kid slipped off his leather trench-coat and handed it to Ivod. Then the three men stepped back into the bushes while Kid combed his long sandy hair back off his shoulders.

Tucking his guns out of sight, he plastered on a worried, very innocent look, pushed the button beside the huge, double wooden doors then stood back so he could easily be seen from inside the house.

Several minutes passed before a voice shouted from inside, "Go away, we don't want anything you're selling."

"I, uh," Kid stammered, glancing around nervously, "uh have a message from a woman, a woman I know, Este Darceaux. Says she's a friend of Mr. Fiorenzo. She has a warning for Mr. Fiorenzo." He could hear noise behind the door. Footsteps leaving. In a minute they returned.

The door eased open slowly, a face peered out at him. A gun quite visible in his hand he said, "Mr. Fiorenzo wants to know who the fuck you are and how did you-"

Kid threw his hands up in fright. Looking as young and harmless as possible, he cried out, "Oh! Sir, please don't shoot! I-I'm just passing on a message. A warning the lady said. She paid me. You wanna see the cash? It's for real, it's really-" as he babbled nervously the other men crept up to the side of the door.

The man behind the door rolled his eyes. "You wait here, ya dumb fuck, lemme go see-"

Vaclav threw his body at the door knocking the guy behind if off his feet.

Before he hit the ground, Vaclav was on him. One punch stilled the man; one twist of his neck broke it. Jumping to his feet, he quickly checked the area making sure no one was about to plug him full of holes.

Griff charged in to stand beside him. Ivod tossed Kid's coat to him and he put it on.

"Looks clear, damn he's stupid," Griff said with a censorious smirk.

"*Da*," Vaclav muttered, "I need to find *mea* wife."

They stood in a dimly lit vestibule of grey and white tile. The walls were painted a lighter grey with the trim and borders white.

The house was ancient. Instead of doors there were arches leading into other rooms. The ceiling was open wood beams. The grey tile led to and down hallways.

Motioning to his men, Vaclav said quietly, "Spread out, question then kill whoever you come upon. Text if you find her."

The four men darted off in different directions.

Vaclav charged into every room he came across.

There were dens and parlors, a large commercial kitchen had modern appliances, but the floor was an antique patterned brown diamond-shaped. The counters light brown, the cupboards carved maple.

A man emerged from the kitchen as Vaclav approached it. Vaclav recognized him as one of Fiorenzo's soldiers.

The guy's eyes popped, he blinked in astonishment. Before he could comprehend Vaclav wasn't a mirage, Vaclav had thrown a knife into the man's neck. He went down without a sound.

Vaclav clomped over, bent and retrieved his knife wiping the blood on the man's shirt.

He didn't run into anyone else as he made his way back to the foyer, and no one had texted him. The alarm raging in his abdomen just kept building the more time passed and he didn't find her.

The other guys got back almost the same time as he did. He knew but asked anyway, "Anything?"

The all shook their heads with concerned despondency.

Griff said, "There are some stairs, not a full set towards the back, let's-"

Vaclav was already stalking off to find them.

Practiced in stealth, they made their way up the wood-planked stairs without a sound.

When they reached the top, Vaclav held his hand up. They stilled, and listened.

Rumbles of men talking spilled down the hall, someone was crying. It sounded like a woman.

Then they heard the crack of a slap, and Raffaele Fiorenzo barked, "You bitch, yeah, I'll show you. You dare leave me for that fucking Russian?" Another slap, another cry out.

His voice a heavy sneer, he was heard shouting, "When I get done with you, you will be begging me to kill you, you cunt, begging me to put you out of your misery. But," there was a foul laugh.

"I won't. I will beat you, whip you, cut you, fuck you, and pimp you out until you draw your last breath, you whore. Starting right now."

There was a grunt, murmurings from other men. Then, "I'm gonna show you whose dick is your boss, fuck you until you call me your master and scream for me to-"

Vaclav didn't wait for the next slap, he charged down the hall.

When he reached the room, he burst in with guns in both hands raised and cocked.

Keeping the impact of the abhorrent scene in the room off his iron face, he commanded, "No one move."

Adara was lying on the floor, Fiorenzo standing, bending over her. Even from the door, Vaclav could see her face was bruised. She wore a white frilly blouse that was ripped open, and white jeans, her blood was on both.

His hands tearing at her jeans, Fiorenzo looked up in shock at Vaclav's sudden entrance.

Griff, Kid and Ivod stood beside Vaclav, weapons drawn. All four men, their trench coats swinging around their ankles like Wild West cowboys on the brink of a shoot-out.

"What the fu-" a man inadvertently moved between them allowing Fiorenzo the split second to haul Adara to her feet.

Instantly, he had his arm across her chest and a gun to her head. "Don't fucking move, not one muscle, Braşov, you fucking cocksucker. One step and I shoot her. You can't kill me before I get her. You ain't taking her from me this time you bastard!"

His arms stretched out taut, a gun in each hand, Vaclav took in the room.

Fiorenzo's men had been taken by such surprise none held a weapon. They all stood speechless looking hopelessly stupid and inept. And afraid. Just like when Vaclav had taken Adara from him the last time.

Vaclav's men's weapons were trained on the other soldiers in the room.

His voice soft, Vaclav said quietly, "You *bine*, baby?" and cringed when Fiorenzo raised his arm jerking it tight across Adara's neck.

Her plush lips were bruised and the upper one had a cut. The huge doe eyes were swollen with tears and Fiorenzo's hits. She blinked back the tears and cried hoarsely, "Shoot him, Vâj."

Breathy with pain, hoarse from screaming, she rasped, "He will kill you and me, all of your friends, kill him. Forget about me-"

"Shut up!" Fiorenzo snapped his arm hard cutting off her words, and her air. Smugly he said to Vaclav with a sneer, "Put down your weapons, and leave my house, or she dies. I will strangle her right in front of you, break her neck or shoot her if you make a move. It's your choice," and he tightened his arm.

Adara clawed at his arm trying to dislodge it from cutting off her windpipe, her feet barely touched the ground, her toes kicked out as she struggled to get free.

No one moved. The room was pin drop quiet, except for Adara's gasping for air.

"Well?" Fiorenzo taunted. "Make your decision. The bitch won't last much longer. She's small, can't hold much air in those little lungs. And this beautiful soft neck of hers," he bent his head, his eyes never leaving Vaclav, and slicked his tongue up her face.

"So delicate, Brașov, a flick of my hand and I could snap it in less than a blink. Now," his eyes glittered furiously, he ordered, "take your men and get the fuck out of here. I swear I will kill her, and then you if you try anything."

Vaclav, standing still as a statue in his long coat, boots planted, arms stretched out with his guns never wavered, said, "Fiorenzo, just tell me, how did you find her mother? We will leave, but I want to put a bullet in Estella's brain. At least do that little bit since I have to leave *mea* wife with you." His brows arched quizzically, blue eyes gleaming with sincerity.

"Ha! I'm about to fuck your wife and that's all you have to say you fucker?" Fiorenzo glanced at his men and chuckled. "Can you believe this asshole? Fucking coward."

While he yapped, Vaclav caught Adara's eye and shifted his eyes almost undetectably down, hard, then did it twice more before Fiorenzo looked back at him.

Adara's skin was translucent as her blood left her brain and she gasped for a last few breaths. She started sagging under Fiorenzo's arm.

But he was strong. He bumped her up. "Tsk tsk, honey, no passing out, not quite yet. And," he looked at Vaclav, "next time she passes out it will be lights out, for good."

She slipped further, he bumped her up again. To keep her where he could hold his forearm over her throat, the hand holding the gun at her temple shifted away from her head.

Adara let her body drop- at the spilt second that Fiorenzo juggled her limp body, Adara reached down to where Vaclav had indicated with his eyes, grabbed the knife in a sheath at Fiorenzo's leg, yanked it out and stabbed it in his thigh.

Fiorenzo screamed and dropped her to grab at his thigh-

Vaclav unloaded both his guns at him while his team barraged the room with gunfire, shooting all of Fiorenzo's men.

Fiorenzo's body jerked and twitched as Vaclav's bullets pounded into him, blood spurted, gushed. His eyes wide at Vaclav, darkened as he realized he had lost.

As he died, Vaclav moved to him. He said, "Checkmate you asshole," kicked his gun away from his hand and kicked him in the head.

"Last time you take what is mine. Last time you fucking lay a finger on a woman you pussy coward." He spat on him while cursing the man, "Hitting and raping helpless women that cannot defend themselves, you prick." He leaned over so his face was close to Fiorenzo's.

As the life wavered from Fiorenzo's eyes, Vaclav said, "Now you will see what helpless and defenseless, torture and hell is like, say hi to Satan for me you fucker." Straightening, he spat on him again then rushed to where Adara lay not moving.

"Fuck," was he too late? "Baby," he gasped. Dropping down, he slid his arm under her back lifting her. "Baby," he whispered, his heart in his throat, "Adara."

He laid her back down and put his fingers on her pulse. It was faint but still beat, her chest rose and fell with shallow breaths.

"*Zue*, baby." Sliding both hands under her, he lifted her in his arms as he stood up. Starting for the door he ordered, "Check they are all dead then torch it."

He carried Adara down the stairs holding her close to his chest. Her head hung over his arm, hair swaying with his movements as he hurried. She was limp, unconscious. He glanced down at her, saw the pulse fluttering in her neck, long and smooth and ivory, like her mother had said, like a ballerina.

He gaze fell lower, and he smiled. She was wearing his favorite bra. He had bought it for her as kind of a joke, but hell, it was sexy as shit too. It was a tiny bra made out of mink. She had matching panties he couldn't wait to see. He had always likened her hair to that of a mink, when he'd seen a picture of the mink lingerie set he knew he had to get it for her.

Leaving the house, once outdoors, his long legs ate up the ground in fast chomps as he strode to their car tucked away in the woods. When he got inside, he climbed in the very back, the third row of seats and settled her on his lap.

It was a while before his men joined him.

Jumping into the car, Griff stuck the key in the ignition and drove them the hell out of there.

Like years before, they all watched out the window as the flames flickered higher and higher, over the treetops licking the sky with their orange tongues.

All the way back to their hotel, Vaclav never took his eyes off his wife. Occasionally he stroked her hair, her cheek. It was hell seeing the damage Fiorenzo had inflicted on her beautiful face and body. Besides the bruises on her face, they were all over her arms.

His stomach sickened at the fingerprints on the top mounds of her breasts. Fiorenzo had to have gripped her hard to leave prints on her fair skin.

Zue, he wished he hadn't killed him. He wished he could have taken him back and played with him for days, weeks, letting the bastard feel what real torture felt like.

After he beat the piss out of him and broke every bone, every so often he would make tiny slits in his body with his knife. His switchblade was the sharpest blade he'd ever possessed. He'd watch the bastard die so slowly, so painfully, listening to him beg, cry for mercy. And he would get the same mercy Fiorenzo had shown to Adara.

Then, as the mobster took his last day's breath, Vaclav would do as he promised another man long ago. He'd gut his stomach, cut off his cock and balls and shove them in the hole, and force him to stare at them as he died. Fucker.

But he had to shoot him. He posed too much of a danger to Adara. If somehow he had managed to overtake Vaclav and his men, Vaclav chuckled at the implausible thought, like that could ever happen. But shit does happen, and if he got past Vaclav, Adara would again be at his mercy.

He could not chance that. He had to shoot him. Whatever, the crud was gone, and he has his beloved wife back in his arms. That was all that mattered.

When they neared the city, Adara's long lashes curling on her pale cheeks fluttered. Her lovely eyes cracked open. She turned blurry peepers up to him, a pained smile bloomed faintly, then she winced at the split lip.

"Ah, baby, be careful," he said tenderly, stroking a soft finger gently over her lips.

Through the swollen lips, she whispered, "You came for me, Vâj."

Nodding, he kissed her lightly avoiding the cut. "*Da*, sweet, always." He bent and kissed her again, "Always and forever, Wife."

Her eyes closed, her mouth too sore to respond to his gentle kisses, she just sighed and enjoyed the loving play of his tender kisses.

Then, her body stiffened. "Vâj," she croaked.

"*Da*, sweet?" He smoothed wisps of hair off her brow.

Her forehead furrowed with despair, "My...mother. She..." Tears burned in the corners of her bruised eyes. Her voice caught, "She sold me, Vâj, she..." Adara gulped back the pain, but the tears slipped out, "She sold me. Just like my uncle, my own mother sold me to that man, that fiend."

"Shh," he soothed, dabbing at her tears with the pads of his thick fingers. "It was Estella that told me where you were." He left out the part of his threatening Estella to talk or he'd kill her.

A sound of disbelief then her mouth curved in the weak smile, "Really? She told you where I was so you could save me?"

Pressing his lips tight to keep in the vitriol that threatened to spurt out for the bitch that bred his beautiful wife, Vaclav nodded. "*Da*. If she had not told, it would have," he clapped his lips shut.

No need to have her think about what would have happened if Estella hadn't squealed like the spineless rat that she was. He would have found her eventually on his own, but by then- he shook the thought out of his head.

"Oh, Vâj, I thought she hated me. She said terrible things to me, that she'd never wanted me. But, I guess she was just scared. She really cares for me."

Her voice small and shaky, the tremulous smile steeped higher, she said weakly, "Maybe when things settle down we can visit her. Do you think we can?" Her dainty hand set on his chest. The smile crooked with her injuries was nonetheless gratified, she sighed with contentment.

"Humph," he grunted. Then, a wicked grin split his hard face making it sinful and loving at the same time. As the car bumped along and his friends grinned ear-to-ear, Vaclav said while casually stroking her arm, "Oh, Adara, *mea* sweet..."

She sighed happily, "Yes, Vâj?"

He leaned over and said quietly so the others couldn't hear, "As soon as you are better, you are so going to get punished for disobeying me and leaving the hotel, and putting me through such hell."

Her lashes blew up, she opened her mouth to protest, but he silenced her with his kiss.

Chapter Twenty-Eight

No one would have ever believed the savage mobster could be so tender and loving, but Vaclav brought Adara to San Francisco where he had a home, for her to heal.

He had a doctor on call that came every few days to check on her.

Thankfully, she'd suffered no broken bones, but her contusions were massive and the doctor was concerned about concussion and internal injuries, so the first couple of days she was in the hospital for observation.

His townhouse was up Jefferson Street, one of the busiest locations in San Francisco. They would have plenty to do and see.

When she was on her feet, Vaclav had plans. He wanted of course first to take her to Fisherman's Wharf, then to see the Golden Gate Bridge, Chinatown, the rest of all the touristy sights, and across the Bay.

After they saw everything there, there so much of California he wanted to show her, Napa, Sonoma, Catalina, Carmel, Muir Woods and on and on.

They had been in the three-bedroom townhouse for a month. The entire length of the wall was glass and there were spectacular views of the city, and in the distance, the ocean. There were skylights in the ceiling.

On chilly nights they could lie in bed, drink hot chocolate and watch the sky sprinkle with stars, on warmer days they ate breakfast on the wide balcony.

For the first week Vaclav never left her side.

Adara floated in and out of consciousness from the strong pain medication the doctor had prescribed.

Vaclav was afraid to hold her, touch her, Fiorenzo had done such damage Vaclav feared hurting her.

He lay beside her every night, the only time he touched her was to stroke her hair or help her eat or drink or use the bathroom.

He carried her to the door but she insisted with a scarlet face she could handle the rest on her own. Her shyness made her irresistibly adorable to him.

When she seemed to be feeling better and more movable, Vaclav carried her downstairs for meals.

At night in bed, he pulled her against him. As she curled in his arms, she would reach for him, to pull his head down to kiss, but he would gently hold her away. "When you are 100% well, baby," he promised, smiling at her pout.

For himself, he spent several times a day in the shower taking care of the pounding hard-on she gave him just by being near her.

After weeks passed, Vaclav took her on longer and longer walks as she grew stronger.

When they started jogging, he finally began to relax, she was well on the mend.

Vaclav had to go do business. He was gone all day until well into the evening. When he returned, they had a late dinner; he practically dozed at the table.

"Come on, big boy," Adara teased, helping him up, and down the hall to stumble to the bedroom.

She pushed him to sit on the bed and then knelt at his feet to undo his boots.

Through a flop of dark blond hair that hung over his eye he smiled impishly. "Hey, while you're down there…"

Not getting the old joke, her pretty smile up at him always did him in. She asked, "Yes? What can I get you?"

Vaclav chuckled. "When you are fully better, babe, I have some things to show you, up close and personal."

She gave him a questioning look. "What, Vâj? I am recovered. You can stop treating me with those kid gloves of yours."

When he was quiet, she started to ask him again what he meant, but he yawned and fell backwards on the mattress. By the time she got up, he was sound asleep.

Her face soft with a loving smile, Adara dragged him the rest of the way on the bed, it wasn't easy, and undressed him.

Putting on her own nightgown, she climbed into bed and snuggled up against him. She had never felt safer, or happier in her life. It could only get better.

The next day Vaclav was up and gone before Adara rose. She had breakfast, put on a workout video in the bedroom. He still didn't want her out without him, even to go on a run by herself or to the store or gym.

To her surprised delight, one morning she had come out and there was this gloriously shining harp beaming in the living room. He had so generously bought it for her.

The next few days that passed, he sat in a chair with his computer working while listening to her play.

At the end of the week when he came home from more meetings, she had dinner ready for him.

Coming in the door, Vaclav peeled off his jacket and tossed it on a chair in the living room, kicked off his boots, and plodded into the kitchen. An incredible aroma wafted right to his nose.

"Wow, baby, that smells amazing." He trod all the way in and saw her setting a tasty looking dish on the table. "What is that? Did you make it?" He let his nose lead him to the table.

"Yes, of course," she replied with a smile and told him, "sit down. It's chicken tagine with lemons and olives."

As he took a seat, she retrieved a bottle of Chablis and poured them each a glass and lit the candles in the center of the table.

They had a dining room, but they preferred the intimacy of the kitchen. It was a big country kitchen with windows overlooking the city. They ate the tagine with pasta and a salad, Vaclav gushed over her homemade rolls.

Shoveling a heavily buttered bun in his mouth, he said while chewing, "I didn't know you could cook. When did you learn? Surely they did not make gourmet food like this in prison?" Swallowing the bite, he picked up his glass of wine and took a sip.

Delicately munching on a slice of tomato, Adara replied, "No, of course not. But, you saw how my mother was."

At his sudden grimace she went on, "Uh, well, she was always too drunk to prepare food for us. We had housekeepers but no one really cooked. So," she shrugged, "I taught myself with cookbooks. I kept Vincenzo and me fed while mama drank her dinner. Daddy was very rarely home."

Setting his glass down, Vaclav reached to her and took her hand, then leaned over and kissed her. "I am so sorry the shitty life you had, sweetheart. If I could have only helped you somehow."

Adara set her elbow on the table and her head on her palm and gazed at her husband's sad face. "Vâj, there was nothing you could have done. While I was growing up, you were a young enforcer, my father was a big crime boss. Anyway, it all turned out for the best, right?"

"*Da,* baby." He sifted the hair from the side of her face back and gave her a gentle kiss.

Her head propped on her hand, she closed her eyes and smiled when his lips gently brushed hers, and then he sat back.

Her eyes opened, a pouty frown punched her lips out. "Hey, you call that a kiss? I want a real one." She set both arms on the table and glowered at him.

Vaclav's brows arched at her. Taking his last bite of chicken, he said, "When you are better, *mea* sweet."

"Vâj..." she complained. "I am better now. Don't you think it's time we..." She awkwardly wiggled her brows like she'd seen others do.

Picking up his wineglass, he peered over the rim at her as he sipped, then set the glass down and wiped his mouth on a napkin.

Shaking his head he said, "I will not jeopardize your health, Adara, when the doctor clears you, we will talk about it."

At her pout, he smiled. "Sweetheart, you do not think that I do not jerk off ten times a day with fantasies of you? I want to as well, but," he shook his head again, the smile turning serious. "Not until you are completely well."

"Oh, poof," she muttered, tossing her napkin down. "I am perfectly fine. Geesh, men. First you have to fight them off, then they marry you and you can't even get a proper kiss."

Laughing at her consternation, he got up and started clearing the dishes. She sat holding onto her wineglass grumbling.

Unaware he was coming up behind her, she continued grumbling to herself.

"Ah, you think you are well enough to take me on, little wife?" He bent over her back from behind and grabbed her breasts. His moan buzzed her ear as he kneaded them. "This what you want, *mândră*?"

Adara arched her back to reach around his neck and turned her head to kiss him. Bending her spine back shoved her breasts into his palms. He netted her rounded flesh in his hands, squeezing, molding them between his long fingers.

Breaking contact, Vaclav scooped her up and sat in her chair with her on his lap. His kiss was hard, voracious; he had to struggle not to be too rough with his mouth, or his hand that roamed up her shirt to clutch her breast. Then he grabbed the bottom of her shirt and pulled it up off her head and tossed it.

Adara leaned her chest against his with a moaning sigh. "It's been so long, Vâj." A shiver roiled through her when she felt his fingers at the clasp of her bra and soon felt the cool air on her bare skin as he removed it.

His hands cupping, clenching her naked breasts, he smiled at her, "*Da*, it has been so long, baby, *Zue* I want you so badly it hurts. Are you sure?" He stroked his palms hard over her plump globes enjoying the moans his hands brought from her parted lips, her beautiful eyes already hazing over.

At her sensuous nod, he shoved his hands under her and lifted her. On his way to their bedroom he seized her mouth and pillaged the hell out of it.

Inside the warm room of shades of blue, Vaclav headed for the king-sized bed and set her on her feet beside it.

Breaking their kiss, he reached for her belt, undid the buckle, the snap, pulled down the zipper and drew her jeans and panties down to the floor where she kicked them off.

"You now," she smiled in the low lighting from the partially pulled drapes, and she grabbed at his belt, but he stopped her. "*Na*, sweet, not yet, I have to do something first."

Puzzled, completely naked, she asked, "What do you-" and she squeaked as he sat down on the bed then grabbed her and threw her over his lap.

"Vâj!" she wailed kicking her legs. "What do you think you're doing? Stop it right now, you can't!"

Smack! He brought his palm down on her bare ass. "Ah but I can, sweet wife. You remember, I warned you," and he smacked her again, she screamed.

"You left the goddamned hotel when I told you again and again not to," smack. "You could have died," smack- smack-

"Please, Vâj, I'm sorry, but it was my mother- ow!" she cried as his hand came down on her tender tush. "Stop!"

He spanked her harder as he recalled the heart-rending terror that coiled in his stomach, choked his throat when he'd realized she'd left the hotel and then worse, when he learned Fiorenzo had her in his filthy clutches.

"You will never put me through that horror again, Wife, never," and he spanked her until she was flailing and her butt was bright red.

Then, cupping a cheek, he bent and kissed it, blew air on it, and she stilled. He put his mouth on her skin and sucked, making the redness redder, and a small cry shuffled from her with a squiggle of her slender hips.

"You hear me, Adara? Never again." He squeezed her cheeks then ran his fingertips down the crease between them.

She groaned, and he chuckled as he reached to fondle her soft girl parts. Pushing her thighs apart, he played with her; she squirmed on his lap with little mewing sounds.

First one long finger slid inside her, at her whimper he added another and as her silk oozed and covered his hand, and her hips writhed, he started moving them.

Soon gasping sounds came from her, and he had to hold her hips still so he could tweak her clit and finger-fuck her sex.

He could feel her body clench, she was about to break out and burst over the moon- and he pulled his fingers out, lifted her and set her on her feet. She swayed from the sudden movement; he held her wrist with a laugh.

Confused, she batted flustered dazed eyes at him. "Vâj, what-"

He stood up and quickly shucked his clothes then pushed her to lie on the bed on her back.

"Real punishment *mea* wayward, recalcitrant wife." Vaclav grinned. "You like the spanking too much. This time you were already wet at the third smack. So, real punishment will be the withholding of your orgasm, eh?"

"But, wait, I don't understand," she whined, her butt wriggled painfully on the mattress.

He climbed on and shoved her legs wide. "You will see, *mea* sweet," he purred, and lowered his body until his mouth was clamped on her pussy.

She jumped, "Oh!" Then, her body melted soft and eager, her hips raised to meet his sucking mouth, his tongue lapping at her clit. His fingers curling back inside her with harder and harder thrusts, stroking her hot spots until- he stopped again.

Hearing her frustrated groan, he lifted his head up from between her legs and grinned at her. "Ah, you see now the punishment, *mea* girl?" And he did it over and over, bringing her to the precipice then stopping right when she was on the edge.

"Dammit, Vâj," she growled, her fingers clutched the sheet in her frustration. She tried to raise her hips to make him let her come, but he chuckled and pushed them down, holding her thighs tight on the bed.

"Hmm," he murmured, titillating her pussy lips, squeezing the folds, suckling her nub, he darted his tongue in and out of her channel. "What did I say about you cursing? I think more punishment is in order."

He reached up to grip her breast, pinching and twisting her nipple at the same time he pinched her clit and she screamed with her hips bucking.

"Do it! Vâj, let me go!"

He only laughed at her, crushing her breast in his strong grasp and biting her clitoris and she screamed again, begged him to let her release.

"*Bine*, sweet." He got on his knees and moved up her body. Melding their mouths, his passion heated flames over them both, and he thrust inside her in one long hard plunge.

A harsh gasp tore from her lips, her pussy crunched his dick, he stopped. "Ah, baby, I am sorry, I teased *meaself* too long with you, and could not go slow. Did I hurt you?"

Her hips straining at his, she wailed, "Yes it hurts, but good hurt, no, don't stop, Vâj, don't stop!"

"Shit babe," he croaked, and let loose pounding into her. He'd wanted to make love to her, slow, gently, take their time, but he had overdone it with teasing her and now neither one of them could wait.

Huffing, rolling an arm around her shoulders to hold her, Vaclav slipped his hand under her butt and lifted it.

She wrapped her legs around his waist, digging her heels into his ass and stabbed her nails in his back as she held on for his wild ride.

Diving deep and too fast for her to keep up, Vaclav rode her, growling and chuffing, he slammed in his little wife again and again until the whimpers strode up her throat, and his chest burned, his balls clinched into tight fists.

He suddenly pulled out, she whined, he lifted her and flipped her over on all fours. His hand on her nape, he pushed her down with her beautiful ass up in the air, and he plunged back in.

His rhythm rough and hard and fast, he plucked at her clit until she writhed under him, then he reached up and grabbed her breast and as her body shook with convulsions, his name shrieking from her lips.

He unleashed and drilled over and over, then he paused way deep, way hard inside her, and his seed erupted, bursting from his raging cock.

Shuddering, he hissed her name, "*Adara*," and his hips went crazy again as he emptied into her thrusting in and out.

His last deep thrust, he growled, "I love you, Adara, *mea* wife," and let the rest go and collapsed.

They lay there, he could still feel his seeds pumping into her, his dick throbbing, her pussy still milking him, spasms still ringing around their bodies, chests panting in unison.

After some time, their hearts slowing, pulses diminishing, breaths deeper and calmer. Curled in his arms, Adara said shyly, "Did you say you loved me, Vâj?"

His hand came up to cradle her head to his chest, his heart beating against her cheek. "*Da*. I always have, you know that. It was you that needed to catch up, *mea* sweet."

His chest rose high with his yawn, then lowered, her head moved with it.

She rolled to her stomach, braced on an elbow and looked up at him. His eyes were closed. She said, "Vâj?"

Smiling with grateful contentment, he murmured, "Hmm?" and tightened his arm around her.

"I do love you, you know."

His eyes cracked open, he peered down at her. The smile lit brighter then broadened across his face. "You do?"

She nodded, her chin rubbing on his chest. "I don't know when it happened. It moved on me slowly. You were so protective, so gentle with me. You kept rescuing me. You stayed by my side and persevered even though I denied you again and again. Your magical hands, your skillful mouth," she leaned up and kissed him softly.

"So brave, fearless, undaunted, you just kept coming and coming…for me. I've seen you brutal with those that threatened you or someone you cared for, but never, ever, did you harm someone that was innocent. Never a woman or a child, only someone that deserved it, knew what they were doing.

"When Fiorenzo had me and I thought I'd never see you again, that's when I fully realized it. That I would just as soon die if I was never to see you again. Yes," she kissed him again, enjoying the sweet wonder in his eyes. I love you, Vaclav Brașov."

He put his hands under her arms and pulled her up and to the side so they could kiss more deeply.

A few minutes later, Adara felt his manhood prodding at her. She smiled, "Wait a second, Husband, I wanted to discuss you moving your syndicate into a legitimate business."

With a groan and a roll of his eyes, he flipped her over, jerked her bottom up, gave it a smack and knelt behind her.

Pushing her thighs apart, his shaft at her entrance, he said, "*Da*, sure, *mândră,* we will talk about that in a minute," and this time he made prolonged, unhurried, passionate love to his wife.

The End